The Nudger
Dilemmas

The Nudger Dilemmas

A Short Story Collection

John Lutz

Five Star • Waterville, Maine

This novel is a work of fiction. Names, characters, places, and incidents are either the product of the author's imagination, or, if real, used fictitiously.

Five Star First Edition Mystery Series.

Published in 2001 in conjunction with Tekno-Books and Ed Gorman.

Set in 11 pt. Plantin by Al Chase.

Printed in the United States on permanent paper.

Library of Congress Cataloging-in-Publication Data

Lutz, John, 1939–
    The Nudger dilemmas : a short story collection / John Lutz.
        p.   cm. — (Five Star first edition mystery series)
    ISBN 0-7862-3147-5 (hc : alk. paper)
    1. Nudger, Alo (Fictitious character)—Fiction.
    2. Private investigators—Missouri—Saint Louis —
    Fiction.   3. Detective and mystery stories, American.
    4. Saint Louis (Mo.)—Fiction.   I. Title.   II. Series.
    PS3562.U854 N84 2001
    813′.54—dc21   2001023901

Contents

Foreword

Somewhere in heaven, or relatively close, in the *Twilight Zone* maybe, but not quite in that genre, is PI Purgatory, where fictional private detectives are all enjoying themselves in (what else?) a bar. Let's call it Chez Purgatory, though you don't have to be dead though you were never really alive to be there. If that makes sense. Or if it docsn't. And let's call it what it is, a bar, all right?

Oh, Miss Marple and her ilk are over in the Cozy Corner where the decor runs to chintz, imbibing innocuously named alcoholic beverages with fruit in them. But it's still a bar. It's always a bar. And Nero Wolfe and Holmes are in the Art Deco Victorian Room, sipping good sherry while bent over some infernal (Oops!) board or card game.

Archie Goodwin is chatting up the barmaid. And there at one of the tables are Sam Spade and Philip Marlowe, knocking them back straight while cracking wise and trying to top one another. They're getting on Mike Hammer's nerves, so he and Lew Archer take their leave, go sit at the bar, and put on lugubrious faces while discussing Spade and Marlowe.

The door opens, and in walks Nudger. He isn't an imposing figure like Spade or Marlowe. A bit taller than average perhaps. His hairline has begun to recede, and he's suffering the beginning of middle-age spread. Not a bad looking guy, with regular features and keen blue eyes that express puzzlement and the kind of resigned wisdom that is the loser's consolation prize.

He gives the Cozy Corner a wide berth, fearing that

wafting cat dander will trigger his allergy. It is Miz's Night, and in the Female Urban PI Room they are practicing kick boxing and doing some sort of aerobic exercise that seems to combine hugs with sudden knee lifts. He only glances in there and hurries on his way.

Wolfe and Holmes look at him, sneer, and turn back to their mind-bending game. Hammer and Archer raise their glasses in a hard-boiled salute to him, but Nudger doesn't want to join them. They're so intense. They make him tired.

So he sits alone at the other end of the bar, checks his pockets, and realizes he doesn't have enough money to pay for a drink. He asks for a glass of water. The bartender brings it with ice, a slice of pineapple and a paper umbrella in it. Sarcasm?

Nudger looks around and sees that just about everyone is here. Over in a corner near where there's enough tobacco smoke to flavor ham, near the restroom ventilating system and where the kitchen's swinging door slams into the chairs of all the customers, sit a few PI's that are much like Nudger. He doesn't join them. He won't even acknowledge or identify them. His creator knows that their creators are nonviolent but can be snide. Nudger sips his water. The cold pineapple wedge bumps his nose, and he almost loses an eye to the umbrella.

That's when the door bursts open and an incredibly attractive blonde enters and skids to a stop on her six-inch spike heels. None of the patrons seems surprised. It happens every night. It's part of the deal at Chez Purgatory. And she always has on the same dress. That's because she and the rest of the place aren't real, but that doesn't concern the patrons, who have themselves never been real.

Nudger watches in the back bar mirror as the woman rushes over to Wolfe and Holmes and throws herself down on her knees, looking adorable and imploring. He sees her become proper and prim and sidle into the Cozy Room. Mad as all get out but with her head held high, she strides into the Female Urban PI Room. She stands hipshot at the table and trades barbs with Spade and Marlowe. Rubs up against Hammer and Archer, who are reacting quite different from each other. And she sits on a stool next to Nudger.

"I hope this stool doesn't already belong to someone," she says.

"It's all yours," he tells her suavely, gesturing with his right hand and spilling the drink with the pineapple and umbrella all over her.

He stammers his apologies, offers to buy her another drink, realizes it was his that he spilled, asks her how he can possibly make it up to her.

"There's a way," she says somberly, "but it's dangerous."

His stomach seems to bite another of his internal organs. It always starts out this way, or some way like this.

PI Purgatory.

Or maybe it's only in the mind.

Of course it's in the mind.

And in these pages.

Ride the Lightning

A slanted sheet of rain swept like a scythe across Placid Cove Trailer Park. For an instant, an intricate web of lightning illumined the park. The rows of mobile homes loomed square and still and pale against the night, reminding Nudger of tombs with awnings and TV antennas. He held his umbrella at a sharp angle to the wind as he walked, putting a hand in his pocket to pull out a scrap of paper and double-check the address he was trying to find in the maze of trailers. Finally, at the end of Tranquility Lane, he found Number 307 and knocked on its metal door.

"I'm Nudger," he said when the door opened.

For several seconds the woman in the doorway stood staring out at him, rain blowing in beneath the metal awning to spot her cornflower-colored dress and ruffle her straw-blonde hair. She was tall but very thin, fragile-looking, and appeared at first glance to be about twelve years old. Second glance revealed her to be in her mid twenties. She had slight crow's feet at the corners of her luminous blue eyes when she winced as a raindrop struck her face, a knowing cast to her oversized, girlish, full-lipped mouth, and slightly buck teeth. Her looks were hers alone. There was no one who could look much like her, no middle ground with her; men would consider her scrawny and homely, or they would see her as uniquely sensuous. Nudger liked coltish girl-women; he catalogued her as attractive.

"Whoeee!" she said at last, as if seeing for the first time beyond Nudger. "Ain't it raining something terrible?"

"It is," Nudger agreed. "And on me."

Her entire thin body gave a quick, nervous kind of jerk as she smiled apologetically. "I'm Holly Ann Adams, Mr. Nudger. And you are getting wet, all right. Come on in."

She moved aside and Nudger stepped up into the trailer. He expected it to be surprisingly spacious; he'd once lived in a trailer and remembered them as such. This one was cramped and confining. The furniture was cheap and its upholstery was threadbare; a portable black and white TV on a tiny table near the Scotch-plaid sofa was blaring shouts of ecstasy emitted by *The Price Is Right* contestants. The air was thick with the smell of something greasy that had been fried too long.

Holly Ann cleared a stack of *People* magazines from a vinyl chair and motioned for Nudger to sit down. He folded his umbrella, left it by the door, and sat. Holly Ann started to say something, then jerked her body in that peculiar way of hers, almost a twitch, as if she'd just remembered something not only with her mind but with her blood and muscle, and walked over and switched off the noisy television. In the abrupt silence, the rain seemed to beat on the metal roof with added fury. "Now we can talk," Holly Ann proclaimed, sitting opposite Nudger on the undersized sofa. "You a sure-enough private investigator?"

"I'm that," Nudger said. "Did someone recommend me to you, Miss Adams?"

"Gotcha out of the Yellow Pages. And if you're gonna work for me, it might as well be Holly Ann without the Adams."

"Except on the check," Nudger said.

She grinned a devilish twelve-year-old's grin. "Oh, sure, don't worry none about that. I wrote you out a check already, just gotta fill in the amount. That is, if you agree to take the job. You might not."

"Why not?"

"It has to do with my fiancé, Curtis Colt."

Nudger listened for a few seconds to the rain crashing on the roof. "The Curtis Colt who's going to be executed next week?"

"That's the one. Only he didn't kill that liquor store woman; I know it for a fact. It ain't right he should have to ride the lightning."

"Ride the lightning?"

"That's what convicts call dying in the electric chair, Mr. Nudger. They call that chair lotsa things: Old Sparky . . . The Lord's Frying Pan. But Curtis don't belong sitting in it wired up, and I can prove it."

"It's a little late for that kind of talk," Nudger said. "Or did you testify for Curtis in court?"

"Nope. Couldn't testify. You'll see why. All them lawyers and the judge and jury don't even know about me. Curtis didn't want them to know, so he never told them." She crossed her legs and swung her right calf jauntily. She was smiling as if trying to flirt him into wanting to know more about the job so he could free Curtis Colt by a governor's reprieve at the last minute, as in an old movie.

Nudger looked at her gauntly pretty, country-girl face and said, "Tell me about Curtis Colt, Holly Ann."

"You mean you didn't read about him in the newspapers or see him on the television?"

"I only scan the media for misinformation. Give me the details."

"Well, they say Curtis was inside the liquor store, sticking it up—him and his partner had done three other places that night, all of 'em gas stations, though—when the old man that owned the place came out of a back room and seen his wife there behind the counter with her hands up and Curtis holding the gun on her. So the old man lost his head and ran at Curtis, and Curtis had to shoot him. Then the woman got mad when she seen that and ran at Curtis, and Curtis shot her. She's the one that died. The old man, he'll live, but he can't talk nor think nor even feed himself."

Nudger remembered more about the case now. Curtis Colt had been found guilty of first degree murder, and because of a debate in the legislature over the merits of cyanide gas versus electricity, the state was breaking out the electric chair to make him its first killer executed by electricity in over a quarter of a century. Those of the back-to-basics school considered that progress.

"They're gonna shoot Curtis full of electricity next Saturday, Mr. Nudger," Holly Ann said plaintively. She sounded like a little girl complaining that the grade on her report card wasn't fair.

"I know," Nudger said. "But I don't see how I can help you. Or, more specifically, help Curtis."

"You know what they say thoughts really are, Mr. Nudger?" Holly Ann said, ignoring his professed helplessness. Her wide blue eyes were vague as she searched for words. "Thoughts ain't really nothing but tiny electrical impulses in the brain. I read that somewheres or other. What I can't help wondering is, when they shoot all that electricity into Curtis what's it gonna be like to his thinking? How long will it seem like to him before he finally dies? Will there be a big burst of crazy thoughts along with the pain? I know it sounds loony, but I can't help laying awake nights thinking about that, and I feel I just gotta do whatever's left to try and help Curtis."

There was a sort of check-out-tabloid logic in that, Nudger conceded; if thoughts were actually weak electrical impulses, then high-voltage electrical impulses could become exaggerated, horrible thoughts. Anyway, try to disprove it to Holly Ann.

"They never did catch Curtis's buddy, the driver who sped away and left him in that service station, did they?" Nudger asked.

"Nope. Curtis never told who the driver was, neither, no matter how much he was threatened. Curtis is a stubborn man."

Nudger was getting the idea.

"But you know who was driving the car."

"Yep. And he told me him and Curtis was miles away from that liquor store at the time it was robbed. When he seen the police closing in on Curtis in that gas station where Curtis was buying cigarettes, he hit the accelerator and got out of the parking lot before they could catch him. The police didn't even get the car's license plate number."

Nudger rubbed a hand across his chin, watching Holly Ann swing her leg as if it were a shapely metronome. She was barefoot and wearing no nylon hose. "The jury thought Curtis not only was at the liquor store, but that he shot the old man and woman in cold blood."

"That ain't true, though. Not according to—" she caught herself before uttering the man's name.

"Curtis's friend," Nudger finished

"That's right. And he ought to know," Holly Ann said righteously, as if that piece of information were the trump card and the argument was over.

"None of this means anything unless the driver comes forward and substantiates that he was with Curtis somewhere other than at the liquor store when it was robbed."

Holly Ann nodded and stopped swinging her leg. "I know. But he won't. He can't. That's where you come in."

"My profession might enjoy a reputation a notch lower than dognapper," Nudger said, "but I don't hire out to do anything illegal."

"What I want you to do is legal," Holly Ann said in a hurt little voice. Nudger looked past her into the dollhouse kitchen and saw an empty gin bottle. He wondered if she might be slightly drunk. "It's the eyewitness accounts that got Curtis convicted," she went on. "And those people are wrong. I want you to figure out some way to convince them it wasn't Curtis they saw that night."

"Four people, two of them customers in the store, picked Curtis out of a police lineup."

"So what? Ain't eyewitnesses often mistaken?"

Nudger had to admit that they were, though he didn't see how they could be in this case. There were, after all, four of them. And yet, Holly Ann was right; it was amazing how people could sometimes be so certain that the wrong man had committed a crime just five feet in front of them.

"I want you to talk to them witnesses," Holly Ann said. "Find out *why* they think Curtis was the killer. Then show them how they might be wrong and get them to change what they said. We got the truth on our side, Mr. Nudger. At least one witness will change his story when he's made to think about it, because Curtis wasn't where they said he was."

"Curtis has exhausted all his appeals," Nudger said. "Even if all the witnesses changed their stories, it wouldn't necessarily mean he'd get a new trial."

"Maybe not, but I betcha they wouldn't kill him. They couldn't stand the publicity if enough witnesses said they was wrong, it was somebody else killed the old woman. Then, just maybe, eventually, he'd get another trial and get out of prison."

Nudger was awed. Here was foolish optimism that transcended even his own. He had to admire Holly Ann.

The leg started pumping again beneath the cornflower-colored dress. When Nudger lowered his gaze to stare at it,

Holly Ann said, "So will you help me, Mr. Nudger?"

"Sure. It sounds easy."

"Why should I worry about it any more?" Randy Gantner asked Nudger, leaning on his shovel. He didn't mind talking to Nudger; it meant a break from his construction job on the new Interstate 170 cloverleaf. "Colt's been found guilty and he's going to the chair, ain't he?"

The afternoon sun was hammering down on Nudger, warming the back of his neck and making his stomach queasy. He thumbed an antacid tablet off the roll he kept in his shirt pocket and popped one of the white disks into his mouth. With his other hand, he was holding up a photograph of Curtis Colt for Gantner to see. It was a snapshot Holly Ann had given him of the wiry, shirtless Colt leaning on a fence post and holding a beer can high in a mock toast: this one's for Death!

"This is a photograph you never saw in court. I just want you to look at it closely and tell me again if you're sure the man you saw in the liquor store was Colt. Even if it makes no difference in whether he's executed, it will help ease the mind of somebody who loves him."

"I'd be a fool to change my story about what happened now that the trial's over," Gantner said logically.

"You'd be a murderer if you really weren't sure."

Gantner sighed, dragged a dirty red handkerchief from his jeans pocket and wiped his beefy, perspiring face. He peered at the photo, then shrugged. "It's him, Colt, the guy I seen shoot the man and woman when I was standing in the back aisle of the liquor store. If he'd known me and Sanders was back there, he'd have probably zapped us along with them old folks."

"You're positive it's the same man?"

17

Gantner spat off to the side and frowned; Nudger was becoming a pest, and the foreman was staring. "I said it to the police and the jury, Nudger; that little twerp Colt did the old lady in. Ask me, he deserves what he's gonna get."

"Did you actually see the shots fired?"

"Nope. Me and Sanders was in the back aisle looking for some reasonable-priced bourbon when we heard the shots, then looked around to see Curtis Colt back away, turn, and run out to the car. Looked like a black or dark green old Ford. Colt fired another shot as it drove away."

"Did you see the driver?"

"Sort of. Skinny dude with curly black hair and a mustache. That's what I told the cops, that's all I seen. That's all I know."

And that was the end of the conversation. The foreman was walking toward them, glaring. *Thunk!* Gantner's shovel sliced deep into the earth, speeding the day when there'd be another place for traffic to get backed up. Nudger thanked him and advised him not to work too hard in the hot sun.

"You wanna help?" Gantner asked, grinning sweatily.

"I'm already doing some digging of my own," Nudger said, walking away before the foreman arrived.

The other witnesses also stood by their identifications. The fourth and last one Nudger talked with, an elderly woman named Iris Langeneckert, who had been walking her dog near the liquor store and had seen Curtis Colt dash out the door and into the getaway car, said something that Gantner had touched on. When she'd described the getaway car driver, like Gantner she said he was a thin man with curly black hair and a beard or mustache, then she had added, "Like Curtis Colt's hair and mustache."

Nudger looked again at the snapshot Holly Ann had given him. Curtis Colt was about five foot nine, skinny, and mean-looking, with a broad bandito mustache and a mop of curly, greasy black hair. Nudger wondered if it was possible that the getaway car driver had been Curtis Colt himself, and his accomplice had killed the shopkeeper. Even Nudger found that one hard to believe.

He drove to his second-floor office in the near suburb of Maplewood and sat behind his desk in the blast of cold air from the window unit, sipping the complimentary paper cup of iced tea he'd brought up from Danny's Donuts directly below. The sweet smell of the doughnuts was heavier than usual in the office; Nudger had never quite gotten used to it and what it did to his sensitive stomach.

When he was cool enough to think clearly again, he decided he needed more information on the holdup, and on Curtis Colt, from a more objective source than Holly Ann Adams. He phoned Lieutenant Jack Hammersmith at home and was told by Hammersmith's son Jed that Hammersmith had just driven away to go to work on the afternoon shift, so it would be a while before he got to his office.

Nudger checked his answering machine, proving that hope did indeed spring eternal in a fool's breast. There was a terse message from his former wife Eileen demanding last month's alimony payment; a solemn-voiced young man reading an address where Nudger could send a check to help pay to form a watchdog committee that would stop the utilities from continually raising their rates; and a cheerful man informing Nudger that with the labels from ten packages of a brand-name hot dog he could get a Cardinals ballgame ticket at half price. (That meant eating over eighty hot dogs. Nudger calculated that baseball season would be over by the time he did that.) Everyone seemed to want some of Nudger's money. No one wanted to pay Nudger any money. Except for Holly Ann Adams. Nudger decided he'd better step up his efforts on the Curtis Colt case.

He tilted back his head, downed the last dribble of iced tea, then tried to eat what was left of the crushed ice. But the ice clung stubbornly to the bottom of the cup, taunting him. Nudger's life was like that.

He crumpled up the paper cup and tossed it, ice and all, into the wastebasket. Then he went downstairs where his Volkswagen was parked in the shade behind the building and drove east on Manchester, toward downtown and the Third District station house.

Police Lieutenant Jack Hammersmith was in his Third District office, sleek, obese and cool-looking behind his wide metal desk. He was pounds and years away from the handsome cop who'd been Nudger's partner a decade ago in a two-man patrol car. Nudger could still see traces of a dashing quality in the flesh-upholstered Hammersmith, but he wondered if that was only because he'd known Hammersmith ten years ago.

"Sit down, Nudge," Hammersmith invited, his lips smiling but his slate-gray, cop's eyes unreadable. If eyes were the windows to the soul, his shades were always down.

Nudger sat in one of the straight-backed chairs in front of Hammersmith's desk. "I need some help," he said.

"Sure," Hammersmith said, "you never come see me just to trade recipes or to sit and rock." Hammersmith was partial to irony; it was a good thing, in his line of work.

"I need to know more about Curtis Colt," Nudger said.

Hammersmith got one of his vile greenish cigars out of his shirt pocket and stared intently at it, as if its paper ring label might reveal some secret of life and death. "Colt, eh? The guy who's going to ride the lightning?"

"That's the second time in the past few days I've heard

that expression. The first time was from Colt's fiancée. She thinks he's innocent."

"Fiancées think along those lines. Is she your client?"

Nudger nodded but didn't volunteer Holly Ann's name.

"Gullibility makes the world go round," Hammersmith said. "I was in charge of the Homicide investigation on that one. There's not a chance Colt is innocent, Nudge."

"Four eyewitness ID's is compelling evidence," Nudger admitted. "What about the getaway car driver? His description is a lot like Colt's. Maybe he's the one who did the shooting and Colt was the driver."

"Colt's lawyer hit on that. The jury didn't buy it. Neither do I. The man is guilty, Nudge."

"You know how inaccurate eyewitness accounts are," Nudger persisted.

That seemed to get Hammersmith mad. He lit the cigar. The office immediately fogged up.

Nudger made his tone more amicable. "Mind if I look at the file on the Colt case?"

Hammersmith gazed thoughtfully at Nudger through a dense greenish haze. He inhaled, exhaled; the haze became a cloud. "How come this fiancée didn't turn up at the trial to testify for Colt? She could have at least lied and said he was with her that night."

"Colt apparently didn't want her subjected to taking the stand."

"How noble," Hammersmith said. "What makes this fiancée think her prince charming is innocent?"

"She knows he was somewhere else when the shopkeepers were shot."

"But not with her?"

"Nope."

"Well, that's refreshing."

21

Maybe it was refreshing enough to make up Hammersmith's mind. He picked up the phone and asked for the Colt file. Nudger could barely make out what he was saying around the fat cigar, but apparently everyone at the Third was used to Hammersmith and could interpret cigarese.

The file didn't reveal much that Nudger didn't know. Fifteen minutes after the liquor store shooting, officers from a two-man patrol car, acting on the broadcast description of the gunman, approached Curtis Colt inside a service station where he was buying a pack of cigarettes from a vending machine. A car that had been parked near the end of the dimly lighted lot had sped away as they'd entered the station office. The officer had gotten only a glimpse of a dark green old Ford; they hadn't made out the license plate number but thought it might start with the letter "L."

Colt had surrendered without a struggle, and that night at the Third District station the four eyewitnesses had picked him out of a lineup. Their description of the getaway car matched that of the car the police had seen speeding from the service station. The loot from the holdup, and several gas station holdups committed earlier that night, wasn't on Colt, but probably it was in the car.

"Colt's innocence just jumps out of the file at you, doesn't it, Nudge?" Hammersmith said. He was grinning a fat grin around the fat cigar.

"What about the murder weapon?"

"Colt was unarmed when we picked him up."

"Seems odd."

"Not really," Hammersmith said. "He was planning to pay for the cigarettes. And maybe the gun was still too hot to touch so he left it in the car. Maybe it's still hot; it got a lot of use for one night."

Closing the file folder and laying it on a corner of Hammersmith's desk, Nudger stood up. "Thanks, Jack. I'll keep you tapped in if I learn anything interesting."

"Don't bother keeping me informed on this one, Nudge. It's over. I don't see how even a fiancée can doubt Colt's guilt."

Nudger shrugged, trying not to breathe too deeply in the smoke-hazed office. "Maybe it's an emotional thing. She thinks that because thought waves are tiny electrical impulses, Colt might experience time warp and all sorts of grotesque thoughts when that voltage shoots through him. She has bad dreams."

"I'll bet she does," Hammersmith said. "I'll bet Colt has bad dreams, too. Only he deserves his. And maybe she's right."

"About what?"

"About all that voltage distorting thought and time. Who's to say?"

"Not Curtis Colt," Nudger said. "Not after they throw the switch."

"It's a nice theory, though," Hammersmith said. "I'll remember it. It might be a comforting thing to tell the murder victim's family."

"Sometimes," Nudger said, "you think just like a cop who's seen too much."

"Any of it's too much, Nudge," Hammersmith said with surprising sadness. He let more greenish smoke drift from his nostrils and the corners of his mouth; he looked like a stone Buddha seated behind the desk, one in which incense burned.

Nudger coughed and said goodbye.

"Only two eyewitnesses are needed to convict," Nudger

said to Holly Ann the next day in her trailer, "and in this case there are four. None of them is at all in doubt about their identification of Curtis Colt as the killer. I have to be honest; it's time you should face the fact that Colt is guilty and that you're wasting your money on my services."

"All them witnesses know what's going to happen to Curtis," Holly Ann said. "They'd never want to live with the notion they might have made a mistake, killed an innocent man, so they've got themselves convinced that they're positive it was Curtis they saw that night."

"Your observation on human psychology is sound," Nudger said, "but I don't think it will help us. The witnesses were just as certain three months ago at the trial. I took the time to read the court transcript; the jury had no choice but to find Colt guilty, and the evidence hasn't changed."

Holly Ann drew her legs up and clasped her knees to her chest with both arms. Her little-girl posture matched her little-girl faith in her lover's innocence. She believed the white knight must arrive at any moment and snatch Curtis Colt from the electrical jaws of death. She believed hard. Nudger could almost hear his armor clank when he walked.

She wanted him to believe just as hard. "I see you need to be convinced of Curtis's innocence," she said wistfully. There was no doubt he'd forced her into some kind of corner. "If you come here tonight at eight, Mr. Nudger, I'll convince you."

"How?"

"I can't say. You'll understand why tonight."

"Why do we have to wait till tonight?"

"Oh, you'll see."

Nudger looked at the waiflike creature curled in the corner of the sofa. He felt as if they were playing a childhood guessing game while Curtis Colt waited his turn in the elec-

24

tric chair. Nudger had never seen an execution; he'd heard it took longer than most people thought for the condemned to die. His stomach actually twitched.

"Can't we do this now with twenty questions?" he asked.

Holly Ann shook her head. "No, Mr. Nudger."

Nudger sighed and stood up, feeling as if he were about to bump his head on the trailer's low ceiling even though he was barely six feet tall.

"Make sure you're on time tonight, Mr. Nudger," Holly Ann said as he went out the door. "It's important."

At eight on the nose that evening Nudger was sitting at the tiny table in Holly Ann's kitchenette. Across from him was a thin, nervous man in his late twenties or early thirties, dressed in a long-sleeved shirt despite the heat, and wearing sunglasses with silver mirror lenses. Holly Ann introduced the man as "Len, but that's not his real name," and said he was Curtis Colt's accomplice and the driver of their getaway car on the night of the murder.

"But me and Curtis was nowhere near the liquor store when them folks got shot," Len said vehemently.

Nudger assumed the sunglasses were so he couldn't effectively identify Len if it came to a showdown in court. Len had lank, dark brown hair that fell to below his shoulders, and when he moved his arm Nudger caught sight of something blue and red on his briefly exposed wrist. A tattoo. Which explained the long-sleeved shirt.

"You can understand why Len couldn't come forth and testify for Curtis in court," Holly Ann said.

Nudger said he could understand that Len would have had to incriminate himself.

"We was way on the other side of town," Len said, "casing another service station, when that liquor store killing went down. Heck, we never held up nothing but service stations. They was our specialty."

Which was true, Nudger had to admit. Colt had done time for armed robbery six years ago after sticking up half a dozen service stations within a week. And all the other holdups he'd been tied to this time around were of service stations. The liquor store was definitely a departure in his M.O., one not noted in court during Curtis Colt's rush to judgment.

"Your hair is in your favor," Nudger said to Len.

"Huh?"

"Your hair didn't grow that long in the three months since the liquor store killing. The witnesses described the getaway car driver as having shorter, curlier hair, like Colt's, and a mustache."

Len shrugged. "I'll be honest with you—it don't help at all. Me and Curtis was kinda the same type. So to confuse any witnesses, in case we got caught, we made each other look even more alike. I'd tuck up my long hair and wear a wig that looked like Curtis's hair. My mustache was real, like Curtis's. I shaved it off a month ago. We did look alike at a glance, sorta like brothers."

Nudger bought that explanation; it wasn't uncommon for a team of holdup men to play tricks to confuse witnesses and the police. Too many lawyers had gotten in the game; the robbers, like the cops, were taking the advice of their attorneys and thinking about a potential trial even before the crime was committed.

"Is there any way, then, to prove you were across town at the time of the murder?" Nudger asked, looking at the two small Nudgers staring back at him from the mirror lenses.

"There's just my word," Len said, rather haughtily.

Nudger didn't bother telling him what that was worth. Why antagonize him?

26

"I just want you to believe Curtis is innocent," Len said with desperation. "Because he is! And so am I!"

And Nudger understood why Len was here, taking the risk. If Colt was guilty of murder, Len was guilty of being an accessory to the crime. Once Curtis Colt had ridden the lightning, Len would have hanging over him the possibility of an almost certain life sentence, and perhaps even his own ride on the lightning, if he were ever caught. It wasn't necessary to actually squeeze the trigger to be convicted of murder.

"I need for you to try extra hard to prove Curtis is innocent," Len said. His thin lips quivered; he was near tears.

"Are you giving Holly Ann the money to pay me?" Nudger asked.

"Some of it, yeah. From what Curtis and me stole. And I gave Curtis's share to Holly Ann, too. Me and her are fifty-fifty on this."

Dirty money, Nudger thought. Dirty job. Still, if Curtis Colt happened to be innocent, trying against the clock to prove it was a job that needed to be done.

"Okay. I stay on the case."

"Thanks," Len said. His narrow hand moved impulsively across the table and squeezed Nudger's arm in gratitude. Len had the look of an addict; Nudger wondered if the long-sleeved shirt was to hide needle tracks as well as the tattoo.

Len stood up. "Stay here with Holly Ann for ten minutes while I make myself scarce. I gotta know I wasn't followed. You understand it ain't that I don't trust you; a man in my position has gotta be sure, is all."

"I understand. Go."

Len gave a spooked smile and went out the door. Nudger heard his running footfalls on the gravel outside the trailer. Nudger was forty-three years old and ten pounds overweight; lean and speedy Len needed a ten-minute head start like

27

Sinatra needed singing lessons.

"Is Len a user?" Nudger asked Holly Ann.

"Sometimes. But my Curtis never touched no dope."

"You know I have to tell the police about this conversation, don't you?"

Holly Ann nodded. "That's why we arranged it this way. They won't be any closer to Len than before."

"They might want to talk to you, Holly Ann."

She shrugged. "It don't matter. I don't know where Len is, nor even his real name nor how to get in touch with him. He'll find out all he needs to know about Curtis by reading the papers."

"You have a deceptively devious mind," Nudger told her, "considering that you look like Barbie Doll's country kid cousin."

Holly Ann smiled, surprised and pleased. "Do you find me attractive, Mr. Nudger?"

"Yes. And painfully young." For just a moment Nudger almost thought of Curtis Colt as a lucky man. Then he looked at his watch, saw that his ten minutes were about up, and said goodbye. If Barbie had a kid cousin, Ken probably had one somewhere, too. And time was something you couldn't deny. Ask Curtis Colt.

"It doesn't wash with me," Hammersmith said from behind his desk, puffing angrily on his cigar. Angrily because it did wash a little bit; he didn't like the possibility, however remote, of sending an innocent man to his death. That was every good homicide cop's nightmare. "This Len character is just trying to keep himself in the clear on a murder charge."

"You could read it that way," Nudger admitted.

"It would help if you gave us a better description of Len," Hammersmith said gruffly, as if Nudger were to blame for

Curtis Colt's accomplice still walking around free.

"I gave you what I could," Nudger said. "Len didn't give me much to pass on. He's streetwise and scared and knows what's at stake."

Hammersmith nodded, his fit of pique past. But the glint of weary frustration remained in his eyes.

"Are you going to question Holly Ann?" Nudger said.

"Sure, but it won't do any good. She's probably telling the truth. Len would figure we'd talk to her; he wouldn't tell her how to find him."

"You could stake out her trailer."

"Do you think Holly Ann and Len might be lovers?"

"No."

Hammersmith shook his head. "Then they'll probably never see each other again. Watching her trailer would be a waste of manpower."

Nudger knew Hammersmith was right. He stood up to go.

"What are you going to do now?" Hammersmith asked.

"I'll talk to the witnesses again. I'll read the court transcript again. And I'd like to talk with Curtis Colt."

"They don't allow visitors on Death Row, Nudge, only temporary boarders."

"This case is an exception," Nudger said. "Will you try to arrange it?"

Hammersmith chewed thoughtfully on his cigar. Since he'd been the officer in charge of the murder investigation, he'd been the one who'd nailed Curtis Colt. That carried an obligation.

"I'll phone you soon," he said, "let you know."

Nudger thanked Hammersmith and walked down the hall into the clear, breathable air of the booking area.

That day he managed to talk again to all four eyewitnesses. Two of them got mad at Nudger for badgering them. They all stuck to their stories. Nudger reported this to Holly Ann at the Right-Steer Steakhouse, where she worked as a waitress. Several customers that afternoon got tears with their baked potatoes.

Hammersmith phoned Nudger that evening.

"I managed to get permission for you to talk to Colt," he said, "but don't get excited. Colt won't talk to you. He won't talk to anyone, not even a clergyman. He'll change his mind about the clergyman, but not about you."

"Did you tell him I was working for Holly Ann?"

"I had that information conveyed to him. He wasn't impressed. He's one of the stoic ones on Death Row."

Nudger's stomach kicked up, growled something that sounded like a hopeless obscenity. If even Curtis Colt wouldn't cooperate, how could he be helped? Absently Nudger peeled back the aluminum foil on a roll of antacid tablets and slipped two chalky white disks into his mouth. Hammersmith knew his nervous stomach and must have heard him chomping away. "Take it easy, Nudge. This isn't your fault."

"Then why do I feel like it is?"

"Because you feel too much of everything. That's why you had to quit the department."

"We've got another day before the execution," Nudger said. "I'm going to go through it all again. I'm going to talk to each of those witnesses even if they try to run when they see me coming. Maybe somebody will say something that will let in some light."

"There's no light out there, Nudge. You're wasting your time. Give up on this one and move on."

"Not yet," Nudger said "There's something elusive here that I can't quite grab."

"And never will," Hammersmith said. "Forget it, Nudge.

Live your life and let Curtis Colt lose his."

Hammersmith was right. Nothing Nudger did helped Curtis Colt in the slightest. At eight o'clock Saturday morning, while Nudger was preparing breakfast in his apartment, Colt was put to death in the electric chair. He'd offered no last words before two thousand volts had turned him from something into nothing.

Nudger heard the news of Colt's death on his kitchen radio. He went ahead and ate his eggs, but he skipped the toast.

That afternoon he consoled a numbed and frequently sobbing Holly Ann and apologized for being powerless to stop her true love's execution. She was polite, trying to be brave. She preferred to suffer alone. Her boss at the Right-Steer gave her the rest of the day off, and Nudger drove her home.

Nudger slept a total of four hours during the next two nights. On Monday, he felt compelled to attend Curtis Colt's funeral. There were about a dozen people clustered around the grave, including the state-appointed clergyman and pallbearers. Nudger stood off to one side during the brief service. Holly Ann, looking like a child playing dress-up in black, stood well off to the other side. They didn't exchange words, only glances.

As the coffin was lowered into the earth, Nudger watched Holly Ann walk to where a taxi was waiting by a weathered stone angel. The cab wound its way slowly along the snaking narrow cemetery road to tall iron gates and the busy street. Holly Ann never looked back.

That night Nudger realized what was bothering him, and for the first time since Curtis Colt's death, he slept well.

In the morning he began watching Holly Ann's trailer.

At seven-thirty she emerged, dressed in her yellow wait-ress uniform, and got into another taxi. Nudger followed in his battered Volkswagen Beetle as the cab drove her the four miles to her job at the Right-Steer Steakhouse. She didn't look around as she paid the driver and walked inside through the molded plastic Old West-saloon swinging doors.

At six that evening another cab drove her home, making a brief stop at a grocery store.

It went that way for the rest of the week, trailer to work to trailer. Holly Ann had no visitors other than the plain brown paper bag she took home every night.

The temperature got up to around ninety-five and the hu-midity rose right along with it. It was one of St. Louis's leg-endary summer heat waves. Sitting melting in the Volkswagen, Nudger wondered if what he was doing was really worthwhile. Curtis Colt was, after all, dead, and had never been his client. Still, there were responsibilities that went beyond the job. Or perhaps they were actually the es-sence of the job.

The next Monday, after Holly Ann had left for work, Nudger used his Visa card to slip the flimsy lock on her trailer door, and let himself in.

It took him over an hour to find what he was searching for. It had been well hidden, in a cardboard box inside the access panel to the bathroom plumbing. After looking at the box's contents—almost seven hundred dollars in loot from Curtis Colt's brief life of crime, and another object Nudger wasn't surprised to see—Nudger resealed the box and replaced the access panel.

He continued to watch and follow Holly Ann, more confi-dent now.

Two weeks after the funeral, when she left work one eve-ning she didn't go home.

Instead her taxi turned the opposite way and drove east on Watson Road. Nudger followed the cab along a series of side streets in South St. Louis, then part way down a dead-end alley to a large garage, above the door of which was lettered "Clifford's Auto Body."

Nudger backed out quickly onto the street then parked the Volkswagen near the mouth of the alley. A few minutes later the cab drove by without a passenger. Within ten minutes, Holly Ann drove past in a shiny red Ford. It's license plate number began with an L.

When Nudger reached Placid Cove Trailer Park, he saw the Ford nosed in next to Holly Ann's trailer.

On the way to the trailer door, he paused and etched the Ford's hood with a key. Even in the lowering evening light he could see that beneath the new red paint the car's color was dark green.

Holly Ann answered the door right away when he knocked. She tried a smile when she saw it was him, but she couldn't quite manage her facial muscles, as if they'd become rigid and uncoordinated. She appeared ten years older. The little-girl look had deserted her; now she was an emaciated, grief-eroded woman, a country Barbie doll whose features some evil child had lined with dark crayon. The shaded crescents beneath her eyes completely took away their innocence. She was holding a glass that had once been a jelly jar. In it were two fingers of a clear liquid. Behind her on the table was a crumpled brown paper bag and a half-empty bottle of gin.

"I figured it out," Nudger told her.

Now she did smile, but it was fleeting, a sickly bluish shadow crossing her taut features. "You're like a dog with a rag, Mr. Nudger. You surely don't know when to let go." She stepped back and he followed her into the trailer. It was warm in there; something was wrong with the air conditioner. "Hot

33

as hell, ain't it," Holly Ann commented. Nudger thought that was apropos.

He sat down at the tiny Formica table, just as he and Len had sat facing each other two weeks ago. She offered him a drink. He declined. She downed the contents of the jelly jar glass and poured herself another, clumsily striking the neck of the bottle on the glass. It made a sharp, flinty sound, as if sparks might fly.

"Now, what's this you've got figured out, Mr. Nudger?" She didn't want to, but she had to hear it. Had to share it.

"It's almost four miles to the Right-Steer Steakhouse," Nudger told her. "The waitresses there make little more than minimum wage, so cab fare to and from work has to eat a big hole in your salary. But then you seem to go everywhere by cab."

"My car's been in the shop."

"I figured it might be, after I found the money and the wig."

She bowed her head slightly and took a sip of gin. "Wig?"

"In the cardboard box inside the bathroom wall."

"You been snooping, Mr. Nudger." There was more resignation than outrage in her voice.

"You're sort of skinny, but not a short girl," Nudger went on. "With a dark curly wig and a fake mustache, sitting in a car, you'd resemble Curtis Colt enough to fool a dozen eyewitnesses who just caught a glimpse of you. It was a smart precaution for the two of you to take."

Holly Ann looked astounded. "Are you saying I was driving the getaway car at the liquor store holdup?"

"Maybe. Then maybe you hired someone to play Len and convince me he was Colt's accomplice and that they were far away from the murder scene when the trigger was pulled. After I found the wig, I talked to some of your neighbors, who told me that until recently you'd driven a green Ford sedan."

Holly Ann ran her tongue along the edges of her protruding teeth.

"So Curtis and Len used my car for their holdups."

"I doubt if Len ever met Curtis. He's somebody you paid in stolen money or drugs to sit there where you're sitting now and lie to me."

"If I was driving that getaway car, Mr. Nudger, and knew Curtis was guilty, why would I have hired a private investigator to try to find a hole in the eyewitnesses' stories?"

"That's what bothered me at first," Nudger said, "until I realized you weren't interested in clearing Curtis. What you were really worried about was Curtis Colt talking in prison. You didn't want those witnesses' stories changed, you wanted them verified. And you wanted the police to learn about not-his-right-name Len."

Holly Ann raised her head to look directly at him with eyes that begged and dreaded. She asked simply, "Why would I want that?"

"Because you were Curtis Colt's accomplice in all of his robberies. And when you hit the liquor store, he stayed in the car to drive. You fired the shot that killed the old woman. He was the one who fired the wild shot from the speeding car. Colt kept quiet about it because he loved you. He never talked, not to the police, not to his lawyer, not even to a priest. Now that he's dead you can trust him forever, but I have a feeling you could have anyway. He loved you more than you loved him, and you'll have to live knowing he didn't deserve to die."

She looked down into her glass as if for answers and didn't say anything for a long time. Nudger felt a bead of perspiration trickle crazily down the back of his neck. Then she said, "I didn't want to shoot that old man, but he didn't leave me no choice. Then the old woman came at me." She looked up at Nudger and smiled ever so slightly. It was a smile Nudger hadn't seen on her before, one he didn't like. "God help me, Mr. Nudger, I can't quit thinking about shooting that old woman."

"You murdered her," Nudger said, "and you murdered Curtis Colt by keeping silent and letting him die for you."

"You can't prove nothing," Holly Ann said, still with her ancient-eyed, eerie smile that had nothing to do with amusement.

"You're right," Nudger told her, "I can't. But I don't think legally proving it is necessary, Holly Ann. You said it: thoughts are actually tiny electrical impulses in the brain. Curtis Colt rode the lightning all at once. With you, it will take years, but the destination is the same. I think you'll come to agree that his way was easier."

She sat very still. She didn't answer. Wasn't going to.

Nudger stood up and wiped his damp forehead with the back of his hand. He felt sticky, dirty, confined by the low ceiling and near walls of the tiny, stifling trailer. He had to get out of there to escape the sensation of being trapped.

He didn't say goodbye to Holly Ann when he walked out. She didn't say goodbye to him. The last sound Nudger heard as he left the trailer was the clink of the bottle on the glass.

What You Don't Know Can Hurt You

"You are Nudger?"

"I am Nudger."

The bulky woman who had leaned over Nudger and confirmed his identity had a halo of dark frizzy hair, a round face, round cheeks, round rimless spectacles, and a small round pursed mouth. She reminded Nudger of one of those dolls made with dried whole apples, whose faces eerily resemble those of aged humans. But the apple dolls' usually are benign; the face looming over Nudger came equipped with tiny dark eyes that danced with malice.

Behind the round-faced woman had stood two silent male companions. She and the two men hadn't spoken when they'd entered Nudger's office without having sounded the buzzer and in workmanlike fashion had begun beating him up.

"Who? What? Why?" a frightened Nudger had asked, wrapping his arms around his head and trying to think of who other than his former wife would want to do this to him. He couldn't divine an answer. "I don't need this!" he'd implored. "Stop it, please!"

And they had stopped. Extent of damage: sore ribs, cut forehead, but no damaged pride. Nudger was still alive; that was the object of his game.

But there was more to it. He'd felt his shirtsleeve being unbuttoned, shoved roughly up his forearm. And the abrupt bite of a dull hypodermic needle as it was inserted just below his elbow. Sodium Pentothal, he deduced, before floating away on a private, agreeable cloud. His mouth seemed to become completely disassociated from his brain. He was vaguely aware that he was answering questions posed by the round-faced woman, that he was rambling uncontrollably. Yet he couldn't remember the questions or his answers a few seconds after they were uttered. Then an emptiness, a breathtaking slippage of light and time.

Nudger opened his eyes and wondered where he'd been dropped. It didn't seem proper that he should be slowly revolving. Then the sensation of motion ceased, and with relief he realized he was lying on his back on his office floor. He felt remarkably heavy and comfortable.

Moving only his eyes, he gazed around and took in the open desk drawers and file cabinets, the papers and yellow file folders strewn about the floor. He remembered the hulking round-faced woman and her greedy pig's eyes and her two silent masculine helpers. He tried to recall the round-faced woman's questions but he couldn't.

Nudger struggled to a sitting position and a headache fell on him like a slab from the ceiling. When he'd become somewhat accustomed to the idea of enduring throbbing pain for the rest of his life, he stood, dizzily staggered to his desk, and sat down. The squeal of his swivel chair penetrated his brain like a hot stiletto.

What was it all about? What could he know that the round-faced woman wanted to know? All he was working on now was a divorce case, like dozens of other divorce cases he'd handled as a private investigator. The husband was sleeping with his secretary, the wife had a compensatory affair going with her hairdresser, the husband had hired Nudger to get the goods on the wife. That would be easy; she was flaunting the affair. All of these people were suburbanites who wouldn't know a round-faced woman who shot up people with Sodium Pentothal; they were mostly concerned about who was going to come away with the TV and the blender.

Nudger made his way over to where the coffeepot sat on the floor by the plug in the corner. He tried to pour a cupful but found that the round-faced woman and friends had emptied the pot and spread the grounds around on the floor. Maybe it was diamonds they were looking for.

Sloshing through a shallow sea of papers and file folders, Nudger got his tan overcoat from its brass hook, wriggled into it, put on his crushproof hat, and went out, not locking the door behind him. He took the steep steps down the narrow stairwell to the door to the street, feeling the temperature drop as he descended. He shoved open the outer door and braced himself as the winter air stiffened the hairs in his nostrils. The sudden rush of cold made his headache go away. He almost smiled as he stepped out onto the treacherous pavement and walked quickly but gingerly in a neat loop through the door of Danny's Donuts, directly above which his office was located.

Nobody was in the place but Danny. That was the usual state of the business. Nudger breathed in deeply the sudden warmth and cloying sweetness of the doughnuts and unbuttoned his coat. He sat on a stool at the end of the stainless steel counter. Without being asked, Danny set a large plastic-coated paper cup of steaming black coffee before him. Danny was Danny Evers, a fortyish guy like Nudger, and, some might say, a loser like Nudger. Even Danny might say that, aware as he was that he made doughnuts like sash weights.

But what he said was, "You cut yourself shaving?" as he pointed at the cut on Nudger's forehead.

Nudger had forgotten about the injury. He raised tentative fingers, felt ridges of blood coagulated by the cold. "I had a

39

visit from some friends," he said.

"Some friends!" Danny said, changing the emphasis. He put some iced cake doughnuts and a couple of glazed into a grease-spotted carryout box. He was a sad-featured man who seemed to do everything with apprehensive intensity, a concerned basset hound.

"Actually I never met them before this morning," Nudger said, sipping the coffee and burning his tongue. "So naturally we were curious about each other, but they asked all the questions."

"Yeah? What kinda questions?"

"That's the odd thing," Nudger said. "I can't remember."

Danny laughed, then cocked his head of thick graying hair and squinted again at the cut on Nudger's forehead. "You serious about not remembering?"

"It's not the knock on the head," Nudger assured him. "They shot me up with a drug that made me a regular mindless talking machine. It's called truth serum. It works even better than cheap scotch."

"Maybe you oughta see a doctor, Nudge."

"Find me one that doesn't charge twenty dollars a stitch."

"I mean about the memory."

"That kind of a doctor charges twenty dollars a question."

Both men were silent while a blonde secretary from the office building across the street came in, paid for the carryout order, and left. Nudger smiled at her but she ignored him. It took a while for the doughnut shop to warm up again.

"I could drive you," Danny offered. "Emil is coming in to take over here in about fifteen minutes." Emil was Danny's hired help, a sometime college student working odd jobs. He made better doughnuts than his boss's.

"I've got my car here," Nudger said.

"But maybe you shouldn't drive."

"I won't drive anywhere for a while," Nudger said. "What I'll do is go back upstairs and straighten up my office. If you'll give me another cup of coffee and a jelly doughnut, and put them on my tab."

"Straighten up why?" Danny asked, reaching into the display case.

"It's always a mess after friends drop by unexpectedly," Nudger told him.

"Some friends, those boys and girls," Danny reiterated, dropping the doughnut into a small white bag. It hit bottom with a solid smack.

As he trudged back up the unheated stairwell to his office, Nudger tried again, with each painful step, to surmise some reason for his interrogation. He could think of none. Business had been slow ever since summer, and he had been a good boy. Danny's horrendous coffee had started his stomach roiling. He'd take a few antacid tablets before drinking a second cup.

He stopped at his office door and stood holding the sack. It was a morning for surprises. In the chair by the desk sat a slender man wearing a camel hair topcoat with a fur collar. On his lap were expensive brown suede gloves. On his gloves rested pale, still, well-manicured hands. The man's bony face was as calm as his hands were.

"There's no need to introduce myself, Mr. Nudger," he said in a smoothly modulated voice. "On your desk is a sealed envelope. In the envelope is five thousand dollars. You've proved yourself a clever man, so you can't be bought cheap." A thin smile did nothing for him. "But, like all men, you can be bought. I know your present financial status, so five thousand should suffice."

The man stood up, unfolding in sections until he was at

least four inches taller than Nudger's six feet. But he was thin, very thin, not a big man. He gazed down his narrow nose at Nudger with the remote interest of a scientist observing familiar bacteria.

"The problem is," Nudger told him, "I don't know who you are or what you're buying."

"I'll make myself clear, Mr. Nudger: stay away from Chaser Heights, or next time you'll be paid a visit of an altogether more unpleasant nature."

He turned and left the office with wolflike loping strides.

Nudger stood stupefied, listening to the man's descending footfalls on the wooden stairs to the street. He heard the street door open and close. The papers on the floor stirred.

Nudger went to the office door and shoved it closed. He walked to his desk, and sure enough there was an envelope, sealed. He opened it and counted out five thousand dollars in bills of various denominations. Earning this money would be a cinch, since he'd never been near any place or anyone named Chaser Heights. Then he reconsidered.

There was little doubt of a connection between the round-faced woman and the tall man. What bothered Nudger was that if these unsettling characters thought he'd been around Chaser Heights at least once when he hadn't, what was going to keep them from thinking he'd been there again? And acting forcefully on their misconception?

Now the five thousand didn't look so good to Nudger. This occupation of his had gotten him into trouble again. He put the money back into its envelope and tucked in the flap. He opened a desk drawer and got out a fresh roll of antacid tablets. He wished he knew how to paint a house.

After his stomach had calmed down, Nudger set about putting his office back together. Small as the place was, the task took the rest of the morning. Most of the time was spent matching the footprinted papers on the floor with the correct file folders. When he was finished he looked around with satisfaction, straightened the shade on his desk lamp, then went out for some lunch.

At a place he knew on Grand Avenue, Nudger drank a glass of milk, picked at the Gardener's Delight lettuce omelet special, and studied the phone directory he'd borrowed from the proprietor. Within a few minutes he found what he was looking for: Chaser Heights Alcoholic Rehabilitation Center, with an Addington Road address way out in the county.

Nudger knew what he had to do, even if it cost him five thousand dollars.

He finished his milk but pushed his omelet away, jotted down the Chaser Heights address on a paper napkin, and put it into his pocket.

Outside, he slammed his Volkswagen's door on the tail of his topcoat, as he invariably did, reopened the door and tried again, and twisted the key in the ignition switch. When the tiny motor was clattering rhythmically, he pulled the dented VW out into traffic.

It had been a large and palatial country home in better days, with sentry-box cupolas, tall colonial pillars, and ivy-covered brick. Now it was called Chaser Heights, which Nudger gathered was a sort of clinic where alcoholics went to tilt the odds in their battle with booze. It was isolated, set well back from the narrow road on a gentle rise, and mostly surrounded by woods that in their present leafless state conveyed a depressing reminder of mortality.

Nudger parked halfway up the long gravel drive to study the house. He realized that the longer he sat there in the cozy warm car, the more difficult it would be to do what he intended. He put the VW in gear and listened to the tires crunch on the gravel as he drove the rest of the way to the house.

He entered a huge foyer with a gleaming tiled floor that smelled of pine disinfectant. There were brown vinyl easy chairs scattered about, and behind a high, horseshoe-shaped desk stood a tall elderly woman wearing a stiff white uniform. The starch seemed to have affected her face.

"May I help you?" she asked without real enthusiasm, as if she risked ripping her lips by parting them to speak.

"I'd like to see whoever's in charge," Nudger told her, removing his hat. He leaned with his elbow on the desk as if it were a bar and he was about to order a drink.

"Do you have an appointment with Dr. Wedgewick?" the woman asked.

"No, but I believe he'll want to see me. Tell Dr. Wedgewell that a Mr. Nudger is here and needs to talk with him."

"Dr. Wedge*wick,*" his mannequin corrected him. She was so lifelike you expected her eyes to move. She picked up a beige telephone and conveyed Nudger's message, then without change of expression directed him down a hall and to the last door on his left.

He entered an anteroom and was told by an efficient-looking young brunette on her way out that he should go right in, Dr. Wedgewick was expecting him.

And Nudger was expecting Dr. Wedgewick to be exactly who he turned out to be: the tall, camel-coated unfriendly man who had delivered the five thousand dollars. He was wearing a dark blue suit and maroon tie and was seated behind a slate-topped desk a bit smaller than a Ping-Pong table. There wasn't so much as a paper clip to break its smooth gray surface. Behind him was a floor-to-ceiling window that overlooked bare-limbed trees and brown grass sloping away toward the distant road. Probably in the summer it was an impressive view. He didn't get up.

"I am surprised to see you here," he said flatly.

"You'll be more surprised by why I came," Nudger told him.

Dr. Wedgewick arched an inquisitive eyebrow impossibly high. Obviously he'd practiced the expression, had it down pat, and knew there was no need for words to accompany it.

"I'm here to return this," Nudger said, and tossed the envelope with the five thousand dollars onto the desk. It looked as lonely as a center fielder there. "Its return should prove to you that you've made a mistake. I can't be who you think; I can't sell you whatever it is you want to buy, because I don't have it and don't know what it is."

"That is nonsense, Mr. Nudger. You've been followed from here several times by Dr. Olander, observed going to your office by the back entrance, observed emerging at times and coming here, snooping around here. Where you hid the pertinent information regarding your client, and how you managed to fool Dr. Olander when she administered her drugs, I can't say, nor do I care."

"I didn't fool her," Nudger said. "I have no client and I didn't know the answers to her questions. But I understand somewhat more of what's going on. Dr. Olander and her two silent helpers couldn't make any progress with me their way, so you came around and tried to buy me."

"We live in a mercantile society."

"The thing is, there was no reason for Dr. Olander to hassle me, and there was nothing I could tell her. I wish there were some way to get you to believe that."

"Oh, I'll bet you do."

"And I wish you'd tell me why a doctor would want to follow me to begin with, me without medical insurance."

Dr. Wedgewick smiled with large, stained, but even teeth. "Dr. Olander is not a medical doctor. You might say hers is an honorary title. She is chief of security here at Chaser Heights."

"Then I needn't expect a bill." He felt in his pocket for his tablets.

"What you should expect, Mr. Nudger, is to suffer the consequences of being stubborn."

Nudger saw Dr. Wedgewick's gaze shift to something over his left shoulder. He turned and saw the round, malicious features of Dr. Olander. She had taken a few silent steps into the office. Now she stood very still, staring through her gleaming spectacles at the bulge of the hand concealed in Nudger's coat.

He realized that she thought he had a gun.

"What's this wimp doing here?" Dr. Olander asked. "I thought he'd been taken care of."

Nudger, still with his hand inside his coat, perspiring fingers wrapped tightly around his roll of antacid tablets, backed to the door, keeping as far as possible from her. His stomach was fluttering a few feet beyond him, beckoning him on.

Dr. Wedgewick said, "He brought back the five thousand dollars." He looked somewhat curiously at Nudger. "Someone must be paying you a great deal of money," he said. His slow, discolored smile wasn't a nice thing to see. "You'll find that it isn't enough to make it worth your while, Mr. Nudger. You can't put a price on your health."

But Nudger was out into the hall and half running to the lobby. There were a few patients in the vinyl armchairs now. One of them, a ruddy old man wearing a pale blue robe and pajamas, glanced up from where he sat reading *People* and smiled at Nudger. The waxwork behind the counter didn't.

Nudger shoved open the outside door and broke into a

46

run. He piled into his car fast, started the engine, and heard the tires fling gravel against the insides of the fenders as he drove toward the twin stone pillars that marked the exit to the road and safety.

All the way down Addington Road to the alternative highway he kept checking his rearview mirror, expecting to be followed by troops from Chaser Heights. But as he turned onto the cloverleaf he realized they didn't have to follow; they knew where to find him.

When he got back to the office he parked in front, out on the busy street, instead of in his slot behind the building. As he climbed out of the car he noticed that the tail of his topcoat was crushed and grease-stained where he'd shut the door on it again. The coattail had flapped in the wind like a flag all the way back from Chaser Heights. For once Nudger didn't care. He went up to his office, locked the door behind him, and sat for a while chomping antacid tablets.

When his stomach had untied itself, he picked up the phone and dialed the number of the Third Precinct and asked for Lieutenant Jack Hammersmith.

Hammersmith had been Nudger's partner a decade ago in a two-man patrol car, before Nudger's jittery nerves had forced him to retire from the police force. Now Hammersmith had rank and authority, and he always had time for Nudger, but not much time.

"What sort of quicksand have you got yourself into this time, Nudge?" Hammersmith asked.

"The sort that might be bottomless. What do you know about a place called Chaser Heights, out on Addington Road?"

"That clinic where drunks dry out?"

Nudger said that was the one.

"It's a second-rate operation, maybe even a front, but it's out of my jurisdiction, Nudge. I got plenty to worry about here in the city limits."

"What about the director out there? Guy named Dr. Wedgewick?"

"He's new in the area. From the East Coast, I been told." Nudger heard the rhythmic wheezing of Hammersmith laboriously firing up one of his foul-smelling cigars and was glad this conversation was by phone. "Anything else, Nudge?" The words were slightly distorted by the cigar.

"How about Wedgewick's assistant and chief of security, a two-hundred-pound chunk of feminine wiles named Dr. Olander?"

"Hah! That would be Millicent Olaphant, and she's no doctor, she's a part-time bone crusher for some of the local loan sharks."

"Isn't that kind of unusual work for a woman?"

"Yes, I would say it is unusual," Hammersmith said dryly, "and I meet all sorts of people in my job. You be careful of that crew, Nudge. The law out there is the Mayfair County sheriff, Dale Caster."

"What kind of help could I expect from Caster if I did get in the soup?"

"He'd drop crackers on you. Let's just say it would be difficult for a place like Chaser Heights to stay in business if they didn't grease the proper palms."

"And they grease palms liberally," Nudger said. He expected Hammersmith to ask him to elaborate, but the very busy lieutenant repeated his suggestion that Nudger be careful and then hung up.

Nudger sat for a long time, leaning back in the swivel chair, gazing at the ceiling's network of cracks that looked like a rough map of Illinois including major highways. He thought. Not about Illinois.

He thought until the telephone rang, then he picked up the receiver and identified himself.

"This is Danny, downstairs, Nudge," came the answering voice. "Your ex, Eileen, was by here about an hour ago looking for you. She was frowning. You behind with your alimony payments?"

"No further than with the rent," Nudger said. "Thanks for the warning, Danny."

"No trouble, Nudge. She bought half a dozen cream horns."

"Then she's doing better than I am."

When Nudger had replaced the receiver in its cradle he sat staring at it instead of Illinois, and he remembered something Danny had said this morning. "Some friends, those boys and girls," he had said. But Nudger hadn't mentioned Dr. Olander-Olaphant's gender.

Nudger put on his coat and tromped downstairs, gaining more understanding as he descended. He went outside, but instead of taking a few steps to the right and entering Danny's Donuts, he cut through the gangway and entered the building through the rear door, then opened another unlocked door and was in the aromatic back room of the doughnut shop. On a coat tree he saw Danny's topcoat, similar to the rumpled tan coat he, Nudger, was wearing and Danny's sold-by-the-thousands brown crushproof hat that was identical with Nudger's. Nudger and Danny were about the same height, and seen from a distance and wearing bulky coats they were of a similar build. Things were making sense at last.

Nudger walked into the greater warmth of the doughnut shop proper, nodded to the surprised Danny, and sat on a stool on the customers' side of the counter. He and Danny were alone in the shop; Emil got off work at two, after the almost nonexistent lunch trade.

"I shoulda said something to you earlier, Nudge," Danny said, no longer looking surprised, nervously wiping the already gleaming counter. "I seen them people from Chaser Heights go up to your place this morning, but I couldn't figure out why until you came down here and told me you'd been roughed up."

"You've been sniffing around there, haven't you?" Nudger said.

Danny nodded. He poured a large cup of his terrible coffee and placed it in front of Nudger like an odious peace offering.

"You were spotted at Chaser Heights," Nudger went on, "and they followed you to find out who you were. You're close to my size, you were wearing a coat and hat like mine, and you came and went the back way. They checked to see who occupied the building and naturally figured it was the private investigator on the second floor. Whoever did the following probably staked out the front of the building and verified the identification when I left my office."

"It was a mistake, Nudge, honest! I didn't mean for you to come to any harm. Absolutely. I wouldn't want that."

Nudger sipped at the coffee, wondering why, if what Danny had said was true, he would serve him a cup of this. "I believe you, Danny," he said, "but what were you doing reconnoitering at Chaser Heights?"

Danny wiped at his forehead with the towel he'd been using on the counter. "My uncle's in there," he said.

"Is he there for the cure?"

Danny looked disgusted. "He's an alcoholic, all right, Nudge. That's how he got conned into admitting himself into Chaser Heights. But what they really specialize in at that place is getting the patients drugged up and having them sign over damn near everything they own in payment for treatment, or as a 'donation' that actually goes into somebody's pocket."

Nudger tried another sip of his formidable coffee. It was easier to get down now that it was cooler. "Does your uncle have much to donate?"

"Plenty. Now don't think small of me, Nudge, but it's no secret he plans to leave most of it to me, his only living relative. And he's not a well man; on top of his alcoholism he's got a weak heart."

"And Chaser Heights is about to get your inheritance before you do. Have you tried talking to your uncle?"

"Sure. They always tell me he's in special care, under detoxification quarantine—whatever that is. So I went back there a few times in secret and hung around thinking I might get a glimpse of old Benj and get to talk to him, at least see what they're doing to him. But they've got him doped up in a locked room with wire mesh on the windows. Some quarantine. I'm worried about him."

"And his money."

"I don't deny it. But that ain't the only consideration."

Danny rinsed his towel, wrung it out, and started wiping the counter again. Nudger sat slowly sipping his coffee. Growl, went his stomach.

"You help me, Nudge, and I'll pay you a couple of thousand—when the inheritance comes."

Nudger eased the coffee cup off to the side. He looked at Danny. "I think it's time your Uncle Benj checked out of Chaser Heights," he said.

"You know a way to manage it?"

Nudger always figured there was a way. That was a two-edged attitude, though, because he always had to figure there

51

was a way for the other guy, too. All of which didn't help Nudger's nervous stomach. Nor did the knowledge that he had to go back out to Chaser Heights that night and case the joint.

The next evening, Nudger and Danny parked Nudger's Volkswagen on a narrow dirt access road that ran through the woods behind Chaser Heights. Nudger was glad to see that Danny was only slightly nervous; the fool had complete faith in him. Both men put on the long black vinyl raincoats with matching hooded caps that Nudger had rented. They pinned badges on the coats and on the fronts of the caps. The sun was down and it was almost totally dark as they made their way through the trees and across the clearing to the rear of Chaser Heights.

They huddled against a brick back wall. Nudger checked the tops of the leafless trees, where the moon seemed to be nibbling at the thin upper branches, to verify which way the breeze was blowing. From a huge pocket of his raincoat he drew a plastic bag stuffed with oil-soaked rags. Danny drew a similar bag from his pocket. They laid the bags near the rear of the building, in tall dry grass that would catch well and produce a maximum amount of smoke. Danny was smiling confidently in the fearlessness born of incomprehension, a kid playing a game.

Nudger used a cigarette lighter to ignite the two bags and their contents. While Danny crept around to the side of the building to set fire to a third bag, Nudger forced open a basement window and lowered himself inside. He had noticed the sprinkler system in the halls on his first visit. Following the yellowish beam of a penlight, he made his way to the system's pressure controls in the basement and turned the lever that built the water pressure all the way to high, hearing an electric pump hum to life and the hiss of rushing water.

With a hatchet strapped inside his coat, Nudger broke the lever from the spigot with one sharp blow and then headed for the stairs to the upper floor. He opened the door to the back first-floor hall and then the rear door to admit Danny. Already he could hear movement, voices. And as Danny stepped inside and both men put on their respirator masks, Nudger saw that the burning bags and weeds were creating plenty of smoke, all of it drifting away from Chaser Heights.

Just then the pressure built up enough to activate the sprinkler system in the halls throughout the building, sending a cold spray on anyone caught outside a room. There were several startled shouts, a few curses.

Each carrying a hatchet, Nudger and Danny bustled down the halls in their badge-adorned black slickers and hoods, the respirators snug over their faces. They pulled the respirators away just enough to yell, "Fire department! Everyone remain calm! Everyone out of the building!" They began kicking doors open and ushering patients through the watery halls toward the exits. Nudger was beginning to enjoy this. Not for nothing did small boys want to be firemen when they grew up.

In the distance they could hear wails of sirens. The genuine fire department had been called and was on the way. A white-uniformed attendant, one of the thugs who had been in Nudger's office, jogged past them with only a worried glance.

"Where do you suppose Wedgewick and Olander are?" Danny asked.

"You can bet they were among the first out," Nudger said. "Go get Uncle Benj and head for the car."

Dr. Wedgewick's office was empty, as he'd thought it would be. Through the wide window behind the slate-topped desk, Nudger could see more than a dozen people gathered on the front grounds. Beyond them flashing red lights were approaching, casting wavering, distorted shadows; the sirens had built to a deafening warble. The Mayfair County fire engine even had a loud bell that jangled with a frantic kind of gaiety, as if fires were fun.

The door of a wall safe was hanging open. Nudger went to it and found that the safe was empty. After glancing again out the front window, he left the office.

Everyone in front of Chaser Heights seemed to be shouting. Volunteer firemen were playing out hose and advancing on the building like an invading army. Patients and staff were milling about, asking questions. Nudger joined them. At the edge of the crowd stood Dr. Wedgewick, holding a large brown briefcase.

"Are you in charge, sir?" Nudger inquired from beneath his respirator.

Dr. Wedgewick hesitated. "Yes, I'm Dr. Wedgewick, chief administrator here."

"Could you come with me, sir?" Nudger asked. "There's something you should see." He wheeled and began walking briskly toward the side of the building. All very official.

Dr. Wedgewick followed.

When they had turned the corner, Nudger removed his respirator. "The briefcase, please," he said, not meaning the please.

"Why, you can't! . . ." Then Dr. Wedgewick's eyes darted to the hatchet Nudger had raised, and remained fixed there. He handed the briefcase to Nudger. His hand was trembling.

"Millicent!" Dr. Wedgewick suddenly whirled and ran back the way they had come, all the time pointing to Nudger.

Nudger saw the unmistakably bulky figure of Millicent Olander-Olaphant. He took off for the woods behind the building. He didn't have to look back to know Millicent and the good doctor were following.

Running desperately through the woods, Nudger shed his cumbersome coat, hood, and respirator. He kept the ax and briefcase, using both to smash through the branches that whipped at his face and arms. Behind him someone was crashing through the dry winter leaves.

Nudger had the advantage. He knew where the car was parked. He put on as much speed as he could. The pounding of his heart was almost as loud as his rasping breath.

As he broke onto the road Nudger saw a dark form in the VW's rear seat. Still wearing raincoat and hood, Danny stood leaning against the left front fender with his arms crossed.

"Quick, get in!" Nudger shouted as he yanked open the driver's side door. He tossed the briefcase and hatchet onto the backseat next to Uncle Benj. His chest ached; his heart was trying to escape from his body.

Danny was barely into the passenger's seat when the engine caught and began its anxious clatter. As Nudger hit first gear and pulled away, he saw the fleeting shadows of pursuing figures in the rearview mirror.

"Who was chasing you?" Danny asked, straining to peer behind them into the darkness.

"My quarrelsome friends from that morning in my office."

"You think they'll get the cops, Nudge?" Danny sounded apprehensive.

Nudger snorted. "I think it's going to be the other way around!" He jerked the VW into a two-wheeled turn, bounced over some ruts, and was back on the main road, picking up speed.

From behind him came a chuckle and Uncle Benj said, "Hey, young fella, where's the fire?"

Nudger thought it wise to stay in the presence of witnesses

55

while he had the briefcase he'd taken from Dr. Wedgewick. He'd known that Dr. Wedgewick wouldn't have paid off the county sheriff, Caster, without keeping some sort of receipts. And when fire supposedly broke out at Chaser Heights and Dr. Wedgewick hurriedly cleaned out the safe, it figured that the doctor would number those receipts among his most valuable possessions.

In Danny's Donuts, Nudger examined the briefcase's contents. There was a great deal of money inside. Also some stock certificates. And among other various papers a notebook containing the dates, times, and amounts of the payoffs to Sheriff Caster. There also were several videocassettes, which the notebook referred to as documentation of the payoffs. Nudger had to admit that Dr. Wedgewick was thorough, but then wasn't the doctor the type?

Nudger went to the phone and called Jack Hammersmith at the Third Precinct. Hammersmith said he'd be around in ten minutes. "I don't understand how you manage to emerge from these misadventures relatively unscathed," he said. He was quite serious.

"Pureness of heart very probably is a factor," Nudger told him. Hammersmith broke the connection without saying goodbye.

"I forgot to give this to you earlier, Nudge," Danny said, holding out a small lavender envelope. "It's from Eileen. She said she could never find you and I was to deliver it."

Nudger grunted and crammed the envelope into his shirt pocket. "Ain't you gonna open it?" Uncle Benj asked, from where he sat near the end of the counter.

"I know what it is," Nudger told him. "It's from my former spouse and makes more than passing reference to neglected alimony payments!"

Uncle Benj chortled. "Women can do that to you—drive

you to drink if you let 'em." He sat up straighter and drew a deep breath. "You know, Danny boy," he said heartily, "despite the drugs and all the arm-twisting out at that place, I ain't had a drop of the sauce for weeks and I think my stay there did help me. I feel great, like I'll live to be a hundred!"

Danny bit his lower lip glumly, then he smiled and ducked behind the counter.

"Have a doughnut, Uncle Benj," he said.

Nudger thought about Danny's inheritance, about the rent due upstairs, about the envelope from Eileen.

"Don't forget to give him some of your coffee," he said to Danny with a meaningful nod.

If Uncle Benj was going to escape the bottle, maybe he'd fall prey to the cup.

Only One Way to Land

July in Del Moray, Florida, south of Fort Myers and east of the Ten Thousand Islands. Hot, steamy, about to storm.

Nudger sat at one of the Del Moray Yacht Club's white metal outside tables, across from Candy Caruthers. In front of each of them was a tall, wet, and greenish creation known as the Tidal Wave, the club's official drink. It was creme de menthe that gave the drink its greenish cast, and that wasn't to Nudger's taste. He took a few polite sips of the artless concoction, then ignored it.

A sea breeze was gusting in hard off the Gulf, pushing low black clouds laden with afternoon rain. The tall palm trees along the beach bent gracefully landward and rhythmically tossed their crowns of lush green fronds, as if dancing to some secret, mad music in the wind.

Candy Caruthers was privy to the music, too. She peeked with a glittering blue eye from between the long strands of honey blonde hair that had blown across her face. "I love the wind," she told Nudger.

"It freshens things."

Candy laughed loudly. "There's no doubt that things around here need freshening." Still smiling, she took a sip of her Tidal Wave. "I don't mean here specifically." She waved a lissome bare arm to encompass the plush yacht club. "I mean it would be oh so nice if the wind could blow away the troubles of the Caruthers family."

Nudger figured that would require a hurricane. Thanks to the voracious news media, the Caruthers family's troubles were no secret. Candy's father, Calvin "Cap" Caruthers, a silver-haired vigorous man in his mid-sixties, was being divorced from his twenty-six-year-old wife Melissa. They were a rich and well known couple; Cap Caruthers had been a war hero, and Melissa would have been a celebrity of sorts on the basis of appearance alone. She was a gaunt, dark-haired beauty who had been a fashion model before her marriage to Caruthers six years ago. Caruthers had noticed her on a glossy magazine cover, decided he wanted her, and turned that wish into reality. Now they were in the middle of a messy divorce in which each party was accusing the other of everything from snoring too loudly to sexual perversion. If anyone other than the principals knew how much of this was true, it would be Candy. She lived in the same house as her father and stepmother, and had in fact been dragged into the case as the alleged participant in some of the bad behavior.

"I assume," Nudger said, "that your father's divorce and all the accompanying sensationalism is why you paid my way down here."

"No," Candy said. "The divorce only complicates matters. And it might disappoint you to know that ninety-nine percent of everything you've heard or read about the Caruthers family and drugs and sex is pure nonsense. It's all charges and countercharges dreamed up by Mom's and Daddy's lawyers."

"Mom?"

"Melissa—my stepmother. We're very close."

"According to the news media—"

"The hell with the news media. We're like sisters, actually. We're both the same age, twenty-six, and we both care about my father."

"Melissa still cares?"

"Yes." She was emphatic. "Oh, Mom wants the divorce,

but in her own way she still *likes* Daddy, even if she doesn't love him. It's impossible not to like him."

"Then why do you need my services? And why not a local PI?"

"You were recommended to me by David Collins," Candy said.

"The man who owns most of New Orleans."

"David is an old friend of Daddy's, and we've met once or twice. I heard you got his daughter Ineida out of trouble. So when I needed someone, I decided on you."

"That makes some sense."

Candy drilled him with an appraising smile. "Some, but not enough. All right, Mr. Nudger, the other reason is that I can't trust a local investigator. With the divorce still in the courts, anyone from Florida I hired might be influenced by Daddy or Mom. They each have a wide circle of acquaintances that could apply pressure if a Florida investigator's license were at stake."

Nudger gazed out at the rolling blue-green Gulf. It was causing the sleek, docked sailboats to bob in unison at their moorings. "Okay," he said, after a pause. "It's savvy of you to recruit your knight from beyond the border."

"What a romantic concept!" she said. She sounded as if she'd just discovered a jewel in a popcorn box.

Nudger shrugged. "The essential me." He knew better, but why puncture her illusions? "Tell me about the offending dragon."

Candy rotated her Tidal Wave on the table's smooth metal surface, staring at the distortion of the damp ring around the glass. "Someone is watching the house."

"That isn't surprising, considering the divorce."

"Perhaps not. But I happen to know something the press, and Mom, don't know. Daddy is almost broke."

"Legal fees, no doubt. I'm a divorced man myself."

"He expects to get a great deal of money shortly; I overheard him talking about it during a phone conversation. That made me wonder how he's been getting his money for the last few years. It's come infrequently, but in huge amounts. He's no longer active in business, so what's the source of his income?"

"There are lots of possibilities," Nudger told her. "Loan payments, stock dividends?"

"No," Candy interrupted. "Lately he's been acting rather furtive. I'm afraid he's involved in something illegal. I'd like you to find out if he is, and if so what that something illegal is."

Nudger felt his nervous stomach give a warning kick. He got out his roll of antacid tablets, thumbed back the aluminum foil, and popped one of the chalky white discs into his mouth. "Why do you want to know this?" he asked.

"So I can protect him."

Nudger sighed, finished chewing, and swallowed. "Candy, I believe you do love your father, which is why I feel I should warn you that the divorce might be wrapped up in whatever he's doing. You might find out something you'll wish you didn't know."

She shook her head firmly, and her plain but pleasant features fell, as if from long practice, into a cast of determination. "I don't live my life trying to avoid painful conclusions, Mr. Nudger. That's a trap that snares too many of the wealthy. It's a temptation to sidestep reality when you can afford to think whatever is most convenient."

"I have the temptation myself, but not the means." Nudger found himself liking Candy Caruthers and wanting to help her. Hers was a world that could easily twist soul and reason. Despite that, she seemed to possess wisdom uncommon to youth. A lot of pain had to go along with it.

"Will you do what I ask, Mr. Nudger?"

Nudger watched a large cabin cruiser drift lazily away from the dock, shifted his gaze to the beach cabanas, the private pool entrance, the restaurant with its designer-labeled diners and drinkers, and the white-coated waiters gliding discreetly and subserviently among them. "All right," he said.

"Thank you, Mr. Nudger." She meant it. She clasped his hand and squeezed it. "What can I tell you that might help?"

"First," Nudger said, "I think we should discuss my fee."

Candy released his hand and grinned apologetically. "I'm sorry. I simply forgot."

"It's been uppermost in my mind."

A waiter drifted near and Candy motioned for two more Tidal Waves. Nudger said he'd prefer bourbon and water.

"Sorry again," Candy said.

Nudger told her that was okay, they'd get along. A gull wheeled in close in an exquisite arc against the wind and screamed before sailing back toward the expanse of sand and sea. The scream sounded human. Female. Maybe it was a warning.

Later that afternoon, after a heavy but brief rain that left the streets damp and steaming in the lowering sun, Nudger took his rented subcompact car from the lot of his motel, the Blynken and Nod, and followed Candy's directions to the Caruthers estate.

The estate's grounds were spacious and well kept, and the house itself was like something off the cover of a Gothic novel. Steep wooden steps near the rear of the staunch Victorian home zigzagged their way down to a private beach and a boathouse and dock. A shaky looking, weathered wood pier jutted like an accusing finger out to sea, into water deep enough to accommodate the small streamlined yacht that was anchored there. Nudger studied the sleek yacht through his binoculars. He admired its lines, but he saw no sign of life on board.

He spent about half an hour looking over the grounds. After determining the safest spots from which he could observe the house from concealment, he decided to drive to a seafood restaurant he'd noticed down the highway and get some supper, then return to the motel for a nap. He would come back to the Caruthers estate after dark. Candy had told him that whoever was watching the place was nocturnal.

The seafood soup Nudger spooned down at the restaurant was authentic enough to taste polluted. It was followed by a fried something that probably Jacques Cousteau hadn't catalogued. Back in his room at the Blynken and Nod, instead of sleeping, Nudger lay on the rumpled bed watching television and chomping antacid tablets. The violence on the small screen was appalling. By the time his stomach calmed down, it was dark outside.

This wasn't his kind of case, Nudger told himself as he drove the bone-rattling subcompact back up the coast highway. He shivered as he passed the seafood restaurant. What exactly was his kind of case he wasn't sure. Maybe no kind. He didn't doubt for a moment that he was in the wrong business, but this was all for which life had prepared him. He wished he were a sponge fisherman, so he could look in the newspaper help wanted ads, get a sane job on the bottom of the sea, and forget this sneaking around nonsense.

But Nudger wasn't the only one sneaking around that evening, and that made the night's work easier.

He hadn't spent more than an hour on the hill overlooking the Caruthers house when he spotted another car parked farther down the winding road, at one of the vantage points he'd noted earlier. The car, a dusty gray sedan, was pulled well off the road and would be practically invisible in the foliage from almost any spot other than Nudger's. He reached for the ignition key, then thought better of it. There was plenty of time; whoever had gone to the trouble of concealing the car was settled in for a long stakeout.

Nudger struggled out of the subcompact and walked along the road toward the other watcher. When he thought he might be visible, he entered the shadows of the scrubby growth alongside the road and, estimating where the gray sedan was parked, cut cross-country toward it. Though he was several hundred yards from the sea, the ground was soft and sandy and clung to his soles, making him strain as if he were trudging through glue. He was short of breath and had a stitch in his side by the time he got near enough to see the parked car.

He had emerged from the underbrush closer to it than he'd anticipated. Less than a hundred feet in front of him, moonlight glistened off a chrome bumper. Nudger put an antacid tablet in his mouth and crouched, watching, knowing that if the man seated behind the car's steering wheel happened to glance at the rearview mirror he might realize Nudger was there. Nudger chose not to think about what action that might prompt.

On the big sedan's rear bumper he saw a rental company's decal. The driver's features were indistinguishable in the darkness. Nudger made a mental note of the license number and retreated as silently as possible into the shadows, feeling a warm fondness for the night.

When he'd returned to his own car, Nudger settled into a cramped position behind the miniature steering wheel and waited for his breathing to even out. He turned on the car's radio, tuned in a Fort Myers station, and tried to relax.

As he sat there with the window rolled down, he heard a door slam several hundred yards away, from the direction of the Caruthers house. Nudger scanned the place with his binoculars, but caught no sign of movement either outside the house or at the lighted window.

Then he saw a tall, dark-clad form descending the wooden steps to the beach. When he focused the binoculars, Nudger could tell that the figure was that of a man wearing a windbreaker and a yachting cap. Despite darkness and distance, he could see the man's thick silver-white hair sprouting out from beneath the pushed-back cap.

The tall figure strode confidently out along the rickety pier, then across a narrow gangplank onto the craft that was docked there. Cap Caruthers boarding his yacht. Yellowish light appeared in two of the portholes, but there was no indication that the yacht, which Nudger estimated must require at least a small crew, might get underway.

At midnight a low red sports car snarled into the Carutherses' circular driveway, veered left, and disappeared into a garage whose door had automatically opened. Nudger figured that would be Candy Caruthers returning from wherever Del Moray rich girls whiled away their evenings.

Within another hour Cap Caruthers left his yacht and returned to the house. The lights in the house winked out window by window. Nudger turned his binoculars and his attention to the car parked on the road below.

At two a.m. the man in the gray car evidently assumed that the night's activities at the Caruthers estate had ended. The sound of the car's motor turning over rose to Nudger, mingled with the whisper of the moonshot surf breaking on the beach beyond the house. The gray sedan nosed slowly out of its place of concealment like a wary animal, turned right, away from Nudger, growled, and picked up speed. Nudger started the subcompact, almost lost a filling as the little car jarred back onto the road, and followed.

Was this the man Candy had seen watching the house? She had glimpsed only a shadowed figure a few times, seen a light-colored car parked up the beach from the boathouse.

The gray sedan traveled all the way into Del Moray and parked in a slot in the lot of the Del Moray Hotel, a rambling, tripled-decked, white stucco building near the center of town. Nudger parked nearby and watched a short, paunchy man with slicked-back dark hair get out of the car. With Napoleonic vigor and purpose he strode toward the hotel's main entrance.

Quickly Nudger unfolded himself from the subcompact. He entered the lobby just in time to hear the paunchy dynamo ask for his room key.

"Two fifty-one," he demanded of the desk clerk, a narrow-faced, elderly man who obeyed with absentminded servility and then returned to reading a true crime magazine.

"Restaurant still open?" the paunchy man asked, hefting the room key in a stubby hand.

The desk clerk nodded his narrow gray head. "Open all night." He flipped a page, a glossy illustration of a desperate looking youth strangling a model who looked as if she belonged in a lingerie ad.

The paunchy man spun like a dancer on his heel and went through the archway into the coffee shop. Nudger waited until someone else came into the lobby, then casually wandered over to the stairs, rounded a corner, and jogged up to the second floor.

It took him less than a minute to locate the door numbered 251, less than another minute to use his honed Visa card to slip the simple hotel lock and enter the room.

The paunchy guy was a slob. Clothes were draped all over

the place; there were cigar ashes on the rumpled bed and on the carpet near the phone. An open black vinyl attaché case sat next to a cheap portable typewriter on the desk. In the attaché case were some sheets of lined notepaper with dates and times scrawled on them. There were also two large yellow envelopes, both addressed to a party in Gainesville, Georgia. One envelope was empty, the other contained something but was sealed.

Nudger took the sealed envelope into the bathroom, ran the basin full of hot water, covered it by draping a towel over it, and inserted the top of the sealed envelope so that the flap was inches above the steaming water.

Within a few minutes the glue had loosened its grip on the flap. Nudger withdrew the envelope and opened it. The typed pages inside contained the same dates and times that appeared on the notepaper, but they were identified as a record of Cap Caruthers' comings and goings for the past several days. There was also a request for more expense money for the envelope's sender, a paunchy private investigator named Raoul DeMent.

While the glue was still moist, Nudger resealed the envelope and returned things to the way they had been in the bathroom. He got out his own notepad and pen and copied the name and Gainesville address from the envelope. Then he placed the envelope back in the attaché case and left the room. His stomach said, "About time!" He had learned to interpret its growls.

Downstairs, as he was leaving the hotel lobby, Nudger glanced into the coffee shop and saw Raoul DeMent ravishing a hamburger.

"The man watching the Caruthers estate is a private investigator observing your father," Nudger told Candy Caruthers the next morning over breakfast in a Waffle King in Del Moray. The place was built to resemble a huge crown, though you'd never know it from inside. "But he isn't working for your stepmother."

Candy paused with her fork halfway to her open mouth, suddenly having lost interest in a large syrupy bite of her Royal Court Strawberry Special. Her blue eyes were puzzled. "Then who hired him?"

"A man named Yasuhiro Oh, a Japanese who owns a large electronics firm in Georgia. Oh is receiving regular reports on your father's activities and the times he's away from home."

"Maybe this Oh is a friend of Mom's."

"Not so's you'd notice. I checked on him. He's a businessman in his mid-sixties. His firm, El-Tron Electronics, manufactures components for a range of products from automatic pilots to pour-through coffee brewers. If there's any relationship between Oh and your stepmother, no one knows about it but them. Possible but not likely."

Candy resumed the transfer of the bite of waffle from plate to palate and seemed to be mulling over this new information as she chewed. When she had swallowed noisily she said, "Find out more, Mr. Nudger."

"About Oh?"

"About everything."

"The task looms larger."

"So does the fee."

"In that case I'll have another Hamlet Sour Cream Danish Delight." He signaled a melancholy waitress and reached into his jacket pocket to fondle the roll of antacid tablets he knew he would need within the hour.

It seemed to Nudger that the most logical way to find out more about Oh's reason for hiring DeMent was to continue observing DeMent. That evening he sat parked in the sub-compact in front of the Del Moray Hotel, and when he saw DeMent's gray sedan leave the lot and turn in the direction of the Caruthers estate Nudger followed.

DeMent parked the sedan where Nudger had first seen it the night before. Nudger drove past without slacking speed, rounded a bend, and then made a U-turn. He drove back the way he'd come until he reached the concealed area where he'd parked before. He situated his car in exactly the same spot. From it, without craning his neck, he could see both the Caruthers estate and DeMent's car. He wondered if anyone was watching the place regularly during daylight hours. Some of Caruthers' daytime arrivals and departures were noted in DeMent's report, but he seemed to be working alone, which suggested that Oh was interested primarily in what Cap Caruthers did at night.

A swishing sound, as of something rushing through the weeds behind him, made Nudger turn. A roar, a squeal, and as a dark shape swept toward him Nudger recognized it as a car with its lights out. No sooner had he realized this than the subcompact lurched forward to the loud crunch of metal on metal and Nudger's body slammed back against the seat. Whoever was driving the lights-out car apparently had parked here before and hadn't suspected another car might be occupying the spot. Which meant . . .

That this was one of those rare times when Nudger wished he carried a gun.

A large man wearing a dark suit got out of the car and walked toward Nudger's smashed rear fender. In the rearview mirror Nudger saw that the man had his right hand in his suit coat pocket. For an instant he contemplated ducking out the door on the passenger's side and running for the dark woods, but if the man had a gun and intended to use it there was no reasonable escape route. He got out of the car slowly.

The large man stopped a few feet from Nudger and looked him over. He was neatly dressed, not only bulky but lean-waisted and athletic, a boxer's build. His face was squarish and all-American-handsome beneath tousled dark hair. The shirt was white, the tie straight and tightly knotted. A daughter's ideal date.

"Who are you and why are you here?" the man asked.

Nudger's jittery stomach growled so loudly that the man glanced at it. "Maybe you should answer those same questions," he suggested, not quite managing to make his voice as authoritative as that of the figure confronting him.

"What right have you to ask?" the man said calmly.

"Squatter's rights, I suppose. I was here first." Nudger was feeling braver. After all, the man didn't know he wasn't armed. "By what authority do you ask me questions?"

"FBI."

"Oh."

The man identified himself as Agent Frank Slayton, flashing a classy two-tone badge of the sort Nudger had seen before. Nudger knew it was genuine. This was a genuine FBI agent. This was genuine trouble.

Nudger showed his own identification, which at the moment seemed to carry as much clout as Monopoly money.

"A private investigator from out of state, eh?" Slayton said with something like disdain, as if what had promised to interest him had turned out to be hardly worth his time. "Who's your client?"

"The Caruthers woman," Nudger said. Not precisely a lie.

"The wife?" Slayton handed back Nudger's wallet and identification. "Divorce doesn't interest us," Slayton said. "We've been trying to stay out of the way of your colleague down there for the past two weeks." He motioned in the direction of DeMent's parked car.

"Colleague?"

Slayton shrugged. "Maybe he's working for the husband. A PI named DeMent."

"I don't know him," Nudger said.

"We don't, either, but we know he's a PI and that's all we want to know. And he doesn't know about us, and we don't want him to know. If you were to tell him it wouldn't go easy for you. Do you understand?"

"Obstruction of justice?"

"Something like that. You wouldn't have known we were around, either, only . . ." Slayton waved a hand toward the crumpled fenders. "The point is, Nudger, we're involved in our own investigation. It has nothing to do with this divorce, and we don't want any interference."

"You'll get none from me," Nudger said. "This encounter is something I won't reveal to my client."

"I'll trust you," Slayton said, "since I have to." He pointed to the damaged subcompact. "A rental? Did you pay extra for the collision insurance?"

"No. I wasn't on an expense account when I leased it."

"Your government will pay for repairs," Slayton told him. "Keep a copy of the damage estimate." He turned back toward his car.

"I was just leaving," Nudger said. "You take this spot."

"No, thanks."

"It's my patriotic duty."

Slayton didn't reply. Probably he had an FBI sense of humor. He got into his car, backed it out onto the road, and drove it away in the direction of the Caruthers house.

Nudger was becoming a bit boggled by all of this. The FBI was watching the Caruthers estate, along with two private detectives whom they logically assumed to be working for the contestants in a nasty divorce. And maybe Cap and Melissa Caruthers had each hired detectives to watch for extramarital meanderings that could prove beneficial in court. The area around the Caruthers estate might be teeming with agents of one kind or another, unsuspectingly passing each other in the night.

Nudger laughed, almost uncontrollably. He leaned on the tiny fender of the subcompact and waited until his fit of mirth subsided. His stomach felt fine. Nothing was better for nervous indigestion than laughter from down deep.

He got back into the dented car, started it, and bounced back onto the road. He drove toward town. Let Raoul DeMent and the rest of them sit in the dark and peer through binoculars while they passed the time listening on their car radios to the inane patter of all-night disc jockeys. Nudger was going back to his room and going to bed.

In the morning he called Candy Caruthers, who said with dramatic emphasis that she was alone but that the phones in the house might be bugged. He waited fifteen minutes while she drove to a public phone and called him back.

"You told me your father might be engaged in an illegal activity," Nudger said. "Do you have the slightest idea what it involves?"

"Not an inkling. Of course there are the rumors."

"Rumors?"

"About drug-running. But everyone in Southern Florida who owns a fast yacht is suspected at one time or another of smuggling narcotics. The Ten Thousand Islands and the Keys are havens for smugglers; it's impossible for the Coast Guard to stop the arrival of drugs by boat from Mexico and South America, even from Cuba."

"Is your father's yacht fast?"

"The *Sea Dreamer*? Very fast."

"Do you think he's involved in drugs?"

She waited a while before answering. This was one suspicion she didn't care to voice, as if making it audible would move it nearer to fact. "I don't know. That's one of the reasons I hired you. Do you have any firm information that Daddy is into something illegal? You sounded so sure."

"I'm not sure," Nudger told her.

"Have you discovered anything more about Oh?"

"Not yet," Nudger said. "But I will." He told Candy Caruthers he would phone her tomorrow and hung up.

A cold shower shocked him awake completely while probably shortening his life several years. By then it was almost ten o'clock. Nudger went back to the Del Moray Hotel.

As he drove into the Del Moray's lot, he saw DeMent's parked car in a slot near the far end of the blacktopped surface. DeMent probably had been up most of last night and was still in bed.

He wasn't, at least, in the coffee shop. Nudger walked to a booth from which he could see into the lobby, sat down, and ordered coffee and a glazed doughnut. The coffee shop was pleasantly cool after the heat already building outside. Someone had left a morning newspaper in the booth. Nudger divided his attention among the doughnut and the lobby and reading about the latest sensational developments in the Caruthers divorce hearings. Melissa allegedly had been having an affair with a teenaged delivery boy; on the other hand it was alleged that Cap Caruthers had discussed the possibility of selling Melissa into bondage to South American slave traders. On such matters hinged the million dollar fortunes of divorce settlement. Nudger thought about his own divorce from Elaine six years ago. She had fought like fury for the color television.

As Nudger was sipping his third cup of coffee, Raoul DeMent, looking tired and rumpled, waddled into the coffee shop and sat down at a table near the door. He was occupied with the waitress when Nudger paid for the coffee and doughnut and left.

Within five minutes Nudger was again in DeMent's disheveled room. He had hung out the "Do Not Disturb" sign and figured he would have at least fifteen uninterrupted minutes while DeMent ate breakfast.

The fifteen minutes yielded no new information other than that DeMent was a devotee of paperback detective novels. Nudger glanced around the room that he had carefully put back together in its original disorder. He knew he had been there long enough, maybe too long. What if he ran into DeMent in the hall as he left? His stomach said, "Get out!"

It aggravated Nudger that he'd wasted his time there. Before leaving, he tore out the last few pages of the paperback mystery novel DeMent had just begun reading. That way it would be more like real life.

But DeMent hadn't planned on returning to his room after breakfast. When Nudger stepped from the elevator into the lobby, he caught a glimpse of the detective shrugging into his suit coat as he pushed through the glass double doors to the parking lot.

DeMent turned his car in the opposite direction from that of the Caruthers estate. He drove for a few blocks, then veered onto an exit ramp and got on the highway leading east, away from the coast. He drove fast. Nudger had to push his whiny little rental car hard to keep DeMent's gray sedan in sight.

Ahead of Nudger a small, propeller driven plane crossed above the highway low and at a downward angle. It disappeared beyond a slight rise. When Nudger looked back at the road, he saw DeMent's sedan turning off the highway onto a road that a sign proclaimed led to the Del Moray airport.

A jet airliner wouldn't have dared to set down at this airport. Nudger parked well away from DeMent on a gravel lot and looked out at a single asphalt runway. To his left was a small brick office and terminal building, on top of which a red wind sock listlessly pointed northeast in the humid hot air. Several light planes were parked toward the far end of the runway. Beyond them squatted three corrugated metal hangars. The plane Nudger had seen land taxied off the runway, gave a hard left rudder, and rolled toward the hangars. Its propeller stopped spinning, and two men emerged from the shadowed hangar entrance to help the pilot roll the plane toward the gaping doors. A red and yellow twin-engined plane took to the air with a roar and went into a climbing turn toward the ocean. DeMent got out of his car and walked over to stand near the terminal building in a waiting attitude.

A single-engine, high-winged silver plane with a red stripe along its fuselage circled the field, dropped lower, and made a smooth landing. On its tail was painted a red circle containing the letter "E" traversed by a lightning streak—El-Tron Electronics' logo. The plane taxied to the hangar entrance and was also pushed inside. A short while later a yellow golf cart emerged from the hangar. There were two men on the cart. One of them was wearing a blue business suit and was the pilot of the silver plane; the other was the driver. DeMent tossed away the cigar he'd been smoking and stepped forward to meet the cart. He and the man in the business suit went into the terminal building while the cart's driver swung the vehicle around and headed back toward the hangars. The man in the blue suit carried a small suitcase, walked with a limp, and had Oriental features.

When they emerged from the building, DeMent was dutifully carrying the suitcase. The two men walked to DeMent's car and got in, and Nudger followed them back to the Del Moray Hotel.

Nudger waited outside for fifteen minutes and then walked in and asked the desk clerk if Mr. Yasuhiro Oh had checked in yet. The clerk told him that Mr. Oh had gone up to Room 358 just a minute ago.

For the benefit of the clerk, Nudger crossed the lobby and pretended to talk for a while on one of the house phones. Then he left and returned to his own meager digs at the Blynken and Nod. He really did use his room phone. He placed a long distance call to Lieutenant Jack Hammersmith, who turned out to be sitting unsuspectingly in the Third Precinct office over a thousand miles north of Del Moray. Hammersmith had been Nudger's partner in a patrol car twenty years ago, during Nudger's brief police career. The bond between the two men had never been broken.

Nudger identified himself and told Hammersmith he was in Florida. "It's plenty hot here," he said.

"The call isn't collect," Hammersmith told him. "We can chat about the weather as long as you want."

"Why I called," Nudger said forgetting about the weather, "is to ask you to get some information from the Gainesville, Georgia, police department. I need to learn about a man there named Yasuhiro Oh."

" 'O' what? Is that a middle initial?"

"He's Japanese. Oh is his last name, like the home run hitter."

Silence. Apparently Hammersmith didn't follow Japanese baseball enough to know about the Oriental equivalent of Babe Ruth.

"There was a famous Japanese baseball player of the same name," Nudger said.

"Oh."

"That's right."

"Huh?"

"He owns a business in Gainesville, El-Tron Electronics."

"This is going to be a lot of trouble, Nudge. Is it important?"

"I wouldn't ask unless it meant the very survival of our world as we know it." Nudger heard the lip-smacking wheezing sound of Hammersmith firing up one of his horrendous cigars.

"Okay, Nudge." The voice was slightly distorted by the cigar. "When do you need this info?"

"As soon as it reaches your hot little hand." Nudger gave Hammersmith the phone number of the Blynken and Nod and told him he appreciated the favor.

"You shoulda waited till winter to go to Florida, Nudge," Hammersmith said. "Now last January me and the wife drove down there and ⟷"

"This isn't a collect call," Nudger reminded him. As he hung up he heard Hammersmith chuckling around the cigar.

The rest of that day and most of the next, Nudger followed Oh, who was driving around in a luxury rental car while DeMent was at his post keeping the Caruthers estate under close watch. Oh had supper in an expensive seafood restaurant while Nudger, outside in his parked car, wolfed down a chili dog. When Oh left the restaurant, he drove to the Del Moray waterfront, where he boarded a large sleek cabin cruiser docked there. He stayed on board for about an hour, talking to a shadowy figure that appeared now and then behind the drawn curtains of the lighted cabin. As the boat bobbed gently at dockside, Nudger made out the name

Dandy Dan lettered across its stern.

Even the breeze off the sea did little to cool the humid evening air, and by the time Oh left the cabin cruiser Nudger was soaked in perspiration and his hands were slippery on the steering wheel. He suspected that he'd done serious harm to the car's engine while trying to keep up with DeMent earlier that morning; heat was rolling up around his feet and something was softly hissing beneath the sloping little hood.

Fortunately he wouldn't have to drive the car harder to keep pace with Oh's larger, more powerful vehicle. Instead of getting into his car, Oh buttoned his suit coat and began walking along the narrow street bordering the glittering dark water. Nudger gratefully climbed out of the subcompact, relieved to find that all his limbs could still extend to their fullest, and followed Oh's erect but limping figure.

On Nudger's left, various souvenir shops and related tourist attractions were open along the street. On his right, an array of docked vessels bobbed in unison with the soft lapping of waves. Nudger heard the occasional muffled thump of a hull bumping a padded dock buffer. Music and sometimes laughter wafted from some of the pleasure boats showing lights. Except for the pressing heat, it was a nice night and a nice place for a walk.

Oh stopped walking, dabbed, at his perspiring forehead with a white handkerchief, and disappeared through a doorway.

Nudger moved nearer, crossed the street to get a better view, and saw that Oh had entered the offices of the Pegasus Steamship Line. Standing in the shadows near a docked sailboat with a mast tall enough to merge with the dark sky, Nudger idly chewed on an antacid tablet and waited.

He didn't move when, twenty minutes later, Oh emerged from the Pegasus office and limped back the way he had come. When Oh had passed, Nudger followed him back to where the cars were parked near *Dandy Dan*.

It was easy to figure out where Oh was driving after they left the dock. As soon as Nudger realized they were taking the route back to the hotel, he dropped back in the struggling subcompact and relaxed, turning the air conditioner on high and ignoring the engine's clattering protests.

Oh treated himself to a drink in the Del Moray Hotel's lounge—presumably a nightcap—then went upstairs to his room. Nudger waited almost an hour on a stool near the end of the bar, from which he could see the elevators, to make sure he was bedded down for the night. Oh was an elderly man with a bad leg, but there was an aura of energy about him that suggested he was tireless.

When Nudger returned to the Blynken and Nod, he checked at the desk to see if Hammersmith had phoned. Hammersmith hadn't. Candy Caruthers had, and left a number where she could be reached.

They met at a lounge overlooking the Gulf. It was ten miles outside of town. Apparently Candy had gotten into the spirit of subversiveness and didn't deem it wise for them to be seen together in her yacht-club-set haunts. They sat near a wide window affording a panoramic view of darkness broken only by a lonely, distant buoy light. And over whisky sours, and a yellowish glowing candle in a mottled glass holder, they talked.

"Daddy's taken a trip," Candy said. "The *Sea Dreamer* is gone."

"When did he leave?"

She shrugged and sipped her drink. The candle glow transformed her plain, attractive features into the serene kind of beauty seen in paintings by old masters. "I noticed that the yacht was missing from its moorings late this afternoon," she said. "I don't know how long it had been gone, and Daddy never tells anyone where he's going. Every few months he simply boards the *Sea Dreamer* and disappears for several days."

"Maybe he's fishing."

"Daddy doesn't fish. What have you learned about Yasuhiro Oh?"

"Not much, but I utilized some of my far-reaching contacts and expect to know a great deal more about him shortly. Also, he's here in Del Moray."

"Is he—?"

"He's not on the *Sea Dreamer*; I saw him go up to his hotel room at around ten o'clock." Nudger sampled his drink and gazed out at the vast blackness of the Gulf. It was disconcerting to imagine how far that black void extended. "Do you know anyone who owns a big cabin cruiser called the *Dandy Dan*?"

Candy screwed up her mouth and searched her memory. For a moment she looked twelve years old. "I don't think so."

"Yasuhiro Oh does. He spent some time on board this evening. Then he visited the offices of the Pegasus ship line."

"Pegasus does commercial shipping," Candy said, "all sorts of cargo to and from South America."

"What do you mean by 'all sorts'?"

"Copper, construction materials, bananas, whatever that kind of ship carries."

"It seems there are no detectives hired by your father or stepmother watching the principals in the divorce," Nudger said. "Maybe I'm cynical, but that strikes me as unusual."

"Not when you realize that Mom and Daddy aren't bitter enemies. They simply want to live apart and unmarried. I told you it was the media that was concocting all those bizarre stories. And of course the divorce lawyers furnish plenty of innuendo."

"Was your father's war record also concocted by the media?"

Candy appeared insulted. She sat back and wore an injured expression, her features in shadowed sharp relief outside the circle of candlelight. "Of course not. He was the second-in-command of a destroyer, the U.S.S. *Latty*, when it was attacked by kamikazes—Japanese suicide planes whose mission it was to dive into U.S. warships—in the South Pacific in 1945. The captain and several crew members were killed, and Daddy took command. He fought off the attackers and brought the ship home. He was decorated for what he did. He became a big hero." She sat forward and stared challengingly at Nudger. "A genuine hero."

"Relax, please," Nudger told her. "You're the only one I can talk to who knows the truth about these things." He saw that their glasses were empty. He looked again at Candy in the soft light and for a moment regretted that he had a rule about fraternizing with his clients, and that she regarded him as a middle-aged creature of relative poverty who no doubt wore plain white underwear from J. C. Penney. The woman had insight. It was time for them to leave and go their separate ways. "I'll phone you when I receive more information about Oh," he said, magnanimously reaching for his wallet.

Candy bent low to pick up her purse from beside her chair. "I'll get the check," she said. "Since you're on an expense account, I'd wind up paying for the drinks anyway."

Insight indeed.

Nudger was in bed at the Blynken and Nod when Hammersmith phoned. With the cool receiver pressed to his ear, he rested his head on his perspiration-soaked, flattened pillow and listened as Hammersmith identified himself in a voice tinged with sadism.

"It's two in the morning," Nudger said groggily.

"I'd have phoned Greenwich if I wanted to check the time," Hammersmith told him. "You said you wanted information on Yasuhiro Oh as soon as possible."

Nudger snapped fully awake at the mention of Oh's name. He sat up and switched on the bedside lamp. "So what did you find out?"

"Oh is of Japanese descent, attended Northwestern University in the early fifties, founded El-Tron twenty years ago, and has been a successful businessman ever since. He was married but his wife died. El-Tron makes electronic components for a variety of products. Recently they lost a big government contract for missile parts, but the company is still financially solid if not prospering."

"Oh sounds like an upstanding citizen," Nudger said with undeniable disappointment.

"He has a police record, but it's been clear for the last ten years. If you go back that far, you'll find that El-Tron was found guilty of fraud involving some kind of tariff violation. Two years before that, Oh himself was dragged into court and forced to pay fines on two parking violations." There was a pause, punctuated by bellows wheezing. One of Hammersmith's abominable cigars being lighted. "Is this useful information, Nudge?"

"No. It sounds like a record of a Chamber of Commerce president."

Hammersmith chuckled. "Oh's military record is more interesting but probably just as useless. He was a kamikaze pilot in the Japanese air force."

Nudger spent several seconds digesting that pithy morsel of information. "He must not have been a very successful kamikaze pilot, since he's alive and walking around Florida."

"It seems he was captured," Hammersmith explained. "In 1945, as he was trying to crash his plane into a U.S. ship in the South Pacific, he was hit and went down in the water. He lost a leg in the crash, but he survived and was pulled from the ocean by the ship's crew."

Despite the heat of the hotel room, a cold sensation snaked its way up the nape of Nudger's neck. "What was the name of the ship?"

"The *Latty*," Hammersmith said. "It was a destroyer."

"I know," Nudger muttered.

"How could you know that?"

"It was Cap Caruthers' ship."

"Caruthers . . . you mean the husband in that messy Florida divorce circus?"

"The same. You've helped a lot, Jack. In fact, you might have explained everything."

"Nothing's been explained to me, Nudge. But I'll try to make something else clear to you. The Caruthers divorce is not only messy, it's dangerous for a small-time out-of-state investigator. Big money is operating there, and now and then big money needs someone like you to throw to someone like me, either dead or alive. Big money means big problems."

"And a big fee," Nudger pointed out.

"Hah! The fee is the bait, Nudge. Betcha there's a hook in it."

Nudger declined the bet. "Thanks for the information," he said.

"Sure," Hammersmith said. "Banzai, Nudge."

"What?"

"That's what the kamikaze pilots yelled just before they disappeared into the clouds on their way to their deaths."

"Then maybe that's what you should yell before you light your cigars," Nudger suggested.

Hammersmith hung up.

Nudger replaced the receiver, switched on the lamp, and lay awake trying to fit his fragmentary thoughts into some meaningful pattern, trying to gain some insight into the mind and role of Yasuhiro Oh. For a kamikaze pilot there must have been the blackest shame in not only failing in one's mission but in also being captured alive by the enemy that was to have been destroyed. More importantly, the kamikaze incident provided a connective thread between Cap Caruthers and Oh. What that thread meant was something Nudger had yet to discover.

It was morning, and Nudger was showering, when it occurred to him that it might be a mistake to assume that the Caruthers divorce, Cap Caruthers alleged drug running, and Oh's interest in Cap Caruthers' movements might all somehow be connected. It could be that none had much if any bearing on the others; possibly Oh hadn't any idea what had become of Cap Caruthers until the divorce publicity, and that in itself had drawn him to Florida.

Then, as he stood beneath the beating needles of the shower watching water swirling at his feet, a disturbing, chilling possibility crept from a corner of Nudger's mind into his consciousness. His flesh began to tingle, and not from the pounding of the water.

He got out of the shower still partially lathered with soap, toweled dry, dressed quickly, and drove to the Del Moray Hotel. When he knocked on the door to Oh's room and got no answer, Nudger used his Visa card to slip the lock and enter. He was getting plenty of practice on the Del Moray Hotel locks.

In contrast to DeMent's room, everything in Oh's room

was neatly arranged. Though the bed was unmade, the covers were turned back symmetrically. Oh's clothes were hung in the closet. Underwear, socks, and shirts were folded in a dresser drawer. In the bathroom, shaving gear and cosmetics were neatly aligned with military precision on the shelf above the washbasin. But the cap wasn't on the toothpaste tube. The bottles of aftershave lotion and cologne also stood uncapped.

Nudger went to the phone and dialed DeMent's room number. When DeMent answered, Nudger said, "I'm a private investigator like yourself, Mr. DeMent. I've been watching you watch Cap Caruthers. We need to talk. I'm sitting on the bed of your employer's room."

Nudger had to admire DeMent. The paunchy little detective wasn't thrown for more than a few seconds. He said, "Sure. I'll be there as soon as I can," and hung up.

A few minutes later, looking sleepy and disheveled, DeMent knocked twice on the door and then pushed into Oh's room.

Nudger introduced himself and the two men shook hands with appropriate wariness.

"Caruthers or his wife hire you?" DeMent asked. He had beady ferret eyes that glared out from padded cheeks. A shrewd and careful man, a man who walked on the edge. This was the small-time investigator that Hammersmith had mentioned, the non-swimmer in the deep end of the pool. Nudger wondered if his own features conveyed the same desperate, calculating expression.

"It doesn't matter who hired me," he said. "What I need to know is, did you report to Oh that Caruthers put to sea night before last in his yacht?"

DeMent shrugged. "Why should I answer you?" He glanced around. "Where's Oh?"

"He's gone," Nudger said. "I hope you collected your fee in advance."

DeMent ran out of patience. "Listen, you . . ." He lowered his head and took a step toward Nudger.

Nudger ignored him, turned, and walked toward the door.

"Hey! Where are you going?" DeMent asked.

"To the Caruthers estate. Want to come along?"

DeMent stood weighing the odds, like a menacing, bewildered bull frozen in puzzlement in the bull ring. He didn't want to go with Nudger, but the alternative was to be left standing and wondering in Oh's room.

"Okay," he said in disgust. "I'm coming with you." He said it as if he were in charge.

"Good," Nudger said. "Let's take your car. It'll be faster, not to mention more comfortable."

When they reached the Caruthers estate, they found Candy Caruthers and a slender, dark-haired woman having breakfast on the patio overlooking the Gulf. Nudger recognized the woman as Melissa Caruthers. She looked as if she could resume her modeling career tomorrow.

Candy glanced from Nudger to DeMent to Melissa. Back to Nudger. "Since Daddy was gone," she said, "I invited Mom here for—"

"Moral support," Melissa finished her stepdaughter's sentence. "Despite what the news media might say." She began to introduce herself.

"I know who you are," Nudger interrupted. He introduced himself and DeMent, who stood in belligerent, watchful stupefaction.

"I assumed you were with the people in the house," Melissa said.

"What people?"

"The FBI," Candy said to Nudger. "They've been here

86

since early this morning. They're waiting for Daddy to return."

"Is there any way to contact your father's yacht?" Nudger asked.

"That's what we're here to prevent," Frank Slayton said as he opened sliding glass doors and stepped out into the sunlight on the patio. A tall man with Latin features, as square-edged clean-cut as Slayton, followed him outside. "This is Agent Sam Ortero," Slayton said. "What's going on, Nudger?"

While the others watched intently, Nudger drew Slayton aside and told him everything.

"We're tracking Caruthers' yacht," Slayton said. "We're sure he picked up a narcotics shipment in Mexico, and we're waiting here to confiscate it and place him under arrest when he docks."

"If he docks," Nudger corrected. "Can we contact him by radio?"

"I can't allow that," Slayton said. "We can't be sure that what you think is true." The agent rubbed his handsome, squarish chin, looked glum. "On the other hand, if you are right, we won't have anyone to interrogate. We're trying to eliminate the regular importation of millions of dollars' worth of illegal drugs."

"Time could be running out," Nudger said. He slipped an antacid tablet into his mouth and chewed with metronome precision, glancing at the others still staring curiously at him and Slayton.

Beyond the patio a pelican swooped low over the sea, seeking its prey. It dived. It missed.

Slayton came to a quick, firm decision in that FBI way of his. "I'm going to have a fast Coast Guard boat pick us up here," he said.

"Us?"

"We're all going," Slayton said. "I don't want anyone staying behind and possibly contacting Cap Caruthers by radio."

After Slayton had hurried back into the house to call the Coast Guard, DeMent swaggered with pugnacious pudginess over to Nudger, his dark eyes narrowed angrily. "You drag me up here and I get tangled up with the FBI and I still don't know what's going on," he growled. "I don't like it a bit."

"What will perk you up," Nudger told him, "is some fresh sea air."

The Coast Guard cutter was a forty-foot craft with speed. Its gray bow was raised high and proud, and its hull slapped over the waves as it headed away from the Caruthers dock out into the blue Gulf. Nudger stood near Slayton by the rail, squinting against the sea spray that was cooling him in the hot glare of the sun off the shimmering water. The Coast Guard had a fix on the *Sea Dreamer*'s position and was on course to reach the unsuspecting Cap Caruthers in the shortest time possible

They'd been out on the Gulf for about forty-five minutes when the captain on the bridge shouted down at Slayton and pointed off the port bow. Nudger stared in the direction the captain had pointed and could make out a tiny dark shape near the horizon. Slayton borrowed the captain's binoculars, aimed and focused them.

"It's the *Sea Dreamer*," he said.

Nudger felt on his face the subtle change of wind direction as the boat altered course. He almost stumbled on the deck as the bow lifted higher and they gained speed. The sound of the waves slapping against the hull was like irregular rifle fire. Candy, Melissa, and DeMent all rushed unsteadily to the side of the deck where Nudger and Slayton stood. They all craned their necks for a view of the *Sea Dreamer*.

Then Nudger glimpsed another dark speck—above the horizon. He snatched the binoculars from Slayton and pressed their rubber cups to his eyes. It took him a few seconds to locate the airborne speck. He prayed that it was a gull, but it hadn't moved like a gull against the sky.

When he focused the binoculars, he saw that the speck was the red and silver aircraft that Oh had landed at the Del Moray airport. He cursed, pointed, and handed the binoculars back to Slayton, who focused on the plane and echoed Nudger's curse.

Within half a minute they could all see the plane quite clearly with the naked eye. They watched the sun glint off its silver wings and its red El-Tron emblem as it soared, dipped, and headed toward the *Sea Dreamer*. It was only a few feet above the waves, bearing down on the yacht in classic kamikaze fashion.

"I wouldn't have believed it," Slayton said almost reverently, "that the shame could last all those years . . ."

"You were never a kamikaze pilot," Nudger said. And then softly, "Banzai."

Cap Caruthers was running illegal cargo, all right. A figure appeared on the *Sea Dreamer*'s aft deck and flung a tarpaulin off a brace of high-caliber machine guns, swiveled the twin barrels toward the oncoming plane, and opened fire. The chattering pop of the guns wafted over the water toward the Coast Guard cutter as it closed the distance between it and the *Sea Dreamer*.

Pieces flew from the small plane. It shuddered but didn't alter course in the face of the machine gun fire. A tall man—Cap Caruthers—appeared on the *Sea Dreamer*'s flying bridge and calmly studied the plane through binoculars. The bullets that missed the plane were raising geysers of water behind it as it droned inexorably toward its target. Nudger stood in breathless, silent fascination. He couldn't have turned away. This was like watching *Victory at Sea* in color.

The plane's left wing dipped and almost touched the water, and for an instant Nudger thought it would go down. But it righted itself, climbed sharply, then dived straight toward the *Sea Dreamer*'s bridge.

There must have been explosives on the plane. Both it and the yacht disappeared in a huge ball of fire that rose like a brilliant sun gone mad into the blue sky. A few seconds later the roar of the explosion hurt Nudger's ears and left them buzzing. The shock wave rocked the Coast Guard boat.

The Gulf breeze soon cleared away black smoke to reveal only a broken tail section, a curve of shattered hull, and various smaller pieces of smoldering debris where the *Sea Dreamer* had floated. Cap Caruthers and his ship were below the waves; a forty-year-old fanatical mission of destruction had been completed.

Melissa was stunned, her face pale and old. One of the crewmen helped her below deck. Candy was sobbing, gasping for breath. She burrowed her face into Nudger's chest, and he felt her body's shuddering merge with the vibration of the boat.

"There goes our source of information," Nudger heard Slayton murmur.

"There goes my fee," DeMent said, and spat over the side.

Nudger pulled Candy closer to him and pressed his hand over her free ear.

The Coast Guard cutter circled for a while, though everyone knew it was pointless to search for survivors. After radioing the exact position of the tragedy, the captain set a course for shore.

It was when they were within eight miles of Del Moray that

Nudger noticed, among the many fishing vessels and pleasure boats, the *Dandy Dan* headed into shore and only a few hundred yards from the docks.

The *Dominique* was a twenty thousand ton freighter of the Pegasus Line. It was loaded with a cargo of heavy construction equipment bound for several South American ports and was due to cast off in an hour.

Nudger sat uncomfortably in a wooden chair in one of the *Dominique*'s few passenger compartments, chewing antacid tablets and waiting. The subtle, steady rocking of the ship at her berth was making him slightly nauseated.

But when the compartment door opened, Nudger forgot his discomfort and smiled at the man who entered.

"We need to talk," Nudger said, not getting up.

Shock crossed Oh's face like a passing shadow. Then he frowned slightly, glanced about, and entered the compartment all the way and closed the door. He had been carrying a large leather suitcase, which he placed carefully beside the bunk, as if the deliberate act would allow him time to think.

"Who are you?" he asked as he straightened and faced Nudger.

Nudger told him. Then he said, "You're a realist, Mr. Oh, a hard-nosed businessman who wouldn't hold a forty-year-old grudge about being prevented from committing suicide."

" 'Grudge' is hardly an adequate term, Mr. Nudger."

"Whatever the term, you've proved by your actions since the war that you're not the suicidal type after all. You're also not the type to let the valuable cargo that Caruthers was carrying on the *Sea Dreamer* go to the bottom of the Gulf—unless of course you'd already been paid for that cargo."

Oh smiled confidently, barely twitching his lips. He had a nifty poker face. "Please explain, Mr. Nudger."

"You and Cap Caruthers were in business together for a long time. You were his narcotics supplier. Then the divorce hearing came up and the news media started digging into Caruthers, and I'm sure you found out the FBI was onto him. You hired a detective to watch Caruthers so you could be sure he hadn't talked yet to the FBI, but exposure of your operation was almost inevitable. You decided to make one more big profit and get out in such a way that everyone would assume you were dead. So you sold Caruthers a final shipment—probably worthless—to smuggle in on the *Sea Dreamer*, pocketed the money, and when he was almost back to the Florida coast, where you could be sure there would be witnesses, you flew the El-Tron company aircraft into the *Sea Dreamer* and sent ship and plane to the bottom, just as you tried to do so many years ago. But this time you were more sensible. You flew your plane from the *Dandy Dan*, by remote control. Banzai. Mission accomplished. Now here you are alive and on your way to the good life in South America under an assumed name. No samurai you."

Oh still seemed unperturbed, as if he'd been listening only absently to Nudger. But he said, "Very nicely thought out, Mr. Nudger."

"And true."

Oh smiled. "Standing here embarrassingly alive as I am, I can hardly deny it. The question is, what now?" He reached into an inside pocket of his suit coat and withdrew a small revolver. "Merely a bargaining chip," he explained, nodding toward the gun. "Don't be alarmed."

Nudger had never looked into a revolver barrel and not been alarmed. And he wasn't deceived by Oh's reassurances. Guns were for killing, and that was what Oh intended doing with this one.

The door from the adjoining compartment opened, and

Slayton and Ortero walked through, also with guns drawn, trained on Oh. Nudger let out a relieved breath when the gun that was aimed at him lowered, but Oh's finger remained firm on the trigger.

For a moment Nudger thought that this elderly executive might actually decide to shoot it out. Oh's eyes were steady and unreadable. Violence had already begun in Nudger's stomach.

But the inclination for suicide had left Oh decades ago. He sensibly handed over the revolver to Slayton and presented no resistance as he was handcuffed and read his rights. He was a businessman cutting his losses, already anticipating long legal wars.

"I assume you were eavesdropping," Oh said to Slayton.

Nudger stood up on shaking legs and grinned. "No one had to eavesdrop," he said to Oh, as he removed a small flat instrument from his breast pocket. "Our conversation is accurately preserved in tone and content, all right here on tape in this small but efficient recorder. It's the best that El-Tron manufactures."

Time Exposure

She was upset about something. All mussed by external and internal stormy weather, all wild blonde hair and wild blue eyes, haunted by the lightning. That was what had driven her to Nudger's office. She made Nudger, who was used to dumpy divorcees and pilfered cash registers, feel like Sam Spade. Nudger liked that.

"Mr. Nudger?' she asked tentatively, brushing water from her raincoat with the back of her hand, lowering her neat frame into the chair before Nudger's desk. The action allowed a glimpse of startlingly pale legs with slender ankles.

Nudger nodded to the ankles. A sheet of rain hit the window as if the wind had flung it there out of malice.

"I'm Adelaide Lacy," the wet blonde said. "I want to hire you."

Nudger sized her up for potential to pay, as was his habit. She was wearing a navy blue dress. Her clothes were expensive but not high fashion; she was about thirty-five, neatly groomed, and wore no wedding ring. She didn't appear to be the sort you'd go to to finance a business venture, but she looked as if she could afford Nudger's piddling fee. Nudger's alternative was another hand of solitaire.

"What's bothering you . . . Miss, is it?" She nodded. "Miss Lacy?"

"These." She removed a squarish brown envelope from her purse and leaned forward to place it on the desk. "You'd better look, then I'll explain."

Nudger opened the damp envelope and withdrew an

eight-by-ten black and white photograph of a downtown street. He recognized the street: Locust Avenue. The photograph was sharp; there were no people or traffic, only buildings. Beneath the first photo was a second, a blow-up of one of the buildings, the Arcade Building, an office building Nudger had been in more than once. There was a curious thing about that photograph. All of the windows in the Arcade Building seemed to reveal empty rooms, all except one. In that window was a heavy-set, balding man seated at a desk, a pencil resting between his fingers, his head slightly bowed. He was in sharp focus; Nudger could count the buttons on his shirt. He looked familiar to Nudger, but Nudger couldn't place him.

"You want something to drink, Miss Lacy?" Nudger asked, putting down the photographs on his desk. He wanted to slow the pace of this encounter; he was experiencing intimations that made him uneasy.

"Call me Adelaide," she said, smiling nervously. "And no thanks. A photographer named Paul Dobbs came to me with those two days ago," she went on. "He said he'd been commissioned by an architectural firm to take photos of certain downtown streets. His employer was interested in the buildings, nothing else. So Dobbs would set up his camera just after sundown, when it was still light out but shadows were minimal and downtown was pretty much deserted. Then with special film he'd take forty-five minute time exposures."

"Very long exposures," Nudger said.

"And for good reason," Adelaide told him. "As Dobbs explained it, at that slow exposure rate, occasional passing cars, buses, or pedestrians wouldn't show up in the photo; they'd be moving too fast for their images to form on the film. There could be a bank holdup on those streets and it wouldn't appear in the photograph."

Nudger understood. The same held true of any movement inside the windows of the photographed buildings. That was why all the rooms appeared empty. All but one. Nudger felt a cold weight in his stomach. He was liking this less and less. Soon his insides would be forcibly reminding him that he was ill-suited by temperament for his work.

Adelaide Lacy confirmed what he was thinking. "Dobbs told me that the only way that man could appear so sharply focused in that window would be if he was as still as the building itself. If he was dead."

Nudger's stomach kicked. He picked up a foil-wrapped roll of antacid tablets, slipped one of the thin white disks onto his tongue, and began to chew. "Dead." Gee, he disliked that word!

"What else did Dobbs say?" he asked. More rain, a sudden noisy downpour. Lightning flashed like a warning; thunder rumbled life fateful laughter.

Adelaide shifted in her chair, obviously made uncomfortable by the thought of what she was about to say. "Dobbs noticed the man in the window in one of his photographs, blew up the scene, and took it to a friend who is a reporter on the *Globe-Democrat*. The reporter told him he was crazy, that the city leased that floor of the Arcade Building, and that the man in the photo was Virgil Hiller, the city comptroller."

Face and name suddenly connected in Nudger's mind. He popped another antacid tablet into his mouth.

"The next day Hiller and his secretary had disappeared," Adelaide said, "along with a million dollars in City funds."

"And that made Dobbs all the more suspicious of murder."

"Sure. But the assistant comptroller and even the mayor claimed they saw Hiller alive the morning *after* Dobbs's photograph was taken."

"Did Dobbs buy their story?"

Adelaide shrugged. "He had no choice. I mean, contradicting the mayor . . ."

"Right, City Hall and all that. So what did Dobbs do?"

Adelaide widened her luminous blue eyes in faint surprise. "Why, he came to me. He told me everything." She saw suddenly that she'd gotten ahead of herself, smiled a nervous, shadowy smile, and sat back. "Virgil Hiller's secretary, the woman he supposedly ran away with, is my sister Mary, Mr. Nudger. And I know what she really thought of her boss. She told me often enough he was a tyrannical creep and a secret drunk. She'd never have run away with him."

"Where is Dobbs now?" Nudger asked.

"He's disappeared."

Nudger felt a growing queasiness. He longed for a nice dull divorce case, a punch in the nose from an irate adulterer.

"Have you told the police all this?" he asked.

"No, Mr. Dobbs cautioned me not to go to the police. So did Mr. Kyle."

"Not Mr. Arnie Kyle, the gambler?"

"Yes," Adelaide said, "do you know him?"

"Only well enough to avoid him like bubonic plague."

Adelaide nodded, brushed back an errant strand of blonde hair that was still damp from the rain. "I can understand that. He came to my apartment the first time Mr. Dobbs was there and asked for the envelope."

"Is this another envelope?" Nudger asked. "What envelope are we talking about now?"

"Two weeks ago Mary came to me with this regular business-size white envelope. She was scared, though trying not to act it. She left the envelope with me and told me to open it only if something happened to her."

"And now something has, apparently. Did you open the envelope?"

"No, when I went to get it from where I kept it on a shelf in the closet, it was gone."

"Did you tell Arnie Kyle that?"

"Yes. He acted angry, though he was very gentlemanly, then he left."

"He was only acting gentlemanly," Nudger assured her. "He probably really was angry. He's the dominant force in bookmaking and prostitution in this city. He's had people killed before breakfast, then had an extra piece of toast."

"That's what Mr. Dobbs said, more or less."

Nudger grunted. "Before Mr. Dobbs disappeared." He rubbed a hand across his mouth and chin, realizing that he was starting to call everyone "mister" like Adelaide.

"Mr. Nudger," Adelaide said, "I need to know what it all means. I need to find Mary, or at least find out what happened to her. And I can pay. I have money saved, and if I have to, I'll use it all."

Nudger absently touched his twisting stomach, rapped a knuckle on the desk. "Why did you come to me in particular, Adelaide?"

"I don't know one private investigator from another," she said candidly. "I picked you out of the Yellow Pages."

"That's apropos," Nudger said.

Adelaide stared at him without blinking. Her wide blue eyes seemed like a child's. Then she brought herself under control and her voice was steady, but pleading. "I need help, Mr. Nudger!"

Nudger gave in. He smiled at her. "And I need money. Let's talk fee."

Ten years ago, when Nudger was a rookie patrolman in

the police department, his partner in a two-man patrol car had been Jack Hammersmith. Nudger's nerves couldn't stand up under the constant strain and the hyped up life of a street cop. When his superiors realized this, he'd been assigned to play Coppy the Clown, appearing with red nose and oversized shoes at benefits and children's parties around town. Then Coppy the Clown had been discontinued by the new police commissioner as cutting too undignified a figure to represent the police department. So Nudger left the department and, after a series of short-lived occupations, discovered that, though he wasn't constitutionally fit for the work, using his police background and contacts to become a private investigator was his best hope to feed, shelter, and clothe himself.

He'd managed with difficulty to do that during the past eight years, often acutely missing Coppy the Clown. During those same years, Nudger had developed a spastic nervous stomach. Hammersmith had risen in the department to become a lieutenant in the Third Precinct, and Nudger's most valuable police contact.

As usual, the rotund, sarcastic, but kind Hammersmith had put aside whatever other business he had and seen Nudger. Nudger had saved Hammersmith's life while on the police force, and almost killed him at the same time by frantically spraying bullets around a large discount store after hours while an armed robbery was in progress. That was the exploit that had earned Nudger his polka-dotted Coppy the Clown suit.

"What's with Virgil Hiller?" Nudger asked, settling into the straight-backed wooden chair at the side of Hammersmith's desk. It was a tough chair to settle into; Nudger and anyone else who sat in it felt an irresistible urge to stand up after about ten minutes. Hammersmith was a workaholic and didn't like visitors hanging around his office distracting him.

"What I like about you, Nudge," he said, "is that you get to the point." Desk work had made the once sleek and handsome Hammersmith a portly, florid man; his image had finally caught up with the long, foul-smelling cigars he'd always smoked. "Hiller fell victim to two of man's greatest temptations: money and a woman." Hammersmith scooted back in his own comfortable leather chair. "The two seem to go together, have you noticed? Anyway, Hiller saw his chance to get his hands on both on a more or less permanent basis, tucked one under each arm, and left the city for pleasure-filled parts unknown."

"Anything in his background to suggest he'd do that?" Nudger asked.

"Nope. There doesn't have to be. We're talking about opportunity. And half a million dollars and the woman he no doubt loves, or thinks he does. Even thee and me, Nudge . . ."

"Me, maybe," Nudger said, "not thee. What about the secretary, Mary Lacy?"

"Thirty-two, straight, hard-working, and homely. But then Virgil Hiller was never offered leading roles in the movies either." Hammersmith fired up one of his abominable cigars and squinted at Nudger through its curiously greenish smoke. "You hired to find Hiller?"

"The secretary," Nudger said.

"Same thing; they're a set. You want a cigar?"

"No thanks; I love life. Did a photographer named Paul Dobbs come to see you?"

"Oh, him, sure. With his time exposure photo that showed Hiller sitting at his desk, maybe asleep."

"Or dead. How do you explain it?"

Hammersmith observed the glowing ember of his cigar

closely, as if something minute had appeared there that gripped his interest. "Question is," he said, "how do you explain it to a grand jury? The date of the photograph can't be firmly substantiated, and who understands all that technical jargon? I know I don't."

"And you've got a caseload up to here," Nudger finished. He'd heard this story before from the police. He understood their point of view, too. They were undermanned and struggling to cope with a backlog of cases they at least might solve. This was one that didn't warrant much time or effort; Hiller and Mary Lacy were probably thousands of miles away, basking on foreign sands.

"I know what you're going to ask next," Hammersmith said "What about Dobbs's disappearance? Well, officially Dobbs hasn't disappeared, despite a phone call we got from a certain young lady named Adelaide Lacy. We checked, Nudge, and Dobbs has dropped out of sight off and on for months at a time for the last ten years. Those kinds of freelance photographers are like that. He's probably in Fiji photographing natives for *National Geographic*, or maybe doing some porno work to turn a fast buck. He's done both those things in his varied career."

Nudger's back was beginning to ache. His ten minutes in the hard chair were almost up. "How does Arnie Kyle fit in with Hiller?" he asked.

Hammersmith wiggled the cigar clamped in his mouth and raised an eyebrow. "I didn't know he did. But I'm not surprised. Kyle's the sort that likes to be seen with any politician. Makes him feel respectable, though I can't imagine why."

Nudger stood to leave, stretching his cramped back muscles. "Thanks, Jack."

"Maybe you can tell *me* where Kyle fits in with Hiller,"

Hammersmith suggested, aiming the cigar at Nudger as if it were a smoking gun.

"When I find out," Nudger said, "you'll be the next to know."

"If there is a next," Hammersmith cautioned. "You be careful of Kyle."

Purely by accident, he blew a perfect smoke ring and glared at it, a bit surprised.

He'd always been skeptical of coincidence.

Nudger left him like that, walked through the crowded, noisy booking area and down the concrete steps to the street.

The place to start was Mary Lacy's apartment. It was in a downtown building that Nudger figured would be converted into condominiums. It wasn't exclusive or wildly expensive, but it was a nice place to live, with a touch of aged luxury and plenty of atmosphere in the long, high-ceilinged halls, stained glass windows, fireplaces, and ornate wrought iron. Mary's apartment was on the fifth floor. According to Adelaide, she'd moved in two years go and liked the place. Adelaide had a spare key and let Nudger in.

"She's paid rent to the end of the month," Adelaide said. "I don't know what to do, start packing her things, or what."

Nudger didn't answer. He was nosing around, not knowing exactly what he was looking for, hoping he'd recognize it if he came across it.

He started with the living room, searching in table drawers, beneath lamp bases, behind drapes. He noticed immediately that Mary Lacy's apartment had been searched by experts, no doubt the police. Yet there was an uncharacteristic care with which things were put back in place; the police didn't have to be that careful, having no reason to conceal the fact that they'd searched the apartment.

For the next hour Nudger gave the apartment a thorough tossing. He found nothing that might give a clue to the whereabouts of Mary Lacy or the mysterious envelope.

Until he stopped halfway out of the bedroom, struck by what had been odd about the dresser drawers. He went back to Mary Lacy's dresser and removed its contents, then withdrew the newspaper she'd used to line the bottoms of the drawers.

"Look at this," Nudger said to Adelaide, who was standing staring at him as if reconsidering having hired him. "These sheets of newspaper are dated five years ago. You told me that Mary had only lived here two years. And this paper isn't the least bit stained; it might have been bought down at the corner newsstand yesterday."

"But why would Mary use such an old newspaper to line her dresser drawers?"

"Because she wanted to save the paper, but she didn't want anyone to know she saved it. Even if they searched the apartment, they might not think anything of old newspaper used to line drawer bottoms; they'd be too interested in the other contents of the drawers."

Adelaide was getting impatient, nervous. "But why that paper?"

"Look at it." Nudger held the five-year-old newspaper's front page up for Adelaide to see. It was a special edition of the *Globe-Democrat*, printed the tragic day Mayor Ollie Lane had been killed in an airplane crash while riding in the back seat of an open-cockpit skywriter as a reelection campaign attention-getter. The biplane was to have spelled out the mayor's initials high in the sky over the city, but something went wrong; the plane began fluttering downward halfway through the capital L, and exploded on contact with the ground. The pilot's mechanic had wisely disappeared. The

CAA had examined the wreckage and determined that one of the wing struts was twisted from its mooring, and the turn at the base of the L had caused the top wing to buckle under the strain of the tight maneuver. There was a large photo of the mayor on the front page, trimmed in black.

"So, what does it mean?" Adelaide asked. "After all these years?"

"It could mean a number of things. Did Mary ever talk about this accident?"

"Not that I remember."

"Did she work for the city at that time?"

"No. She was a secretary at a chemical firm. She went to work for Virgil Hiller three years ago."

Nudger began returning things to the way he'd found them, but he folded the newspaper carefully and tucked it beneath his arm.

"What now?" Adelaide asked.

"Research," Nudger told her. "I'll drop you off at your place, then phone you and tell you the results."

After half an hour at the city's main library, Nudger had a late supper and then drove across town to Paul Dobbs's apartment.

Dobbs's place was on the top floor of one of several modern three-story apartment projects that looked like elaborate motels. Their rent was cheap, and seemed like even more of a bargain because they had a pool where boy could meet girl.

Nudger stood for a moment on the third-floor front balcony, looking down at the deserted parking lot. Then he rang the doorbell. Who could say, maybe Paul Dobbs had gotten back from Fiji.

But Nudger knew better. After a few minutes, he used his

honed Visa card to slip the pathetic lock and entered Dobbs's apartment. Breaking and entering this was called in courts of law. Nudger's stomach was fluttering like hummingbirds' wings.

What calmed him somewhat was that he knew he wouldn't be here long. He knew what he was searching for and he found it in less than five minutes, the place where Paul Dobbs kept his photography equipment.

It took up most of the closet in the second bedroom: The inside of the closet was a mess; there was undeveloped film unraveled all over the place, and three expensive thirty-five millimeter cameras lay on the floor with their backs open.

A sudden noise from the living room made Nudger suck in a harsh breath, fear clawing at his insides.

Someone else was in Dobbs's apartment, walking slowly toward the main bedroom. Nudger heard the floor creak. This bedroom would be next, he was sure. He doubted if he was hearing Paul Dobbs lightfooting it around his own apartment.

Nudger eased his way out the sliding glass doors onto the rear balcony. He saw the pool glimmering darkly in the moonlight three stories below.

A deep, amused voice said from the room he'd just left, "Come out, come out, wherever you are." Sadistic and coaxing.

Nudger moved to the side of the balcony, almost running into a huge fern in a ceramic planter, pressing himself against the cool hard bricks. There was no way off the small balcony other than through the bedroom, or by a Tarzan-caliber three-story dive into the pool, and it occurred to Nudger that he didn't know which end was the deep one.

"Getting a breath of night air, are you?" the voice said, nearer, moving toward the open glass doors.

Nudger found sudden strength and lifted the ceramic planter to hurl at the man. Then he had a better idea. He yelled and tossed the heavy planter, fern and all, out over the pool. Then he drew back into the shadows at the very end of the balcony.

A large man wearing a gray suit cursed and ran to the railing, gazed down for a second at the foam and ripples in the dark pool. Then he wheeled and ran back into Dobbs's apartment. Nudger saw that he was carrying a gun.

Nudger waited five seconds before he followed the man's path through the empty apartment. He could hear descending footfalls clattering on the back stairs. Nudger ran as silently as he could down the front stairs. Then he was out the front entrance and racing across the parking lot to his car.

"Hey!" a voice yelled behind him. Nudger didn't know whose voice, didn't pause or look back to find out. He had his key in his hand when he yanked open the car door, had it in the ignition switch even before he was in the seat. The engine came to life on the second try and he sped from the blacktop lot, the right front fender ticking one of the brick pillars flanking the driveway.

He took every side street at top speed in the old Volkswagen, skidding around each corner, checking the rearview mirror on the straightaways.

Ten minutes had passed before he could assure himself that he wasn't being followed. And it was a wonder he hadn't picked up a cop, speeding around like a teenage leadfoot. Where were the traffic cops when you needed them? Out chasing crooks? He'd talk to Hammersmith about this.

But if he was right about Dobbs, he'd have more important things to discuss with Hammersmith. He came to a major intersection and got his bearings, then popped three antacid tablets into his mouth and drove toward Adelaide Lacy's apartment.

Adelaide was in bed. It took her about five minutes to come to the door and let Nudger in. She was wearing no makeup and had her hair wrapped in some kind of scarf to preserve her hairdo. Her drab flannel robe was tied crookedly about her waist with a sash, and brown furry slippers destroyed the grace of her ankles.

"Mr. Nudger? . . . What . . . ?"

Nudger looked her over. For the first time he didn't mind that she'd called him mister.

"I've just come from Paul Dobbs's apartment," he told her.

"Did you find anything?" She walked halfway across the living room and turned to look at him. "Do you want some coffee?"

"I found confirmation of a sort. Yes, thanks, cream and sugar."

"I drink mine black," said a voice from the doorway

Nudger turned and saw a small dapper man wearing a checked sportcoat, with a luminous striped silk tie that appeared almost metallic. He recognized Arnie Kyle. And he recognized the large man with Arnie Kyle; he'd seen him earlier in Paul Dobbs's apartment.

"That was good," the big man said admiringly to Nudger. "I really thought you'd jumped off that balcony into the swimming pool."

"Actually," Nudger said, his stomach beginning to pulsate, "I don't even swim, especially with my clothes on."

Arnie Kyle smiled. "That might be good to know." He looked at Adelaide, then back at Nudger. "Forget the coffee. Both of you can sit down."

The large man was holding a revolver with the casual respect of an expert marksman.

Nudger sat on the sofa, and Adelaide sat down next to him. She absently rested a hand on his wrist. He hoped she wouldn't pick up his trembling and become unsettled.

"You're a lot smarter than you look," Kyle said to Nudger. "But as soon as Riley here told me what you were looking for in Dobbs's place, I came to the same conclusion you did. That's why I showed up here, apparently just in time."

"What's he talking about, Mr. Nudger?" Adelaide said.

"Five years ago," Nudger said, "Arnie Kyle was in on the scheme to murder the incumbent mayor so the election would go to his man. The city comptroller, Virgil Hiller, was the only member of the previous administration in on the murder, which explains why the library reveals he was the only member who kept his job all these years. But Hiller was becoming a risk, drinking too much, talking too much. He talked to his secretary, your sister Mary. Naturally she was afraid to go to the authorities in an administration corrupt from the mayor on down. To protect herself she sealed something incriminating in an envelope and left it with you. Dobbs figured she might have done something like that for insurance, so he searched your apartment without your knowing, found the envelope, then came to you and pretended to be there for the first time."

"But why come see me if he already had the envelope?"

"To put it back," Nudger said. "Dobbs was a small-time photographer who'd stumbled onto something big. He knew that if that envelope turned up missing, he'd be suspected of having stolen it, and that would put him in danger. So he took it, photographed its contents, and then put it back—not on the first visit with you, because Arnie Kyle interrupted him. But I remembered your mentioning a second Dobbs visit.

Since the envelope hasn't been found in his apartment, or anywhere else, I think he managed to slip it back onto your closet shelf during the second visit. You were supposed to find it later and assume you simply missed it the first time you looked."

"Dobbs was like you," Kyle pointed out, "just smart enough to get himself in serious trouble by playing out of his league."

Nudger tried to ignore that unnerving comparison and continued. "When Arnie Kyle found photographs of the contents but no envelope in Dobbs's possession, he knew the original was still missing and started frantically searching for it. It never occurred to him that Dobbs would want to photograph its contents and then bring the envelope back here where he got it."

"Until tonight," Kyle said. "When it occurred to you."

"I had the advantage," Nudger said sportingly. "I knew about Dobbs's second visit with Adelaide. It wasn't difficult to figure out the purpose of that visit."

"Everybody seems to have some kind of angle in this world," Kyle said. "Ain't it depressing? It causes this kind of trouble. The question now is, what are we gonna do about it?"

Nudger shrugged. He knew there was no question in Kyle's mind, except possibly how to dispose of the bodies. "I have no idea. That's why I stopped on the way here and phoned Police Lieutenant Hammersmith, to ask him to meet me here so we can figure this thing out."

"Don't waste my time with bluffing," Kyle said. He had a shark's underslung smile. "It doesn't become you to lie. You never talked to Hammersmith, admit it."

"I admit it." Nudger said, as sirens began to wail in the distance. "But I left a message on his recorder."

109

Doubt crossed Kyle's intense features like a subtle change of light.

"You haven't personally killed anyone," Nudger told him. "But being in the vicinity here while Riley does would amount to the same thing."

"He really is bluffing," Riley said. He had more nerve than Kyle and he seemed eager to kill whereas Kyle was merely willing. Nudger wondered if Riley was the one who had made Mary Lacy reveal the whereabouts of the envelope. Who had killed Mary Lacy and Virgil Hiller.

The sirens were getting louder, getting closer.

"If you wait around to find out for sure if I'm bluffing," Nudger said, "it will be too late for you to slip out of the building."

"Those might be fire engine sirens, Arnie," Riley said.

Kyle shook his head.

"They ain't fire engines."

Nudger's stomach did flip after flip as Kyle stared appraisingly at him. Riley was standing very straight and tall, breathing rapidly.

Then Kyle gave a sort of snarl and took a few steps toward Adelaide's bedroom.

"Knowing where that envelope is might hang you in court," Nudger pointed out. "Not to mention what might happen if it were found in your possession."

Kyle stopped and glared at him. The sirens were quite close now. He sighed. "You really aren't as dumb as you look," he said.

"No," Nudger agreed, "I ain't."

With a snake-like hiss, Kyle spat on the carpet. "Come on," he said to Riley. "Let's get out by the fire stairs." He beat Riley out the door.

Riley tucked his gun into a shoulder holster and smiled

faintly at Nudger as he followed, as if he derived some satisfaction at least out of seeing his boss outsmarted.

Adelaide let out a long breath and removed her hand from Nudger's wrist. She stared at him. "*Were* you bluffing?"

Nudger stood and began to pace to help get rid of his heartburn. He reached into a shirt pocket, peeled back the silver paper on a roll of antacid tablets, popped three of them into his mouth, and chewed. "I wasn't bluffing," he said, as the sirens growled to silence in the street below. Car doors slammed. Within a minute footsteps sounded on the stairs and in the hall.

When Hammersmith arrived, they found the envelope shoved to the back of the top shelf of Adelaide's closet. Inside was a blueprint of the downtown convention center that had been constructed five years ago at the time of the mayor's death. There was an X in red ink on the blueprint and a footnote, indicating where the body of Fred Carter, the missing mechanic paid by Arnie Kyle to sabotage the mayor's plane, was encased in the building's concrete piering.

Hammersmith stared at the blueprint and shook his head sadly. "It's gonna take this city years to get over what's coming."

"The dead legitimate mayor, the skywriter pilot, Paul Dobbs, Mary Lacy . . . they were all victims, too," Nudger said. "They'll never get over anything again."

Hammersmith admitted Nudger had a point. After ordering a pickup bulletin for Arnie Kyle and Riley, he stormed out of Adelaide's apartment, leaving behind a greenish haze of cigar smoke.

When they were alone, Adelaide said, "It didn't turn out at all the way I wanted when I hired you, Mr. Nudger."

"Things seldom do," Nudger told her, "but sometimes

they turn out better than they might have. I guess that has to be good enough."

Adelaide smiled a tight, resigned smile and nodded, her eyes moist.

Nudger took her out and bought her several double scotches. He drank warm milk.

Typographical Error

Nudger walked into the Kit-Kat lounge and looked around, waiting for his eyes to adjust to the dimness. It was ten a.m. and the lounge was barren of customers. That was okay. The person he wanted to talk with stood behind the long, vinyl-padded bar, idly leafing through a newspaper. Lani Katlo was her name, proprietor and manager of the Kit-Kat. She was a woman sneaking up on menopause, attractive in a still youthful if shopworn fashion. When she saw Nudger approaching the bar, she smiled and nodded, waiting for him to order.

"Coffee if you have it," Nudger told her.

"We don't. There's a restaurant across the street." Her smile remained, taking any edge off her words.

"Never mind," Nudger said. "What I really want is to talk, Lani." He handed her one of his cards with his Saint Louis address.

She appeared vaguely surprised that he knew her name as she accepted the card and folded the newspaper closed. "You're in what line of work," she asked, studying the card, "that brings you to Florida?"

"I'm a private detective," Nudger told her.

"This says defective, with an 'f.' "

"That's a printer's error."

"Why don't you return the cards?"

"I had a thousand of them made up, then the printer went out of business. What can I do but use the cards anyway?"

"I see your point," Lani Katlo said. "These cards aren't

113

cheap. But what would a private detective from Saint Louie want to talk to me about?"

"Harmon Medlark. And nobody from Saint Louis says 'Saint Louie.'"

"You mean Meadowlark?"

"Medlark." Nudger spelled the name for her.

Lani Katlo shrugged. "I thought maybe he was somebody who'd used your printer."

"Medlark was in business over in Clearwater six months ago, selling time shares in vacation condominium units. The deal where the customers purchase part ownership in a unit and have the right to use it one or two weeks out of each year before turning it over to the next part owner."

"I'm in familiar with the system," Lani said. "I own one fifty-second of a unit in Hawaii myself."

Nudger settled himself onto a soft barstool. "Harmon Medlark ran into problems when he used his own peculiar calendar that divided the year into hundreds of weeks. After collecting big down payments he managed to finagle by offering ridiculously low interest rates on loans, he disappeared with the money. Some of the Saint Louis fleeced have hired me to find him and recover the wool."

"Did he build any of the condominiums?"

Nudger shook his head sadly. "There is a tract of graded ground in Clearwater supporting only weeds and a sign reading 'Sun Joy Vacation Limited.' That is all. Medlark bought the ground with a small deposit and a large smile then defaulted on the loan when he disappeared."

"With all that wool."

Nudger nodded. He watched Lani Katlo pour herself two fingers of Scotch in a monogrammed glass and winced at the thought of hundred proof booze cascading down a throat at ten in the morning.

Lani downed half the Scotch without visible effect and asked, "Why are you telling me all this?"

"Because your name and address were found among the few items Medlark left behind in his hasty departure."

Lani Katlo appeared mystified. "Honest, Nudger, I never heard of the man."

Nudger reached into an inside pocket of his sports coat and withdrew a fuzzy snapshot of a graying man with regular features and kindly blue eyes. He showed the photograph to Lani Katlo.

"Him I think I know," she said. "I thought his name was Herman Manners. He's a friend of Eddie Regal, who owns a florist shop over on Citrus Drive. They used to come in here together now and then, a few times they came in with Eddie's wife and a tall oversexed-acting redhead that looked like a watermelon festival queen." Lani used cupped hands before her own gaunt torso to illustrate her meaning.

"Do you know the redhead's name?" Nudger asked. That could be useful information even if there was no longer a connection with the evasive Medlark.

"No," Lani said, "I only saw her maybe twice. Eddie Regal could probably tell you."

Nudger reached into his pocket again, unfolded a slip of beige notepaper and laid it on the bar, "Does this note we found along with your name tell you anything?" he asked Lani Katlo. The neatly typed note read:

Dear Mrs Cupcake,
    I still can't believe you love an old greybeard like me, but I'll keep living in a dream. See you in Shangri-la.
                                                    Mr Moneybags

"It doesn't mean a thing to me," Lani Katlo said, handing

115

back the note. "Where's Shangri-la, anyway. Isn't that a place up the coast?"

"It's a place in a book," Nudger told her. "Not real."

"Maybe it's the name of a night spot or resort or something. Ever think of that?"

"Thought of it and checked," Nudger said. "It's possible that was what Medlark meant when and if he typed the note."

"Maybe Eddie Regal can tell you something about it," Lani Katlo suggested. She unfolded her newspaper again, as a signal that she was losing interest in the conversation.

Nudger thanked her for her cooperation and left.

On the sidewalk he stood in the heat and glare of the Florida sun and felt his stomach contract. Talking with people like Lani Katlo did that to him. Nerves. She was hiding something and Nudger knew it but couldn't pinpoint how he knew. He couldn't draw her out of concealment. Frustration. He wished, as he had so many times, that he knew another trade, was in some other line of work. But he didn't. He wasn't. He regretted the Spanish omelet he'd eaten for breakfast, popped an antacid tablet into his mouth and walked toward his dented Volkswagen Beetle.

"This card says defective," Eddie Regal said from behind a display of chrysanthemums. He was a swarthy, hairy man with oversized knuckles. He did not look like a florist.

"A typographical error," Nudger said. "I use them anyway. Have you ever heard of a man named Harmon Medlark?"

"You mean Meadowlark?"

Nudger explained that he didn't. "Possibly you knew him as Herman Manners." Nudger flashed the obscure photograph of Medlark.

"Sure," Regal said, "that's Herman. I met him a few

116

months ago at a place called the Kit-Kat. We talked a while over drinks and found we were both interested in the dog races. So we went a few times."

"Alone?"

"Sometimes. A couple of times we took my wife Madge and a girl Herman went out with, a redhead name of Delores."

"Do you know where I can find Delores?"

Regal snipped a bud and shook his head no. "I only met her a few times, when she was with Herman. I think she lives around Orlando, near Disney World."

"Did Manners ever mention where he lived?"

"Nope. It wasn't that kind of friendship. And Herman is a kind of tight-lipped guy anyway."

"What's Delores's last name?"

"That I remember because it's unusual. Bookbinder. It stuck in my mind because she isn't a bookish kind of girl at all."

"So I hear," Nudger said. "Did Manners ever mention a timesharing deal in a condominium project in Clearwater?"

"Nope. We talked dogs and women and that's about all."

"Okay, Mr. Regal. You have my card with my motel phone number penned on it. Will you call me if you think of anything else about Manners?"

"Oh, be glad to, Mr. Nudger. It interests me, how a detective works. Where you going now? Back to Saint Louie?"

"To Orlando, to try to find Delores Bookbinder."

"We specialize in funeral wreaths," Regal said, "but we got a special today on long-stemmed roses if you're interested."

"Thanks," Nudger said, "but I don't think I'll need either." He walked from the aromatic shop and heard the little bell above the door tinkle cheerily behind him.

Bookbinder, he thought. That is an unusual name.

She was easy to find, Delores Bookbinder. She lived in Orlando proper and was listed in the phone directory. When Nudger called her she readily agreed to see him after learning only his name and hearing Regal's name mentioned. She gave directions to her apartment in a sultry telephone voice that kicked his imagination around like a bent tin can.

Delores's directions led Nudger to a long, two-story stucco apartment building on Soltice Avenue, just off the Bee-line expressway. She lived on the top floor, and when he knocked she answered the door wearing a simple green dress that hugged her curves the way he found himself yearning to hug. Delores was a tall, lushly proportioned woman in her early thirties, with that flawless milky complexion possessed by only a minority of natural redheads.

"Nudger?" she asked.

He nodded, and she stepped back to usher him into a small but neatly furnished apartment that featured thick blue carpet, cool white walls and a large oil painting of a leopard luxuriously sunning itself on some far away African plain. A window airconditioner was humming a gurgly, suggestive melody. Nudger handed Delores one of his cards.

"This says defective," she told him.

"Don't let it fool you."

Delores smiled and motioned for Nudger to sit on a low cream-colored sofa. She sat across from him in a dainty chair and crossed her long legs with a calculated exaggerated modesty that brought a familiar tightness to his groin. He decided he was an idiot for what he was thinking. He reached for the foil-wrapped cylinder in his shirt pocket, thumbnailed off an antacid tablet and popped it into his mouth.

Delores was staring at him curiously.

"Sensitive stomach," Nudger explained. "Nerves."

"Isn't that something of a drawback in your profession?"

"Yes and no," he answered. "It causes me discomfort, but it sometimes acts as a warning signal." As it was doing now. Nudger decided not to lay a hand or anything else on Delores Bookbinder, if that was her name.

"Do you know a man named Herman Manners?" he asked.

She threw him the kind of curve he wasn't thinking about. "You mean Harmon Medlark?"

"The same." Nudger was becoming uncomfortable on the underslung soft sofa; it was for lying down, not sitting. "Eddie Regal and a number of other people seem to know him as Herman Manners."

Delores waved an elegant, ring-adorned hand. "Oh, that's a name Harmon sometimes uses."

Nudger showed her the photograph. "Is this the man we're talking about?"

She crossed the room, leaned over Nudger with a heavy scent of perfume and squinted at the photo. "That's so fuzzy it could be anyone," she said, "but I can say with some certainty it's Harmon." Her hand rested very lightly on Nudger's shoulder. He wondered if she could feel his heartbeat. He chomped down hard on the antacid tablet to create a diversionary vibration.

"Where can I get in touch with Medlark?" he asked as casually as possible.

"I don't know exactly," Delores said. "We had an argument. I haven't seen Harmon for over a week."

"What did you argue about?"

Delores didn't seem offended by Nudger's nosiness. Her hand remained steady on his shoulder and he could feel the warmth of her breath on the back of his neck, as if she still

119

needed to study the photograph that he'd now replaced in his pocket. "His drinking," she said. "Harmon drinks too much. Between the two of us, he's a sick man." She gave a mindless little laugh. "I do pick the losers. You look like a winner."

Now that was fairly direct. Nudger turned to say something to her and they were kissing. After what seemed an enjoyable full minute, he pulled away. He stood up.

"I don't see this as a wise move in the game," he said.

Delores appeared mystified, her green eyes wide. "What game?"

"I'm not sure. That's why it's not a wise move." He smiled at her. "I'm going to leave while I still can, Delores."

She frowned and ran a long-fingered hand over her svelte curves, as if to reassure herself that they were still there. "You're nuts," she said, "or something else."

"Nuts," Nudger assured her.

"If you're really leaving," Delores said in a resigned and disappointed voice, "I guess I ought to tell you about a rumor I heard that Harmon is in a 'rest home' that's actually a place for alcoholics to dry out and take the cure."

"Rest home where?" Nudger asked.

"Over near Vero Beach. Shady Retreat, it's called, like it's a religious place for meditation or something. Well it's not; it's for problem drinkers."

Nudger moved toward the door.

"After I told you that," Delores said in an injured tone, "you're not still leaving, are you?"

Nudger got out of there. The tropical Florida sun seemed cool.

Vero Beach was a resort town on the Atlantic coast, a few hours' drive from Orlando. Nudger gassed up the Beetle and drove there.

Shady Retreat was south of the town, one of several buildings erected on relatively undeveloped beachfront property secluded from the highway by thick brush and palm trees. It was a converted large beach-house, behind a mobile home office that rested with an air of permanence on a stone foundation that hid any sign of wheels or axles. The sunlight glinted brightly off the mobile home's white aluminum siding, causing Nudger's eyes to ache as he approached along a brick walkway flanked by azaleas. The sea slapped at the beach beyond the cast concrete structure behind the mobile home. Nudger pressed a button beside the glass storm door and heard a faint buzzing that reminded him of a fly trapped in a jar.

A dark-eyed man with black hair and wire-rimmed glasses opened the door. He was wearing a neat blue business suit with a maroon tie. He introduced himself as Dr. Mortimer and invited Nudger inside.

Nudger stepped into the coolness of the sparsely furnished office and handed Dr. Mortimer his card. The doctor glanced at it and slipped it into his pocket, then sat behind a tan metal desk, and in the manner of doctors asked Nudger how he could help him.

"Do you have a patient here named Harmon Medlark?" Nudger asked.

The doctor's face didn't change expression. "We don't ordinarily give out information on our patients."

"How many patients do you have at one time?" Nudger asked.

"Sometimes ten, at maximum. Right now we have five."

"And Harmon Medlark is one of them?"

The doctor seemed to struggle with his sense of ethics.

"The information is very important to a lot of people, Doctor," Nudger said.

121

Doctor Mortimer nodded and finally said, "Yes, Mr. Medlark is here."

"For treatment of chronic alcoholism?"

Dr. Mortimer nodded. "As are all our patients."

Nudger's stomach was kicking up violently.

"Could you describe Harmon Medlark?"

"Average height, middle-aged, a rather handsome man." The doctor reached into a desk drawer and handed Nudger a slip of yellow paper. "Here's his admission form, filled out and signed by Medlark himself. His description and vital statistics are on it."

Nudger read: "Mr Harmon Medlark/age 46/hgt. 5' 10"/wgt. 160/hair: gray/eyes: blue/occupation: real estate." He handed Doctor Mortimer the photograph. "Is this Medlark?" he asked.

Dr. Mortimer nodded.

"Would you mind doing me a favor, Doctor?" Nudger asked. "Just jot down Medlark's description on the back of the photo. It's kind of fuzzy and the color of hair and eyes and complexion couldn't be right. Here, just copy off this if you want." Nudger laid the yellow admission form on the desk before the doctor.

"Certainly," Dr. Mortimer agreed with a smile, withdrew a gold pen from his pocket and took a few minutes to comply with Nudger's request.

Nudger took the photograph the doctor handed back and read: Mr. Harmon Medlark/age 46/hgt. 5' 10"/wgt. 160/hair: grey/eyes: blue/occupation: real estate.

"Now, do you mind if I see Mr. Medlark?" Nudger said.

"How important is it, Mr. Nudger?"

"Very. And if I don't see him now, someone with authority certainly will later."

Dr. Mortimer sighed and laced his manicured fingers together tightly. "All right, if it's necessary, though I don't like the patient disturbed during withdrawal. Mr. Medlark is in Unit C."

Nudger thanked the doctor and left the office. He walked back along an extension of the brick path to the main building. A white-uniformed attendant seated in a webbed chair near the front door smiled and nodded to him. Nudger returned the smile but said nothing as he walked past and inside.

Unit C was one of the four ground floor units. Nudger knocked on the door, heard a muffled voice invite him to enter, and went in.

Before him in a white wicker tucking chair, reading a *Time* magazine sat his quarry.

"Harmon Medlark?" Nudger asked.

The handsome gray-haired man nodded. "I am. Are you Doctor Mortimer's assistant?"

"I am not. My name is Nudger. I'm a private detective hired by the so called owners of Sun Joy Vacation Limited."

The wicker rocker stopped its gentle movement. "I know nothing about such a development."

"Who said it was a development? I might have been talking about a travel club."

"I'm not a travel agent, Mr. Nudger, I'm in real estate."

"Delores Bookbinder told me where to find you," Nudger said.

For an instant surprise showed in the blue eyes that surveyed Nudger. "Never heard of her. She sounds like a librarian."

"How about Eddie Regal?"

"I knew an Eddie Rogers once. Sold billiard accessories."

"Not the same fella, Herman."

"It's Harmon." The chair resumed its gentle back-and-forth motion. Its occupant ignored Nudger and crackingly turned a page of *Time*.

Nudger stood listening to the creak of the wicker runners for a while, then turned and left the room. He asked the attendant if it was okay to use the telephone he'd noticed on the way in. The attendant said sure.

After using the phone, Nudger returned to the office in the white aluminum trailer. Dr. Mortimer was still at his desk, ostensibly studying an open file. He smiled at Nudger.

"Did you see Mr. Medlark?" he asked.

"I'm impressed," Nudger told him.

"We try to keep our facilities modern and—"

"I mean I'm impressed by the way I was led by the nose," Nudger said. "From Lani Katlo to Eddie Regal to Delores Bookbinder to here. Of course, I wouldn't have come here at all if Delores had been able to entice and derail me with her own special diversion. And then there was the deliberate absence of periods in Medlark's note to 'Mrs Cupcake'— Delores no doubt—and signed 'Mr Moneybags,' and the same absence of a period in the admission form you showed me. And let's not forget the fuzzy photograph."

"This is somewhat confusing," Dr. Mortimer said, raising an eyebrow at Nudger.

"It's simple once you have the key," Nudger said. "A network was set up in case anyone came looking for Medlark. That network guided me to Delores, where I would have wound up anyway in time, and if Delores couldn't deal with me she was to send me here and phone to warn you I was on my way. I was supposed to collar the wrong man then, and give the right man plenty of time to make other hideaway arrangements."

"Wrong man?" Dr. Mortimer asked.

"That isn't Harmon Medlark in Unit C," Nudger said. "That's someone hired to play a role as long as possible for the police while the heat is off the real Medlark. You're Harmon Medlark, behind that dyed hair and dark contact lenses. And that sound you hear is the law from Vero Beach turning into your driveway."

Dr. Mortimer seemed to absorb a powerful kick in the solar plexus. He slumped back in his chair, and his head lolled forward over his maroon tie that suddenly resembled a long tongue.

"It was a good idea, attempting to deflect rather than simply stonewall an investigator," Nudger said. "It might have worked. It was the note that put me onto you."

"The note?" Medlark-Mortimer croaked.

Nudger nodded. "The British spelling of gray, with an 'e,' was in the note to Mrs Cupcake." The form filled out by the man in Unit C contained 'gray' with an 'a,' the common American spelling. But your description jotted on the back of the photograph contains 'grey' 'with an 'e,' like on the Medlark note. That was a genuine unconscious similarity you hadn't intended."

Car doors slammed outside.

"But it was our introduction that really tipped me," Nudger said.

Medlark glared at him from behind the desk, counting his remaining seconds of freedom. "I don't understand."

"You're the only one I gave a business card to who didn't comment on the misspelling of detective. You were expecting me today, Mr. Medlark, and knew who and what I was, so you barely glanced at my card."

The police were pounding on the door.

"I'll let them in," Nudger said.

Harmon Medlark was studying the card Nudger had handed him earlier. "Defective," he muttered. "That isn't true at all."

Where Is Harry Beal?

"Mr. Nudger?" she said.

I said yes.

"It ain't every private detective that has a leaky trailer for an office." She closed her umbrella and stepped into my twelve-by-forty home and office.

"I like it," I told her. "I'm into moss and mushrooms."

She was a weary-looking blonde, about forty, with brown eyes, a squareish homely face, and a nice shape except for thick ankles. "I want to hire you to find Harry Beal," she said.

"Who is?"

"My friend. More than a friend—my lover for the past year."

"How do you mean he's lost?"

"The police found his coat, shoes, and tie on the Jefferson Bridge last week."

"He sounds lost in the worst way," I said, motioning for the woman to sit down on the undersized sofa. "You haven't told me your name."

"Helen Farrow. I'm a cocktail waitress at the Blue Bull on Seventh Avenue."

I poured myself another cup of morning coffee, offering a cup to Helen Farrow, who refused. "So you've gone to the police?"

"They think Harry committed suicide."

"Why don't you think that?"

"The evening of his death, the police received a call from a public phone booth near the bridge. It was Harry, saying

126

someone had threatened to kill him and was following him. When a patrol car got to the booth there was no one around, but they found Harry's clothes on the bridge."

"If someone murdered him, it isn't likely they'd remove his coat, shoes, and tie. Is that what leads the police to believe it was suicide?"

"That's what they say."

But I knew that what had led to the easy conclusion of suicide was an undermanned and overworked police force. Lieutenant Catlin had told me about the department's troubles often enough.

"Have you got a photograph of Beal?"

She shook her head no.

"If it was murder, Beal's as dead as if it was suicide," I told her. "Either way, if a body hasn't washed up, the river's still got him—or maybe the ocean. People have jumped from that bridge and never been found."

"I don't think it was murder or suicide," she said stubbornly. "Neither one makes sense. I've drawn out all my savings. I want you to try to find Harry—alive."

"That sounds impossible."

"I know. But I'm paying your price and then some." A light came into her tired eyes that suggested a flinty toughness, an unexpected fineness of character to complement her desperation. She was one of those people who refuse to acknowledge hopelessness until they absolutely have to. "Harry was sort of my last chance, Mr. Nudger. And you're my last chance to find him."

I sighed, slid open a shallow desk drawer, and got out one of my contracts for Helen Farrow to sign, reflecting that it was this type of case that invariably brought me pain and eventually would kill me. Still, I would take it. "Don't be optimistic," I told her.

But she was. I could tell. What's the matter with people?

Lieutenant Charles Catlin looked up from behind the desk in his sparse, efficient office at police headquarters. The office was the standard pale green that needed a fresh coat of paint, and the drone of a dispatcher directing squad cars drifted in from a speaker in the booking area. From a portrait on the wall behind the desk, the commissioner seemed to be looking with stern disapproval over Catlin's shoulder.

"Hello, Nudger," Catlin said indifferently. He is a hulking man whose primal features belie a keen mind. "What brings you to this den of anti-crime."

"I'm on a job."

"The Yellow Pages strike again."

I sat down in the uncomfortable wooden chair alongside Catlin's desk. "Harry Beal," I said.

He nodded. "I talked to the girl he left behind him. She refuses to believe."

"She needs reassurance," I told him, "one way or the other. Fill me in on the case."

I knew Catlin would honor my request. We trade favors like Monopoly money. We both know neither of us is going to get rich in the real world.

Catlin repeated, in essence, Helen Farrow's short sad account of the night of Beal's disappearance.

"So why a finding of suicide?" I asked.

"Because there's more evidence suggesting suicide than there's evidence suggesting murder or accidental death—this year's budget being what it is."

"What about Beal himself?"

"Forty-eight years old, Caucasian, worked as an office-equipment salesman, no living relatives."

"Did his clothes tell you anything?"

"Check with Denning in the lab if you want. I'm busy with important things." He made a slight waving motion with the back of his hand and began filling out a form on his desk. Charm wasn't his strong suit.

I left and took the elevator down to the lab.

Denning recognized me and nodded a friendly hello. We discussed our mutual revulsion for Catlin, then I asked Denning to tell me whatever he could about Harry Beal.

"He wore a size ten shoe, a 44-regular coat, and favored loud neckties."

He led me to where Beal's effects were stored, sliding open a metal file drawer long enough to contain a body.

The shoes were black wingtips, the suit coat was a medium-priced material and blue, the tie, a violent red, yellow, and gray. The soles of the shoes were about half worn, and there had been nothing in the suitcoat pockets.

"Anything off the record?" I asked.

"There were a few strands of red hair on the suit coat," Denning said. "Dyed, I think."

"Helen Farrow's hair is dyed blonde."

"Who's Helen Farrow?"

"Beal's girl friend. My client."

"Poor woman." He looked at me with his lab-man's myopic gaze.

I left him without a kind word and drove my battered brown VW Rabbit to Helen Farrow's apartment. On the way I reviewed what I knew about the case, managed to start my nervous stomach churning, and popped an antacid tablet into my mouth. I have the knack but not the nerves for my profession.

Helen Farrow's apartment was in a declining part of town, on the third floor of a drab brick building with a chipped gargoyle on each side of the entrance. The apartment itself was small, cheaply furnished, and almost antiseptically clean and ordered. Helen Farrow was the kind who needed to know where things were and why. She let me in and I told her I'd come from headquarters.

"What did you find out?" she asked me.

"That Beal wore wingtip shoes. It's a start." I sat in a small vinyl chair and watched her pace. She stopped near a window overlooking the street and lighted a cigarette.

"Where did Beal work?" I asked.

"Gavner Enterprises, downtown. The police questioned Mr. Gavner, and I talked to him on the phone. He says Harry seemed depressed before his disappearance."

"I'll talk to Gavner," I told her, "but he'll most likely give me the same answers he gave the police."

She turned and stared at me, inhaling smoke from her cigarette as if it hurt her. I knew she wanted some words of encouragement. My opinion was that at the moment Harry Beal was somewhere underwater, being nibbled by the fishes. But Helen wouldn't have been encouraged to hear that, so I left the apartment without saying anything.

Gavner Enterprises occupied an inconspicuous suite of offices in an inconspicuous building downtown. There was no receptionist in the small modern outer office, so I followed instructions on a sign telling visitors to press a button and wait.

Soon a voice boomed from the inner office, telling me to enter. I thought it was a bit unbusinesslike but I went in anyway.

The round-shouldered, gray-haired man behind the cluttered desk didn't stand as he acknowledged he was Gerald P. Gavner, but he offered his hand. He appeared to be in his early fifties, but there was a keen and vital gleam in his eyes that suggested he might be an aging Romeo who chased the office girls around their desks.

I soon discovered I'd misinterpreted that gleam.

"I didn't approve of Beal living with that woman out of wedlock," Gavner said in a clipped, concise voice. "That might be an old-fashioned point of view, but I think that kind of behavior reflects on the company. Still, the man was my best salesman and I attribute his living with the woman to the depression he seemed to slide into the year before his suicide."

"Depression?"

"Oh, some people probably wouldn't have noticed. But Beal was usually such an enthusiastic person that for him normal behavior constituted depression. The woman probably never saw his real character and didn't realize he was in a depressed state."

"A year is a long time to stay depressed," I said.

"He might have pulled out of it if it hadn't been for the Farnworth murder."

My stomach jumped at the word "murder." "I don't know the case."

"Farnworth was the man who was tried and acquitted six years ago for the murder of Beal's wife and daughter in Texas. The feeling is that he was actually guilty but that he bought his way out of a conviction. Then, when Farnworth was killed last month, the police naturally suspected Beal. He had an ironclad alibi—wasn't within a thousand miles of the crime—but he was still questioned. Old wounds must have been opened, and I think that's what led him to do what he threatened."

"Beal had threatened suicide?"

"He'd made subtle references to it." Gavner folded his waxy hands, flashing a diamond pinky ring and raised quizzical eyebrows. "Did the police tell you?"

"Our relationship is such that they seldom go into great detail."

I left Gavner and drove back to headquarters, where I was lucky enough to find Catlin still in.

"Tell me about the murder of Beal's wife and daughter," I said.

"It's irrelevant," he answered, "so I don't mind telling you." He leaned back in his squeaky swivel chair and clasped his hands behind his head. "Six years ago a wealthy woman-izer named Farnworth was having an affair with Beal's wife. He turned out to be more than a little kinky. He strangled the wife and fourteen-year-old daughter—or at least he was ar-rested and tried for the murders. Money being all-important in this world, some key witnesses changed their testimony and Farnworth was acquitted."

"How did Beal react?"

"He took his insurance money and moved north to start over."

"What about Farnworth being murdered?" I asked.

"That happened two months ago, in Galveston. His body was discovered in a hotel. He'd been tortured before he was killed."

"So the law went to Beal as the logical suspect."

Catlin nodded. "Only Beal couldn't have killed Farnworth. He was in New York at the time, at a company meeting. His boss, Gavner, and William Davis, Gavner En-terprises' New York office manager, swore to it. At the exact time of Farnworth's death in Galveston Beal was in confer-ence in New York discussing a new line of interlocking file cabinets. I can show you Gavner's statement and the signed deposition the NYPD obtained from Davis." He smiled his ugly smile. "Like I told you—it's irrelevant."

I was prepared to admit that the Farnworth murder probably had nothing to do with Beal's disappearance, but my stomach sensed otherwise. I unpeeled the foil from a roll of white discs, popped one into my mouth, and chewed reflectively.

"I bet you're developing an ulcer," Catlin said concernedly. "For your own sake, why don't you get into some other line of work and never come back here?"

"Tempting," I said, and meant it.

After leaving Catlin, I decided to pay another visit to Gavner and find out what, if anything, Beal had said to him about the Farnworth murder, and to discover Beal's reaction when he'd been informed of Farnworth's death. I phoned Gavner Enterprises from a booth on Twelfth Street, but a recorded voice informed me that Mr. Gavner was out and asked if I'd like to leave a message. After the tone, I informed the recorder that I had no message to leave and hung up. Apparently Gavner had departed for home after a hard day's work.

I stopped for a quick supper at a Culinary Cow steakhouse, took two antacid tablets, drove back to my trailer, and went to bed.

After sleeping late the next morning, I drove downtown to Gavner Enterprises and found the door locked. The building manager told me that Gavner had moved out the day before. He'd rented the office on a month-to-month basis and had left no forwarding address. I talked the manager into letting me into the empty office in the hope of finding some clue as to where Gavner had gone, but the place was so bare it might as well have been hosed clean.

When I phoned Catlin to tell him about Gavner's sudden move, he seemed surprised but not particularly aroused.

"Moving isn't a crime," he said, "even if it is unusually fast."

"Maybe you ought to tell me what your investigation turned up on Gerald Gavner," I said.

"I'll indulge you," he said, and excused himself to get the file on Gavner. "Gavner was born in Plinton, Georgia," Catlin said, "on August 20th, 1929. He lived in Georgia most of his life, then moved north to start Gavner Enterprises, which sells business equipment to various companies nationwide." Gavner had told the police he was single and listed his address as the Hawthorn Arms, a luxury apartment building on the west side of town.

"If you turn anything up," Catlin told me, "share it."

"You'd probably consider it irrelevant," I said, and hung up.

I was perspiring, and my stomach felt as if it were trying to digest metal filings. This wasn't my kind of case. When you get involved with murderers, things can get violent. The last time one of my cases turned violent I was badly hurt. Though I didn't want that to happen again, I knew I was caught in currents I couldn't control. I drove to the plush Hawthorn Arms, asked for Gerald P. Gavner.

I was told the expected—that Gerald P. Gavner had moved out. He'd paid the last two months of the lease on his furnished apartment the day before, and the doorman had helped him with his two large suitcases and summoned a taxi.

I phoned Helen Farrow from the lobby and brought her up to date. She asked me to meet her at her apartment in an hour.

"I want you to find out about Gavner for me," she said as soon as I'd stepped in from the hall. "Whatever happened to Harry, Gavner knows about it."

"Not necessarily," I cautioned her. "There might be no connection. Gavner could have something to hide, and the police questioning him about Beal's death might have made him figure it was time to move on. Anyone investigating Beal's disappearance would be likely to tumble onto anything illegal Gavner Enterprises might have been involved in."

"I want you to investigate Gavner anyway," Helen persisted. She was smoking another cigarette in that seemingly painful manner. "Go to wherever he's from—find out everything."

"You're talking about money, Helen. More than I want to charge and more than you can pay."

She smiled and handed me something small, neatly folded and faintly scented. It was a thousand-dollar bill.

"Ten of those came yesterday in the mail," she said. "There wasn't any note or anything in the envelope—just the ten bills." Her drab eyes brightened with the hope she was living on. "It means Harry's alive. I think you can find him through Gavner."

I asked her to show me the envelope the money had arrived in. It was a cheap manila envelope with her name and address typed on it. There was no return address.

"This could be Beal's way of telling you thanks and goodbye," I told her. She'd thought of that, judging by her guarded expression and the glint of tears in her eyes. "But what I think is happening," I continued, "is that we've scared somebody, and the money is that person's way of trying to buy you off so you'll stop searching for Beal."

"I want to use the money to find him," she said fervently.

"I don't know if that's smart, Helen. If it is someone trying to buy you off, he may try to stop you some other way."

Her answer was to hand me another thousand-dollar bill. "Use as much of it as you have to," she said. "Buy whatever information you need. I can't think of any way I'd rather spend the money." She glared challengingly at me. "I'm not afraid, are you?"

"Yes. But I'll go to Gavner's hometown and start digging if you'll promise to put the rest of the money in the bank and keep your doors locked."

She smiled again. Soft light from the curtained window highlighted her features, and I decided that twenty years ago she must have been passable. "It's a deal," she said.

I was on the afternoon flight to Atlanta, and from the Atlanta airport I drove a rented car west to Plinton, Georgia. Plinton was a small town, and it didn't take me long to discover that the Gavner family, with their boy Gerald, had moved in 1930 to Carver, a hundred miles south.

In the small farming town of Carver I discovered some members of the Gavner family still living there. They told me that Gerald Gavner had died of internal injuries after being struck by a car. They gave me directions to his grave, and I stood in the neatly kept little cemetery and looked at the dates carved on the weather-smoothed tombstone: August 20, 1929—June 12, 1933.

I knew then what had happened. Someone had assumed Gerald Gavner's identity, obtaining a copy of his birth certificate from Plinton and using it to obtain various identification documents from library cards and gasoline credit cards to a driver's license, possibly even working up to a social-security card. It's often done in the underworld, and the identification will stand up under a cursory investigation. The name on all the identification belongs to someone long dead, but someone who existed long enough to provide the foundation for the structure of phony identification. It's handy if the bearer of all that ID wants to engage in something illegal—

like the operation of a dummy company to serve as a front for something profitable but risky.

I wanted to find out more about Gavner Enterprises, and I knew who could tell me. After booking into a motel on the outskirts of Carver, I phoned Helen and told her I was flying to New York the next day.

William Davis had vacated the New York office of Gavner Enterprises with the same abruptness with which Gavner himself had vacated the home office. So if Gavner had been involved in something crooked, Davis was too.

The New York office, in an undistinguished building on East Fifty-third Street, had been emptied as thoroughly as the home office, except for a skinny girl who was cleaning out the receptionist's desk and looking forlorn.

She said her name was Millie Ann and that Mr. Davis had given her notice the day before and left immediately.

"Left for where?" I asked.

She shook her frizzy blonde head. "He didn't say. I didn't think it was my place to ask. I've only been working here a few months, part-time."

"Don't you have any idea? It's important, and I know he'd want to see me."

Millie Ann paused in her efforts to stuff several magazines and bottles of nail polish into a small paper bag. I could see she was debating with herself—and that she was miffed at losing her job on such short notice.

"You might try the Hangout—it's a bar on Fifty-second Street. Mr. Davis went there sometimes. Talk to Frank, the bartender."

"Were Frank and Mr. Davis friendly beyond a bartender-customer relationship?"

"I don't know." She rolled a romance magazine tightly.

"But I was in there last night with my boy friend and I saw Mr. Davis come in, talk to Frank, and hand him a big yellow envelope and some money. He acted real nervous. The skin under one of his eyes was jumping around, like."

"Did he see you?"

"No."

"What does Mr. Davis look like?" I asked.

She frowned. "Average size, I guess. About forty-five, maybe a little more. Not too bad-looking—red hair, a nice smile. He dressed pretty neat."

I thanked Millie Ann, told her I hoped she'd find work soon, and left.

The Hangout was a respectable-looking if dim lounge with a long padded bar worked by a lanky man with a gleaming bald head and a down-turned moustache.

"Frank the bartender, I presume," I said, sitting near the end of the bar where he was stacking glasses.

He nodded and gave me a puzzled smile. I ordered a beer.

When he'd brought the beer I asked him if he knew where I could find Bill Davis.

He didn't pretend not to know Davis, but he shrugged and shook his head.

"It's important to both Davis and me that I find him," I said, placing a hundred-dollar bill on the bar.

Frank looked solemnly at the hundred. "I don't know where he is. If I did know, I'd tell you for sure."

"What about the envelope he gave you?"

Frank seemed surprised.

"That won't tell you where he's at."

"Did Davis say what was in the envelope?" My hand reached out as if to withdraw the crinkled bill on the bar.

"Sure," Frank said hastily, and my hand paused. He

watched my hand. "All that's in it are some other smaller envelopes, addressed to somebody I never heard of. I'm supposed to mail one the first of every month for the next year."

"Let me look at one of those envelopes," I said. "Mr. Davis would want you to show it to me—believe me." I drew another hundred-dollar bill from my pocket and held it casually.

Frank shrugged as if the matter were really of no importance, went to a small safe in a cabinet behind the bar, and bent over it for a few minutes. Then he returned with a small white envelope. When I released my grip on the second bill and let it drop on top of the first, he set the envelope on the bar so I could read the address: "Mr. Norman Llewelyn, Hill Manor, Hillsboro, Missouri."

The next afternoon I turned my rented Chevy into a driveway beside a freshly painted metal sign lettered HILL MANOR—REST HOME. Though only about fifty miles southwest of the St. Louis city limits, Hillsboro was very country, and Hill Manor was secluded well off the main highway in low, densely wooded hills.

As I followed the curve of the narrow blacktop drive, the rest home came into view. It was a rambling three-story white frame structure that looked like a modernized and enlarged farmhouse. The grounds were neatly kept, the grass green and mowed beneath the two large elms that flanked the steps onto a wide gray-floored porch. A few people sat reading in the rocking chairs that lined the porch. They ignored me as I parked the car and went in through the double-doored entrance.

I was in a large, cool reception area. A television room off to the left emitted the sounds of a soap opera. Beneath a large brass chandelier was a counter, and behind the counter stood a bespectacled elderly woman in a white uniform.

"I'm here to see Mr. Norman Llewelyn," I told her through one of my best smiles.

"He's in 326, at the end of the hall on the third floor," the woman said. "I'll ring upstairs and have someone tell him you're on your way up. What name should I give?"

"I'd rather surprise him," I said, and before she could answer I leaned over the counter and spoke confidentially. "I'm an old friend, and I came here primarily to make sure all of his bills are being paid."

"Oh, there's no problem there," she assured me. "Mr. Llewelyn has a wealthy aunt who sends cash every month to cover his expenses."

I nodded to her and walked toward the wide stairway.

When I entered Room 326 without knocking, Llewelyn was sitting in a wicker chair by a tall window, gazing down at something. His back was to me, and I saw only a slumping, gray-haired form haloed by the fading afternoon light. One finger was rhythmically tapping the arm of the chair.

I said, "Hello, Harry Beal."

He turned and jumped halfway out of the chair, then sank back. His mobile face went through a series of expressions and settled on a pasty, resigned smile.

"I don't know what you're talking about or who you are," he said in a calm voice, but without real conviction. "My name is Norman Llewelyn. I'm here for a rest cure."

"You'd have succeeded but for Helen Farrow," I told him. "You had to murder Farnworth; you devoted your life to his death, planned it for six years. But with such a strong motive to kill him, you knew that even if he had seemed to die accidentally the police would suspect you of killing him. So you manufactured the perfect alibi for yourself. You used the names of dead people and their records of birth to build several identities—taking months, maybe years to establish them. You created synthetic lives—witnesses to provide you with a completely leakproof alibi for the time of Farnworth's murder."

"Whoever Farnworth is or was, I've never heard of him before." The wicker chair creaked softly.

"You were in New York, Gavner said—but *you* were Gavner. Davis corroborated your presence there—but *you* were Davis. You knew the Davis statement would be done by deposition, without the same people seeing either Gavner or Davis. But you effected mild disguises so your descriptions would differ. You wore a red wig as Davis, and you were careful not to stand up in your phony Gavner Enterprises office as Gavner so I wouldn't get an estimate of your height or build."

He began to squirm, a tic began under his right eye. "You're insane," he told me. Then his voice slipped into the concise efficient cadence of Gavner. "I demand that you leave—now!" Again his face and voice changed. He seemed to be slipping from personality to personality of the identities he'd created, as if the real Harry Beal had been lost among the long-dead.

"I didn't figure on her loving me," he said finally, in a slow natural voice that probably was his own.

"You needed someone like Helen Farrow to substantiate your death," I said. "You phoned her to establish the possibility of murder, but left your clothes on the bridge to suggest suicide. That way, if the police suspected anything it would be your murder—and that would throw off the idea of you faking a suicide to go underground after killing Farnworth. Helen would keep the law moving in that direction if it was disposed to investigate your death."

"I didn't figure on her loving me," Beal repeated in a hoarse voice. "Not that much . . ."

I didn't know if he was actually mad or not. Llewelyn was just another of his carefully contrived false identities, the one he'd kept in reserve to slip into when his scheme was finished. He planned to stay at Hill Manor until he felt well enough to check out and return to New York, to reclaim what was left of the money he'd earmarked for his recuperation and left to be mailed regularly from the Hangout.

Leaving him slumped in the wicker chair, I walked from the suddenly stifling room and went downstairs to use the phone at the desk.

But I never completed the call.

I heard screams, then a commotion beyond the French windows at the far end of the reception area. I put down the receiver and went with the white-uniformed woman from behind the counter as she ran to open the French windows.

Beal was sprawled on the stones of the patio, where he had landed after plunging from his window.

This time he was definitely dead.

Standing there staring at his pathetically contorted corpse, I saw no real point in contacting the law. The easiest course for everyone was to keep Beal's death a suicide on the Jefferson Bridge—in another place, another time.

Amid hushed voices, sobbing, and confusion, I made my way around the side of the building to my car and drove away.

I would go home and explain to Helen Farrow that Beal was dead and better off that way, and that now she should pick up what was rest of her life and forget him. I cringed at the thought of telling her—but hadn't I warned her when I accepted the case that she'd be disappointed.

As Beal had discovered, sometimes it's impossible to con-

Where Is Harry Beal?

vince the Helen Farrows of the world of anything they refuse to believe.

I stopped for a red light and chewed an antacid tablet as I waited for it to change.

143

Flotsam and Jetsam

When a customer hefted a grease-spotted box of glazed-to-go and cracked, "You'd make more money selling these by the pound," Danny didn't smile his customary good-business grimace to hide the hurt.

After the customer had left and Nudger was the only one other than Danny in Danny's Donuts, Nudger sipped his horrendous coffee and studied Danny over the stained rim of the Styrofoam cup. Danny, who resembled a scrawny basset hound, had larger, deeper, and darker circles than usual beneath his sad brown eyes, and the lines on his drooping features appeared longer and more defined. Something was gnawing on him. If this kept up, he would go from basset hound to bloodhound, a less lovable breed.

"What's bothering you, Danny?" Nudger asked, partly to make conversation, partly to divert Danny's attention from the fact that he hadn't been able to get down more than half of the Dunker Delite Danny had bestowed upon him for breakfast.

Danny sighed, then removed the grayish towel he kept tucked in his belt and flicked some crumbs off the stainless steel counter. "Friend of mine died," he said.

Nudger grunted and nodded, surreptitiously folding his napkin to conceal the half-carcass of the doughnut before him when Danny glanced away. "Natural death or accidental?"

"He died in a fall," Danny said, "off a wagon."

"Old friend?"

Danny tucked the towel back beneath his belt and nodded. "We went back over twenty years. Then we wound up in AA together."

"That kind of wagon," Nudger said. He knew that Danny had been a member of Alcoholics Anonymous for the past seven years, and in that time hadn't touched alcohol. The organization had convinced Danny, finally and forever, that he would always be an alcoholic and the best he could do was to be one who never drank alcohol. If Danny had a religion, it was AA. And the organization had done more for him than religion had done for most people.

"Artie Akron hadn't touched a drop of liquor for five years, Nudge," Danny said, leaning on the counter with both elbows. "Then they find him last night down on North Broadway with his head bashed in and his wallet missing. They say he had a point twenty-eight alcohol content in what was left of his blood."

"It happens that way sometimes," Nudger said. "Some punk probably rolled him for his money and hit him too hard." He wondered, was Danny only mourning his old friend, or was he also considering that the same kind of fate might someday be his own? It was a tough life for those who'd inherited the wrong genes and a thirst for alcohol. "You'll make it okay, Danny," Nudger said.

Danny glanced over at him and smiled sadly; he knew what Nudger had been thinking and appreciated the concern. "You want another doughnut, Nudge?"

"Er, no, thanks, I'm full, I'd better get upstairs and do some work." Nudger's office was on the second floor of the old brick building, directly above the doughnut shop.

Danny picked up Nudger's cup and ran some more gritty dark coffee into it from the big steel urn. "One for the road, Nudge."

Nudger thanked him, carefully picked up his wadded napkin as if it were empty, and tossed it into the plastic-lined trash can by the window counter on his way out. The napkin-wrapped doughnut struck the can's bottom like a piece of stone sculpture.

The morning was already heating up; a typical St. Louis July day. It would also be typical of St. Louis weather if it were sixty degrees and hailing by nightfall. The only thing that changed rapidly in this city was the weather.

Nudger quickly entered a door next-door to Danny's Donuts and climbed a narrow wooden stairway to his office. He picked up the morning mail from where it lay on the landing, then unlocked the office door and pushed inside.

Warm, stifling, stale. The small office still seemed to contain heat from yesterday's record-breaking temperature, as well as, the sweet, cloying scent from the doughnut shop below. It was the kind of scent that permeated everything: furniture, drapes, clothes, even flesh. Wherever Nudger went, he gave off the faint scent of a Dunker Delite. It didn't drive women wild.

He switched on the window air conditioner, then sat down in his squealing swivel chair and did nothing until the cool breeze from the humming, gurgling window unit had made the office air more breathable. Finally, he picked up the stack of mail from where he'd tossed it on the desk and leafed through it.

The usual: a mail-order catalog from International Investigators Supply Company, featuring an inflatable boat that would fit into a shirt pocket when deflated; a letter from his former wife Eileen, no doubt threatening stark horror unless alimony money showed up via return mail; an enticement to join a home-video club specializing in X-rated movies full of snickering adolescent sex, for adults only; an envelope from the electric company that looked disturbingly like a bill. Nudger tossed the entire mess into the wastebasket.

Then he glanced at his watch, made sure his phone-answering machine was on Record, and left the office. He had to follow a cigarette delivery-truck on its route, to discover if the driver had anything to do with why certain figures didn't coincide.

A week later, when the cigarette pilfering case had ended (the supervisor—the man who had hired Nudger—turned out to be the thief; there was some debate over paying Nudger's fee), Nudger was sitting at his desk wondering what next when there was a knock on the door.

Client! Nudger thought hopefully. He leaned forward, his swivel chair squealing at the same time he called for the visitor to enter.

The door opened and Danny walked in.

"You don't seem glad to see me, Nudge," Danny said.

"It's not that," Nudger said. "I was expecting someone else."

"I think I need to talk to somebody, Nudge. You know how it is, I got no family, nobody."

"Sit down," Nudger said. "Talk."

Danny sat in the chair by the window, aging ten years in the harsh morning light. "Another friend of mine died last night," he said. "Found on the north side in a rough neighborhood, shot in the back of the head. Robbery again."

"Who was this one?" Nudger asked.

"Mack Perry, another member of my AA chapter, another old shipmate."

"Shipmate?"

"Yeah. Perry, Akron, and I served on the USS *Kelso* during the Vietnam War. This was in the mid-sixties, before the war heated up, when the Navy got young guys to join by promising them they'd go through training and service together. We were in a St. Louis unit. Lots of guys on the *Kelso* were from St. Louis, until after it was hit and recommissioned later as a minesweeper."

"Hit?"

"By a North Vietnamese torpedo boat. The ship didn't sink, but we limped back to port with two dead, including the captain, and fifteen wounded. They dug metal out of us and pinned medals on us and took the *Kelso* out of service for repairs."

"I didn't know *you* were a war hero, Danny."

"Wrong place, wrong time," Danny said simply. "And me and a few others were just drunk enough to be brave."

Nudger could see he didn't want to talk about the violent years, so he concentrated on violent yesterday. "You said Perry was another old shipmate, Danny. Was the other fellow who was killed, Artie Akron, on the *Kelso*, too?"

Danny nodded, "Yeah. That's when the three of us really started drinking hard, in Honolulu after the *Kelso* got hit and we were in the last stages of our recuperation. Of course, lots of other guys were drinking hard then, too, and didn't go on to let it ruin their lives."

Nudger sat staring out the window beyond Danny, at the pigeons strutting along a stained ledge of the building across the street. He really didn't like pigeons—messy birds. "Are any other old shipmates in your AA chapter?" he asked.

"Nope," Danny said. "But there's a lot more of them around town, I told you we were mostly recruited together here and formed a kind of unit throughout training and part of our service."

"Kind of odd," Nudger said, "two old *Kelso* crewmen being murdered within a week of each other."

Danny's furrowed forehead lowered in a frown. "You figure it could be part of a pattern, Nudge?"

"Can you think of any reason there might be a pattern?"

Danny sat silently for a moment, then shook his head. "No, there was nothing between Akron and Perry except that they served on the *Kelso* and were alcoholics."

"You know anybody else fits that description, Danny?"

"No, not really." Danny's somber brown eyes suddenly widened. Fear gleamed in them briefly like a signal light: a call for help. "Jeez, Nudge, you don't think somebody might try snuffing me, do you?"

"I wish I could tell you, Danny. I guess I'd better try to find out more about what's going on."

Danny looked embarrassed. "I can't pay you for this right away, Nudge, but I will eventually. And you've got free doughnuts forever."

Nudger tried to mask the distress on his face, but he was sure Danny caught it. The man was sensitive about his doughnuts. Nudger would have to make amends.

"And coffee?" he said, bargaining hard.

Danny smiled. "Coffee, too, Nudge."

It was laborious but sure, the process of getting a list of the *Kelso*'s crew members in 1965. Naval Records even supplied a list of the crew's hometown addresses. Thorough, was the military. We should all learn.

Fifteen of the *Kelso*'s crew had been from St. Louis. Nudger sat down with his crew list and the phone directory and matched five names besides Danny's, Akron's, and Perry's. He began phoning, setting up appointments. When told that the subject of their conversation would be the *Kelso*, the four crew members he was able to contact eagerly agreed to talk with Nudger.

The first *Kelso* crewman Nudger met with was Edward Waite, who took time out from his job as some sort of technician at a chemical plant to sit in a corner of the employees' lounge with Nudger over coffee. The place was empty except for them; a long, narrow room with plastic chairs, Formica tables, and a bank of vending machines displaying questionable food.

Waite was a large, muscular man with a florid face, powerful and immaculately manicured hands, and a clownlike fringe of reddish unruly hair around his ears, grown long as if to compensate for his bald pate. He squinted at Nudger with his small blue eyes, as if he needed glasses, and said, "Sure, I was below deck when the *Kelso* took the torpedo. The concussion rolled me out of my bunk. I heard valves exploding, steam hissing, shipmates yelling. None of us near the bow were in any real danger, though; the torpedo hit amidships. But I can tell you I wanted to see the sky worse than anything when I managed to stand up. I could smell the sea and hear water rushing and figured we might be going down."

"You lost two crewmen," Nudger said.

Waite nodded, gazing down at the Styrofoam coffee cup that was barely visible steaming in his huge hand. "Yeah, a signalman name of Hopper, and Captain Stevenson. They were on the bridge when the *Kelso* got hit; damage was heavy there. Artie Akron tried to pull the captain out of the flames, but he was already dead. That's how Akron got wounded, going onto the burning part of the bridge after the captain. Won himself a Navy Cross, and now he got himself drunk and killed in a bad part of town. Hard to figure."

"It is that," Nudger agreed. "Did Akron do much drinking on board the *Kelso*?"

Waite thought about that, looking beyond Nudger at the sandwich machine. "No more than any of us, as far as I can remember."

"Who did Akron pal around with who might know more about him?"

"Nobody in particular on the *Kelso*, but when we were laid up in Honolulu he did a lot of bumming around with Mack Perry. A lot of serious drinking, come to think of it. I guess they both got too far into the bottle there. Maybe that's what led to their alcohol problem. Odd, though, them both getting rolled and killed within a week of each other."

"How come Akron and Perry all of a sudden became buddies on shore, but hadn't been on board ship?" Nudger asked.

Waite shrugged. "Hell, who knows? Maybe they were bunked next to each other in the hospital there. Perry was on the bridge, too, when the *Kelso* and that torpedo met. He picked up some shrapnel and got burned some. It makes sense that he and Artie Akron were in the hospital burn unit together."

"Makes sense," Nudger agreed. "Did anyone else from St. Louis get wounded in the torpedo attack?"

"Jack Mays, Danny Evers, Milt Wile, maybe a few others. None of them got badly hurt, though, just enough to earn some medals and some hospital leave. I got injured myself, in the stampede to get up on deck after the ship got hit. All hell erupts when a little ship like a destroyer takes a hit, Nudger. For a few minutes there's terror and panic. It's nothing like in the movies."

"Not much is," Nudger said. He checked his list. Milt Wile had died in an auto accident four years ago. Running his forefinger down the list, Nudger said, "Jack Mays is one of the ten crewmen who moved away from St. Louis."

"Yeah. I saw him at our five- and ten-year reunions, but he wasn't at the fifteen-year get-together." Waite sipped his coffee. "He's in prison somewhere, I heard, mixed up in narcotics trafficking."

"Do you know the whereabouts of the other crew members who moved from the city?"

"Most of them. I talked to them at the last reunion, five years ago. We decided not to have a twenty-year reunion, though. You know how it is, other interests, lives gone in different directions. Only eight of us showed up at the fifteen-year reunion."

Waite told Nudger about the other crew members. Two more of them had died within the past five years. Now Artie Akron and Mack Perry were dead. Nudger could see that Waite was depressed just talking about it. Time did that to people who went to reunions. Another *Kelso* crewman, Ralph Angenero, had done seven years for extortion before being released from the state prison in Jefferson City two years ago. Other than Mays and Angenero, the crewmen had, as far as Waite knew, stayed on the sunny side of the law.

Nudger spent the rest of that day and part of the next talking to the *Kelso* crew members still in the city. They all more or less substantiated what Waite had said. The series of interviews hadn't given Nudger anything to work with; no new insights, no new direction. He was still at sea.

From time to time in that situation, Police Lieutenant Jack Hammersmith had tossed Nudger a life preserver. Though it would be difficult to discern from their conversation, the two men had a deep respect and affection for each other that went back over ten years to when they shared a two-man patrol car. Nudger had saved Hammersmith's life; Hammersmith never forgot or considered the scales even. His sense of obligation hadn't flagged even after Nudger's nervous stomach had caused him to quit the force and go private.

Nudger sat now in one of the torturous straight-backed oak chairs in front of Hammersmith's desk at the Third District. He watched with trepidation as Hammersmith's smooth, pudgy hand fondled the greenish cigar in his shirt pocket then absently withdrew. Close. Smoke from Hammersmith's cigars had the capacity to kill insects and small animals. Even secondhand, it was more than mildly toxic to humans.

"Who are these people?" Hammersmith asked, studying the list of names that Nudger had handed him. "Is this the infield of the Minnesota Twins?"

"They're former crewmen of a destroyer in the Vietnam War," Nudger said. "As were Artie Akron and Mack Perry. All presently St. Louisans."

"Those last two names strike a chord. Murder victims, right? A couple of alkies who got themselves rolled and killed."

"Making any progress on those cases?" Nudger asked, with an edge of sarcasm.

Hammersmith's pale blue eyes glared at Nudger from his smooth, flesh-padded features. He sure had put on weight during the past ten years. "You know there actually are no cases, Nudge. It's not unusual to find alkies rolled and dead in this city or any big city. It's virtually impossible to find a suspect. Maybe some bum or small-timer we pick up on another charge will confess to one of the killings, but probably not. The risk of dying comes with the territory for alcoholics. It's an American tradition."

"These two men were members of the same Alcoholics Anonymous chapter," Nudger said. "They hadn't consumed any alcohol for months, maybe years, before they were found dead."

"Maybe. Anyway, that's when an alkie really goes on a big bender, Nudge, coming off a long dry spell." He shook the paper in his hand. "What do you want me to do with this list?"

"Check with Records and see if you have anything on the names."

"That's what I thought you wanted," Hammersmith said. "Unauthorized use of police files." He drew the cigar from his pocket, methodically unwrapped it, and lit it. Greenish smoke billowed. Nudger's remaining time in the office was very limited. Hammersmith intended it to be that way. He was a busy man; crimefighting was a demanding profession.

After Hammersmith had phoned Records and given them his request, he leaned his corpulent self back in his padded desk chair and puffed on the cigar with a rhythmic wheezing sound, fouling the room with a greenish haze. Nudger was going to earn this information.

"You're going to kill yourself with those poisonous things," Nudger said, to fill the silence in the hazy office.

"You'll probably get to me first," Hammersmith said. "You and your pestiness."

Nudger was sure there was no such word as pestiness, but he thought it best not to correct Hammersmith's diction. Anyway, the message was clear. He sat quietly until a young clerk who knew better than to mention the smoke in the office came in and laid some computer print-out paper on Hammersmith's desk.

"Not very interesting," Hammersmith said around his cigar, even before the pale clerk had gone. He removed the cigar and placed it in an ashtray, carefully propping it at an angle so it wouldn't go out. "Nobody here has anything on this sheet more serious than a traffic violation. Well, here's a five-year-old assault charge against one Edward Waite. Disturbance at a tavern. Other than that, not a black hat in the bunch. Your two deceased drunks, however, had a string of alcohol-related offenses until about six years ago. They've been clean since then. I checked last week, Nudge. Your police department does care when a corpus delicti is noticed at the curb."

"Reassuring," Nudger said, standing up from the uncomfortable chair. The smoke was thicker nearer the ceiling; he stifled a cough. "Thanks for your help, Jack." He moved toward the door and fresh air.

Hammersmith's voice stopped him. "Keep me tapped in on this one, Nudge. If there's a chance to collar whoever killed either of those alkies, I want to know."

"You'll be the first I'll tell," Nudger promised.

Hammersmith smiled and exhaled a greenish thundercloud. "You feel okay? You look a little sickly."

"Oh, that's probably because my lungs are collapsing," Nudger said, opening the door and pointing his nose toward the sweet, breathable air of the booking area.

"So who invited you here?" Hammersmith said behind him.

Nudger didn't recall inviting anyone to drop by at four a.m. at his apartment on Sutton, but there seemed to be someone in the hall, pounding on his door with a sledgehammer. He sat up in bed, rubbing his eyes, trying to convince himself this was a dream and he wouldn't have to cope and could go back to sleep.

The pounding continued. Even the walls were shaking.

"Nudge?"

Nudger recognized the voice filtering in through the locked door. Danny.

"Hey, Nudge!"

Nudger's stomach came belatedly awake and gave him a swift mulelike kick that helped to propel him out of bed. Soon the neighbors would be on the phone, in the hall, shouting, threatening to call the landlord or the police, meaning it all.

The muscle-bound drug-head down the hall in 4-C might get violent; he'd almost killed a meter reader last month.

"Damn!" Nudger stubbed his toe on the nightstand. He managed to switch on the reading lamp, which provided enough light for him to find his way out of the bedroom and into the living room. Switching on another lamp, he made it to the door and unlocked it.

It was like opening the door to a distillery. Danny was slouched against the wall in the hall. He staggered back with a dumb grin on his long face, almost losing his balance, and stared at Nudger. "You ain't got nothin' on, Nudge. You're naked."

Which was true, Nudger suddenly realized, coming one hundred percent awake just in time to see the door across the hall open and old Mrs. Hobson peer out above her gold-rimmed spectacles. The Hobson door quickly closed, then opened again a fraction of an inch.

"Shut up down there or let me join the party!" a deep voice yelled from the landing upstairs.

Nudger quickly grabbed Danny and yanked him inside, then shut and relocked the door. He went back into the bedroom and put on a robe and the leather slippers his true love Claudia Bettencourt had given him on an expensive whim, then he returned to the living room. Danny was now slumped in Nudger's favorite armchair, his head lolling. He had vomited on the chair and on the carpet. He looked as pale and sick as Nudger had ever seen him.

"What happened, Danny?" But Nudger knew what had happened.

"Smallish drink," Danny said, his voice slurred.

"How many?" Nudger asked.

"Thousands."

"Stay there," Nudger said. He went into the kitchen and

got Mr. Coffee going. When he came back, he saw that Danny had passed out.

"The hell with this," Nudger said. He would let Danny sleep. He got some wet towels, cleaned up Danny, cleaned the armchair and the carpet. Then he wrestled the limp Danny until he'd removed his shirt and shoes and dumped him onto the sofa.

"Doughnuts," Danny said, snuggling in.

"What?"

"Remember when you caught that old guy in my shop and chased him, thought he had a bag of the day's receipts. But all he had was doughnuts. He was hungry, was all. Two dozen glazed doughnuts. His name was Masterson, gray guy about ninety years old. Bum with a hole in his shoe with newspaper sticking out of it. Hell, we let him have the doughnuts. What did I care; I was drunk at the time. That's when I was drinkin' heavy, Nudge."

Nudger thought back. "That's been over seven years ago, Danny."

"Eight at least," Danny said, his voice still thick.

"How come you remembered that?" Nudger asked.

Danny ignored him. "He'd have got sick if he'd eaten all them doughnuts," he said. He would never have said that if he'd been sober. Fiercely proud of his weighty cuisine, was Danny. Soft snoring began to drift up from the sofa.

Nudger poured himself a cup of coffee and let Danny sleep.

He sat at the kitchen table, sipping coffee and thinking, until almost dawn. Then he went back to bed and tried to sleep for a while, but that didn't work. At eight in the morning, he felt almost as bad as Danny looked.

Danny probably felt even worse than he looked. He sat on the edge of the sofa, holding his head with both bands as if it were fragile crystal. "Fell off the wagon," he said sheepishly, when he'd managed to free his tongue from the roof of his mouth.

"Why?" Nudger asked.

Danny shrugged, wincing. "Got to thinking about Akron and Perry. It ain't right, how they stayed dry so long and then wound up booze-soaked and dead. It ain't fair."

"Life isn't renowned for its evenhandedness."

"Don't I know it, Nudge." Danny brought off a smile. Brave man, risking having his cheeks shatter. "You know it, too, what with people pounding on your door in the middle of the night."

"What made you think of the old bum with the doughnuts?" Nudger asked.

Danny looked bewildered. "Huh? What old bum?"

"Take a shower," Nudger said. "I'll get us some breakfast."

"Nothing to eat for me, Nudge," Danny said, making it to his feet. "Just black coffee and a gallon of orange juice." He stumbled bleary-eyed into the bathroom. Nudger listened to the tap water run as Danny drank glass after glass of water from the washbasin faucet before climbing into the shower.

Over his third glass of orange juice, Danny said, "I ain't been that far gone in over six years, Nudge, except for when Uncle Benj died and didn't leave me any money. He got to be a mean old bastard, a dry drunk who wouldn't drink or admit his problem. They're the worst kind of alcoholic."

Maybe, Nudger thought, but Uncle Benj's liver might have disagreed.

After breakfast, Danny looked, and seemed to feel, reasonably human. While Nudger listened, he phoned someone named Ernie, an AA buddy and confidant who promised to meet him that morning. Then, assuring Nudger that he was all right and would stay sober, he left to open the doughnut shop.

Nudger picked up the phone and made a ten o'clock appointment with Dr. Abe Addleman, a reformed alcoholic and the head physician at the Pickering Alcoholic Rehabilitation Center, who knew more about alcoholism firsthand and textbook than anyone else in the city.

Mays was still in town, registered under his own name at the Mayfair, a classy old downtown hotel with acres of carpeting and wood paneling. Hammersmith's check of major hotels had located him within an hour. The age of the computer. Nudger elevatored to the hotel's fifth floor, chomping antacid tablets as he rose. In the hall, he adjusted his clothing and buttoned his sport coat.

He knocked on Mays's door, heard movement inside the room, and within a few seconds the door opened. Jack Mays, older and heavier than the grinning, tow-headed sailor Danny had pointed out in the *Kelso* crew photograph, stood staring blankly at Nudger.

"I was expecting Room Service."

"Sorry," Nudger said. "I'm a friend of a friend of Artie Akron and Mack Perry. Can I come in so we can talk?"

"Talk about what?"

"Old times. I'll talk, and you interrupt me if I'm wrong about something. Though I suspect I've got everything pretty well figured out."

Wariness glimmered for a moment in Mays's flat gray eyes. Desperation crossed his face like a shadow, and he ran a hand through his thinning blonde hair. He had his white shirtsleeves rolled up; when he raised an arm to lean on the doorjamb, Nudger glimpsed a faded blue anchor tattoo high on his forearm. "This a shakedown?" he asked.

Nudger didn't answer. Mays stepped back to let him in, then closed the door and walked to the window. He stared down at the traffic on St. Charles, studiously not looking at Nudger. Nudger could almost hear the gears in Mays's mind whirring.

"You got out of Raiford Prison in Florida last month," Nudger said, "after serving seven years on a narcotics charge."

Mays snorted. "Those aren't old times."

"But they pertain to old times on the *Kelso*. You peddled drugs and bootleg liquor on board ship back then, didn't you?"

"Sure. No big deal. Half the guys in Nam used one thing or another. It was a bad war."

"Especially for you, Mays. The *Kelso*'s captain found out about your drug-dealing and was going to have you court-martialed. There was a confrontation on the bridge, when the two of you were alone for a few minutes. That's when the North Vietnamese attack occurred and the ship was hit. You used the opportunity to kill the captain so he couldn't make good on his court-martial threat. When Artie Akron and Danny Evers got to their feet after the explosion, they saw the captain still standing. After the bridge had burned, his body was found in the debris."

"They were mistaken about Captain Stevenson," Mays said, looking at Nudger now. "They were disoriented. He was killed in the explosion on the bridge. Akron knew they'd been wrong about seeing the captain on his feet five minutes after they thought they saw him. Akron was trying to pull him from the flames—got a medal for it even though he couldn't reach Stevenson. It didn't matter, though, because Captain Stevenson was already dead. He was killed almost instantly when the torpedo hit."

"That's what they thought all these years. But that's not what you admitted to them in Honolulu, when the three of you were drunk."

Mays smiled a mean smile. "You got to Danny Evers."

"Sure. Danny and I are old friends. I did what you planned to do, what you were hanging around town waiting for the opportunity to do when enough time had passed after Mack Perry's death. I got Danny drunk this afternoon. Only I did it with his permission, and in the presence of a doctor. And a stenographer."

Mays took a step toward Nudger, then stood still, poised. Dangerous. Sweat beaded on his upper lip. His eyes were the color of a flat gray-green sea where sharks swam. Nudger's stomach turned over, but he talked on despite fear.

"You, Akron, and Danny were falling-down drunk in Honolulu when you admitted having killed the captain and told how you did it. Then you tried to make amends for your slip of the tongue and your booze-affected judgment by saying you were only joking. But you all knew it hadn't been a joke. The next morning, Akron and Danny didn't remember any of the conversation, or didn't seem to. And you weren't about to bring it up. But you watched them, and whenever there was a *Kelso* St. Louis reunion, you showed up and reassured yourself that they still didn't recall the drunken conversation in Hawaii so many years ago. When you got out of prison, you came here for the twentieth reunion, found out there wasn't going to be one, and also discovered that Akron, Danny, and Mack Perry were attending Alcoholics Anonymous meetings. You didn't know they'd become problem drinkers, but you knew what I confirmed this afternoon: When something happens to someone while very drunk, he tends to forget it when sober, but he might just remember it when he's drunk again, even years later. Some doctors even say that's the reason alcoholics drink, to try, usually futilely, to get in touch with the part of their lives they can only recall when extremely drunk; it's as if a piece of their past is missing. You were afraid Akron or Danny would fall off the wagon, get blind drunk, and happen to remember the Honolulu conversation and mention it to the wrong party. But why did you kill Mack Perry?"

"He was going to AA meetings with Artie Akron and Danny. When alkies get into the bottle they sometimes spill their guts to a fellow AA member, especially if he's an old friend and shipmate. If they'd just been social drinkers, I could have let them live. Perry always had a drinking problem, but how do you figure the other two, Danny and Akron, becoming alcoholics?"

"Maybe you gave them their reason to drink," Nudger said. "One that was buried in their subconscious minds."

"Freud stuff," Mays said, grinning. He shrugged. "They couldn't prove anything, not after all those years."

"Sure they could. You told them you shot the *Kelso*'s captain with a pistol you stole from ordnance. If his body was exhumed, even now, the bullet might be there in the coffin with him."

"Might," Mays said. "The bullet might have passed through him when I shot him. Or even fallen out of his body; he was burned almost to a cinder."

"It's a big might," Nudger told him. "Too big not to act on if a murder charge is at stake. You could take a chance on your old shipmates not remembering, until you found out they were problem drinkers, alcoholics. Enough deep drunks, if any of them started drinking again, and the secret might unexpectedly pop out of the past. The only sure way to prevent that from happening was to kill them. But first you got them drunk, to make sure they were capable of falling off the wagon and might repeat what was said in Honolulu, to somehow justify the murders as well as to provide a cover for the deaths. You knew the police wouldn't make a connection or look too closely into the street murders of a few middle-aged drunks, killed and rolled for their wallets. The thing about your old shipmates that frightened you, their alcoholism, was what provided a safe means of getting rid of them."

A gradual change came over Mays, a darkening of his complexion and a hardening of his broad features. It was as if something in a far, shadowed corner of his mind had been flushed out of hiding. "I could live knowing they might have a few too many now and then," he said. "It was unlikely they'd remember what I said all those years ago. But to a gut-deep, genuine alcoholic, time means nothing. Anything might surface. Twenty years ago is like twenty minutes ago. You're right. I couldn't take the chance anymore that they might talk." He moved around so he was between Nudger and the door. "And I can't take the chance that you might talk, no matter how much you shake me down for." He scooped up a heavy glass ashtray and sprang at Nudger.

Nudger yelled in surprise, tried to back away, and lost his footing. It was a good thing; as he fell backward onto the carpet, he felt a swish of air and glimpsed the bulky ashtray arc past his head. Mays lost his grip on the ashtray at the end of his swing. It went skipping across the room and broke against the far wall. Snarling, he lunged at Nudger just as Nudger had gotten up on one knee.

They went down together, rolling on the floor and seeking handholds on each other. Nudger shoved the palm of his hand against Mays's perspiring face; it slipped off, and he had the brief satisfaction of feeling his elbow crack into Mays's cheekbone. He tried to grasp Mays's hair, but there wasn't enough of it to grip, and Nudger's hand shot away with a few blonde strands between the fingers of his clenched fist. Mays had one hand against Nudger's chest, pressing him to the floor. His other hand found Nudger's eyes and tried to gouge them out. Nudger twisted his neck, turning his face to the carpet. He could smell something garlicky Mays had had for lunch. He could hear Mays's labored, rasping breathing. Or was that his own rasping struggle for air? Two middle-aged guys out of shape and fighting for their lives.

Then Mays was sitting up, one hand beneath Nudger's shirt. There was amazement and rage in his contorted features. "You bastard! You're wired! Everything we said's been recorded!"

With strength exploding from this fresh infusion of rage, he lunged again at Nudger, trying for a chokehold. This time Nudger managed to bend his knee and place a foot against Mays's soft midsection. He shoved hard and Mays grunted and lurched backward into a crouch, slamming into the wall and hitting his head hard. He glared at Nudger and felt around on the floor for one of the jagged pieces of the broken ashtray.

"Lose a contact lens?" Hammersmith asked. His bulk suddenly loomed over Mays. Two blue uniforms flanked him, behind Police Special revolvers aimed steady and ready at Mays.

"Did you get enough of that on tape?" Nudger asked, peeling adhesive strips and transmitter from his bare chest, wincing with pain.

"Every incriminating word," Hammersmith said. He began reading Mays his rights as two more uniforms came in and jerked Mays to his feet, frisked him, and handcuffed his wrists behind his back.

"I didn't have any choice about what I did," Mays was saying, looking at Nudger now as if pleading for under-

164

standing and pity. "They knew about me, even if they didn't realize it. The knowledge was out there, floating around like something rotten in their memories. It could have washed ashore on alcohol anytime, with any unexpected change in the current. I couldn't live knowing that, so the three of them had to die."

"Two out of three isn't bad," Hammersmith told him. "It might win you the gas chamber."

The Thunder of Guilt

It didn't begin as anything unusual. The big guy, Arthur Leland, came into Nudger's office and hired him to follow his wife, Beatrice. Nudger got a lot of that kind of work; his seedy address seemed to attract it. Even if clients had plenty of money, like Leland, and lived in a good part of town, also like Leland, they seemed to think they should hire a private investigator they considered to be from the unwashed underside of life to follow an errant spouse. Dirty folks for dirty work.

Leland owned and managed a construction company specializing in commercial projects. There was real agony on his veiny, ruddy face as he told Nudger, "Bea is a good woman. She's had some strain lately. We're both forty-one, Nudger. She became pregnant six months ago and had an abortion. It went against her grain, and I guess I talked her into it. A week later our youngest child, Alice, was killed in an automobile crash. She was our last child at home. It . . . ruined both of us for a while. We didn't know what to do. The church didn't seem to help. I tried to talk Bea into professional counseling, but she wouldn't go. We suffered a lot. We came out of it different people."

"And now you think she's seeing another man," Nudger said. He picked up the pity in his voice and was embarrassed; he felt sorry for both the Lelands, with their dead child and their dead or dying marriage. He didn't like the idea of following the wife to some motel, where she'd meet a man, they'd have a few drinks in the lounge, and then rent a room at the four-hour rate. The prospect of watching and reporting

166

that made Nudger feel like the cheap goods Leland probably thought he was.

"She goes out at odd hours during the day, doesn't tell anyone where she's going. And she lies to me at times; I know because the odometer on her car doesn't register the mileage it would if she was telling me the truth." Leland shifted his husky frame awkwardly. "I'm not looking for ammunition for a divorce, Nudger. I'm worried about Bea; I just want to know what's going on. I need to know, damn it!"

"And you will know," Nudger told him, trying to spike the man's anger with the old positive approach.

He thought Leland was going to snap the ballpoint pen in half when he signed a contract for Nudger's services. Leland's jaw muscles were working as if he were chewing raw leather, and when he leaned near, he smelled like desperation. It was tough, the tricks love played on some people.

The big man counted out the retainer in cash almost absently and left it on Nudger's desk, then buttoned his overcoat to the neck and left the office.

Beatrice Leland was middle-aged plump but still attractive, with a head of thick, wavy dark hair and pale blue, gentle eyes. There was a subtle sadness to her, even at first glance. She would appeal to those men who could sense a vague helplessness in women; predators who picked off the cripples.

At three o'clock on the afternoon of her husband's visit to Nudger's office, she got into her blue Toyota sedan and drove from the driveway of her comfortably plush home in Des Peres. She was wearing a gray dress and red high heels, carrying a large red purse. There was a jacket-length fur draped over her shoulders. Nudger classified her as dressed up, not just on her way to pick up some crackers and dip. She wasn't running errands; the lady was going somewhere that meant something.

He followed as she headed south, then as she turned east on Manchester, back toward Nudger's office. For a moment Nudger wondered inanely if she were on her way to hire him to follow her husband.

Her first stop surprised him. She parked on Sutton Avenue in Maplewood and crossed the street to enter a plumbing supply company. She had a graceful, alluring walk despite her extra ten or fifteen pounds. Nice ankles and pro-portioned curve of hip. Maybe she was having an extramarital affair with a plumber, Nudger mused, as he sat in his dented Volkswagen Beetle and shivered in the January cold.

But ten minutes later she came out of the plumbing supply place, carrying her purse as if it were heavier. She got back into the Toyota and U-turned to head north on Sutton. Nudger followed her as she made a left and drove west on Manchester, away from the city.

At the Holiday Inn on Craigshire, she parked and walked directly to a second-floor door. She knocked lightly twice, as if whoever was in the room was expecting her. The door opened almost immediately, and she disappeared inside. The number 201 was visible in a glint of sunlight when the door swung closed.

Keeping an eye on her parked car, Nudger left the Volks-wagen nestled out of sight behind a van and walked into the office. He tried to slip the pimply-faced young desk clerk ten dollars of Arthur Leland's money to give him the name of whoever was in 201. The desk clerk was a guy who probably never went to the movies or read detective novels. He told Nudger to go to hell, the motel's guests were entitled to their privacy. Nudger shrugged and slunk back to his car. It was much colder there than in hell.

Beatrice Leland emerged from the room an hour later. She looked the same as when she'd entered; hair not mussed, clothes still unwrinkled. There were too many cars parked in the lot for Nudger to be able to tell which belonged with room 201, so he didn't write down a license number before following her out of the parking lot.

He expected her to go home. Instead, she drove for twenty minutes and made a left turn into the Howard Johnson's Motel on South Lindbergh. She was staying with franchises.

Again she went directly to one of the rooms. This time the desk clerk was more cooperative because Nudger didn't discourage the impression that he was a policeman. The man in the room had registered an hour ago as James Smith. Actually Smith.

But this time there was little doubt which car went with the room. Business was slow today; the only car parked on that side of the lot was a dark gray Lincoln with black-tinted windows. Nudger jotted down its license plate number in his spiral pocket notebook.

Apparently Beatrice Leland had done enough of whatever it was she was doing. When she left Howard Johnson's and Mr. Smith, she drove straight home. She looked upset when she went into the house, and she didn't leave again that day. Nudger waited in the stifling little Volkswagen until he saw Arthur Leland arrive home from work, then he went home himself and had a high old time with a frozen turkey dinner and a cold beer.

After supper he watched a "Barney Miller" rerun on TV and thought about Beatrice Leland and the woman in his own life, Claudia Bettencourt, who was in Chicago for a week-long teachers' convention. If the husband was the last to know, could it be that the boyfriend never found out at all?

★ ★ ★ ★ ★

In the morning he phoned Lieutenant Jack Hammersmith at the Third District police station and asked him please, please if he'd run a check with the Department of Motor Vehicles to see who owned the gray Lincoln. Hammersmith didn't like it, or pretended he didn't like it, as he puffed and smacked his lips on his foul cigar over the phone and copied the license number Nudger read to him. Then Nudger went down to Danny's Donuts, directly below his second-floor office, and had a Dunker Delite, coffee, and an antacid tablet for breakfast.

Forced by Danny to accept a free second cup of acidic coffee, he sat at the stainless steel counter and wondered about Beatrice Leland. Was this a flare-up of middle-aged sexuality? He'd seen it before, in women as well as men. Maybe Beatrice Leland was having a final sexual fling, or maybe her daughter's death had inspired some sort of nymphomaniacal clinging to sex as a symbol of life. Nudger had seen that before, too, this compulsion for sex after having dealings with death; he'd felt that one and knew how powerful it might be to a lonely, bereaved woman like Beatrice Leland.

Danny looked at Nudger with his doleful brown eyes and nodded toward the grease-spotted frosty window beyond the low counter. "Looks like business, Nudge," he said.

Nudger swiveled on his stool just in time to see Arthur Leland open the door next to the doughnut shop; he heard the door swing shut and the heavy tramp of Leland's footfalls as he climbed the narrow stairs to the door to Nudger's office.

"I guess I'd better be in," Nudger said. He carried his coffee with him so as not to offend Danny and joined Leland on the second-floor landing outside the door.

"She left the house yesterday and lied to me about where

170

she went," Leland said without preliminaries. "Where did she go?"

Nudger unlocked the door and ushered Leland inside. Leland stood with his arms crossed while Nudger opened the drapes to let in more winter gloom, then turned up the valve on the steam radiator and sat down behind his desk. "She drove to the Holiday Inn on Craigshire," Nudger said, "then to the Howard Johnson's motel on South Lindbergh. Both times she stayed in a room about an hour."

A sheen Nudger didn't like slid into Leland's hard eyes. Leland uncrossed his arms and unbuttoned his bulky overcoat. "Who did she see in these rooms?"

"I don't know yet. I'm finding out who she met at Howard Johnson's; I got the license number of his car."

"You saw him?" Leland asked, a sharp edge to his voice.

"No, I saw his name on the registration card. James Smith."

Leland grunted and began to pace.

"Don't jump to conclusions," Nudger cautioned, wondering at the value of that advice.

Leland grinned. It had nothing to do with humor. "My wife sees two men at motels in the middle of the afternoon and one of them registered under the name Smith, and you tell me not to draw any conclusion?"

"We don't even know if the person at the Holiday Inn was a man."

"Worse still," Leland said, his imagination really taking hold. "You know how to cheer up a client, Nudger."

"All I'm doing is passing on what I've learned," Nudger said. "That's why you hired me. I'm also advising you not to waste your anger and frustration yet, because we don't know the story."

"You telling me my wife is supplying these motels with

Gideon Bibles, Nudger?"

"Somebody does."

"Don't smart off," Leland said. "That I didn't hire you for." He sighed and wiped a hand over his forehead, gazed at his fingers as if to see if they were soiled by his thoughts. "I'm not upset for the usual reason, Nudger. If my wife needs professional help, I want to see that she gets it. She's entering menopause, and she's suffering a terrible grief and strain." He looked at Nudger, his beefy face contorted by agony. "I can forgive her, whatever she's done."

"Do you want me off the case?" Nudger asked. "You get a refund. Maybe you don't want to learn anything more."

Leland shook his big head. "No, find out the rest of it." He walked heavily to the door, staring at the floor. "You have my work number; call me if anything urgent comes up."

"I'll phone you when I learn anything else," Nudger said, and watched Leland wedge his wide body through the doorframe. He listened to the big man's steps as Leland descended the stairs to the street. Cold air stirred briefly around Nudger's ankles a moment after he heard the outside door open and close. He picked up his foam coffee cup from the desk, took a sip, and was about to get up and pour the rest of the coffee down the washbasin in the office's half bath when the telephone rang.

It was Hammersmith. "What are you up to with this one, Nudge?" he asked around his cigar.

"Errant spouse case. Why?"

Hammersmith chuckled and slurped at the cigar. "You might be a bit errant yourself this time."

Nudger knew Hammersmith relished the dramatic pause. He waited patiently, silently, listening to the wheeze of the cigar being smoked, glad he was talking to Hammersmith by phone and not in person in Hammersmith's clouded office.

He'd expected only a name and address out of this conversation, and Hammersmith knew it. Nudger thought about the big, fancy Lincoln. It crossed his mind that James Smith might be a known pimp, and Beatrice Leland was working for him, turning over her share of the profits. Arthur Leland would be thrilled to learn that.

"That license plate you asked me to run for you," Hammersmith said, "it belongs to a new Lincoln, gray on gray, registered to the Archdiocese of St. Louis."

"What?"

"The Church," Hammersmith said. "A priest drives it. Father Adam Tooley of St. Luke's Parish; the address is St. Luke's Cathedral over on Hanley." Hammersmith wheezed and chuckled again around the fat cigar. "I think you got the wrong car, Nudge."

He hung up, still chuckling.

But Nudger wasn't even smiling.

He followed Beatrice Leland again that afternoon. This time she was wearing jeans and a red quilted ski jacket. She appeared nervous; maybe she'd had a talk with her husband and suspected she was being followed. She drove around most of the afternoon, going nowhere, stopping only once, to buy gas.

When Nudger reported this to Arthur Leland that evening, Leland seemed relieved. He shouldn't have been; Beatrice surely was hiding something from him.

Nudger slept uneasily that night, nagged by his subconscious. He was up at 1:00 a.m. with heartburn and didn't fall asleep again until almost 2:30, an antacid tablet dissolving on his tongue.

He felt better at 8:30 after a shower and shave. As he sat eating the leathery omelet he'd prepared for breakfast, sipping coffee, he watched the morning local news on the black and white portable Sony in his apartment kitchen. Another mugging in the West End, the pretty blonde anchorwoman said disconsolately, as a shot of some buildings that might have been anywhere in town came on the screen. She was happier about the mayor's new cleanup campaign to get unemployed youths off the street. There was a piece of videotape of a surly kid spearing a crumpled paper bag with a spiked pole. Nudger wondered if he might be the one doing the mugging in the West End.

After a commercial the news came back on with tape of a group of people picketing an abortion clinic and tying up yesterday evening's downtown rush-hour traffic. A concerned-looking doctor inside the clinic was interviewed and said that tomorrow was the thirteenth anniversary of the Supreme Court's decision to legalize abortion, and he feared there might be violence. The right-to-lifers outside didn't look violent to Nudger. The newsman was talking to a fiftyish, balding man in a trenchcoat now. One of the picketers. His gentle gaze was firm, and he didn't blink once as he spoke. The wintry breeze blew his coat partly open and revealed a white clerical collar. After the interview, which Nudger didn't bother listening to, the newsman referred to the man as "Father Tooley, the militant priest."

Nudger dropped the piece of toast he was buttering. Then he realized the "tomorrow" the clinic doctor had referred to was today.

He went into the living room and picked up the phone.

Arthur Leland sounded as if he'd been awakened by the call. Nudger didn't care. He quickly identified himself and said, "Mr. Leland, this question might not make much sense to you, but are you having plumbing problems?"

"Is this a joke, Nudger?"

"No."

"All right, then. No. No plumbing problems—of any kind."

"Is your wife home?"

"No. She went shopping with her sister, early, before the stores get crowded. At least, that's what I was told."

"Did you see your sister-in-law?"

"No, Bea took our car and picked her up. Listen, Nudger—!"

Nudger hung up the phone, then lifted the receiver again and dialed Hammersmith at the Third.

Then he left the apartment. Fast.

He tried to sort things out as he drove along Manchester in the bouncing Volkswagen, hoping he was wrong, knowing he wasn't. The first person Beatrice Leland had met was probably a demolitions expert—or more likely an amateur who thought he was an expert—a member of a violent antiabortion organization. The second person, Father Tooley, possibly gave her exact instructions, or simply fortified her with faith.

There was nothing Nudger could do. Or Hammersmith and the power of the law. It had been too late when Nudger phoned.

Ten minutes from the apartment the news came over the car radio. The Woman's Clinic Downtown had been destroyed by a bomb blast. Apparently it was assumed that the building would be empty, but staff members had early abortions and consultations scheduled. Two staff members were killed, and three patients. Along with a woman thought to be carrying the bomb, who was seen entering the clinic with a large red purse a few minutes before the explosion. Police speculated that something had gone wrong with the explosive device. They were still trying to determine the identity of the woman with the purse, and what kind of explosive device was used.

Nudger knew who the woman was: Beatrice Leland. And he knew what kind of explosive device had been in her purse: a pipe bomb. Assembled at the Holiday Inn on Craigshire.

The bomb was supposed to stop abortions at the clinic and to draw attention to the anti-abortion cause. No one was supposed to die. Right-to-life groups didn't stand for death. Priests didn't stand for death. Six people were dead.

Nudger pulled the Volkswagen to the curb and sat still for a long time, staring out the windshield at nothing beyond the car's sloping, dented hood. He felt angry, guilty for not having figured out everything sooner. That guilt was unreasonable, maybe, but there it was, resting heavily on him like a pall, and he couldn't do anything about it.

Eventually he realized he was cold.

He started the engine, jammed the car into gear, and drove on toward St. Luke's Cathedral.

The massive church's parking lot was almost empty when Nudger left the Volkswagen in a No Parking area near the front entrance. He hurried up veined marble steps and through ornate doors, then down the wide, carpeted center aisle of the cavernous cathedral. Above him towered ancient Gothic arches, carved stone, and softly glowing stained glass. Statuary was set in the walls on each side of the wide rows of dark-stained wooden pews; St. Luke himself on Nudger's right, on Nudger's left a stone Holy Mother and Child. Spiraling organ pipes rose on one side of the pulpit, where a young altar boy stood near wooden stairs. Except for half a dozen worshipers seated or kneeling in the vastness of the church, the altar boy seemed to be the only one around.

"Where can I find Father Tooley?" Nudger asked.

"In the rectory," the boy stammered, seeing the intensity in Nudger's face.

An elderly, gray man Nudger hadn't noticed stood up from the organ bench and said, "He's in his office, I believe. I saw him go in there earlier this morning." He pointed to a door behind the pulpit. "You'll have to check with Miss Hammond."

Nudger nodded and walked through the door, then down a richly paneled hall to a tall closed oak door.

He opened the door to find himself in a large outer office. The walls were lined with books and paintings. Behind a massive carved-wood desk sat a dark, fiftyish woman with stern eyes and a severe skinned-back hairdo. Miss Hammond, no doubt.

"I want to see Father Tooley," Nudger said.

Miss Hammond didn't like the way he'd asked. Her sharp eyes darted to a closed door on her left, back to Nudger. "He's preparing for Mass. I'm afraid—"

She stood up as Nudger ignored her and strode to the office door, his rage building. He wasn't sure what he was going to say once he got in to see Father Tooley. He figured that would take care of itself. Before the capable Miss Hammond could stop him, he opened the door and stepped inside.

Behind him Miss Hammond gasped. Then her harsh intake of air exploded outward in a scream.

Father Tooley was hanging motionless by a red sash looped around his distended neck. He was in his full and colorful priest's vestments, eyes bulging and grotesquely swollen purple tongue protruding. He resembled a huge, exotic tropical bird that had been garroted; bird of paradise profaned.

Miss Hammond seemed to be screaming from far away, though she was standing right next to Nudger. He turned and left her, and with that slight distance her shrieks became almost deafeningly loud. The altar boy and the gray old organist rushed past Nudger at exactly the same pace, as if drawn magnetically by the screams; several people who had joined the worshipers in the church passed him indistinctly, moving more slowly, hesitantly, sensing the worst, shadow figures in a dark dream.

Nudger's stomach was kicking around violently. He staggered up the wide center aisle toward the doors. The Holy Mother's calm stone eyes seemed to follow him as he passed. From high on the cross behind the altar, a crucified Christ gazed down on the scene through His suffering.

The echoing wails and cries of the parishioners racketed off the high arches and stone and stained glass of the great cathedral as Nudger found his way outside. He felt the stinging coldness of tears on his cheeks as he slumped on the marble steps.

He knew he wasn't crying for the dead at the clinic or for Father Tooley, but for everyone left behind in the wilderness.

The Right to Sing the Blues

"There's this that you need to know about jazz," Fat Jack McGee told Nudger with a smile. "You don't need to know a thing about it to enjoy it, and that's all you need to know." He tossed back his huge head, jowls quivering, and drained the final sip of brandy from his crystal snifter. "It's feel." He used a white napkin to dab at his lips with a very fat man's peculiar delicacy. "Jazz is pure feel."

"Does Willy Hollister have the feel?" Nudger asked. He pushed his plate away, feeling full to the point of being bloated. The only portion of the gourmet lunch Fat Jack had bought him that remained untouched was the grits.

"Willy Hollister," Fat Jack said, with something like reverence, "plays ultra-fine piano."

A white-vested waiter appeared like a native from around a potted palm, carrying chicory coffee on a silver tray, and placed cups before Nudger and Fat Jack. "Then what's your problem with Hollister?" Nudger asked, sipping the thick rich brew. He rated it delicious. "Didn't you hire him to play his best piano at your club?"

"Hey, there's no problem with his music," Fat Jack said. "But first, Nudger, I gotta know if you can hang around New Orleans till you can clear up this matter." Fat Jack's tiny pinkish eyes glittered with mean humor. "For a fat fee, of course."

Nudger knew the fee would be adequate. Fat Jack had a bank account as obese as his body, and he had, in fact, paid Nudger a sizable sum just to travel to New Orleans and sit in

179

the Magnolia Blossom restaurant over lunch and listen while Fat Jack talked. The question Nudger now voiced was: "Why me?"

"Because I know a lady from your fair city." Fat Jack mentioned a name. "She says you're tops at your job; she don't say that about many.

". . . And because of your collection," Fat Jack added. An ebony dribble of coffee dangled in liquid suspension from his triple chin, glittering as he talked. "I hear you collect old jazz records."

"I used to," Nudger said a bit wistfully. "I had Willie the Lion. Duke Ellington and Mary Ann Williams from their Kansas City days."

"How come had?" Fat Jack asked.

"I sold the collection," Nudger said. "To pay the rent one dark month." He gazed beyond green palm fronds, out the window and through filigreed black wrought iron, at the tourists half a block away on Bourbon Street, at the odd combination of French and Spanish architecture and black America and white suits and broiling half-tropical sun that was New Orleans, where jazz lived as in no other place. "Damned rent," he muttered.

"Amen." Fat Jack was kidding not even himself. He hadn't worried about paying the rent in years. The drop of coffee released its grip on his chin, plummeted, and stained his white shirtfront. "So will you stay around town a while?"

Nudger nodded. His social and business calendars weren't exactly booked solid.

"Hey, it's not Hollister himself who worries me," Fat Jack said, "it's Ineida Collins. She's singing at the club now, and if she keeps practicing, someday she'll be mediocre. I'm not digging at her, Nudger; that's an honest assessment."

"Then why did you hire her?"

"Because of David Collins. He owns a lot of the French Quarter. He owns a piece of the highly successful restaurant where we now sit. In every parish in New Orleans, he has more clout than a ton of charge cards. And he's as skinny and ornery as I am fat and nice."

Nudger took another sip of coffee.

"And he asked you to hire Ineida Collins?"

"You're onto it. Ineida is his daughter. She wants to make it as a singer. And she will, if Dad has to buy her a recording studio, at double the fair price. Since David Collins also owns the building my club is in, I thought I'd acquiesce when his daughter auditioned for a job. And Ineida isn't really so bad that she embarrasses anyone but herself. I call it diplomacy."

"I thought you were calling it trouble," Nudger said. "I thought that was why you hired me."

Fat Jack nodded, ample jowls spilling over his white collar. "So it became," he said. "Hollister, you see, is a handsome young dude, and within the first week Ineida was at the club, he put some moves on her. They became fast friends. They've now progressed beyond mere friendship."

"You figure he's attracted to Dad's money?"

"Nothing like that," Fat Jack said. "When I hired Ineida, David Collins insisted I keep her identity a secret. It was part of the deal. So she sings under the stage name Ineida Mann, which most likely is a gem from her dad's advertising department."

"I still don't see your problem," Nudger said.

"Hollister doesn't set right with me, and I don't know exactly why. I do know that if he messes up Ineida in some way, David Collins will see to it that I'm playing jazz on the Butte-Boise-Anchorage circuit."

"Nice cities," Nudger remarked, "but not jazz towns. I see your problem."

"So find out about Willy Hollister for me," Fat Jack implored. "Check him out, declare him pass or fail, but put my mind at ease either way. That's all I want, an easeful mind."

"Even we tough private eye guys want that," Nudger said.

Fat Jack removed his napkin from his lap and raised a languid plump hand. A waiter who had been born just to respond to that signal scampered over with the check. Fat Jack accepted a tiny ballpoint pen and signed with a ponderous yet elegant flourish. Nudger watched him help himself to a mint. It was like watching the grace and dexterity of an elephant picking up a peanut. Huge as Fat Jack was, he moved as if he weighed no more than ten or twelve pounds.

"I gotta get back, Nudger. Do some paperwork, count some money." He stood up, surprisingly tall in his tan slacks and white linen sport coat. Nudger thought it was a neat coat; he decided he might buy one and wear it winter and summer. "Drop around the club about eight o'clock tonight," Fat Jack said. "I'll fill you in on whatever else you need to know, and I'll show you Willy Hollister and Ineida. Maybe you'll get to hear her sing."

"While she's singing," Nudger said, "maybe we can discuss my fee."

Fat Jack grinned, his vast jowls defying gravity grandly. "Hey, you and me're gonna get along fine." He winked and moved away among the tables, tacking toward the door, dwarfing the other diners.

The waiter refilled Nudger's coffee cup. He sat sipping chicory brew and watching Fat Jack McGee walk down the sunny sidewalk toward Bourbon Street. He sure had a jaunty, bouncy kind of walk for a fat man.

Nudger wasn't as anxious about the fee as Fat Jack thought, though the subject was of more than passing interest. Actually, he had readily taken the case because years ago, at a club in St. Louis, he'd heard Fat Jack McGee play clarinet in the manner that had made him something of a jazz legend, and he'd never forgotten. Real jazz fans are hooked forever.

He needed to hear that clarinet again.

Fat Jack's club was on Dexter, half a block off Bourbon Street. Nudger paused at the entrance and looked up at its red and green neon sign. There was a red neon Fat Jack himself, a portly, herky-jerky, illuminated figure that jumped about with the same seeming lightness and jauntiness as the real Fat Jack.

Trumpet music from inside the club was wafting out almost palpably into the hot humid night. People were coming and going, among them a few obvious tourists, making the Bourbon Street rounds. But Nudger got the impression that most of Fat Jack's customers were folks who took their jazz seriously, and were there for music, not atmosphere.

The trumpet stairstepped up to an admirable high C and wild applause. Nudger went inside and looked around. Dim, smoky, lots of people at lots of tables, men in suits and in jeans and T-shirts, women in long dresses and in casual slacks. The small stage was empty now; the band was between sets. Customers were milling around, stacking up at the bar along one wall. Waitresses in "Fat Jack's" T-shirts were bustling about with trays of drinks. Near the left of the stage was a polished, dark, upright piano that gleamed like a new car even in the dimness. Fat Jack's was everything a jazz club should be, Nudger decided.

Feeling at home, he made his way to the bar and after a five-minute wait ordered a mug of draft beer. The mug was frosted, the beer ice-flecked.

The lights brightened and dimmed three times, apparently a signal the regulars at Fat Jack's understood, for they began a general movement back toward their tables. Then the lights dimmed considerably, and the stage, with its gleaming piano, was suddenly the only illuminated area in the place. A tall, graceful man in his early thirties walked onstage to the kind of scattered but enthusiastic applause that suggests respect and a common bond between performer and audience. The man smiled faintly at the applause and sat down at the piano. He had pained, haughty features, and blond hair that curled above the collar of his black Fat Jack's shirt. The muscles in his bare arms were corded; his hands appeared elegant yet very strong. He was Willy Hollister, the main gig, the one the paying customers had come to hear. The place got quiet, and he began to play.

The song was a variation of "Good Woman Gone Bad," an old number originally written for tenor sax. Hollister played it his way, and two bars into it Nudger knew he was better than good and nothing but bad luck could keep him from being great. He was backed by brass and a snare drum, but he didn't need it; he didn't need a thing in this world but that piano and you could tell it just by looking at the rapt expression on his aristocratic face.

"Didn't I tell you it was all there?" Fat Jack said softly beside Nudger. "Whatever else there is about him, the man can play piano."

Nudger nodded silently. Jazz basically is black music, but the fair, blond Hollister played it with all the soul and pain of its genesis. He finished up the number to riotous applause that quieted only when he swung into another, a blues piece. He sang that one while his hands worked the piano. His voice was as black as his music; in his tone, his inflection, there seemed to dwell centuries of suffering.

"I'm impressed," Nudger said, when the applause for the blues number had died down.

"You and everyone else." Fat Jack was sipping absinthe from a gold-rimmed glass. "Hollister won't be playing here much longer before moving up the show business ladder—not for what I'm paying him, and I'm paying him plenty."

"How did you happen to hire him?"

"He came recommended by a club owner in Chicago. Seems he started out in Cleveland playing small rooms, then moved up to better things in Kansas City, then Rush Street in Chicago. All I had to do was hear him play for five minutes to know I wanted to hire him. It's like catching a Ray Charles or a Garner on the way up."

"So what specifically is there about Hollister that bothers you?" Nudger asked. "Why shouldn't he be seeing Ineida Collins?"

Fat Jack scrunched up his padded features, seeking the word that might convey the thought. "His music is . . . uneven."

"That's hardly a crime," Nudger said, "especially if he can play so well when he's right."

"He ain't as right as I've heard him," Fat Jack said. "Believe me, Hollister can be even better than he was tonight. But it's not really his music that concerns me. Hollister acts strange at times, secretive. Sam Judman, the drummer, went by his apartment last week, found the door unlocked, and let himself in to wait for Hollister to get home. When Hollister discovered him there, he beat him up—with his fists. Can you imagine a piano player like Hollister using his hands for that?" Fat Jack looked as if he'd discovered a hair in his drink.

"So he's obsessively secretive. What else?" What am I doing, Nudger asked himself, trying to talk myself out of a job?

But Fat Jack went on. "Hollister has seemed troubled, jumpy and unpredictable, for the last month. He's got problems, and like I told you, if he's seeing Ineida Collins, I got problems. I figure it'd be wise to learn some more about Mr. Hollister."

"The better to know his intentions, as they used to say."

"And in some quarters still say."

The lights did their dimming routine again, the crowd quieted, and Willy Hollister was back at the piano. But this time the center of attention was the tall, dark-haired girl leaning with one hand on the piano, her other hand delicately holding a microphone. Inside her plain navy blue dress was a trim figure. She had nice ankles, a nice smile. Nice was a word that might have been coined for her. A stage name like Ineida Mann didn't fit her at all. She was prom queen and Girl Scouts and PTA and looked as if she'd blush at an off-color joke. But it crossed Nudger's mind that maybe it was simply a role; maybe she was playing for contrast.

Fat Jack knew what Nudger was thinking. "She's as straight and naive as she looks," he said. "But she'd like to be something else, to learn all about life and love in a few easy lessons."

Someone in the backup band had announced Ineida Mann, and she began to sing, the plaintive lyrics of an old blues standard. She had control but no range. Nudger found himself listening to the backup music, which included a smooth clarinet solo. The band liked Ineida and went all out to envelop her in good sound, but the audience at Fat Jack's was too smart for that. Ineida finished to light applause, bowed prettily, and made her exit. Competent but nothing special, and looking as if she'd just wandered in from suburbia. But this was what she wanted and her rich father was getting it for her. Parental love could be as blind as the other kind.

"So how are you going to get started on this thing?" Fat Jack asked. "You want me to introduce you to Hollister and Ineida?"

"Usually I begin a case by discussing my fee and signing a contract," Nudger said.

Fat Jack waved an immaculately manicured, ring-adorned hand. "Don't worry about the fee," he said. "Hey, let's make it whatever you usually charge plus twenty percent plus expenses. Trust me on that."

That sounded fine to Nudger, all except the trusting part. He reached into his inside coat pocket, withdrew his roll of antacid tablets, thumbed back the aluminum foil, and popped one of the white disks into his mouth, all in one practiced, smooth motion.

"What's that stuff for?" Fat Jack asked.

"Nervous stomach," Nudger explained.

"You oughta try this," Fat Jack said, nodding toward his absinthe. "Eventually it eliminates the stomach altogether."

Nudger winced. "I want to talk with Ineida," he said, "but it would be best if we had our conversation away from the club."

Fat Jack pursed his lips and nodded. "I can give you her address. She doesn't live at home with her father; she's in a little apartment over on Beulah Street. It's all part of the making-it-on-her-own illusion. Anything else?"

"Maybe. Do you still play the clarinet?"

Fat Jack cocked his head and looked curiously at Nudger, one tiny eye squinting through the tobacco smoke that hazed the air around the bar. "Now and again, but only on special occasions."

"Why don't we make the price of this job my usual fee plus only ten percent plus you do a set with the clarinet this Saturday night?"

Fat Jack beamed, then threw back his head and let out a roaring laugh that turned heads and seemed to shake the bottles on the back bar. "Agreed! You're a find, Nudger! First you trust me to pay you without a contract, then you lower your fee and ask for a clarinet solo instead of money. There's no place you can spend a clarinet solo! Hey, I like you, but you're not much of a businessman."

Nudger smiled and sipped his beer. Fat Jack hadn't bothered to find out the amount of Nudger's usual fee, so all this talk about percentages meant nothing. If detectives weren't good businessmen, neither were jazz musicians. He handed Fat Jack a pen and a club matchbook. "How about that address?"

Beulah Street was narrow and crooked, lined with low houses of French-Spanish architecture, an array of arches, pastel stucco, and ornamental wrought iron. The houses had long ago been divided into apartments, each with a separate entrance. Behind each apartment was a small courtyard.

Nudger found Ineida Collins' address. It belonged to a pale yellow structure with a weathered tile roof and a riot of multicolored bougainvillea blooming wild halfway up one cracked and often-patched stucco wall.

He glanced at his wristwatch. Ten o'clock. If Ineida wasn't awake by now, he decided, she should be. He stepped up onto the small red brick front porch and worked the lion's head knocker on a plank door supported by huge black iron hinges.

Ineida came to the door without delay. She didn't appear at all sleepy after her late-night stint at Fat Jack's. Her dark hair was tied back in a French braid. She was wearing slacks and a peach-colored silky blouse. Even the harsh sunlight was kind to her; she looked young, as inexperienced and naive as Fat Jack said she was.

Nudger told her he was a writer doing a piece on Fat Jack's club. "I heard you sing last night," he said. "It really was something to see. I thought it might be a good idea if we talked."

It was impossible for her to turn down what in her mind was a celebrity interview. She lit up bright enough to pale the sunlight and invited Nudger inside.

Her apartment was tastefully but inexpensively furnished. There was an imitation Oriental rug on the hardwood floor, lots of rattan furniture, a Casablanca overhead fan rotating its wide flat blades slowly and casting soothing, flickering shadows. Through sheer beige curtains the apartment's courtyard was visible, well tended and colorful.

"Can I get you a cup of coffee, Mr. Nudger?" Ineida asked.

Nudger told her thanks, watched the switch of her trim hips as she walked into the small kitchen. From where he sat he could see a Mr. Coffee brewer on the sink, its glass pot half full. Ineida poured, returned with two mugs of coffee.

"How old are you, Ineida?" he asked.

"Twenty-three."

"Then you haven't been singing for all that many years."

She sat down, placed her steaming coffee mug on a coaster. "About five, actually. I sang in school productions, then studied for a while in New York. I've been singing at Fat Jack's for about two months. I love it."

"The crowd there seems to like you," Nudger lied. He watched her smile and figured the lie was a worthy one. He pretended to take notes while he asked her a string of writer-like questions, pumping up her ego. It was an ego that would inflate only so far. Nudger decided that he liked Ineida Collins and hoped she would hurry up and realize she wasn't Ineida Mann.

"I'm told that you and Willy Hollister are pretty good friends." .

Her mood changed abruptly. Suspicion shone in her dark eyes, and the youthful smiling mouth became taut and suddenly ten years older.

"You're not a magazine writer," she said, in a betrayed voice.

Nudger's stomach gave a mule-like kick. "No, I'm not," he admitted.

"Then who are you?"

"Someone concerned about your well being." Antacid time. He popped one of the white tablets into his mouth and chewed.

"Father sent you."

"No," Nudger said.

"Liar," she told him. "Get out."

"I'd like to talk with you about Willy Hollister," Nudger persisted. In his business persistence paid, one way or the other. He could only hope it wouldn't be the other.

"Get out," Ineida repeated. "Or I'll call the police."

Within half a minute Nudger was outside again on Beulah Street, looking at the uncompromising barrier of Ineida's closed door. Apparently she was touchy on the subject of Willy Hollister. Nudger slipped another antacid between his lips, turned his back to the warming sun, and began walking.

He'd gone half a block when he realized that he was casting three shadows. He stopped. The middle shadow stopped also, but the larger shadows on either side kept advancing. The large bodies that cast those shadows were suddenly standing in front of Nudger, and two very big men were staring down it him. One was smiling, one wasn't. Considering the kind of smile it was, that didn't make much difference.

"We noticed you talking to Miss Mann," the one on the left said. He had wide cheekbones, dark, pockmarked skin, and gray eyes that gave no quarter. "Whatever you said seemed to upset her." His accent was a cross between a southern drawl and clipped French. Nudger recognized it as Cajun. The Cajuns were a tough, predominantly French people who had settled southern Louisiana but never themselves.

Nudger let himself hope and started to walk on. The second man, who was shorter but had a massive neck and shoulders, shuffled forward like a heavyweight boxer, to block his way. Nudger swallowed his antacid tablet.

"You nervous, friend?" the boxer asked in the same rich Cajun accent.

"Habitually."

Pockmarked said, "We have an interest in Miss Mann's welfare. What were you talking to her about?"

"The conversation was private. Do you two fellows mind introducing yourselves?"

"We mind," the boxer said. He was smiling again, nastily. Nudger noticed that the tip of his right eyebrow had turned white where it was crossed by a thin scar.

"Then I'm sorry, but we have nothing to talk about."

Pockmarked shook his head patiently in disagreement. "We have this to talk about, my friend. There are parts of this great state of Looziahna that are vast swampland. Not far from where we stand, the bayou is wild. It's the home of a surprising number of alligators. People go into the bayou, and some of them never come out. Who knows about them? After a while, who cares?" The cold gray eyes had diamond chips in them. "You understand my meaning?"

Nudger nodded. He understood. His stomach understood.

"I think we've made ourselves clear," the boxer said. "We aren't nice men, sir. It's our business not to be nice, and it's our pleasure. So a man like yourself, sir, a reasonable man in good health, should listen to us and stay away from Miss Mann."

"You mean Miss Collins."

"I mean Miss Ineida Mann." He said it with the straight face of a true professional.

"Why don't you tell Willy Hollister to stay away from her?" Nudger asked.

"Mr. Hollister is a nice young man of Miss Mann's own choosing," Pockmarked said with an odd courtliness. "You she obviously doesn't like. You upset her. That upsets us."

"And me and Frick don't like to be upset," the boxer said. He closed a powerful hand on the lapel of Nudger's sport jacket, not pushing or pulling in the slightest, merely squeezing the material. Nudger could feel the vibrant force of the man's strength as if it were electrical current. "Behave yourself," the boxer hissed through his fixed smile.

He abruptly released his grip, and both men turned and walked away.

Nudger looked down at his abused lapel. It was as crimped as if it had been wrinkled in a vise for days. He wondered if the dry cleaners could do anything about it when they pressed the coat.

Then he realized he was shaking. He loathed danger and had no taste for violence. He needed another antacid tablet and then, even though it was early, a drink.

New Orleans was turning out to be an exciting city, but not in the way the travel agencies and the chamber of commerce advertised.

★ ★ ★ ★ ★

"You're no jazz writer," Willy Hollister said to Nudger, in a small back room of Fat Jack's club. It wasn't exactly a dressing room, though at times it served as such. It was a sort of all-purpose place where quick costume changes were made and breaks were taken between sets. The room's pale green paint was faded and peeling, and a steam pipe jutted from floor to ceiling against one wall. Yellowed show posters featuring jazz greats were taped here and there behind the odd assortment of worn furniture. There were mingled scents of stale booze and tobacco smoke.

"But I am a jazz fan," Nudger said. "Enough of one to know how good you are, and that you play piano in a way that wasn't self-taught." He smiled. "I'll bet you even read music."

"You have to read music," Hollister said rather haughtily, "to graduate from Juilliard."

Even Nudger knew that Juilliard graduates weren't slouches. "So you have a classical background," he said.

"That's nothing rare; lots of jazz musicians have classical roots."

Nudger studied Hollister as the pianist spoke. Offstage, Hollister appeared older. His blond hair was thinning on top and his features were losing their boyishness, becoming craggy. His complexion was an unhealthy yellowish hue. He was a hunter, was this boy. Life's sad wisdom was in his eyes, resting on its haunches and ready to spring.

"How well do you know Ineida Mann?" Nudger asked.

"Well enough to know you've been bothering her," Hollister replied, with a bored yet wary expression. "We don't know what your angle is, but I suggest you stop. Don't bother trying to get any information out of me, either."

"I'm interested in jazz," Nudger said.

193

"Among other things."

"Like most people, I have more than one interest."

"Not like me, though," Hollister said. "My only interest is my music."

"What about Miss Mann?"

"That's none of your business." Hollister stood up, neatly but ineffectively snubbed out the cigarette he'd been smoking, and seemed to relish leaving it to smolder to death in the ashtray. "I've got a number coming up in a few minutes." He tucked in his Fat Jack's T-shirt and looked severe. "I don't particularly want to see you any more, Nudger. Whoever, whatever you are, it doesn't mean burned grits to me as long as you leave Ineida alone."

"Before you leave," Nudger said, "can I have your autograph?"

Incredibly, far from being insulted by this sarcasm, Hollister scrawled his signature on a nearby folded newspaper and tossed it to him. Nudger took that as a measure of the man's artistic ego, and despite himself he was impressed. All the ingredients of greatness resided in Willy Hollister, along with something else.

Nudger went back out into the club proper. He peered through the throng of jazz lovers and saw Fat Jack leaning against the bar. As Nudger was making his way across the dim room toward him, he spotted Ineida at one of the tables. She was wearing a green sequined blouse that set off her dark hair and eyes, and Nudger regretted that she couldn't sing as well as she looked. She glanced at him, recognized him, and quickly turned away to listen to a graying, bearded man who was one of her party.

"Hey, Nudger," Fat Jack said, when Nudger had reached the bar, "you sure you know what you're doing, old sleuth? You ain't exactly pussy-footing. Ineida asked me about you, said you'd bothered her at home. Hollister asked me who you were. The precinct captain asked me the same question."

Nudger's stomach tightened. "A New Orleans police captain?"

Fat Jack nodded. "Captain Marrivale." He smiled broad and bold, took a sip of absinthe. "You make ripples big enough to swamp boats."

"What I'd like to do now," Nudger said, "is take a short trip."

"Lots of folks would like for you to do that."

"I need to go to Cleveland, Kansas City, and Chicago," Nudger said. "A couple of days in each city. I've got to find out more about Willy Hollister. Are you willing to pick up the tab?"

"I don't suppose you could get this information with long-distance phone calls?"

"Not and get it right."

"When do you plan on leaving?"

"As soon as I can. Tonight."

Fat Jack nodded. He produced an alligator-covered checkbook, scribbled in it, tore out a check, and handed it to Nudger. Nudger couldn't make out the amount in the faint light. "If you need more, let me know," Fat Jack said. His smile was luminous in the dimness. "Hey, make it a fast trip, Nudger."

A week later Nudger was back in New Orleans, sitting across from Fat Jack McGee in the club owner's second floor office. "There's a pattern," he said, "sometimes subtle, sometimes strong, but always there, like in a forties Ellington piece."

"So tell me about it," Fat Jack said. "I'm an Ellington fan."

"I did some research," Nudger said, "read some old reviews, went to clubs and musicians' union halls and talked to people in the jazz communities where Willy Hollister played. He always started strong, but his musical career was checkered with flat spots, lapses. During those times, Hollister was just an ordinary performer."

Fat Jack appeared concerned, tucked his chin back into folds of flesh, and said, "That explains why he's falling off here."

"But the man is still making great music," Nudger said.

"Slipping from great to good," Fat Jack said. "Good jazz artists in New Orleans I can hire by the barrelful."

"There's something else about Willy Hollister," Nudger said. "Something that nobody picked up on because it spanned several years and three cities."

Fat Jack looked interested. If his ears hadn't been almost enveloped by overblown flesh, they would have perked up.

"Hollister had a steady girlfriend in each of these cities. All three women disappeared. Two were rumored to have left town on their own, but nobody knows where they went. The girlfriend in Cleveland, the first one, simply disappeared. She's still on the missing persons list."

"Whoo boy!" Fat Jack said. He began to sweat. He pulled a white handkerchief the size of a flag from the pocket of his sport jacket and mopped his brow, just like Satchmo but without the grin and trumpet.

"Sorry," Nudger said. "I didn't mean to make you uncomfortable."

"You're doing your job, is all," Fat Jack assured him. "But that's bad information to lay on me. You think Hollister had anything to do with the disappearances?"

Nudger shrugged. "Maybe the women themselves, and not Hollister, had to do with it. They were all the sort that traveled light and often. Maybe they left town of their own accord. Maybe for some reason they felt they had to get away from Hollister."

"I wish Ineida would want to get away from him," Fat Jack muttered. "But Jeez, not like that. Her old man'd boil me down for axle grease. But then she's not cut from the same mold as those other girls; she's not what she's trying to be and she's strictly local."

"The only thing she and those other women have in common is Willy Hollister."

Fat Jack leaned back, and the desk chair creaked in protest. Nudger, who had been hired to solve a problem, had so far only brought to light the seriousness of that problem. The big man didn't have to ask "What now?" It was written in capital letters on his face.

"You could fire Willy Hollister," Nudger said.

Fat Jack shook his head. "Ineida would follow him, maybe get mad at me and sic her dad on the club."

"And Hollister is still packing customers into the club every night."

"That, too," Fat Jack admitted. Even the loosest businessman could see the profit in Willy Hollister's genius. "For now," he said, "we'll let things slide while you continue to watch." He dabbed at his forehead again with the wadded handkerchief.

"Hollister doesn't know who I am," Nudger said, "but he knows who I'm not and he's worried. My presence might keep him aboveboard for a while."

"Fine, as long as a change of scenery isn't involved. I can't afford to have her wind up like those other women, Nudger."

"Speaking of winding up," Nudger said, "do you know anything about a couple of muscular robots? One has a scar across his right eyebrow and a face like an ex-pug's. His partner has a dark mustache, sniper's eyes, and is named Frick. Possibly the other is Frack. They both talk with thick Cajun accents."

Fat Jack raised his eyebrows. "Rocko Boudreau and Dwayne Frick," he said, with soft, terror-inspired awe. "They work for David Collins."

"I figured they did. They warned me to stay away from Ineida." Nudger felt his intestines twist into advanced Boy Scout knots. He got out his antacid tablets. "They suggested I might take up postmortem residence in the swamp." As he recalled his conversation with Frick and Frack, Nudger again felt a dark near-panic well up in him. Maybe it was because he was here in this small office with the huge and terrified Fat Jack McGee; maybe fear actually was contagious. He offered Fat Jack an antacid tablet.

Fat Jack accepted.

"I'm sure their job is to look after Ineida without her knowing it," Nudger said. "Incidentally, they seem to approve of her seeing Willy Hollister."

"That won't help me if anything happens to Ineida that's in any way connected to the club," Fat Jack said.

Nudger stood up. He was tired. His back still ached from sitting in an airline seat that wouldn't recline, and his stomach was still busy trying to digest itself. "I'll phone you if I hear any more good news."

Fat Jack mumbled something unintelligible and nodded, lost in his own dark apprehensions, a ponderous man grappling with ponderous problems. One of his inflated hands floated up in a parting gesture as Nudger left the stifling office. What he hadn't told Fat Jack was that immediately after each woman had disappeared, Hollister had regained his tragic, soulful touch on the piano.

★ ★ ★ ★ ★

When Nudger got back to his hotel, he was surprised to open the door to his room and see a man sitting in a chair by the window. It was the big blue armchair that belonged near the door.

When Nudger entered, the man turned as if resenting the interruption, as if it were his room and Nudger the interloper. He stood up and smoothed his light tan suit coat. He was a smallish man with a triangular face and very springy red hair that grew in a sharp widow's peak. His eyes were dark and intense. He resembled a fox. With a quick and graceful motion he put a paw into a pocket for a wallet-sized leather folder, flipped it open to reveal a badge.

"Police Captain Marrivale, I presume," Nudger said. He shut the door.

The redheaded man nodded and replaced his badge in his pocket. "I'm Fred Marrivale," he confirmed. "I heard you were back in town. I think we should talk." He shoved the armchair around to face the room instead of the window and sat back down, as familiar as old shoes.

Nudger pulled out the small wooden desk chair and also sat, facing Marrivale. "Are you here on official business, Captain Marrivale?"

Marrivale smiled. He had tiny sharp teeth behind thin lips. "You know how it is, Nudger, a cop is always a cop."

"Sure. And that's the way it is when we go private," Nudger told him. "A confidential investigator is always that, no matter where he is or whom he's talking to."

"Which is kinda why I'm here," Marrivale said. "It might be better if you were someplace else."

Nudger was incredulous. His nervous stomach believed what he'd just heard, but he didn't. "You're actually telling me to get out of town?"

Marrivale gave a kind of laugh, but there was no glint of amusement in his sharp eyes. "I'm not authorized to tell anybody to get out of town, Nudger. I'm not the sheriff and this isn't Dodge City."

"I'm glad you realize that," Nudger told him, "because I can't leave yet. I've got business here."

"I know about your business."

"Did David Collins send you to talk to me?"

Marrivale had a good face for policework; there was only the slightest change of expression. "We can let that question go by," he said, "and I'll ask you one. Why did Fat Jack McGee hire you?"

"Have you asked him?"

"No."

"He'd rather I kept his reasons confidential," Nudger said.

"You don't have a Louisiana PI license," Marrivale pointed out.

Nudger smiled. "I know. Nothing to be revoked."

"There are consequences a lot more serious than having your investigator's license pulled, Nudger. Mr. Collins would prefer that you stay away from Ineida Mann."

"You mean Ineida Collins."

"I mean what I say."

"David Collins already had someone deliver that message to me."

"It's not a message from anyone but me," Marrivale said. "I'm telling you this because I'm concerned about your safety while you're within my jurisdiction. It's part of my job."

Nudger kept a straight face, got up and walked to the door, and opened it. He said, "I appreciate your concern, Captain. Right now I've got things to do."

Marrivale smiled with his mean little mouth. He didn't

seem rattled by Nudger's impolite invitation to leave; he'd said what needed saying. He got up out of the armchair and adjusted his suit. Nudger noticed that the suit hung on him just right and must have been tailored and expensive. No cop's-salary, J. C. Penney wardrobe for Marrivale.

As he walked past Nudger, Marrivale paused and said, "It'd behoove you to learn to discern friend from enemy, Nudger." He went out and trod lightly down the hall toward the elevators, not looking back.

Nudger shut and locked the door. Then he went over to the bed, removed his shoes, and stretched out on his back on the mattress, his fingers laced behind his head. He studied the faint water stains on the ceiling in the corner above him. They were covered by a thin film of mold. That reminded Nudger of the bayou

He had to admit that Marrivale had left him with solid parting advice.

Though plenty of interested parties had warned Nudger to stay away from Ineida Collins, everyone seemed to have neglected to tell him to give a wide berth to Willy Hollister. And after breakfast, it was Hollister who claimed Nudger's interest.

Hollister lived on St. Francois, within a few blocks of Ineida Collins's apartment. Their apartments were similar. Hollister's was the end unit of a low tan stucco building that sat almost flush with the sidewalk. What yard there was had to be in the rear. Through the low branches of a huge magnolia tree, Nudger saw some of the raw cedar fencing that sectioned the back premises into private courtyards.

Hollister might be home, sleeping after his late-night gig at Fat Jack's. But whether he was home or not, Nudger decided that his next move would be to knock on Hollister's door.

He rapped on the wooden door three times, casually leaned toward it and listened. He heard no sound from inside. No one in the street seemed to be paying much attention to him, so after a few minutes Nudger idly gave the doorknob a twist.

It rotated all the way, clicked. The door opened about six inches. Nudger pushed the door open farther and stepped quietly inside.

The apartment no doubt came furnished. The furniture was old but not too worn; some of it probably had antique value. The floor was dull hardwood where it showed around the borders of a faded blue carpet. From where he stood, Nudger could see into the bedroom. The bed was unmade but empty.

The living room was dim. The wooden shutters on its windows were closed, allowing slanted light to come in through narrow slits. Most of the illumination in the room came from the bedroom and a short hall that led to a bathroom, then to a small kitchen and sliding glass doors that opened to the courtyard.

To make sure he was alone, Nudger called, "Mr. Hollister? Avon lady!"

No answer. Fine.

Nudger looked around the living room for a few minutes, examining the contents of drawers, picking up some sealed mail that turned out to be an insurance pitch and a utility bill.

He had just entered the bedroom when he heard a sound from outside the curtained window, open about six inches. It was a dull thunking sound that Nudger thought he recognized. He went to the window, parted the breeze-swayed gauzy white curtains, and bent low to peer outside.

The window looked out on the courtyard. What Nudger saw confirmed his guess about the sound. A shovel knifing into soft earth. Willy Hollister was in the courtyard garden, digging. Nudger crouched down so he could see better.

Hollister was planting rosebushes. They were young plants, but they already had red and white roses on them. Hollister had started on the left with the red roses and was alternating colors. He was planting half a dozen bushes and was working on the fifth plant, which lay with its roots wrapped in burlap beside the waiting, freshly dug hole.

Hollister was on both knees on the ground, using his hands to scoop some dirt back into the hole. He was forming a small dome over which to spread the rosebush's soon-to-be-exposed roots. He knew how to plant rosebushes, all right, and he was trying to ensure that these would live.

Nudger's stomach went into a series of spasms as Hollister stood and glanced at the apartment as if he had sensed someone's presence. He drew one of the rolled-up sleeves of his white dress shirt across his perspiring forehead. For a few seconds he seemed to debate about whether to return to the apartment. Then he turned, picked up the shovel, and began digging the sixth and final hole.

Letting out a long breath, Nudger drew back from the open window and stood up straight. He'd go out by the front door and then walk around to the courtyard and call Hollister's name, as if he'd just arrived. He wanted to get Hollister's own version of his past.

As Nudger was leaving the bedroom, he noticed a stack of pale blue envelopes on the dresser, beside a comb and brush set monogrammed with Hollister's initials. The envelopes were held together by a fat rubber band. Nudger saw Hollister's address, saw the Beulah Street return address penned neatly in black ink in a corner of the top envelope. He paused for just a few seconds, picked up the envelopes, and slipped them into his pocket. Then he left Hollister's apartment the same way he'd entered.

There was no point in talking to Hollister now. It would be foolish to place himself in the apartment at the approximate time of the disappearance of the stack of letters written by Ineida Collins.

Nudger walked up St. Francois for several blocks, then took a cab to his hotel. Though the morning hadn't yet heated up, the cab's air conditioner was on high and the interior was near freezing. The letters seemed to grow heavier and heavier in Nudger's jacket pocket, and to glow with a kind of warmth that gave no comfort.

Nudger had room service bring up a plain omelet and a glass of milk. He sat with his early lunch, his customary meal (it had a soothing effect on a nervous stomach), at the desk in his hotel room and ate slowly as he read Ineida Collins's letters to Hollister. He understood now why they had felt warm in his pocket. The love affair was, from Ineida's point of view at least, as soaring and serious as such an affair can get. Nudger felt cheapened by his crass invasion of Ineida's privacy. These were thoughts meant to be shared by no one but the two of them, thoughts not meant to be tramped through by a middle-aged detective not under the spell of love.

On the other hand, Nudger told himself, there was no way for him to know what the letters contained until he read them and determined that he shouldn't have. This was the sort of professional quandary he got himself into frequently but never got used to.

The last letter, the one with the latest postmark, was the most revealing and made the tacky side of Nudger's profession seem worthwhile. Ineida Collins was planning to run away with Willy Hollister; he had told her he loved her and that they would be married. Then, after the fact, they would return to New Orleans and inform friends and relatives of the blessed reunion. It all seemed quaint, Nudger thought, and not very believable unless you happened to be twenty-three and love struck and had lived Ineida Collins's sheltered existence.

Ineida also referred in the last letter to something important she had to tell Hollister. Nudger could guess what that important bit of information was. That she was Ineida Collins and she was David Collins's daughter and she was rich, and that she was oh so glad that Hollister hadn't known about her until that moment. Because that meant he wanted her for her own true self alone. Ah, love! It made Nudger's business go round.

Nudger refolded the letter, replaced it in its envelope, and dropped it onto the desk. He tried to finish his omelet but couldn't. He wasn't really hungry, and his stomach had reached a tolerable level of comfort. He knew it was time to report to Fat Jack. After all, the man had hired him to uncover information, but not so Nudger would keep it to himself.

Nudger slid the rubber band back around the stack of letters, snapped it, and stood up. He considered having the letters placed in the hotel safe, but the security of any hotel safe was questionable. A paper napkin bearing the hotel logo lay next to his half-eaten omelet. He wrapped the envelopes in the napkin and dropped the bundle in the wastebasket by the desk. The maid wasn't due back in the room until tomorrow morning, and it wasn't likely that anyone would think Nudger would throw away such important letters. And the sort of person who would bother to search a wastebasket would search everywhere else and find the letters anyway.

He placed the tray with his dishes on it in the hall outside his door, hung the "Do Not Disturb" sign on the knob, and left to see Fat Jack McGee.

They told Nudger at the club that Fat Jack was out. Nobody was sure when he'd be back; he might not return until this evening when business started picking up, or he might have just strolled over to the Magnolia Blossom for a croissant and coffee and would be back any minute.

Nudger sat at the end of the bar, nursing a beer he didn't really want, and waited.

After an hour, the bartender began blatantly staring at him from time to time. Mid-afternoon or not, Nudger was occupying a bar stool and had an obligation. And maybe the man was right. Nudger was about to give in to the weighty responsibility of earning his place at the bar by ordering another drink he didn't want when Fat Jack appeared through the dimness like a light-footed, obese spirit in a white vested suit.

He saw Nudger, smiled his fat man's beaming smile, and veered toward him, diamond rings and gold jewelry flashing fire beneath pale coat sleeves. There was even a large diamond stickpin in his bib-like tie. He was a vision of sartorial immensity.

"We need to talk," Nudger told him.

"That's easy enough," Fat Jack said. "My office, hey?" He led the way, making Nudger feel somewhat like a pilot fish trailing a whale.

When they were settled in Fat Jack's office, Nudger said, "I came across some letters that Ineida wrote to Hollister. She and Hollister plan to run away together, get married."

Fat Jack raised his eyebrows so high Nudger was afraid they might become detached. "Hollister ain't the marrying kind, Nudger."

"What kind is he?"

"I don't want to answer that."

"Maybe Ineida and Hollister will elope and live happily—"

"Stop!" Fat Jack interrupted him. He leaned forward, wide forehead glistening. "When are they planning on leaving?"

"I don't know. The letter didn't say."

"You gotta find out, Nudger!"

"I could ask. But Captain Marrivale wouldn't approve."

"Marrivale has talked with you?"

"In my hotel room. He assured me he had my best interests at heart."

Fat Jack appeared thoughtful. He swivelled in his chair and switched on the auxiliary window air conditioner. Its breeze stirred the papers on the desk, ruffled Fat Jack's graying, gingery hair.

The telephone rang. Fat Jack picked it up, identified himself. His face went as white as his suit. "Yes, sir," he said. His jowls began to quiver; loose flesh beneath his left eye started to dance. Nudger was getting nervous just looking at him. "You can't mean it," Fat Jack said. "Hey, maybe it's a joke. Okay, it ain't a joke." He listened a while longer and then said, "Yes, sir," again and hung up. He didn't say anything else for a long time. Nudger didn't say anything either.

Fat Jack spoke first. "That was David Collins. Ineida's gone. Not home, bed hasn't been slept in."

"Then she and Hollister have left as they planned."

"You mean as Hollister planned. Collins got a note in the mail."

"Note?" Nudger asked. His stomach did a flip; it was way ahead of his brain, reacting to a suspicion not yet fully formed.

"A ransom note," Fat Jack confirmed. "Unsigned, in cutout newspaper words. Collins said Marrivale is on his way over here now to talk to me about Hollister. Hollister's disappeared, too. And his clothes are missing from his closet." Fat Jack's little pink eyes were bulging in his blanched face. "I better not tell Marrivale about the letters."

"Not unless he asks," Nudger said. "And he won't." He stood up.

"Where are you going?"

"I'm leaving," Nudger said, "before Marrivale gets here. There's no sense in making this easy for him."

"Or difficult for you."

"It works out that way, for a change."

Fat Jack nodded, his eyes unfocused yet thoughtful, already rehearsing in his mind the lines he would use on Marrivale. He wasn't a man to bow easily or gracefully to trouble, and he had seen plenty of trouble in his life. He knew a multitude of moves and would use them all.

He didn't seem to notice when Nudger left.

Hollister's apartment was shuttered, and the day's mail delivery sprouted like a white bouquet from the mailbox next to his door. Nudger doubted that David Collins had officially notified the police; his first, his safest, step would be to seek the personal help of Captain Marrivale, who was probably on the Collins payroll already. So it was unlikely that Hollister's apartment was under surveillance, unless by Frick and Frack, who, like Marrivale, probably knew about Ineida's disappearance.

Nudger walked unhesitatingly up to the front door and tried the knob. The door was locked this time. He walked around the corner, toward the back of the building, and unhitched the loop of rope that held shut the high wooden gate to the courtyard.

In the privacy of the fenced courtyard, Nudger quickly

forced the sliding glass doors and entered Hollister's apartment.

The place seemed almost exactly as Nudger had left it earlier that day. The matched comb and brush set was still on the dresser, though in a different position. Nudger checked the dresser drawers. They held only a few pairs of undershorts, a wadded dirty shirt, and some socks with holes in the toes. He crossed the bedroom and opened the closet door. The closet's blank back wall stared out at him. Empty. The apartment's kitchen was only lightly stocked with food; the refrigerator held a stick of butter, half a gallon of milk, various half-used condiments, and three cans of beer. It was dirty and needed defrosting. Hollister had been a lousy housekeeper.

The rest of the apartment seemed oddly quiet and in vague disorder, as if getting used to its new state of vacancy. There was definitely a deserted air about the place that suggested its occupant had shunned it and left in a hurry.

Nudger decided that there was nothing to learn here. No matchbooks with messages written inside them, no hastily scrawled, forgotten addresses or revealing ticket stubs. He never got the help that fictional detectives got—well, almost never—though it was always worth seeking.

As he was about to open the courtyard gate and step back into the street, Nudger paused. He stood still, feeling a cold stab of apprehension, of dread knowledge, in the pit of his stomach.

He was staring at the rosebushes that Hollister had planted that morning. At the end of the garden were two newly planted bushes bearing red rosebuds. Hollister hadn't planted them that way. He had alternated the bushes by color, one red one white. Their order now was white, red, white, white, red, red.

Which meant that the bushes had been dug up. Replanted.

Nudger walked to the row of rosebushes. The earth around them was loose, as it had been earlier, but now it seemed more sloppily spread about, and one of the bushes was leaning at an angle. Not the work of a methodical gardener; more the work of someone in a hurry.

As he backed away from the freshly turned soil, Nudger's legs came in contact with a small wrought iron bench. He sat down. He thought for a while, oblivious of the warm sunshine, the colorful geraniums and bougainvillea. He became aware of the frantic chirping of birds on their lifelong hunt for sustenance, of the soft yet vibrant buzzing of insects. Sounds of life, sounds of death. He stood up and got out of there fast, his stomach churning.

When he returned to his hotel room, Nudger found on the floor by the desk the napkin that had been wadded in the bottom of the wastebasket. He checked the wastebasket, but it was only a gesture to confirm what he already knew. The letters that Ineida Collins had written to Willy Hollister were gone.

Fat Jack was in his office. Marrivale had come and gone hours ago. Nudger sat down across the desk from Fat Jack and looked appraisingly at the harried club owner. Fat Jack appeared wrung out by worry. The Marrivale visit had taken a lot out of him. Or maybe he'd had another conversation with David Collins. Whatever his problems, Nudger knew that, to paraphrase the great Al Jolyon, Fat Jack hadn't seen nothin' yet.

"David Collins just phoned," Fat Jack said. He was visibly uncomfortable, a veritable Niagara of nervous perspiration. "He got a call from the kidnappers. They want half a million in cash by tomorrow night, or Ineida starts being delivered in the mail piece by piece."

Nudger wasn't surprised. He knew where the phone call had originated.

"When I was looking into Hollister's past," he said to Fat Jack, "I happened to discover something that seemed ordinary enough then, but now has gotten kind of interesting." He watched the perspiration flow down Fat Jack's wide forehead.

"So I'm interested," Fat Jack said irritably. He reached behind him and slapped at the air conditioner, as if to coax more cold air despite the frigid thermostat setting.

"There's something about being a fat man, a man as large as you. After a while he takes his size for granted, accepts it as a normal fact of his life. But other people don't. A really fat man is more memorable than he realizes, especially if he's called Fat Jack."

Fat Jack drew his head back into fleshy folds and shot a tortured, wary look at Nudger. "Hey, what are you talking toward, old sleuth?"

"You had a series of failed clubs in the cities where Willy Hollister played his music, and you were there at the times when Hollister's women disappeared."

"That ain't unusual, Nudger. Jazz is a tight little world."

"I said people remember you," Nudger told him. "And they remember you knowing Willy Hollister. But you told me you saw him for the first time when he came here to play in your club. And when I went to see Ineida for the first time, she knew my name. She bought the idea that I was a magazine writer; it fell right into place and it took her a while to get uncooperative. Then she assumed I was working for her father—as you knew she would."

Fat Jack stood halfway up, then decided he hadn't the energy for the total effort and sat back down in his groaning chair. "You missed a beat, Nudger. Are you saying I'm in on this kidnapping with Hollister? If that's true, why would I have hired you?"

"You needed someone like me to substantiate Hollister's involvement with Ineida, to find out about Hollister's missing women. It would help you to set him up. You knew him better than you pretended. You knew that he murdered those three women to add some insane, tragic dimension to his music—the sound that made him great. You knew what he had planned for Ineida."

"He didn't even know who she really was!" Fat Jack sputtered.

"But you knew from the time you hired her that she was David Collins's daughter. You schemed from the beginning to use Hollister as the fall guy in your kidnapping plan."

"Hollister is a killer—you said so yourself. I wouldn't want to get involved in any kind of scam with him."

"He didn't know you were involved," Nudger explained. "When you'd used me to make it clear that Hollister was the natural suspect, you kidnapped Ineida and demanded the ransom, figuring Hollister's past and his disappearance would divert the law's attention away from you."

Fat Jack's wide face was a study in agitation, but it was relatively calm compared to what must have been going on inside his head. His body was squirming uncontrollably, and the pain in his eyes was difficult to look into. He didn't want to ask the question, but he had to and he knew it. "If all this is true," he moaned, "where is Hollister?"

"I did a little digging in his garden," Nudger said. "He's under his roses, where he thought Ineida was going to wind up, but where you had space for him reserved all along."

Fat Jack's head dropped. His suit suddenly seemed to get two sizes too large. As his body trembled, tears joined the perspiration on his quivering cheeks. "When did you know?" he asked.

"When I got back to my hotel and found the letters from Ineida to Hollister missing. You were the only one other than myself who knew about them." Nudger leaned over the desk to look Fat Jack in the eye. "Where is Ineida?" he asked.

"She's still alive," was Fat Jack's only answer. Crushed as he was, he was still too wily to reveal his hole card. It was as if his fat were a kind of rubber, lending inexhaustible resilience to body and mind.

"It's negotiation time," Nudger told him, "and we don't have very long to reach an agreement. While we're sitting here talking, the police are digging in the dirt I replaced in Hollister's garden."

"You called them?"

"I did. But right now, they expect to find Ineida. When they find Hollister, they'll put all the pieces together the way I did and get the same puzzle-picture of you."

Fat Jack nodded sadly, seeing the truth in that prognosis. "So what's your proposition?"

"You release Ineida, and I keep quiet until tomorrow morning. That'll give you a reasonable head start on the law. The police don't know who phoned them about the body in Hollister's garden, so I can stall them for at least that long without arousing suspicion."

Fat Jack didn't deliberate for more than a few seconds. He nodded again, then stood up, supporting his ponderous weight with both hands on the desk. "What about money?" he whined. "I can't run far without money."

"I've got nothing to lend you," Nudger said. "Not even the fee I'm not going to get from you."

"All right," Fat Jack sighed.

"I'm going to phone David Collins in one hour," Nudger

told him. "If Ineida isn't there, I'll put down the receiver and dial the number of the New Orleans police department."

"She'll be there," Fat Jack said. He tucked in his sweat-plastered shirt beneath his huge stomach paunch, buttoned his suit coat, and without a backward glance at Nudger glided majestically from the room. He would have his old jaunty stride back in no time.

Nudger glanced at his watch. He sipped Fat Jack's best whiskey from the club's private stock while he waited for an hour to pass. Then he phoned David Collins, and from the tone of Collins's voice he guessed the answer to his question even before he asked it.

Ineida was home.

When Nudger answered the knock on his hotel room door early the next morning, he wasn't really surprised to find Frick and Frack looming in the hall. They pushed into the room without being invited. There was a sneer on Frick's pockmarked face. Frack gave his boxer's nifty little shuffle and stood between Nudger and the door, smiling politely.

"We brought you something from Mr. Collins," Frick said, reaching into an inside pocket of his pale green sport jacket. It just about matched Nudger's complexion.

All Frick brought out, though, was an envelope. Nudger was surprised to see that his hands were steady as he opened it.

The envelope contained an airline ticket for a noon flight to St. Louis.

"You did okay, my friend," Frick said. "You did what was right for Ineida. Mr. Collins appreciates that."

"What about Fat Jack?" Nudger asked. Frack's polite smile changed subtly. It became a dreamy, unpleasant sort of smile.

"Where Fat Jack is now," Frack said, "most of his friends are alligators."

"After Fat Jack talked to you," said Frick, "he went to Mr. Collins. He couldn't make himself walk out on all that possible money; some guys just have to play all their cards. He told Mr. Collins that for a certain amount of cash he would reveal Ineida's whereabouts, but it all had to be done in a hurry." Now Frick also smiled. "He revealed her whereabouts in a hurry, all right, and for free. In fact, he kept talking till nobody was listening, till he couldn't talk any more."

Nudger swallowed dryly. He forgot about breakfast. Fat Jack had been a bad businessman to the end, dealing in desperation instead of distance. Maybe he'd had too much of the easy life; maybe he couldn't picture going on without it. That was no problem for him now.

When Nudger got home, he found a flat, padded package with a New Orleans postmark waiting for him. He placed it on his desk and cautiously opened it. The package contained two items: A check from David Collins made out to Nudger for more than twice the amount of Fat Jack's uncollectable fee. And an old jazz record in its original wrapper, a fifties rendition of *You Got the Reach but Not the Grasp.*

It featured Fat Jack McGee on clarinet.

Before You Leap

Nudger was being attacked by snakes. The telephone jangled, halfway waking him. He groped for it, got the cord tangled around his wrist. Huh? *Help!*

He awoke all the way, trying to throttle the plastic receiver and keep it from sinking long fangs into him.

When he realized the snake was a phone and he'd been dreaming, he pressed the receiver to his ear, still not completely comfortable about doing that. He'd just finished investigating the theft of some endangered species from the zoo, some sort of cute little rodent, and a snake not so cute. The guy who'd stolen them had returned the snake, but couldn't say what had happened to the rodent.

"Nudge?" Hammersmith's voice. What was a police lieutenant doing calling him at—Nudger squinted at the luminous digital numbers of the clock—3:00 a.m.? Oh God, was it only 3:00 a.m.?

"Nudge?"

"You know what time it is?" Nudger mumbled thickly.

"Sure. Temperature, too. But that's not what I called about."

Hammersmith and his sadistic sense of humor. Still rising toward total wakefulness, Nudger realized he should maybe worry about the reason for this odd-hour call. "What did you call about?"

"You know a guy name of Ernest Gate?"

"Think not."

"Well, he knows you. He's asking for you."

A long pause. Hammersmith and his telephone games. "So put Ernest whatsisname on the line."

"Can't. He's perched on a ledge of the Merrimont Hotel, threatening to walk out into the night thirty stories high."

"Wait a minute. You got a jumper, and he's asking for me?"

"You and no one else, Nudge. Demands to talk to you, in fact, and human life being held to be of high value, he's in a position to make demands. So the department figured I'd be the guy to call you, see if you might wanna chat with this Gate character."

"Bates?"

"Gate."

"Well, I know nobody name of Gate. Bates, either."

"Maybe by some other name."

Nudger, his mind still clouded with night webs, couldn't deny it was possible. Three a.m. Whew!

"You coming downtown to try and talk this guy in off the ledge?" Hammersmith asked.

Nudger said, "That sounds like a scene from an old movie. There gonna be a priest there, and the demure Mrs. Gates, maybe?"

"Just you," Hammersmith said. "He wants you and you alone."

Nudger's nervous stomach kicked. He hated heights. But what was he supposed to do, let this Ernest Gates fly?

"Nudge?"

"The Merrimont you say?"

"Right. On Pine Street."

Nudger said he knew where it was, but Hammersmith had already hung up. Hammersmith had a thing about hanging up first.

Nudger struggled out of bed and got his legs working. He

chewed two antacid tablets while he was getting dressed.

After parking the Granada behind a blue unmarked Chevy that screamed POLICE! Nudger walked through the sultry night toward the department barricades. Typical July weather in St. Louis; the temperature was still over eighty degrees and the humidity was almost high enough to float ships. It was possible that if this Ernest Gate did jump, he'd sink slow enough not to break when he hit.

The sweating and irritable uniform near the barricade must have been told Nudger was on his way. As soon as Nudger identified himself, he said, "See if you can make this guy go one way or the other, okay, Nudger?"

"That's not exactly the idea."

"It'd solve things short term for a lotta people," the uniform said.

Nudger thought that was an odd concept of civic duty, but he let the remark pass and the uniform let him pass.

The Merrimont was bathed in spotlights, and high above the sidewalk a figure was outlined pressed against the stonework at a point precisely between two windows. Windows on either side of the man were open, and people were leaning out looking at him, probably talking to keep his mind off death. Lit up like it was, Nudger couldn't help noticing how beautiful it looked now that it had been bought and refurbished by one of the major chains. Downtown sure was coming back.

The uniform who accompanied him up on the elevator was also appreciative. "They done a great job on this place, huh?" He caressed the oak-paneled wall above the control panel. "I tell you, some of the architecture in these old buildings—"

He shut up as the elevator doors opened onto the thirtieth floor and he saw Hammersmith waiting in the hall like an impatient Buddha, puffing on one of his greenish and abominable cigars.

"Glad to shee you, Nudge," he said around the cigar. "Maybe you can shave this guy an' we can all go home an' get shome shleep."

"If you don't put out that cigar, I'm not gonna talk to him," Nudger said. "Even if he jumps, you and everybody near you might be dead before he is."

"Shorry," Hammersmith said. He buried the cigar's glowing ember in the sand of a nearby pedestal ashtray. It died hard, emitting a green mushroom cloud that looked like a miniature nuclear mishap. "I forgot about your delicate stomach."

"Fear bothers it, too," Nudger said.

Hammersmith said, "I know That's why you quit the department."

"And I guess that's why you called me to help cope with this problem thirty stories high."

"No choice in the matter." Hammersmith actually sounded apologetic. Graceful for such an obese man, he seemed to glide over the red-and-blue carpet as he led Nudger to a room near the end of the hall. The door was open, and Nudger could see a uniform and several plainclothes types milling around inside. Everyone stopped talking and looked at Nudger and Hammersmith when they stepped into the room. "You go in the bathroom, there's even a complimentary shower ca—" a plainclothesman was saying before he clamped his lips together. Even the guy leaning halfway out the window turned and stared.

Hammersmith said, "Here he is at last."

"Great!" said the guy on the windowsill. He immediately straightened up and moved back away from the window. Everyone looked relieved, as if Nudger had the strength of ten men and could fly and would wrap this thing up in a few minutes.

Nudger said, "You got a net set up?"

"Sure," Hammersmith said, "but I don't know how much good it'll do thirty stories down even if he hits it like a dart nails a bull's-eye. We're trying to set up something to snag him on the twenty-fifth floor, but it's a slow process 'cause we don't want him to see what's going on and jump before the device gets strung below him. Also, it's a new contraption still in the testing stage. Anyway, see how this guy knows you and maybe you can convince him to come back in and end this thing without anybody getting hurt."

Nudger moved to the window and leaned outside, looked down, got dizzy. He clasped a hand on the window frame and swallowed a burned metal taste.

" 'S matter, you don't like heights?" a voice asked from outside.

Nudger leaned out a little farther and peered over at Ernest Gate.

Gate was a small, moon-faced man about fifty. He had thinning hair combed straight back but mussed by the wind, a dark widow's peak, and old-fashioned-back-in-style round glasses. He was wearing baggy pants whose legs were whipping like sails in the high, warm breeze, a button-down white shirt with perspiration stains under the arms, a tightly knotted narrow red tie. He looked like an accountant gone mad, which for all Nudger knew he maybe was, because Nudger was sure he'd never seen Gate before.

"Do we know each other?" Nudger asked.

Gate laughed. Spat. They probably appreciated that down on twenty-five.

"I don't get the joke," Nudger said.

"You got your money, though, you bastard. And you

caused what's about to happen here. So how's it feel?"

"Listen, there's been some mistake. For God's sake, come in and let's talk about it." Nudger couldn't bear to think about what this average and pleasant-featured little man would become down on the sidewalk if he stepped off the ledge. "Nothing's worth what you're considering doing."

"You figure I'll live to regret it?" Gate asked.

"Well," Nudger said, "not for long." His stomach seemed to zoom out beyond the Merrimont's stone facade and plunge through the floodlit night. "Just come back in, please, and we'll iron this thing out." Iron. Flat. Oh Christ!

"So you're begging me, huh?" Gate said, sneering. "You afraid of your conscience or something? I've gotta say I'm surprised. Pleased, though. This is better'n I hoped for. I knew you'd never agree to holding my hand when I stepped off."

"Why me?" Nudger asked. "Why did you ask to talk to me? I'd at least like to understand what this is all about."

"Why you, huh? It's because you're responsible for everything. You're the reason I'm standing here. The reason I'm gonna do what I'm gonna do, my friend." Gate's eyes were glowing feverishly behind the round lenses now; he seemed to be working up to something, all right.

"If you were to calm down and come in here," Nudger said, trying not to look down again, "I bet we could straighten out this misunderstanding in no time at all."

"Sure, I'll be right in," Gate said. "I'll take a shortcut, Nubber."

Nubber? "Hey, wait a minute!"

But Gate had casually stepped off into space.

He seemed to be suspended by wires there for just an instant, then he plunged into the haze of light.

Nudger groaned and leaned out, saw Gate change his

mind and begin to flap his arms wildly, heard him scream as he passed twenty-five and the horrified faces of the uniforms setting up an awkward arrangement of metal arms and netting that didn't look as if it would stop a pillow.

Gate frantically beat his arms like wings all the way down. Nudger watched the rescue workers with the round net, far, far below, desperately maneuvering to meet him at street level.

They succeeded.

Gate rocketed through the net as if it were made of paper.

Ten minutes later, down on the sidewalk, Hammersmith said, "That's okay, Nudge, you tried. They go whacko, sometimes there's nothing anybody can do to stop them."

They were standing about twenty feet from where Gate's body lay covered with a dark blanket. Fluids were soaking through the blanket. After the first glance, Nudger couldn't look at it again.

"You wanna take another peek at what's left of his face?" Hammersmith asked. "Make sure beyond any doubt you don't know him?"

"I don't know him," Nudger said, gulping down bile. "And I don't think he knew me."

"Really? Why not?"

"He called me Nubber."

"Oh? You sure about that? It mighta been the wind distorting his words."

"I'm sure. Nubber."

"People mispronounce names under stress sometimes. Or hear them wrong."

"Nubber, Nubber, Nubber!"

"Okay, okay." Hammersmith raised a bloated hand in a halt signal. "The wallet we got from the body says he checked in under his real name, Ernest Gate. Address is out in Chesterfield. The doorman says he thinks he arrived in a cab, and there's no driver's license, only forty-two dollars in cash, a Visa card, and one of those ID forms that come with wallets. Looks like a fairly new wallet, though it's hard to say for sure 'cause it got a little messy."

Nudger's stomach took off again. He swallowed, willing his abdomen to stop twitching against his belt buckle. "Let me know what else you find out, all right?"

Hammersmith fondled an unlit cigar and looked puzzled. "Else? Find out?"

"When you investigate."

"Nothing to investigate," Hammersmith said. "The guy's dead 'cause you couldn't talk him in off the ledge. We notify the next of kin and it's case closed."

"But he obviously had me mixed up with somebody else."

"That was his problem, not ours. Hey, there's an all-out war on drugs! We only got time and manpower for so much other'n that, you know?"

Nudger knew.

Hammersmith laid sausage-like fingers gently on his shoulder. "Why don't you go back to your apartment and see if you can get some sleep. It's not even"—he rotated his thick wrist and glanced at his watch—"four o'clock."

Nudger nodded, then turned and walked away.

He drove home chomping antacid tablets and knowing his sleep was finished for the night. For the next several hours he'd slump on the sofa in front of the TV and watch gold chains being sold on the home shopping network. He was afraid even to doze off, not knowing what terrors his dreams might hold.

The next morning, Nudger sat in his office above

223

Danny's Donuts, nibbling on a greasy and weighty Dunker Delite and sipping a foam cup of Danny's acidic coffee. A breakfast like that could hurt you, but it tended to keep you awake. "Nooooo," his stomach seemed to growl, so he shoved the Dunker Delite, lying like a lumpy corpse on its white paper napkin, off the side of the desk and listened to it *thunk!* into the metal wastebasket. A nutritionist would cheer.

After brushing sugar from his hands, he got the phone directory out of the desk's bottom drawer and turned to the back section where businesses were listed.

There it was, "A. Nubber, Private Investigations," right above Nudger's listing. A. Nubber had to be who Gate had mistaken Nudger for. Had to be.

Nudger copied Nubber's address, poured the rest of the coffee down the drain in the office's tiny washroom, then descended the creaking stairs to the street door. He pushed outside into the morning glare and heat, knocked on the donut shop's grease-coated window, and signaled to owner and manager Danny Evers that he was leaving for a while. Danny waved and nodded, then mopped his face with the gray towel he kept tucked in his belt. It was hot in the donut shop, with all that determined baking going on; each Dunker Delite was forged with great effort and sacrifice. It was a shame about the way they tasted.

A. Nubber's office was classier than Nudger's. It was in the Central West End, on the ground floor of a large Victorian house that had been converted to an office building. Nubber had his own private entrance, a colonial-blue door that bore his name on an antique brass plaque.

As Nudger reached for the doorknob the door swung open and a beautiful blonde woman emerged. She was wearing a lightweight blue business suit, but had the jacket slung over her shoulder. Her silky sleeveless blouse revealed shapely tanned arms. She nodded to Nudger and smiled. His stomach and his knees felt it in a big way. Probably she was an A. Nubber client. People like this never came to see Nudger in his office above the donut shop. Where was justice?

Nubber had a classy waiting room. A classy receptionist, who took Nudger's name, spoke into an intercom, then ushered him into a large, high-ceilinged office with a mammoth antique desk beneath a slowly revolving paddle fan. This would impress clients, Nudger thought, and Nubber wouldn't smell like a Dunker Delite and scare them away by seeming low-class and high in cholesterol.

Nubber himself was seated behind the desk, wearing a black-and-white-checkered sport jacket and a yellow tie. He was a smiling, bland-faced man, but with glittering dark eyes that gave him the look of the tiger. He seemed the sort who should be hawking used cars or life insurance rather than working as a private detective. The tennis court-size desk made Nubber look smaller. When he stood up, Nudger saw that he was about his size—just under six feet tall—though a bit on the pudgy side. Well, Nudger was getting a little paunchy himself.

Nubber shook hands with Nudger and said, "What can I do for you, Mr. Nudger?"

"Fill me in on a few things," Nudger said. "I'm not a prospective client; you and I are in the same business, have similar names. I'm A. Nudger. You're"—he looked at the name plaque on the desk—"Abner Nubber."

"What's your 'A' stand for?" Nubber asked.

"Doesn't matter," Nudger said. "Thing is, you're listed above me in the phone directory, and it appears somebody got us mixed up."

"Mixed up?" The cheerful but feral dark eyes became

wary but no less predatory. "Maybe you're mixed up, I'm sure I'm not."

"Mistook me for you." Nudger explained to Nubber what had happened last night at the Merrimont Hotel. While he talked Nubber sat swiveling this way and that in his padded desk chair, listening carefully and tapping a cheekbone with a gold pen.

"I read in the morning paper about that poor guy," he said, when Nudger was finished. "Gates, or Bates was his name. Went right through the net, hit the pavement—splat!" Nubber slapped the desk with his palm. Nudger winced. The stained, bunched blanket on the sidewalk in front of the Merrimont flashed on the screen of his mind. His stomach grumbled.

"Ernest Gate was his name," he said.

"Ah, yeah."

"So what's the connection?" Nudger asked.

"Connection? Why, there is none. I never heard of this guy Ernest Bate."

"Gate."

"Whatever."

Nudger was surprised. This had all seemed so logical. "You positive about that?"

"Sure am," Nubber said. He began to tap on the desk with the pen, holding it as if it were a drumstick and beating out a soft but insistent rhythm. "Never crossed paths with the unfortunate gentleman." His mouth was always smiling even if his eyes were fierce.

"Might you have known him under another name?"

"Nope. His photograph was in the paper. Guy looked like everybody's accountant, but I never met him."

There seemed nothing more to say. Nudger thanked Nubber, who stood up again behind the huge desk, becoming

Nudger-size once more, and smilingly walked Nudger to the door.

"Sorry I couldn't help you, pal," Nubber said. "But we both know how it is. Coincidence is what keeps us working and what makes our jobs so hard."

Nudger hadn't thought of that and wasn't sure if it was true, but he nodded agreement, thanked Nubber again, and went out into the anteroom. A young and attractive couple was seated on the Early American sofa, waiting to see Nubber. The man looked away from Nudger. The woman was engrossed in a glossy fashion magazine. Nubber's red-headed receptionist smiled dazzlingly at Nudger and said, "Something sure smells good."

"Like a donut?"

Her smile widened. "That's it exactly. Wonder what it is."

Nudger told her he had no idea, then went out into the shade of the Victorian front porch. He left it grudgingly and walked across the street to where the Granada sat with its broken air conditioner. Sweat was already zigzagging down his ribs. This was going to be another day on the griddle.

He drove back to his office, checked with Danny, and was told no one had been by. There were no messages on his answering machine. Business as usual. He got the rickety window air conditioner gurgling and humming away, and sat behind his desk, sipping a glass of water and feeling the cool push of air from the plastic grille caress his bare arm.

When the glass was empty and he was reasonably cool, he called Hammersmith at the Third District station.

"Ah," Hammersmith said, "I was gonna call you, Nudge."

Nudger doubted it but said nothing.

"You remember that jumper last night, Ernest Gate?"

"I remember him," Nudger said.

"Well, that address out in Chesterfield is three years old.

His last address, was the state penitentiary in Jefferson City, where he did a stretch for embezzlement. He was released two days ago."

"What about the Visa card you found on him? The issuing bank got an address on Gate?"

"No, he was sent that card in prison, just before his release."

"You said his wallet was new and the address was written on its identification form. Why would he write an address three years old?"

"Only address he could think of, I guess. The guy didn't live in the Jeff City pen anymore. Or at the Merrimont Hotel. He was only there about an hour before somebody spotted him on the ledge."

"What about his family? Where do they live?"

"No known next of kin," Hammersmith said. "Gate was alone in the world."

And left it mad as hell at me, Nudger thought. He couldn't get that off his mind.

"He had a wife before he went into prison," Hammersmith said. "She divorced him just before he began his stretch, never visited him until about six months ago, and she apparently said something that got him in a crazy rage. The guards had to restrain him. Other than that, no visitors except for his lawyer in three years."

"Who was his lawyer?"

Hammersmith was quiet while he apparently studied the file on Ernest Gate. "Guy named Buddy Witherton. I know him; he's still practicing criminal law. Hasn't gotten it right yet."

Nudger said, "How can you not go to prison with a lawyer named Buddy?"

"Well," Hammersmith said, "Gate did go. Just like most

of Witherton's clients. And I better go, myself—back to work."

"I'm gonna call this Witherton—"

But there was a click on the line and Hammersmith was gone, returned to the front in the War on Drugs.

After depressing the cradle button for a dial tone, Nudger phoned Buddy Witherton. He wasn't in his office, but his secretary took Nudger's number. Everybody had a secretary but Nudger.

Half an hour later, Witherton returned Nudger's call from his car phone. Sure, he remembered Ernest Gate. He was sorry to read about Gate's death last night. He'd done what he could in court, but frankly Gate had been guilty as Charles Manson. He'd embezzled twenty-thousand dollars from the catering firm he worked for and used it to finance an illicit romance, but his wife found out about the other woman and everything else, and revealed the embezzlement out of spite during the divorce proceedings. Witherton had represented Gate in the divorce, too. Gate had apparently been the kind of guy who stayed with a winner. Did Witherton remember the wife's name? "Let's see," he said, "Edna or Irma, it was. She lived out in Chesterfield."

Nudger phoned Hammersmith and got the Chesterfield address that was in Ernest Gate's wallet.

The name on the mailbox was Edna Vickers. Nudger figured Gate's wife had gone back to using her maiden name; stigma of prison and all that, and not wanting to be reminded of Ernest while he was rotting away in his cell. Her conscience must be eating her alive. Hell hath no fury, but after the fury died, maybe hell was all that remains for some scorned women.

The woman who came to the door was in her mid-forties,

at least five feet ten inches tall even without her high heels, and wearing a red halter and blue shorts that displayed a fine figure, most of it legs. She was attractive in a gaunt sort of way, with a smooth complexion and large dark eyes. The eyes took a moment to focus on Nudger, and he realized something wasn't quite right about them.

He identified himself and said he'd like to talk to her about her former husband.

"Late former husband," she corrected, slurring the words and filling the air with eau de gin fumes. It was early to be so smashed, but then ex-hubby had died only the night before—this morning, really—and possibly had been extinguished before what was left of the flame of love. "He was a son of a bitch," she said, and Nudger forgot that flame-of-love idea.

"Kind of warm out here on the porch," he said, and she seemed to get flustered about forgetting her manners. She stepped back and invited him in.

The inside of the house was cool, dim, and furnished modern, with lots of angled smoked glass and stainless steel. The leather sling-sofa looked like a torture rack, and the matching chairs looked like futuristic birthing stools. Nudger couldn't imagine being comfortable there.

"Wanna siddown?" Edna Vickers slurred at him.

Well, maybe he should, if he wanted to gain her boozy confidence. He lowered himself into one of the chairs. The leather squeaked like a new pair of boots. Edna Vickers perched her trim little rear on the sofa and crossed her long, long legs. The house was so cool there were goose bumps on her thighs, even where her shorts had worked up to reveal the curve of her buttock. She didn't seem to notice. Nudger did.

"Is Vickers your maiden leg—er, name?" he asked.

"Yep. I ain't gonna call myself Gate, that's for sure. I really hate—or I guess hated—that son of a bitch. Late son of a bitch." She seemed openly pleased by Ernest's new prefix.

"He asked to talk to me before he jumped," Nudger said. "Do you have any idea why?"

"Nope. Ain't talked to the bastard in almost three years. Since right after I caught him going out on me, and he got caught embezzling money to support his other woman."

"I guess that's what caused the divorce, the other woman."

"You betcha. No man plays me for that kinda fool. I nailed him good. Hired a detective and caught him in the act. In flagrante delicto, it's called. I learned that from the legal proceedings, which didn't take long, because I had his hide nailed to the wall in court, what with photographs and everything. You shoulda seen what him and that woman were doing. He never showed that kinda imagination with me."

"Did Ernest write to you from prison?"

"Nope. I told you, we had no contact and I didn't want any. If he eventually realized the mistake he made dumping me, that's tough cheese, the way I figure."

"But prison records indicate you saw him about six months ago, and after your visit he was in an agitated state."

Her gin-blurred eyes suddenly became cunning. "Well, some mistake musta been made, there at the prison. Maybe it was that other woman who visited him. It's been years since I seen Ernest, and the fact he's passed on is no sorrow to me." She stood up, looking very tall and a bit wobbly on her high heels. Nudger wondered if she always wandered around the house in shorts and high heels, or if she'd peeked out the door and seen him and thought she might impress him. He could have that effect on some women.

Taking her rise from the sofa as his signal that the conversation was over, he stood up also, gave her the old sweet smile, though he had to look up at her to do it.

"Whoa, I almost fell down," she mumbled. "Trying to break in these new shoes. Anyways, I said all that needs saying about the late Ernest R. Gate. I don't even wanna think about that scuzzball ever again, and I don't hafta."

"No, you don't," Nudger agreed. From where he stood he could see into the kitchen. An empty gin bottle and a glass sat on a counter near the sink, next to a Mr. Coffee. "Maybe you oughta make yourself some strong coffee, Mrs. Vickers," he suggested.

She looked perplexed. "Why? I ain't gonna drive."

She had him there. He thanked her for taking time to talk with him, then moved toward the door.

"And it's Miss Vickers," she said. "Far as I'm concerned, I never been married to any of the species of man, and I never even met the late and unlamented Ernest R. Gate. That's how I got my memory arranged, and that's how it's gonna stay."

"One thing," Nudger said, his hand on the doorknob. "You mentioned you hired a detective to get evidence against Ernest. Remember his name?"

"I just said it: Ernest R. Gate. The 'R' stands—stood—for Robert."

"I meant the detective's name."

"I'm not sure."

"Was it Abner Nubber?"

"Mighta been." She slumped back down on the creaky leather sofa, looking pale and ill. Her mouth went slack and she swallowed laboriously, her Adam's apple working beneath the smooth flesh of her long neck. "Yeah, Abner Nubber."

"Better think again about that coffee," Nudger told her, then went out into the July suburban heat.

Something was bothering Miss Edna Vickers. Maybe she

still loved Ernest Gate more than she cared to admit to herself. Or maybe something else was causing her to drink and not drive.

Maybe it had something to do with Albert Nubber lying about not knowing her former husband.

Late former husband.

Since Nubber had lied, Nudger figured the next logical step in the investigation would be to watch and follow him. He parked the sweltering Granada in the shade half a block down from Nubber's office. He wasn't too worried about Nubber spotting him; detectives were geared to tail people, but not necessarily to spot a tail.

Nubber stayed in his office most of the day, leaving only for lunch at a restaurant a few blocks away. Only a few people came and went in the big Victorian house. Nudger couldn't be sure if they were there to see Nubber or visit the other tenants. The three women who'd come and gone were remarkably attractive, or maybe Nudger just thought so because he hadn't seen his lady love, Claudia Bettencourt, for almost a week. She'd been following her psychiatrist's advice for her self-actualization and seeing Biff Archway, the volleyball coach and sex-education teacher at the girls' high school where she taught English. Nudger didn't like to think about the two of them together, so maybe it was natural he'd see something special and immediate about these other women.

At five o'clock the classy redheaded receptionist left. Ten minutes later Abner Nubber, who must have had a parking space in back, roared around the corner in a red Corvette convertible. Nudger only got a glimpse of him, but he seemed to be smiling.

The Corvette had no luck with traffic signals, which allowed Nudger to keep the Granada close and watch Nubber pull into the underground parking garage of a modern condominium on Skinker Boulevard.

A little after six o'clock, the Corvette snarled back out of the shadowed mouth of the garage. Nudger gulped down the rest of the Big Mac he'd taken time to buy at a McDonald's drive-through, shoved the Granada into drive, and followed.

Nubber had changed into an expensive-looking cream-colored jacket, white shirt, and mauve tie. At an apartment building on Lindell he parked and went inside, and came out a few minutes later with an elegant dark-haired woman on his arm. Something about her reminded Nudger of Claudia.

Nubber and the woman drove downtown and entered Tony's on Broadway, probably the city's best restaurant. Nudger had never eaten there.

He finished his french fries and chocolate milkshake and waited, watching Tony's entrance.

Nubber and the woman came out at nine o'clock and drove back to her condo. Nudger caught a glimpse of her at one of the windows and got a fix on which unit was hers. The lights stayed low in the condo; maybe she and Nubber were watching television. The Cardinals' game with the Mets was televised tonight; Nudger ordinarily would be home watching it.

He listened to the game on his static-filled car radio, rooting for the Cards to hold on to their one-run lead.

They didn't. They lost three to two after committing an error in the ninth inning. Nudger often lost that way.

He kept an eye on the woman's windows until ten o'clock, when all of the lights went out.

Hating Abner Nubber, really hating him, he drove back to his apartment and tried to get some sleep.

The next morning Nudger missed Nubber at the woman's

apartment but located his car parked behind the Victorian office building. At ten o'clock he followed Nubber to a house in St. Louis Hills, where a heavyset woman with dark bangs answered the door and invited him in.

Fifteen minutes later Nubber left the house and drove to the Branton Hotel downtown, where he met a blonde woman in the cocktail lounge. This Nubber was something with women.

As he stood in the lobby pretending to talk on a pay phone, watching Abner Nubber and the woman at a table near the bar, Nudger realized the woman was the striking blonde he'd seen leaving Nubber's office yesterday as he was entering.

He moved away from the phones and sat out of sight in the plush lobby, where he could watch the lounge entrance.

After about half an hour the blonde woman left the lounge and walked to the elevators. She was the only one who got in the elevator when it arrived.

Nudger watched the floor indicator and saw that the elevator stopped on nine, then started back down.

Oh-oh, he'd almost missed Nubber coming out of the lounge. Nudger followed him outside and back to where the red Corvette was parked at the curb a block away.

Nubber lowered himself into the car, but he didn't drive away, merely sat chain-smoking cigarettes. Nudger found some shade and leaned against a building with his hands in his pockets, playing Mr. Casual, sweating profusely and keeping an eye on Nubber. After the third cigarette, Nubber started the Corvette's engine and Nudger thought he might have to sprint for where he'd parked the Granada. But Nubber only wanted the car running so he could switch on the air conditioner. Nudger stood back and watched, not liking this, thinking even his fingernails were sweating.

Two cigarettes later Abner Nubber climbed out of the

Corvette, stretched languidly, then stooped to get something out of the car. Carrying a large leather overnight case and what looked like a folded black umbrella, he walked back to the Branton. Nudger followed, and wasn't surprised to see Nubber file into an elevator with half a dozen hotel guests. Nudger got in the next elevator that arrived at lobby level and pressed the "9" button.

When the elevator doors opened on nine, a family of a man, wife, and four boisterous preschool kids was waiting to pile in. They almost knocked Nudger over as he wedged out into the hall and looked both ways. Nubber was nowhere in sight. Other than a maid listlessly pushing a linen cart far down the hall, the ninth floor appeared deserted.

Some detective, Nudger thought, and rode the elevator back down to the lobby.

He sat in one of the lobby's soft armchairs, pretending to read a newspaper, like a character in late-night film noir, for almost two hours. Then he saw the blonde woman leave, not with Nubber but with a husky, crewcut man wearing a wrinkled blue business suit without a tie. Hmmm.

This was getting involved. Nudger didn't know who to follow.

He decided to wait for Nubber, who hadn't checked in and would surely be back downstairs soon.

Right. Nubber stepped out of an elevator fifteen minutes later, left the hotel, and drove back to his office.

More waiting, this time in the hot Granada, using a cleverly altered plastic water bottle to relieve himself while he watched Nubber's office. Nudger wiped his forehead with the back of his wrist, looked at Nubber's parked Corvette, looked at the plastic bottle, wondered if he might be in the wrong line of work. He could get a job selling appliances, probably make more money, meet his alimony payments easier. His former wife, Eileen, would like that. Maybe that was why he remained in his strange and sometimes ugly occupation.

Okay, here was Nubber roaring away in the Corvette at 4:30, probably heading for the apartment of the woman he'd stayed with last night. Nudger wondered what Claudia was doing tonight, and where was Biff Archway, as he gunned the old Granada and barely managed to keep the sleek red trunk of Nubber's car in sight.

That was when things began to shape up. Nubber drove back to St. Louis Hills and turned on the block where he'd visited the heavyset woman with the dark bangs. Only this time he didn't stop the car. The red Corvette slowed momentarily near the house, then its rear end dropped low and it accelerated down the street and around the comer.

A man was in the woman's front yard, cutting the lawn with a power mower. He was short, muscular, had a close haircut, and Nudger was sure he was the man who'd left the Branton Hotel with the blonde woman.

Nudger drove around the corner but didn't bother trying to keep up with Nubber. Instead he pulled the Granada to the curb and sat for a while letting his brain idle with the engine.

After about five minutes, he said, "I'll be damned," and drove away. He wanted to talk one more time with Edna Vickers, be she drunk or sober.

She was home. At first she stood motionless in the doorway squinting at Nudger, as if he were some gift of the cat and she couldn't quite place what she was looking at. Then she recognized him. "You again." She sounded disappointed. Not as if she'd been expecting someone else, though, just disappointed. She seemed sober enough this time and was wearing form-hugging red slacks and a white blouse pulled tight at the waist. Still had on her high heels, which made her seem to loom over Nudger. "Didn't know you at first," she said.

Nudger shrugged. "I've got one of those faces."

"Wouldn't have remembered you at all except for that funny cologne."

"Cologne?"

"Smells like dough and sugar baking."

"Oh. Mind if I come in? I need to ask you a few more questions. Won't take long."

"About Ernest?"

He nodded.

"Then the answer's no." She started to close the door.

"It'll be me or the police," Nudger said.

"I got nothing to fear from the police."

"Maybe not, but it's a maybe. Nothing to lose by talking to me."

"You offering me some kinda deal?"

"Why? Do you need a deal?"

"Nope. I haven't done a thing illegal. I know because I checked with my attorney."

Nudger said, "Your attorney didn't steer you wrong. So why not talk to me? I'm definitely more pleasant than the cops."

She gnawed her lip, glaring down at him. She'd probably been stunningly attractive five years and a lot of bottles ago. "Oh, all right, but let's get it over with in a hurry. I got someplace to go."

He followed her inside and sat down on the creaking leather sofa. She remained standing, towering as a pro basketball player, ready to block his best shots.

"I've got it figured out," he said, driving toward the basket.

"What? Today's crossword puzzle?" She fancied herself

cute when she was sober.

"The puzzle about how you got the evidence on your husband that enabled you to divorce him on your terms. Ernest had an affair, Abner Nubber provided you with proof—probably videotapes—and also told you about your husband's embezzlement from his employer."

"Nothing illegal there on my part. And it was photographs, not videotape."

"Except that you paid Nubber to arrange the affair so you could get the evidence. That's what Nubber does, has charismatic employees who seduce the spouses of his clients and set up the right odds in divorce cases. Very ingenious."

"And provides him a good living, I'm sure, considering the rates he charges. But I guess business is business."

"Some kinda business he's in."

"It fills a need."

"For a lotta people," Nudger had to agree.

She paced, then wheeled and stared down with open distaste at him. "The thing is, nobody forced Ernest to go to bed with that woman!"

"But he got a lot of expert coaxing. You probably even provided Nubber with information to make it easier for his female employee to seduce poor Ernest. What about the woman? Who was she?"

"Some blonde pro. What's the difference who she was? It was part of the deal that she disappear after the photos were taken. Nobody, not even Ernest's lawyers, were ever able to find her, but the photographs were proof enough Ernest had been unfaithful. Even kinky unfaithful. The fact he didn't so much as know the woman's real name or address just made it look all the worse for him. I could never catch the little weasel cheating on me any other way, so I did it this way. Fair's fair, I say."

Nudger said, "I'd call it entrapment."

"Call it what you will. I didn't intend to send the poor schmuck to prison, but there was no way to clue the law in on the affair with the blonde without revealing the embezzlement to the police—so tough cheese."

Nudger stood up. "You're a hard woman."

She smiled. "Better believe it. And a smart one. I wouldn't be telling you any of this if the law could touch me."

"Your lawyer must have mentioned that the law can touch Abner Nubber."

"Tough cheese there, too. Nubber can just figure that as part of the cost of doing business. He supplies male and female heartbreakers to seduce unfaithful spouses, then he provides proof and favorable conditions for divorce, he has to know he's running a risk. That's why he gets paid so much and has a swank office and drives around in a nifty car. You're a private investigator, you got an office and car like that?"

Nudger had to get out of there. He'd had enough of Edna Vickers. Ernest Gate might be better off.

He told her he didn't have an office or car like Abner Nubber's. Pointed out that he didn't have a future like Nubber's, either. Then he told her goodbye and went to the door. She didn't move except to prop her fists on her hips and stand there like a female colossus.

"You gonna tell the cops about this?" she asked.

"Sure."

"Make it a point to also tell them Ernest was a son of a bitch."

"*Late* son of a bitch," Nudger said, and went out the door. He could sense her edging toward the phone behind him.

Abner Nubber's redheaded receptionist said Nubber had left the city on urgent business. But when Hammersmith and a couple of uniforms arrived, she soon buckled and revealed the name of the hotel he'd fled to where he could hole up after Edna Vickers had called him. It was the Emporium, a sleazy near flophouse down by the river. Nubber was seeking his level.

Hammersmith was a homicide cop and was there only because of his previous involvement and his friendship with Nudger, so they waited for a lieutenant named Giardello from the bunko squad to arrive at the hotel before going inside.

A one-eyed desk clerk stared wildly at Hammersmith's badge and said there was no one named Nubber registered but that someone who looked like the man Nudger described had checked in a little over an hour ago and was in Room 815. Uniforms were posted in the lobby and at the base of the fire stairs, and Lieutenant Giardello led the way into the clanking and thrumming elevator that carried them to the eighth floor.

The knock on the door of 815 wasn't answered, but the faintest of sounds came from inside the room. A slight scraping of wood on wood.

Hammersmith knew what it was an instant before anyone else, and he raised a tree-trunk leg and smashed his foot into the door with all his weight behind it.

The doorjamb splintered and the door crashed and caromed off the wall so hard it nearly closed again. But Hammersmith and Giardello almost made the doorway wider rushing inside. Nudger and the uniform they'd brought with them followed.

Almost in time.

Nubber's pants leg and shoe disappeared outside as he scampered out the window he'd just forced wide open.

At first Nudger thought he was trying to get down the fire escape, but there was no outside fire escape.

Nudger was ahead of everyone else getting to the window, and when he looked outside, there was Nubber poised on the ledge exactly the way Ernest Gate had been three days ago. The same desperate backward lean against the safe solidity of the wall, and the same something dreadful and magnetic that seemed to contaminate reason and pull toward space and death.

Nubber was staring at Nudger as if now they belonged to two different worlds, and maybe they really were close to that status. The breeze was playing over Nubber, plucking at his clothes as if trying to coax him off the ledge; come out and play, flying's so much fun.

"It's over," Nudger said. "Don't make things worse for yourself. Get in here. Please!" he added. God, he didn't want to see it again, Ernest Gate making like a featherless bird too soon out of the nest. Ernest Gate plummeting like a stone to challenge the pavement with soft flesh and brittle bone. Nudger looked down. The foreshortened people that had gathered and were staring up, the downscaled cars, the tops of streetlights, all of it started to spin and he leaned forward, forward . . .

A hand clutched his belt and yanked him safely back into the room.

Hammersmith.

"Lemme talk to the asshole, Nudge."

He leaned his great bulk out the window and stared angrily over at Nubber. "You ain't gonna jump, 'cause you're too smart. Think this situation through. You get a good lawyer, you might walk away acquitted of a fraud charge. You get a bad lawyer, you'll probably do at most two years of a five-year stretch. Not nearly as long a time as what you're thinking about. So walk yourself back in here, Nubber, or else step off, but don't waste our time. You ain't worth it."

Hammersmith moved back away from the window and exchanged glances with Giardello.

They waited.

After about a minute a gray cuff and a black shoe appeared on the ledge, and Nubber clumsily backed himself into the room, falling onto the threadbare carpet and scrambling to his feet. The uniform had him immediately and cuffed his hands behind his back. Giardello read him his rights.

"That the truth?" Nudger asked Hammersmith. "About him only doing a few years at most?"

Hammersmith looked grim. " 'Fraid so, Nudge. He's a businessman who went too far, that's all. These days, even the federal government does the kinda thing Nubber'll plead guilty to."

Where was justice? Nudger wondered, watching Abner Nubber being led away, thinking about Ernest Gate and the man mowing the lawn in St. Louis Hills. About the many other men and women who might not have dreamed of being unfaithful to their spouses, except for the amorality and entrepreneurship of Abner Nubber, and temptation too professional and potent to be resisted. Where was justice? And where would it be when Nubber was set free?

As they wrestled Nubber out the door he glanced back at Nudger.

He was smiling, his eyes fierce as a tiger's.

The Litigants

Nudger thought there was no good reason why Lawrence Fleck should be alive. The pugnacious little attorney in the cheap chalk-stripe black suit, and the surrounding aroma of cut-rate, cloying cologne stood with his fists on his hips in front of Nudger's desk and glared down at him.

When Nudger merely stared back, Fleck picked up his coat from where he'd tossed it on a chair, brushed it off, then folded it, and laid it over the chair's arm, where it might stay cleaner. It was made of some kind of mottled, curly fur Nudger had never seen before. Fleck glanced around and scrunched up his bulldog face as if he'd just inhaled a bug. "You got an office looks like a rat hole, Nudger."

"Now that you walked in."

Fleck snorted contemptuously in his best courtroom manner—his only courtroom manner. "We got business to discuss. I'm here to hire you."

"I don't work for ambulance chasers."

"You're listening but you're not hearing, Nudger. Just like always. I said the word hire. That means the word money. Exactly what losers like you need."

Hmm. Nudger knew Fleck was right about that last part. Nudger's former wife, Eileen, had joined a militant feminist group called WOO—Women on the Offensive—whose pro bono lawyer was planning on dragging Nudger back into court to attach damages onto his alimony payments. Eileen and her attorney were claiming that Nudger was responsible

244

for the marriage's failure, which deprived Eileen of children in her prime fertile years, for which deprivation Nudger should pay compensation. Sort of nonchild-support payments. The attorney, a truly frightening woman named Shirley Knott, was attempting to make history with this test case by establishing legal precedent. Important new ground might be broken. She'd chosen Nudger for her plow.

"Money up front?" Nudger asked.

"A little way back," Fleck said with a shrug. "There's a big settlement waiting to happen in this case, and when I get my money you'll get yours."

"I can't eat pie in the sky," Nudger said. "But maybe we can barter. Trade services."

Fleck looked suspicious, dishonest, tempted. "We wouldn't have to claim income on our tax returns . . ." he said thoughtfully.

"It'd be a wash anyway," Nudger pointed out, "but it would still be fun not to claim it. Tell me why you want to hire me, then I'll tell you about someone named Shirley Knott. I think you two should meet."

"Here's the deal," Fleck said, pacing with short, lurching strides and flailing his arms for emphasis as he talked. "Client named Arty Mason comes to me, says a woman ran into his old Chevy. She's driving a Mercedes, barely gets scratched. Just about totals Arty's car, he says."

"What do you mean, 'he says'? Have you seen the car, the estimates for repairs?"

"All that stuff," Fleck said with a backhanded wave of dismissal. "There are some questions from the insurance company as to how old a lot of the damages are, but that's insignificant. In fact, the whole accident might be insignificant, because Arty tells me the collider came to him and offered to pay fifteen hundred to him, leave the insurance companies and any sort of police accident report out of it."

"Collider?"

"Legal term, Nudger. She ran into him. Collider's this bit of eye candy named Nora Bosca."

" 'Eye Candy' is a legal term, too, I guess. Nora Bosca was driving the other car?"

"What I said. You were listening but not hearing again, Nudger. I advised my client not to accept the collider's offer. Know why?"

"Sure. She was a wealthy woman who might have something to hide. So you and this Arty might be able to extort money from her."

Fleck backed away as if slapped and glared down at Nudger with nostrils flared. "That's an insult to me and my profession, and coming from a cheap keyhole peeper."

"Did it work?"

"Yes. She came across with five thousand. Arty said no to that, too, so she gave him ten thousand. Plenty angry about it, though. I don't think we could have gotten any more."

"Seems like the end of the case," Nudger said.

"It was, until Arty's back started acting up because of the accident. A week ago we filed against Nora Bosca for medical expenses."

"I'm not surprised. You got greedy and figured out a way to go back for seconds."

"Don't be so judgmental, Nudger. I'm sworn to get all I can for my client. And you oughta see poor Arty. He can barely get around. Wears a brace."

When someone's looking, Nudger thought.

"But you're right," Fleck said. "I figured the rich babe'd come around with more money, ask us to drop the charges. But she hasn't, and we haven't heard from her attorney." Fleck scratched his head, moving his bargain toupee another half inch toward his right ear. "What I got is guys watching me, I think. Following me."

"You think?"

"It's just an inkling, I admit. But Arty called me yesterday. He's got the same inkling. I—we figured it'd be smart to hire somebody to look into this, see what's happening."

"See if that somebody gets beaten to a pulp or killed," Nudger said, "so you'd know for sure something serious is going on."

"It could occur like that," Fleck admitted. "Are those pigeons over there on that ledge?" He was staring out the window at the building across the street.

Fleck knew he hated pigeons and was trying to divert the conversation away from personal injury at the hands of thugs unknown. "I'd rather not be hurt or killed," Nudger said.

"Goes without saying. How come they don't fly south in the winter like other birds? You'd think something smart as a pigeon would know to do that."

Nudger considered calling off the deal. Then he thought about Eileen. About Shirley Knott. He shuddered. Both women were natural colliders.

"I'm supposed to give a deposition tomorrow," he said to Fleck. "You're coming with me."

At three the next afternoon, Nudger and Fleck sat side by side at a large mahogany table in a legal office across the street from the country courthouse. On the walls were framed photographs of Old West scenes. Some of them were shots of public hangings.

"They rent these rooms for depositions," Fleck whispered knowledgeably to Nudger.

A court stenographer was seated at the end of the table. The door opened and the despicable Henry Mercado,

Eileen's divorce lawyer and live-in lover, entered with Shirley Knott. Mercado nodded and smiled. Even Nudger knew he was there not just as a witness but to shake Nudger's confidence.

Shirley Knott was a small, erect woman in a severely tailored purple suit. She was wearing a white blouse with a man's tie that had on it what to Nudger looked like a design of tiny swastikas. Her black hair was combed in a high arc above a wide forehead and piercing dark eyes. Her features were harsh and symmetrical, with bloodless, thin lips set in a straight, thin fine. Had those lips ever kissed or smiled?

She sat down across from Fleck and said, "You bastard! Is that real fur?"

Fleck looked down at his cheap, mottled coat draped over the chair near him. "Of course not. I'd only wear synthetic fur. I'm a recovering hunter."

Pretty nifty, Nudger thought. Fleck did have a survivor's quick instincts.

Formality took over. All present gave names and addresses to the court stenographer, and the deposition began.

"Remember you're under oath," Shirley Knott told Nudger. "Any of your lies will come back to haunt you."

Nudger looked over at Fleck.

"She's right," Fleck said.

"You were the one in the marriage who didn't want children, Mr. Nudger?"

"It was a joint decision. I was a cop and I—"

"So that's why you alone decided?"

"No! We agreed to wait."

"And there was a period of . . . dysfunction on your part?"

Nudger glanced at the court stenographer, a prim woman in her sixties. She was staring silently over the rims of her glasses at him. "Temporary. Only temporary. I was distressed because of a shooting incident. I've hated guns ever since."

"Sometimes a gun isn't a gun, Mr. Nudger. Don't you agree?"

Nudger looked at Fleck. "What does she mean?"

"Technically, anything with grooves inside the barrel isn't a gun. Legal terminology, splitting hairs. I object to the question."

"*You* are irrelevant," Shirley Knott told Nudger's attorney.

The deposition went downhill then.

Still trembling with anger and humiliation from both the deposition and his argument with Fleck afterward in the parking lot, Nudger drove across to talk with the aggrieved and litigious Arty Mason.

Mason opened the door to his low-rent apartment and ushered Nudger in. He was a wizened little guy about fifty, wearing wrinkled blue pajamas. On his feet were gray fuzzy slippers that were supposed to look like rabbits, only the head was missing from the one on his right foot. He was moving with difficulty because of some kind of aluminum brace attached to his back. Nudger was suspicious of the brace. It was held together with adhesive tape and looked like something made from parts of a disassembled walker. It was, in fact, the only back brace Nudger had ever seen that had a wheel.

"How's the back?" Nudger asked, watching Mason lower himself sideways into a chair.

"Pure agony," he said, wincing with pain. "I gotta lie flat or wear this thing." Nudger could see beyond him into the bedroom. The bed was made, and unruffled.

Mason answered all Nudger's questions politely and through a grimace, pretty much substantiating what Fleck had said about the accident.

"What makes you think you and Fleck are being watched?" Nudger asked, folding the sheet of paper he was taking notes on and slipping it into his pocket.

Mason looked undeniably afraid. "Listen, Nudger, I used to work for a guy who ran a gambling joint, before the state horned in on the business. I know when I got the orange mark on me."

"Orange mark?"

"Like on a tree when it's scheduled to be chopped down."

Nudger swallowed. He'd never heard that one. "You think somebody's going to try to kill you?"

Mason nodded. "I know the signs. Somebody's tailing me, watching, sizing up the best place and time to act. Believe me, I know exactly how it's done."

Nudger stared at him. "Do you know about this because you've done the same thing yourself?"

"I done lots of things in my misguided youth," Mason said noncommittally.

Good Lord! Nudger thought. What has Fleck got me into?

He couldn't help checking his rearview mirror every few seconds as he drove away from his meeting with Mason.

On Grand Avenue he stopped at White Castle and bought some of their little square hamburgers in a take-out sack, then went to Claudia's South Side apartment. Over an aromatic lunch of hamburgers, French fries, and an old bottle of refrigerated wine Nudger had uncapped, he discussed the case with Claudia. She loved him. She would understand and perhaps offer some advice.

When he was finished talking she said, "There might be something to this nonchild-support idea."

"I was thinking, is somebody going to try to kill me over this?" Nudger said.

Claudia slowly tore a corner of bun off her last hamburger,

then poked it in her mouth and chewed thoughtfully. "The ticking biological clock . . ."

"Just because lots of divorced women say they wasted the best years of their lives on their ex-husbands doesn't mean they're owed money," Nudger said.

"What do I have to show for it?"

"Huh?"

"That's the rest of what women say about those wasted years, the question they ask. Especially if they don't even have children. Maybe they *should* be compensated for all that lost time, have something to show for it. I don't see why the ability to bear children couldn't be viewed legally as a diminishing asset."

Nudger was getting frustrated. There was a disconnect here. "Right now I'm thinking I could have the orange mark on me. I might have to defend myself at some point. I'm wondering if I should go to the safety deposit box and get my gun."

"They wouldn't necessarily need to have been married," Claudia said.

My God! Nudger thought. He took a swig of wine. Years ago he'd saved Claudia from suicide. She was emotionally delicate and might go to see her psychiatrist, Dr. Oliver. As far as Nudger was concerned, Dr. Oliver caused more problems than he solved. From time to time he advised Claudia to see men other than Nudger in order to achieve self-actualization. Nudger wasn't sure what self-actualization was. He thought Claudia was actual. He should never have told her about Shirley Knott and WOO. Fleck should never have told him about Arty Mason and the collider. But Nudger had. Fleck had. Nudger was knee-deep in it.

Maybe sinking.

The next morning Nudger decided to follow Nora Bosca.

He sat parked in his old Ford Granada where he could watch the luxury condo on Hanley Road that matched the address Fleck had given him. His assumption was that eventually the Mercedes would exit the underground garage.

A woman emerged from the building and strode to a nearby parking lot. She was eye candy even if she wasn't Nora Bosca, tall, mink-coated and blonde, with a model's way of walking that drew stares.

And she was Nora Bosca. A few minutes after she'd disappeared, a late-model black Mercedes with her license number turned north from the lot onto Hanley. The big car's right front fender was dented, but not badly. It hadn't taken much to total Mason's old Chevy.

Nudger started the Granada and chugged along behind the gliding Mercedes in heavy traffic.

Nora Bosca didn't drive far, only to the Flam Building on Meramec Avenue, which Nudger knew housed a million lawyers, all of them more expensive and effective than Lawrence Fleck.

He trailed along behind her when she entered the building; then he rode the elevator with her and three other women to the fifth floor. Nudger stepped out of the elevator when Nora Bosca did. He walked fifteen paces, pretended to have forgotten something, and turned around just in time to see her enter the offices of Gird and Gird, Attorneys at Law.

Nudger went back to his car and waited. It had become colder and the sky was spitting a combination of snow and sleet. The Granada's heater was keeping the interior warm, but the windshield kept fogging up on the inside where the wipers couldn't help.

If Nora Bosca came out of the Flam Building within the next two hours Nudger missed seeing her. The gas gauge was almost on empty now, and he was getting drowsy. Exhaust leaks were a worry in the old car. He decided to give up on tailing Nora Bosca, at least for today and drove to his office.

Before going upstairs, he ducked into Danny's Donuts, which was located directly below his office, and asked his ersatz receptionist Danny if anybody had been by to see him.

Danny, who was wearing a greasy white apron and his usual basset hound expression, was alone in the shop, standing behind the stainless steel counter and reading a newspaper. The place smelled cloyingly of baked sugar, as did Nudger's office, as did Nudger. Sometimes women thought he was wearing cologne and were repelled.

"Big guy looked something like a horse," Danny said, "wearing an expensive suit. 'Bout an hour ago. Didn't leave his name. Didn't have to."

"Why's that? You recognize him?"

"Recognized him as trouble, Nudge. You best be careful."

"Did he leave a message?"

"Said he'd be back is all."

"Anything else about him?"

"Breathed through his mouth instead of his nose. That kinda guy. That kinda nose." Danny's gaze slid to the fresh-baked lineup of Dunker Delites lying like feces on white butcher paper in the display case. "You had lunch?"

"Sure did," Nudger said, moving toward the door. "Thanks anyway."

"You best be careful, Nudge," Danny repeated, and went back to reading the sports pages spread out on the counter before him.

Nudger chewed an antacid tablet as he entered through the street door next to the doughnut shop and climbed the creaking wood stairs to his office. The higher he climbed the warmer he got, until he entered the office, which was cold. The radiator was malfunctioning again.

He kicked the old iron radiator, then swivelled its valve handle. It hissed angrily at him. Leaving his coat on, he sat at his desk, slid the phone over to him, and called Police Lieutenant Jack Hammersmith at the Third District station house. Hammersmith had been Nudger's partner years ago when they were uniformed officers in the St. Louis Police Department. That was before Nudger's nervous stomach and fear of guns had proved to be career obstacles and led to his present occupation.

"I need a favor, Jack," Nudger said when finally he was put through to Hammersmith.

"Couple of hundred," Hammersmith said.

"I don't need money, Jack."

"I didn't mean money. I meant that when you ask for a favor, you always wind up asking for a couple of hundred more of them."

"I want to give you a woman's name. Also her car's license number. I'd like to know more about her. She was involved in a simple fender bender and offered to settle out of court with Lawrence Fleck's client rather than draw attention from the police or courts."

"Fleck the lawyer? Why do you keep getting mixed up with that little ferret?"

"So I don't have to borrow money from you, Jack."

"Hmm. Give me the details."

Nudger did.

"I can tell you a lot without even checking," Hammersmith said when Nudger was finished. "Gird and Gird is a mob-connected law firm. Nora Bosca is the widow of Manny Boscanarro."

Nudger gripped the receiver harder and sat back in his desk chair. The old radiator was hissing and clanking loudly now as if laughing uproariously at him, hurling heat into the room. He unbuttoned his coat. "Manny Boscanarro the drug czar?"

"The same, Nudge."

Six months ago Boscanarro's body had been found stuffed in a trash can, minus arms and legs. It took a while to identify him. Plastic surgery had been attempted and botched. He still looked enough like his old self for a rival drug cartel to recognize him and kill him. And for narcotics detectives and his wife, Nora, to identify him. The killer or killers were still at large.

"The widow didn't seem too broke up over his death," Hammersmith said. "Just enough sentimentality to ask for the expensive gold chain and engraved heart the corpse was wearing as a necklace."

"That could explain the guy who looked like a horse . . ."

"Don't know who he'd be," Hammersmith said, "but I'd bet he's dangerous."

"Speaking of dangerous," Nudger said, "you ever heard of WOO?"

"Who?"

"WOO."

"Haven't a clue. He a Chinese gangster or something?"

"Never mind," Nudger said.

"I do know Fleck might not be dealing straight with you. If you're mixed up with Nora Bosca and Fleck, be extra careful."

Nudger swallowed an antacid tablet almost whole. "I always am."

"Sometimes to the point of paralysis," Hammersmith said, and hung up the phone.

Nudger kept the receiver to his ear, depressed the phone's cradle button, then called Fleck and filled him in on the day's activities.

"Don't believe everything Hammersmith tells you," Fleck said. "He's a cop; they got their own agenda."

"There's something in your voice. You sound scared."

"I am. So should you be, Nudger. It's unhealthy to be involved with drug criminals or their widows. But it could explain why Arty and I are being watched. Somebody probably wonders why the grieving widow's seeing a lawyer. I'm gonna call Arty and tell him we better drop the case."

"Count me out, too."

"Hah! You can't quit. You owe me, my friend. Remember, we're bartering here. I need to know for sure. I want you to find out exactly who's on my tail. Just like we agreed. Don't you recall me representing you during that deposition?"

"I recall you were in the room," Nudger said.

"Well, I got some other info for you. Listen and hear, Nudger. I met with Shirley Knott and found out Eileen's been examined by a doctor who's willing to testify she's forty percent fertile."

"Forty percent what? I don't understand."

"She's medically certified to be sixty percent less capable of achieving pregnancy than when she was married to you. The other side's got itself an expert witness."

"What's all that mean?" Nudger asked, befuddled.

"Means a whole lot of nonchild support, my friend."

Nudger sank lower into his chair. He was sweating, full of woe, cursing WOO. "I already pay alimony," he said numbly. "Why should I have to pay for children? We never even had any children."

"That's precisely the point. Didn't you hear, Nudger?"

Nudger wanted to kill Fleck.

"We still bartering, Nudger?"

"Still are," Nudger said wearily. "Have you noticed a guy hanging around who looks something like a horse?"

"What kind of horse?"

"Dammit! What difference does it make?"

"Well, a thoroughbred would be a tall, lean guy. A quarter horse or Shetland pony—"

"A big, mean horse!" Nudger said.

"No," Fleck said thoughtfully. "I noticed a guy you might say looked a lot like an ox."

"Are you insane?"

"No, and I'm a better lawyer than you think, Nudger. You'll see. I'm going to help you. But you've gotta keep working hard for me or—"

Nudger slammed down the receiver.

He fled from the sweatbox office and drove down Manchester to Citizen's Bank, where he reluctantly withdrew his old service revolver from his safety deposit box.

After a late breakfast the next day he decided to drive to Fleck's office and looked the Napoleonic little lawyer in the eye when they talked about Arty Mason's suit against Nora Bosca, and about Eileen's claim for nonchild support.

Fleck's office was in a small strip shopping center. It was sandwiched between a dollar store and a place called Hot Plants, which sold indoor and outdoor decorative plastic foliage.

Nudger had parked and was about to get out of the Granada when he saw Fleck and Shirley Knott emerge from Fleck's office. Fleck was wearing an obviously vinyl jacket today. Shirley was bundled in blue denim with studs all over it. Nudger watched them walk together to a restaurant at the far end of the shopping strip. Fleck politely held the door open for Shirley Knott. They were probably going to have their idea of a power breakfast. Probably going to talk about Nudger. The prospect nauseated him so that he climbed back

257

into his car. He sat for a while, sucking but not chewing an antacid tablet until the sizable chalky disk was completely dissolved. It brought some relief, though not much.

The notion of joining two of the most contemptible people he'd ever met was out of the question. Who Nudger wanted to see was Claudia. Maybe he could meet her somewhere for coffee and they could talk. Maybe they could go to her apartment afterward.

When he called from a public phone just inside the entrance of a supermarket, she was cool to his invitation.

"Is something wrong?" Nudger asked.

"*Very* wrong. I don't think we should see each other for awhile, Nudger."

His stomach seemed to be devouring his other organs. This was pain. "Have you gone back to Dr. Oliver?"

"Far from it. I've begun to realize he's the one who's caused most of my problems. His advice to see other men so I might attain self-actualization, the sedatives that dulled my senses, the long sessions that went nowhere productive . . ."

Nudger was heartened.

"I sought other advice and I've decided to sue Dr. Oliver," Claudia said firmly.

Nudger was shocked. "He's an established medical professional, Claudia. He has malpractice insurance, squads of lawyers. You can't afford to sue Oliver."

"I have help, Nudger. I've joined WOO."

"We need to talk."

"We shouldn't, under the circumstances. It would be legally unwise for both of us."

"Claudia—"

"I'm sorry, Nudger, but I have to learn who I am to be who I am. I'm confident I'll find I'm a better person, one who I know I can be."

"What on earth does that mean? I know who you are. You're the woman who likes—"

She hung up.

He stood traumatized. He turned right. He turned left. He didn't know where to turn next. Finally he decided to seek solace in his work. He'd stake out the condo and follow Nora Bosca again. He would be doing his job, holding up his end of his agreement with Fleck. This was what it had come down to. This was all he had. Driven by obligation and dismay, he got his legs moving so he was lurching toward the automatic doors, dodging grocery carts and cursing his stars.

The big Mercedes with the dented fender nosed like a prowling shark out of the underground garage this time. Nudger thought Nora Bosca was going to take the same route today and visit her attorney. Instead she turned left, on Delmar, then took the Inner Belt north. Nudger swiped at the Granada's windshield with one of his old undershirts that he used as a rag, aiding the defrosters as he stayed behind the Mercedes in heavy traffic.

The sleek black car exited on Natural Bridge, then turned down a side street and pulled into the parking lot of a small motel near the airport. Nudger parked near the entrance and watched the Mercedes drive to the far end of the lot and stop almost out of sight next to a large dented green Dumpster. He felt like the cheap peeper. Fleck had called him, aware that his metabolism had picked up. Something was happening here, all right. And some part of him was enjoying it.

Large snowflakes started to fall, obscuring his vision. Also Nora Bosca's. Nudger got out of his car and unobtrusively walked parallel to the front of the motel, staying away from the office. Then he moved along a row of parked cars until he was out of sight of the Mercedes. He crouched behind a red pickup truck.

Nora Bosca had gotten out of her car. She strode into Nudger's line of sight, kicking out with her long legs and fur-topped boots, glancing around furtively. Nudger ducked low and watched over the truck's hood. The door, opened as she arrived. She didn't even have to break stride before she was inside the room and out of sight.

But Nudger had seen enough.

He drove to a phone and called Hammersmith, then returned to the motel through the driving snow.

There were so many red lights blinking there it looked like the place was on fire.

The county police wouldn't let him get close until Hammersmith arrived, sirens screaming, in the first of two Major Case Squad units. He nodded to Nudger and they walked toward the motel room Nora Bosca had entered. Its door was wide open and people were packed into the room. Thick uniform coats made everyone look bulky and immovable. When Nudger and Hammersmith were five feet from the door, they were stopped by a big man in a blue parka who flashed a badge and said he was Captain Farmington of the county police and he was in charge. The corpulent Hammersmith, bulkiest of the bulky in his tentlike camel-hair coat, puffed up even larger and said this was a Major Case Squad investigation and he was the officer in charge. Two deadpan guys in identical tan trench coats arrived and said they were FBI and they were in charge. There was a lot of arguing and shoving, and it seemed somebody from all three units took part in hustling Manny Boscanarro and his wife, Nora, to a waiting unmarked Pontiac with tinted windows and a stubby antenna on its trunk. They were the only ones without coats.

★ ★ ★ ★ ★

"But Boscanarro was found dead!" Fleck said incredulously.

They were in Nudger's office. The radiator was working okay for a change, and the winter sun was brilliant through the half-melted sheet of ice on the window. "You're listening but you're not hearing," Nudger told Fleck. "The plastic surgery on the dead man in the trash barrel wasn't actually botched. It was made to seem that way, done on some poor guy who resembled Manny Boscanarro enough that he'd pass for him with a botched face-lift. Since the victim's arms had been cut off there were no fingerprints. And Boscanarro had no dental records in this country. Six people identified the body, even his wife. And she claimed a gold necklace with their names engraved on it."

Fleck started to pace, grinning and flailing his pudgy little arms. "Well, I'll be flamboozled!"

"Wouldn't be the first time," Nudger said.

"Our barter deal worked out just fine!" he said.

"For you," Nudger told him.

"You too, my friend!" Fleck said triumphantly. "Shirley has advised Eileen to drop the nonchild-support case."

Nudger was astounded. "*Shirley Knott* did that?"

Fleck actually looked embarrassed. "I persuaded her. Or we persuaded each other. We've uh, become close. Neither of us planned on it, but it happened."

There truly is someone for everyone, Nudger thought. Wolf and gray wolf.

"What about WOO?" he asked. "What about making legal history?"

"Shirley and I are preparing to press another historic case, this time in the field of animal rights."

"Animals?"

261

"Primates, specifically."

"Primates don't have legal rights."

"You are a primate, Nudger."

That gave Nudger pause.

"The Constitution refers to men only," Fleck continued, "but obviously women are also meant to enjoy its rights and protections. Who's to say that women are the only primates excluded by the literal language? It's the kind of legal technicality that might change the world."

"Which particular primates are your clients?"

"The ones in the Primate House at the zoo. Shirley—and I—think three of the chimpanzees have occupied the premises long enough to claim squatter's rights by law."

Nudger was momentarily dizzy. "You can't claim the chimpanzees own the building!"

"Possession is nine points of the—"

"Get out!" Nudger screamed. "Get out!" Then, calmer "No, wait."

Fleck paused at the door and cocked his head in the opposite direction that his cheap toupee was tilted. He was looking at Nudger with an uncharacteristic injured expression on his puggy little features. "What?"

"Thanks."

"You too," Fleck said. "I'll send my bill." And he was out the door and gone.

Nudger sat with his face cupped in his hands, trying to fathom it all. He heard the door open and close and knew Fleck had returned.

But when he peeked through his fingers he saw that it wasn't Fleck.

It was an enormous man in a neat brown suit. He was breathing through his mouth and had a long, narrow face with a bent nose and wide-set eyes that made him look like a horse.

"You're Nudger," he said, and proffered a giant hand.

Instinctively Nudger shook it and his own hand was mashed painfully before it was released.

The horselike man sat down. Nudger wondered which breed Fleck would choose to categorize him. Clydesdale, maybe. He stared at Nudger in a way that was unnerving. Nudger unobtrusively opened his top desk drawer and slid his throbbing hand inside, toward the gun that rested there.

"My name's Clyde Davis, Mr. Nudger. Can you guess why I'm here?"

Nudger's heart was hammering, his stomach writhing. "Because of Manny Boscanarro?"

Clyde Davis looked puzzled, crossed his legs, and smiled in a way somehow more bovine than equine. "I don't know anyone by that name. I'm here because you've been harassed. We've learned that an accusation against you was recently withdrawn, but not until after you suffered monetary loss and great emotional stress in a frivolous lawsuit that made mockery and misuse of the courts. You deserve compensation, Mr. Nudger."

Nudger stayed his hand over the gun. "*We've* learned? You're from a law firm?"

"No, Mr. Nudger, but I'm here to help guide you through future litigation as you press your case. I'm from MOO."

Nudger began to withdraw his hand from the drawer but found that he couldn't.

He just couldn't.

He sat staring at the man from MOO.

His hand hovered over the gun.

The Man in the Morgue

It was a big house, with enough gables, dormers, and cupolas to resemble a maniac's chessboard. I smoothly braked and curbed my beige Volkswagen Beetle in the semicircular driveway, conscious of the car's faded paint and character-forming dents in contrast to the symmetrically bricked and shrubbed entranceway to the house. The engine turned over a few times after I'd killed the ignition.

I half expected a butler to answer my ring. Instead, a large cop in a sweat-stained blue uniform opened the door and stared at me. He was about fifty with shrewd gray eyes, a shaggy gray moustache that turned down at the corners, a bulging stomach that dictated he shop in the big men's department.

"Mr. Aloysius Nudger to see Mrs. Emily Stein," I told him.

"If you had a hat and coat," he said, "I could take them from you and hang them up." He stepped back so I could enter. "She's expecting you, Nudger. I'm Chief Gladstone, Marlville Police."

I followed him down a tile-floored hall into a large room furnished in dainty French provincial. The carpet was the same deep pearl color as the grips in the revolver in Gladstone's leather hip holster, and ceiling-to-floor powder-blue drapes were opened to admit soft light through white sheer curtains. The walls were papered in light gold patterned in darker gold fleurs-de-lis. It struck me as the sort of place where it might be difficult to read the menu.

Emily Stein rose from a fragile-looking sofa and smiled a strained smile at me. She was more beautiful now than she was twenty years ago when her name was Emily Colter and she was still single and chasing a modeling career. I couldn't understand how she'd failed to catch that career. She was tall and slender but curvaceous, and she had angular faintly oriental cheekbones and oversized compassionate blue eyes. I'd been in love with her once, back in Plainton, Missouri. But that was over twenty years ago, and she'd considered us only good friends even then. She had phoned me at my office yesterday and said she'd found herself in trouble, would I drive out and talk with her about it. I said yes, what were friends for?

"Thank you for coming Alo," she said, simply. There were circles of worry beneath her large eyes. "This is Chief Fred Gladstone of the Marlville Police Department."

I nodded and we all sat down politely, Gladstone and I on silkily upholstered, breakable-looking matching chairs that were too well bred to creak.

"Chief Gladstone agreed it might be a good idea to call you in on this," Emily said, "when I told him we were old friends and you're a private detective in the city."

When I glanced over at Gladstone's gone-to-fat craggy features, my impression was that he hadn't had much choice.

"Larry's been kidnapped," Emily said.

I waited while she paused for what they call in drama circles "a dramatic beat." Emily had always been stagy in an appealing way. Larry Stein was the man she married five years ago, a wealthy importer of leather goods, dark-haired, handsome, still in his thirties. I'd been at the wedding.

"Or do you use the term 'kidnapped' for a grown man?" Emily asked.

"You do," I told her. "When was Larry kidnapped?"

"Yesterday at three p.m., by the statue of Admiral Farragut in the park."

"Was there a ransom demand?"

"Even before the kidnapping," Gladstone cut in.

"Three days ago," Emily said, "Larry got a letter in the mail here at home. It was to the point and unsigned. If he didn't deliver five thousand dollars to the sender at three yesterday afternoon near the Farragut statue, I would be killed."

Gladstone stood up from his chair, moved to a secretary near the window, and handed me a white envelope. "It's already been checked for prints," he said. "Nothing there. Postmarked locally, widely sold cheap typing paper, typed on a Royal electric portable."

The folded note inside the envelope was as Emily had described—short, direct, neat, and grammatically correct. I asked her, "Did Larry follow these instructions?"

Emily nodded. "And he told me to call you if anything happened to him. He thinks a lot of you professionally."

I found it odd that he'd think of me at all, since I'd only met him twice. But then I'm sure he knew, in that instinctive way husbands have, that I greatly admired Emily.

"Larry knew something wasn't right about it, even as a straight extortion demand," Emily went on. "He said the amount of money they demanded was too small and what they really might want was an opportunity to grab him with enough money on him for them to be able to hold out while they waited for a huge ransom."

"It turns out Larry was right," Gladstone said. "Emily got this in this morning's mail." He handed me another envelope, identical to the first—same paper, same typing—but this time with a demand for $100,000. Otherwise dead Larry. The kidnappers ended the note by assuring Emily they'd stay in touch.

I looked at the postmark. Yesterday's date, time 11:00 a.m., local.

"Right," Gladstone said, following my thoughts. "Mailed before Larry was snatched. So it was planned, not spontaneous."

"How about the FBI?" I said.

Emily shook her head no, her lips a firm, thin line.

"She refused," Gladstone told me. "She wants you instead."

I sat back in my chair digesting what I'd learned. It gave me a stomach ache. Extortion, kidnapping, threatened murder, a ransom demand from someone or some group that seemed to know what moves to make. I didn't have the nerves for my profession. Automatically, I reached into my shirt pocket, peeled back some tinfoil, and popped a thin white antacid tablet into my mouth.

"Call the FBI, Emily," I said. "The odds are better that way."

"Larry told me not to do that. He said it would be a sure way to get him killed. The FBI has a file on him. In the sixties he was what you might call a student radical—nothing serious, but his photograph was taken with the wrong people and he was in the wrong spot when a building burned down. It's all behind him, but they might not believe that."

From student radical to Larry the capitalist.

"What now?" Emily asked in a lost voice.

"We wait for instructions and take it from there. It wouldn't be a bad idea to get a recorder on the phone in case they decide to stop using the mail."

"That's been taken care of," Gladstone said.

"Can you get the hundred thousand?" I asked Emily.

"I can." No hesitation.

"Do you have any idea who might be doing this? Sometimes a kidnapping is a personal matter."

"No one I can think of." Outside a jay started a shrill chatter on the patio. The strident notes seemed to set Emily more on edge. "Larry never told me much about his business; he knows people I don't know. But he was—is—the type who never made enemies."

"Except for the FBI," I said, rising from my fragile chair. The sheer curtains were parted slightly, and beyond the brick patio I could see a tilled garden about twelve by nine feet, lined with cabbage, lettuce and staked tomato plants. Near the center of the garden were two rows of young tomato vines that would mature toward the end of summer and keep the Steins in tomatoes all season long. The garden was neglected now and needed weeding. Still, it was a garden. I smiled. Plainton, Missouri. A part of Emily would always remain a country girl.

"Maybe somebody ought to stay here with you nights," Gladstone said.

"No," Emily said. "I'll be fine. The house is equipped with dead bolt locks and has a burglar-alarm system. And I have Bruno."

Emily got up and walked to the door at the other end of the room. When she opened the door, a huge black and tan German Shepherd ambled in and sat, his white teeth glinting against his black lips and lolling pink tongue. Bruno was a factor.

Before I left, I gave Emily and Gladstone each one of my printed cards with my home and office numbers. I told Emily to try to keep occupied and worry as little as possible. Hollow advice but my best under the circumstances.

The Volkswagen's oil-starved engine beat like a busy machine shop as I drove past Marlville's exclusive shopping area of boutiques, service stations bordered by artificial green grass and shrubbery that would fool you at a thousand feet, and a red-brick and yellow-plastic McDonald's harboring half a dozen scraggly teenagers with nothing better to do on a sunny June day in swank suburbia.

I turned onto the cloverleaf and headed east toward the city, glad to be away from all that manicured spaciousness.

From a phone booth on Davis Avenue, I checked with my answering service. No one had called, and I didn't feel like returning to my desolate office to reread my mail.

My apartment was also a lonely place, but the loneliness was in me, wherever I went. I phoned a colleague at police headquarters who had an FBI connection and promised to get me information on Larry Stein in a hurry and call back. Then I took a quick shower, leaving the bathroom door open so I could hear the phone.

It rang while I was toweling myself dry.

Larry Stein had been a member of a short-lived left-wing student organization called LIFT, Leftist Insurgents for Tomorrow. He had attended some demonstrations that turned violent and had been photographed near the R.O.T.C. building at Washington University when it burned down. He was never formally charged with arson, and someone else was eventually convicted of the crime. This was in 1966. Who cared now? Probably no one.

I cooked up some hamburger steaks and stewed tomatoes and sat down with them and a glass of beer to watch a ball game on television.

At a few minutes after five, the jangle of the phone woke me from a sound sleep in front of the TV.

"Nudger?"

"I think."

"Chief Gladstone. I got a call from the city police. Larry Stein is at the morgue."

I could think of nothing to say. I wasn't sure myself how I was taking the news.

"Refuse collectors found his body this afternoon in a big cardboard box behind a restaurant. He was shot to death. How about going down and making the ID?"

"Does Emily know?"

"Not yet."

"I'll tell her," I said. "I'll let you know when I get done at the morgue."

I replaced the receiver and stood for a moment, despising myself. I knew that hidden in my compassion for Emily was a secret joyous voice reminding me that she was a widow now, she was free.

But when I got to the morgue and old Eagan slid Drawer #16 out on its metal casters, I found that I wasn't looking at Larry Stein. This man had been close to Stein's height and weight, and his hair was dark brown, if not black, but his face was broader than Stein's and slightly pockmarked.

Whoever he was, he'd been shot five times in the chest.

When I phoned police headquarters and told them it wasn't Stein, they told me to come down. I took an antacid tablet and went.

Lieutenant Jack Keough, an old friend from when I was on the force, talked to me. He's a few years older than I am, with candid brown eyes and an often-broken nose that wasn't Roman to begin with. His office is so barren and battered that even after the morgue it was depressing.

"We sent the prints to Washington," Keough said, "so we should know soon who we got chilled." Then he dumped the contents of a large brown envelope onto his desk. He didn't have to tell me it was what was found in the pockets of the corpse. An expensive kidskin wallet—Larry Stein's wallet with all his identification, credit cards, driver's license, photographs of Emily, and a few worn business cards. There were two tens and a five in the bill compartment. Besides the wallet, there were a leather key case, a black pocket comb, and some loose change. While I was sorting through it, I told Keough about the kidnap case.

"Now it's in our ball park too," Keough said. "We can help you."

"I wish there were a way," I told him. "You'd better phone Chief Gladstone and let him know about this. Maybe he can put a name on the dead man."

"We're never that lucky," Keough said.

Armed with some head shots of the corpse, I drove the next morning to Marlville to talk to Emily. As I was about to turn into the semicircular driveway, I saw a dark blue Pontiac sedan turning out of the other end of the drive onto the street.

When Emily answered my knock, I could see that she was badly shaken. I wished I'd had the presence of mind to jot down the license number of the Pontiac.

"Have you found out anything?" she asked, opening the door wide.

"I'm not sure," I told her, stepping inside. Bruno ambled over and licked my hand. "I'm afraid I have to show you some unpleasant photographs, Emily."

She backed a step, supported herself with exaggerated casualness on a low table. "Not . . ."

"Not Larry," I said quickly. "A man was killed, and Larry's identification was in his pockets. We need to know who that man was."

"Killed . . . how?"

"Shot to death." I removed the photographs from the envelope and showed them to her.

271

She seemed relieved to find herself staring at a peaceful composed face. "I don't know him," she said. "At least, not that I can recall."

I followed her into the living room, where she sat bent and exhausted on the sofa.

"Do you know someone who drives a blue Pontiac?" I asked.

She used a graceful hand to brush her hair back from her face. "No, I don't think so. Why?"

"I thought I saw one pulling away from the house as I drove up."

Emily shrugged. "He must have been turning around. We're the end house; they do that all the time."

But she had said "he," and there had been a man driving the car.

That night I began keeping watch on the Stein house. And learned nothing. At midnight, when all the lights in the house had gone out, I went home.

The next morning I learned from Keough that the man in the morgue was still unidentified. His fingerprints weren't in the master files, which meant that he had never been in the armed forces or acquired a police record. His good behavior had earned him five bullets—according to Keough, thirty-eight-caliber bullets, probably fired from a Colt automatic.

I watched the Stein house most of the next day and that evening until Emily went to bed at 11:45. Again nothing. Maybe Emily had been telling the truth; maybe the car I'd seen had only been using the driveway to turn around.

But on the way home I saw the blue Pontiac in the McDonald's lot in Marlville. Of course I'd only caught a glimpse of the car at Emily's and couldn't be positive this was the same one, but after writing down the license number I parked in a spot near the rear of the lot where I could watch it.

McDonald's was closing. After a while some of the parking lot lights winked out and the swarms of insects that had been circling them disappeared.

A man walked from the red and yellow building, munching a hamburger as he strode toward the Pontiac. He seemed to be in his thirties, medium-height, and muscular rather than stocky—a lean-waisted weightlifter's build. He was wearing dark slacks and a blue short-sleeved sport shirt open at the collar. I couldn't see his face clearly.

When the Pontiac pulled from the lot, I popped an antacid tablet into my mouth and followed.

It took him about two minutes to reach Emily's house. As I sat parked up the street, watching, he knocked on the front door. Lights came on, the door opened, and he entered. Twenty minutes later he came back outside, got into the Pontiac, and drove away. I stayed with him.

He drove toward the city, getting off the highway at Vine and turning south on Twentieth. Ten minutes later, he made a right onto Belt Street and parked in front of a six-story brick apartment building just this side of being condemned. We were in one of those neighborhoods on the edge of a genuine slum. As I watched, he entered the building and a while later a light came on in one of the fourth-floor windows.

I climbed stiffly out of the Volkswagen, crossed the street, and entered the vestibule of the building. There was a dim overhead lightbulb and a row of tarnished metal mailboxes. Two of the names on the fourth-floor boxes were women's. 4-D was listed as B. Darris, 4-B as Charles L. Coil.

After copying all the names and the address, I walked back to the Volkswagen, waited until the light had gone out in the fourth-floor window, then drove home weary for bed.

★ ★ ★ ★ ★

Ten o'clock. I got up slowly, sat for a while on the edge of the mattress, then made my way into the bathroom and under a cool shower. Ten minutes later I turned on the burner beneath the coffee before returning to the bedroom to dress. After a breakfast of grapefruit juice, poached eggs, and black coffee I was sufficiently awake to ask myself what it had all meant last night.

Emily was seeing the man in the Pontiac and wanted it kept secret. Was he one of the kidnappers? Anyone unconnected with the case? A clandestine lover?

The telephone rang and I carried my coffee into the other room to answer. It was Keough. They had an identification on the body in the morgue—Harold Vinceno, 122 Edison Avenue. He'd been reported missing by his wife three days ago and his general description fit that of the dead man. Mrs. Vinceno had made the positive identification this morning.

I asked Keough to get me an owner from Records on the blue Pontiac's plate numbers, then asked him to find out what he could about the car's owner. When he asked me why, I told him it was nothing solid, just a hunch I was following.

By the time I'd finished my coffee and examined the mail, drops of rain were pecking at the window. Keough might not call back for hours. I went to the closet and put on a lightweight waterproof jacket, then I left to visit Mrs. Vinceno.

Edison Avenue was near the west edge of the city, medium-priced neat tract houses, on small lots with trimmed lawns that were being watered by the steady pattering rain. The Vinceno house was a white-frame ranch with empty flower boxes beneath the front windows.

Mrs. Vinceno answered the door on the third ring. She was a small haggard woman, probably pretty in ordinary circumstances, with large dark eyes that were red from crying.

"My name's Nudger, Mrs. Vinceno. I'm a detective. I know it's an awkward time, but I need to talk to you about your husband."

She nodded without expression and stepped back.

We sat at opposite ends of the sofa. But for a new-looking console TV, everything in the small living room was slightly worn.

"I'm sure the police have asked you, Mrs. Vinceno, but do you have any idea what happened to your husband?"

She shook her head no. "When I saw Harold I was—surprised," she said in a husky voice. "Not because he was dead, but because he'd been shot."

I waited.

"Harold left here three days ago with the intention of committing suicide, Mr. Nudger. We hadn't been getting along. We had money problems—personal problems. He left here in one of his rages, saying he would end everything for himself."

I watched her battle the trembling of her hands to light a cigarette.

"Then he called here the next morning and told me our problems were solved. He said he'd stumbled across a deal that couldn't miss and he'd let me know more about it when the time came. I begged him to come home, but he wouldn't.

"I didn't take his talk about money seriously. Harold was kind of incoherent on the phone, and he was always stumbling into rainbows without pots of gold at the end of them." She bowed her head and her disarranged black hair fell down to hide her face.

It didn't boost my self-esteem to keep at her, but I did. "Did your husband ever mention Larry Stein, the man whose identification was on him?" She shook her head no. "How about B. Darris? Charles L. Coil?" No and no. Her shoulders began to quake.

Driving to my office, I tried to draw some conclusions and only came up with more questions. Was Vinceno one of the kidnappers? Had he actually intended to commit suicide or had he been playing for his wife's pity? Had he known Emily? The man in the Pontiac? The only person involved in the case I could be sure Vinceno had crossed paths with alive or dead was Larry Stein.

My office is on the second floor of a Victorian apartment building that was converted into oddly shaped bay-windowed offices when the neighborhood had declined. It has a certain ornate charm and the exterminator comes every six months.

I was informed by my answering service that Lieutenant Keough had called and left a number where he could be reached. When I dialed the number, Keough came to the phone and told me that the Pontiac was registered to William Darris, thirty-four years old, of 6534 Belt Street, apartment 4-D. Darris had a record—B and E, Plainton, Missouri, August third of '69, placed on probation; armed robbery, Union, Missouri, May seventh of '71, convicted and served three years. There were also a raft of moving traffic violations and a minor drug charge.

"You're from Plainton," Keough said. "Do you know this Darris?"

The name in conjunction with Plainton had already opened a door in my memory. "I know the Darris family. There were two boys in their early teens when I left. They'd be in their thirties now."

"What connection might they have with Vinceno?" Keough asked.

"I don't know yet. I saw Darris leaving the Stein home late last night. And he was there before, but Emily Stein denied it."

"That's all?"

"All I have."

Keough sighed. "It could mean anything. Maybe we ought to talk to Darris."

"I wouldn't now. If he's mixed up in the kidnapping, we might be putting Stein's life in danger. I think the thing to do is watch him."

"All right," Keough said. "We put somebody on Darris. What are you going to be doing?"

"I'm going to Plainton."

I didn't tell him what I was going to do before I left for Plainton.

When Darris was gone from his apartment, along with his tail, I entered the building on Belt Street and climbed the stairs to the fourth floor. Ignoring my fluttering stomach, I used my Visa card to slip the lock so I could enter apartment 4-D.

The tiny apartment was a mess, the bed unmade, rumpled Levis and a pair of dirty socks in one corner, hot stale air. I knew the places to look and how to look, and I worked hard at looking to stifle my fear.

Within ten minutes I found it, a sealed white envelope taped to the outside of the back panel of a kitchen cabinet drawer. I took it into the bathroom and ran hot water into the basin until steam rose. Then I held the envelope over the rising steam until the glue had softened enough for me to pry the flap open. Inside was five thousand dollars.

Resealing the envelope with the money inside, I replaced it on the back of the cabinet drawer, then, after making sure everything was in the same disorder in which I'd found it, I left.

* * * * *

Plainton existed in reality much as it did in my memory—white frame houses, small shopping area, unhurried pedestrians. I'd taken a flight to Saint Louis and connected with an Ozark Airlines flight to Jefferson City, where I'd rented an air-conditioned Pinto for the drive to Plainton. Now I was driving along the streets where I'd spent my childhood and adolescence, before my family moved to Kansas City.

I parked in one of the angled slots near the sloping lawn that led up to the city hall, fed coins to an ancient parking meter, and left the car in the shade of a huge cottonwood tree.

Benny Shaver was the man I wanted to talk to. We'd been good friends in high school, and now he owned a restaurant on Alternate Route 3, Plainton's main street.

Benny had taken out a liquor license in the twelve years since I'd been through town, and now the sign atop the low brick building read SHAVER'S PUB AND RESTAURANT.

The air conditioner was on high in Shaver's. There was a counter with upholstered stools and a number of tables, each with a red checked tablecloth and an artificial rose in a tall glass vase. The pub had been added on. There was a door near the counter over which the word PUB was lettered, along with what might have been Benny's family crest. The crest wasn't crossed pitchforks against a field of guernseys; it was crossed swords over a shield engraved with something in Latin, maybe the hours. I walked into the pub and saw a man and a blonde woman in one of the booths, and behind the bar where it wasn't so dim stood Benny. Less hair and more jowl, but Benny.

I walked to the bar, sat on a stool, and called for a draft beer. Benny sauntered over and set a frosty mug on a red coaster, then squinted at me. I noticed that the scar on his forehead from the accident we'd had as teenagers was less vivid now.

"God's great acorns, it's Nudger!"

We both laughed and shook hands and Benny reached a beefy arm over the bar and slapped my right shoulder until it hurt. "Twelve years," I told him.

"It is at that," he said, and looked momentarily frightened by the press of time.

After three beers' worth of reminiscence I said, "I need some information on William Darris."

"Is he in trouble?" Benny asked.

"Possibly."

"I haven't seen Billy in about two years. I don't miss him, Alo."

"Why not?"

"He came in here a lot and couldn't drink like he thought he could. This was after he got out of prison and thought he was rougher than he was. I had to break up a couple of fights he got into, mostly over women."

"Married women?"

"Some. Billy claimed he was trying to make up for time lost in prison. I never saw him, though, after he took up with the Colter girl."

"Who?"

"You remember Emily Colter. She was a looker, moved away a long time ago to become a model or something. Well, she was back in town a few years ago to visit her cousin, and she kinda fell in with Billy. About a month after she left town, he left too, claimed he got a job in the East. I wished him luck and hoped he'd stay where he was going. He was always in trouble and prison made him worse."

I didn't think Benny could guess how much worse. After

declining lunch and saying goodbye, I left town.

I was splashing cold water on my face in the office the next morning when the phone rang. It was Keough.

"Emily Stein got the ransom-delivery instructions in the mail," he said. "They want the hundred thousand tonight."

"I'll bet," I said. My stomach came alive and wielded claws.

"The tail on Darris hasn't brought us much," Keough went on. "He's been getting together with an ex-con named Louis Enwood, extortion and armed robbery. We put a tail on Enwood too."

"Have they been near a mailbox or post office?"

"Nope. I don't think they're it, Nudger."

"Are you going to be in your office all morning?"

"Most of it."

"I'll phone you back later," I said.

I combed my hair, rinsed my mouth with cold water, opened a fresh roll of antacid tablets, and left the office to see Emily Stein.

She was home. Her Mercedes convertible was parked near the garage at the side of the house where I'd seen it before. I walked around to the rear of the house, then returned to the front porch and rang the doorbell. A sprinkler on the wide front lawn was flinging a revolving fan of water with a staccato hissing sound. Bruno was lying in the shade near the corner of the house, staring at me like the good watch dog he was.

When she opened the door, Emily smiled at me. She was wearing a pale-pink dress. Her smile lost its luminescence when she saw my face.

"You heard about the ransom instructions," she said. "I was just on my way to draw the money from Marlville Bank."

"Why don't you write him a check and give it to him next time he comes by the house?" I suggested.

She stepped back into the cool entry hall, and it was as if she'd stepped across time and aged twenty years.

"You, Darris, and his friend Enwood are in it together," I said.

She turned and walked into the big room with the French furniture and powder-blue drapes. I followed her.

"You called me into it to make it look like an authentic kidnapping and give you an even better excuse not to call in the FBI. After all, you didn't have anything to fear if it went right."

She sat on the sofa and swayed slightly. The drapes were open, and a pitiless slanted light fell on her.

"You typed and mailed the notes to yourself," I told her, "even the last ransom note. Larry Stein cared about you enough to set out for a lonely meeting with only five thousand dollars when he was sure the extortionists would want something more. Only Larry was smart, and an angle-shooter. Somewhere along the line he ran into Harold Vinceno, contemplating suicide, maybe pumping up his courage over a few drinks. Larry talked Vinceno into delivering the five thousand, maybe offering to pay him a thousand for the job, and they exchanged identification in case the extortionists would check. And Darris and Enwood, who'd never seen your husband close-up, were not only interested in the money but in killing Larry."

"Billy made me do it," Emily murmured.

"No," I said. "He and Enwood wouldn't have killed Larry just for the five thousand dollars. When a married man is murdered, the wife is always at least initially suspected. You needed a cover, like a phony kidnapping scheme complete with notes, ransom money, and a bumbling gumshoe who wasn't much of a threat. Only the hundred thousand wasn't ransom money, it was the final payment to Darris for killing Larry. You probably never really loved Larry Stein, and half his money as he saw fit to dole it out to you wasn't enough." I watched her close her eyes, felt my own eyes brim as tears tracked down her makeup. "When did Larry come back?"

"Yesterday," she said, her eyes still clenched shut, "when he read in the papers about Vinceno being identified by his wife. That's the only time anything about the case got in the papers. Until then, Larry wanted to stay dead to the kidnappers. He was afraid for me."

"And you were afraid of Darris," I said, "afraid he'd think you double-crossed him and he'd want revenge. Darris found out the same way Larry did that he'd killed Vinceno—the wrong man. That's why Darris came here to see you, to demand the hundred thousand, to continue with the original plan."

"I was afraid of him," Emily admitted, opening her eyes. "That's why I wanted you—nearby. I should have known you'd figure it out. You were always smart, you always saw things differently. This hundred thousand, Alo, it's only a fraction of what's left . . ."

"There was only one way you'd be able to mail that final note to yourself," I told her, "and only one more thing I have to know for sure before I phone Chief Gladstone."

She knew what I meant and something buckled inside her. But she had enough strength to stand and walk with me through the house and out the back door into the yard. She waited while I went into the garage and got a disturbingly handy shovel.

Despite everything, I found myself still admiring her. She had masterminded everything from seducing Darris to hiring me on the recommendation of my noted lack of success. And but for Vinceno's impersonation of her husband, it all would have worked. In this or in any other world, I would never find another Emily.

She was leaning on me like a lover and sobbing as we walked to the dark, churned earth of the now meticulously weeded garden, to where the freshly planted tomato vines were flourishing in the hot sun.

The Romantics

Jake Adler was a high-tone downtown attorney of the corporate breed. Why he was slumming in Nudger's office promised to be interesting.

Nudger figured the suave, fortyish fashion plate with the graying hair and hawk-handsome features wasn't here to hire him to investigate anything in relation to a lawsuit. And he was sure he didn't owe money to anyone important enough to have retained Adler. This one figured to be personal, something Adler wouldn't want his society friends or clients to know about. Marital infidelity? A ghost from his past? Nudger leaned back in his *eeep*ing swivel chair, into the cool breeze from the laboring window air conditioner, waiting for Adler to unfold.

"When I'm finished talking," Adler said, "it might seem to you I've come here on something of a whim, but it's not that way at all." He was obviously more than a little ill at ease; it didn't go with his well-tailored, commanding physical presence. Signs of humanity on such Leaders of Men showed as glaring flaws.

"I'm nothing if not confidential," Nudger said, trying to relax Adler, trying to imagine the man as the recipient of a whim.

"I know. I checked." Adler glanced around the sparse Maplewood office, sniffed the sugary aroma from the doughnut shop directly below. "And you're honest. Which is why you're here in this burrow with a desk instead of downtown or out in Clayton."

"Your office is downtown," Nudger pointed out, not very tactfully.

"I'm not always honest."

Nudger thought, at least he's honest about it.

Adler crossed his legs, then used thumb and forefinger to sharpen the crease in his expensive pin-striped pants. "But I will be honest with you," he said. "That's why I came here. Can you believe that?"

"It's a stretch."

"Well, maybe it doesn't matter. I want you to follow someone, find out about her."

"Who's her?"

Adler cocked his head to the side, smiling faintly. "Ever think about love, Nudger?"

Huh? Another whim? "I've been known to swoon now and then. It usually doesn't work out."

"I don't mean long-term love, where you and a woman share a mutual respect and make an investment in each other's happiness. I had that with my wife until she died last year. And I don't mean temporary lust. I mean *real* love, the kind you remember from your teens, maybe. Or earlier."

Down on Manchester Avenue a horn honked. A bus accelerated with a roar like a lion. The air conditioner drew in some diesel fumes to merge with the pervasive scent of fresh-baked doughnuts. Nudger said, "There are lots of definitions of true love." He couldn't help it; he had the feeling Adler was being candid and had come here to bare his soul. The guy was some lawyer.

"True love is unexpected and instantaneous," Adler said. "It's when you pass a woman on the street, or glimpse her through the window of a passing train, and you know you'll never forget that lightning instant, never forget her face. Something in the eyes, the tilt of the chin, the planes of the face. Has that ever happened to you?"

"It happens to all men," Nudger said, trying to pull Adler back to earth. "If we actually got to meet these women, they might have bad breath. We might not even like them."

"I still remember the girl I sat behind in my high school math class. I was too shy to talk to her, but even now I can recall the nape of her neck, the gentle upsweep of her blonde hair, the graceful line of her cheek. That was over twenty years ago, and if I had artistic talent I could sketch her likeness for you with exactness today." An expression of pain and puzzlement crossed Adler's features. "Why is that, Nudger?"

Nudger sighed. "No one knows. It happens, that's all. Something passes between two people, and maybe only one of them realizes it, then they go on their way to their homes or offices and—"

"—And never forget it," Adler interrupted.

"Sometimes. Is that who you want me to find out about, someone you glimpsed through a train window?"

"Bus window," Adler corrected, as if the mode of transportation were important. "Every morning I eat breakfast at the Edgemore Café in the Wellington Building downtown. At exactly seven forty-five, a bus slows down and swings wide to take the corner, and I see a woman like the ones we've been talking about."

"She see you?"

"Our eyes have met. And it happens, that arc of emotion. I'm sure she feels it, too. I don't want it to end the way it usually does, with propriety, inaction, and then recollections and regrets thirty years later. All my life I've been a creature of logic, of planning and pragmatism. Not this time. This time I want to find out about her. I want to get to know her."

"You sure about that? I mean, maybe you're still grieving about your wife, not thinking straight."

"That's what a lot of people would say. But why *shouldn't* I learn something about this woman? And prudently, before I approach her? I'm afraid that if she does return my affection, things might get out of control. I want to know about her first, then maybe introduce myself."

"That's a logical and pragmatic plan," Nudger said, "even if it is to satisfy a whim." *Eeep!* He dropped forward in his chair. "Know what? You're a romantic."

"So are you, my friend. I found that out about you."

"But you're a rich and successful romantic. That's contradictory. It doesn't make sense."

"It does if you take into account I'm unscrupulous."

Nudger said, "I can see why you don't want anyone downtown knowing about this. They'd view it as a weakness."

"But you don't."

"No, I guess not."

"I don't want anything in writing," Adler said. "I'll pay you in cash, and I'll want only a verbal report. I need to know about this woman. I need to know what she is to me, why I look forward to seeing her weekday mornings, and why, when I look at her, the moment is so electric."

Nudger's nervous stomach was warning him to be cautious here. "This is crazy," he said. "It'll be a waste of time, won't get you anywhere. She's probably married, might have children. Might have a boyfriend with muscles and meanness. What romantics do is lie to themselves and get in trouble. You defend them in court all the time. Think again about this."

Adler's square jaw set like a building block beneath his handsome smile. He was obviously determined and a man used to having his way, whatever the cost to anyone. "Indulge me, Mr. Nudger."

Nudger considered, then said, "Indulge me."

Adler laid ten crisp hundred-dollar bills on the desk. He knew how to indulge, all right.

Nudger was hired.

He followed the bus until the woman got off at Fourth and Pine, only blocks from Adler's office in the Wayne Building. Nudger recognized her easily from the description Adler had given him: thin, with delicate features and blonde upswept hair. He remembered the girl who'd sat in front of Adler in high school; maybe that old chemistry was what was haunting Adler. More likely it was that his wife had died recently. Maybe he was searching for her among the living.

This was no time for amateur psychology, Nudger told himself, as he quickly pulled his old Ford Granada into a No Parking zone and killed the engine. His job was to find out the woman's name, where she worked and lived. And he was a professional and a practical businessman, right?

Right. And one who needed the business.

The woman walked west on Pine. He had to take the chance his car would be towed. The day wasn't starting right. He got out of the car, slammed the door behind him, and jogged across the street to fall in behind the woman.

She had a nice figure, a graceful, hip-switching walk without much motion of the upper body, like an aspiring model practicing crossing the room with a book on her head to improve her posture. Adler wouldn't know that, if he'd only seen her sitting down, through a bus window. Nudger wondered if he should include it in his report. Such a romantic he was after all, as Adler had said. Nudger knew that Claudia, his lady love, would have another word for him.

The blonde woman surprised him. He'd been expecting her to enter an office building. Instead she walked north on

Fifth Street, then entered the old but elegant Victoria Hotel on Locust.

Nudger went in behind her, closing the distance between them in the crowded lobby.

He got a better look at her then. She was attractive, but not strikingly beautiful. And older than he'd first thought—probably around forty. There was a remote sadness to her features that made her interesting, but she wouldn't launch more than a few ships.

She paused and studied a placard listing the day's activities in the large and luxurious hotel, then walked toward the restaurant.

Nudger found a place at the counter and ordered a cup of coffee, watching in the mirrored wall as the woman sat down at a table with a man with dark hair and a dark mustache. He was about thirty, broad-shouldered inside a tan sport coat that was too tight on him. When he turned to summon a waiter, Nudger saw that he was wearing a ponytail. He was the type that could get away with it and not seem sissified. This was not the kind of guy Adler would be glad to hear about.

The blonde woman and ponytail talked until the waiter brought a single order of eggs and toast. Then ponytail stood up, leaned over, and kissed the woman's cheek. She didn't seem to pay too much attention to that, kept chewing toast. Ponytail paid his check at the cashier's counter and walked from the restaurant, not looking back.

The woman ate slowly, daintily, then sat for a long time sipping coffee. She extended her little finger whenever she lifted her cup to her lips. Her cool blue glance slid over the other diners, most of whom had entered the restaurant within the last half-hour.

About nine-fifteen, the restaurant was only half full.

Nudger had walked out into the lobby and bought a news-paper from the overpriced gift shop, then returned to the counter and pretended to read while he managed to down his fourth cup of black coffee.

Too much coffee. He had to go to the bathroom, desper-ately, and wondered if he should chance it. The woman didn't show any inclination to get up and leave.

Had to! The hell with it. His stomach was killing him.

He hurried to the rest room at the far end of the restau-rant. Spent only a few minutes there.

When he emerged, the woman was leaning toward an ad-jacent table and talking to a redheaded man with a plastic name tag pinned to the lapel of his dark business suit. She was grinning with apparent embarrassment, shrugging and holding out her small black purse.

The redheaded guy studied her through his rimless spectacles, then smiled and tossed down the rest of his coffee. An ice-hearted executive type who'd been melted on the spot.

He and the woman talked for a few more minutes, then they both stood up and the man snatched the check from her table. So gallant. A romantic himself. He paid for both break-fasts on the way out of the restaurant.

Out in the lobby, the woman smiled at him and touched his arm lightly, then turned to walk away. The same walk that had fascinated Nudger after she'd climbed down from the bus and set off down the sidewalk.

She stopped when the man said something, then she turned back to face him. Smiled.

He smiled back at her.

Then she shrugged, and they walked from the lobby to-gether.

Nudger told himself she'd misplaced or forgotten her

money or credit cards, asked the man to lend her the amount of her breakfast, then charmed him and graciously returned his favor by accompanying him outside. Maybe she was going to give him directions, or show him the sights.

But really he knew that something more than that had occurred between the woman and the redheaded executive type. She'd managed to pick him up smoothly, professionally.

More bad news for Adler.

As he left the Victoria lobby to follow them, Nudger noticed the man with the ponytail seated in a leather armchair near some potted palms and reading *USA Today*.

He got outside just in time to see the redheaded man and the woman climb into a cab and drive away. Three middle-aged women were in line for the next cab the doorman could wave to the curb. Trouble was, no second cab was in sight, much less a third cab for Nudger. Then the light at the corner changed, and the traffic flow on Locust dried up. Terrific.

Nudger watched helplessly as the taxi carrying the blonde woman and her pickup turned the opposite corner just before the traffic light changed, and disappeared into glittering and relentless downtown traffic.

He stood frustrated in the increasing morning heat for a while, then decided the only course left to him was to go back in the hotel and start keeping tabs on the man with the ponytail. Maybe he and the woman would get together again before the day ended.

Almost surely they would. Nudger was getting the idea.

Ponytail stood up from his chair and moved around the lobby from time to time, stretching his muscles. He'd apparently lost all interest in his newspaper, which he'd folded and laid on a table for someone else to read. Twice he sauntered outside to smoke a cigarette.

He was back in the leather armchair when the blonde woman and the redheaded man came into the hotel. The man had his arm around her waist but removed it just inside the door, and he was no longer wearing his plastic convention ID tag. The woman said something to him, smiling up at him like a flower seeking sun, as they walked to the elevator and he pressed the up button.

Nudger idly wandered over and stood near them, among a knot of people waiting for an elevator. He deliberately didn't so much as glance at them, and he figured they were too interested in each other to look his way.

When the elevator arrived, empty of guests from the upper floors, he pushed in with the other passengers and stood to the side, near the door.

Everyone observed elevator etiquette and didn't speak. The blonde woman and the man, and a fat guy with a plastic name tag like the one the redheaded man had removed, got off on the tenth floor.

Nudger followed. The man and woman turned right. Nudger and the guy with a name tag turned left. The chubby conventioneer kept going straight, but Nudger ducked into an alcove with an ice dispenser and soda machines. He peeked around the corner and watched the man and woman enter a room near the end of the long hall.

After checking to find out the room's number, he returned to the lobby.

Ponytail was still seated in the leather armchair. He was staring off into space, absently drumming his fingertips on the chair arms.

Nudger went back into the restaurant, this time ordered a Pepsi, and observed ponytail through the white latticework that divided restaurant and lobby.

"Wasn't you in here earlier drinking coffee?" the waitress asked.

"I'm on a caffeine diet," Nudger told her, realizing he had to use the rest room again, though not so desperately.

The woman stared at him, decided he might be serious, then sashayed down the counter to wait on yet another man wearing a plastic name tag. They were all part of a national luggage wholesalers' convention, according to the placard in the lobby.

The waitress, who had a faint dark mustache and was not a particularly attractive woman, started to walk away, but the guy with the name tag called her back. Gave her a wide, phony smile. Seemed to be flirting with her. Maybe another arc of emotion like Adler described had just occurred and Nudger had missed it. Hadn't even seen a flash.

He didn't miss it when ponytail raised his arm to glance at his watch, then stood up from the leather armchair and swaggered with an air of purpose toward the elevator.

Two elevators were at lobby level. Nudger slowed his pace, then got in the one on the right after ponytail had entered the one on the left.

Then a dozen people began filing slowly into Nudger's elevator. Pressed against the back wall, he heard the adjacent elevator begin its ascent.

Nudger wondered if he'd ever in his life have any luck that wasn't bad.

His elevator made four stops before it reached the tenth floor.

Ponytail had gotten there ahead of him, but Nudger was just in time to see him pause before the same room the blonde woman and the man had entered, give a tight little grin, then quickly push inside.

Nudger rode the elevator back down and used a house phone to call Security.

"I don't know what to tell him," Nudger said to Claudia Bettencourt that afternoon in her apartment. She wasn't teaching summer classes this year, and Nudger found himself spending far too much time with her during the day, when he should have been working. Or trying to find work to do, anyway.

Claudia, lean, dark, beautiful, with eyes that held depths Nudger could never fathom, languidly stretched out a tan arm and poured herself a second glass of the wine Nudger had brought with him. It was a spirited Chablis and had a Nevada label. Without looking at Nudger as she poured the bargain vintage, she said, "Tell him the truth."

"The truth will hurt him."

She put down the bottle and toyed with the threads on the glass neck for the cap that lay beside it. It had been a long time since Nudger had brought her wine in a bottle with a cork. He figured, What did it matter? Neither of them was a connoisseur. "I thought you said Adler was a hotshot lawyer," she told him. "Those guys aren't exactly sensitive souls."

"True, but consider why he hired me. I mean, it isn't like a downtown legal shark to ask for that kind of thing. Completely out of character."

"A trick?"

Nudger poured himself another glass of Chablis and took a swallow. He didn't usually drink wine in the afternoon, but this thing with Adler was bothering him. "I thought it might be a trick, but if it is, I don't understand it."

"That's the idea of a trick, Nudger."

He couldn't dispute her on that one. He took another pull

of wine, noticing that it tickled his throat. No, more than tickled—burned. Was wine supposed to do that?

"Attorneys are devious," Claudia said. "Consider Henry Mercato."

Nudger did. More often than he would have chosen. Mercato was the divorce lawyer of his former wife Eileen. Was in fact sleeping with Eileen. Which gave Henry a personal interest in helping her to extract as much alimony as possible from Nudger even if it meant dragging him back into court and snatching food from beneath his nose. Not child support, which Nudger would gladly have paid if he and Eileen had been blessed with children, but alimony. No one paid alimony these days. No one other than Nudger. Henry Mercato was that skilled and devious. Eileen, who was at the pinnacle of one of those barely legal home product pyramid sales scams and collected large commissions for doing nothing, needed the money not at all. But she hated Nudger and was motivated. And good at motivating Mercato.

But there was something about Adler. He was like Mercato in some ways. But then he wasn't. There was something else in the man, glowing like a fire beneath a lake. A kind of melancholy that hinted at vulnerability in someone in Adler's profession.

Nudger put down his plastic glass so hard that wine sloshed onto the table. "Damn it, I can't explain why, but even if he is a lawyer, I just don't want to hurt the guy."

Claudia smiled. "That's why he hired you, because you had a heart. What he didn't figure on was that you were such a marshmallow."

"Adler called me a romantic."

She studied him over the green neck of the bottle. "Well, I guess you're that, too. You're also a professional who was hired to do a job. Tell your client what you found out,

Nudger. In this instance, revealing the truth is the kindest thing you can do for him, though maybe it won't seem that way at the time. Trust me, okay?"

He thought about it. He didn't usually trust people who urged him to do so, but he trusted Claudia. He said, "Okay, he gets the truth."

She smiled at him and he felt something flutter deep in his nervous stomach. Not unpleasantly, though. He reached out a hand and ran his fingertips over her cool wrist.

She said, "You don't have to tell him right away, do you?"

"I'm not meeting him until this evening."

"So there's time to spare for me," she said.

"Always." He meant it. Always.

She got up and walked around the table. The cold breeze from the air conditioner played over her as she passed the window, momentarily molding the thin material of her summer blouse to her lean torso, her teacup-sized breasts, the gentle curve of her waist and hip.

She sat on his lap and he kissed her.

"Adler was right about you," she said.

"That's why he's an ace criminal lawyer," Nudger said, "he has instincts about people."

Claudia didn't answer. She wasn't listening.

She didn't seem to be listening later when he asked her if he could come back tonight after reporting to Adler. He slept over with Claudia often, and tonight in particular he felt like it. Not for more sex. He knew he'd bleed along with Adler when the truth cut deep; he'd need company.

But Claudia was vague about telling him he could return. He suspected why.

He said, "Is it Biff Archway?" Archway was the soccer coach and taught sex education at the girls' high school where Claudia taught English. She'd been involved with him for a while, but supposedly that was over.

"Is what Biff Archway?" she replied, obviously irritated. "Did you see or hear something, Nudger?"

"Is Archway coming over here after I leave?"

"I don't think it's any of your concern."

"I think it is. I don't see how you can say it isn't."

"I told you there was nothing between us other than that we're on the same faculty. We have no choice but to see each other, to get along."

"Well," Nudger said.

"You should trust me. If Biff and I are alone together, you can be sure it's business."

"It's not that I don't trust you," Nudger said. "I don't trust Archway."

"You don't have to." She kissed him lightly on the cheek. "It's me you need to have faith in. I have faith in you."

Guilt, he thought. She knew how to work him.

He glanced at his wristwatch. He had to get moving if he was going to be on time to meet with Adler. He didn't want to leave, but he had no choice.

Claudia said, "Don't worry, Nudger. Really."

His stomach twitched. He couldn't remember a day in his life when he hadn't worried.

"Her name's Doris Vandervort," Nudger told Adler that evening at the counter in Danny's Donuts, downstairs from Nudger's office. He'd jumped right in there with the truth, though he knew it would cause pain.

They were having Dunker Delites and coffee and were the only customers. The shop was usually conducive to confidential conversations. Danny was in the back room boxing up cream horns to sell at a discount by the dozen before they went stale. Staler.

Gazing morosely into his terrible coffee, Adler said, "She didn't look the type." He lifted his half-eaten Dunker Delite, then plunked it down on its plate in disgust.

"She is, though. Security found her undressed in the room, pretending to be her accomplice's wife caught in the act with a lover. She'd managed to unlock the door so they could be interrupted. The mark would figure he'd forgotten or hadn't locked it all the way in his anticipation. The so-called husband graciously accepted money in return for not telling the conventioneer's co-workers and wife back in Tulsa about his indiscretion, and not naming him as correspondent in an alienation-of-affections suit. The woman pretended to help the mark talk the husband into that forgiving and profitable gesture."

"The badger game."

"That's what they call it."

"I thought she was on her way to work every morning when I saw her on the bus. I guess, in a way, she was."

"No," Nudger said, "she was actually coming home from her job as a waitress in an all-night restaurant. A couple of mornings a month, though, she wouldn't go home. She'd go to wherever she and her accomplice were planning to work the con."

"I'm not a criminal lawyer, Nudger. You think there's enough evidence to convict?"

"There would be if the guy she picked up would testify, but he won't. He still doesn't want his wife to find out about his indiscretion, so he'll decide not to bring charges. That's what makes it such a safe con game."

Adler absently prodded his Dunker Delite with a forefinger, as if checking for signs of life. "So she'll walk, after doing something like that."

"Not for a while. She can't make bail, and it'll take the

mark a day or so to buckle and drop charges. He'll probably want to make the woman and her accomplice sweat for a few days."

"Still, she'll eventually walk."

"Some of your clients have done far worse and walked," Nudger pointed out. He wasn't sure how Adler was taking this, whether he was angry as well as disappointed. Love could be rough in the real world.

"Well, I wanted to know what she was," Adler said, "and now I do know." He used a paper napkin to wipe sugar from his fingers, then slid off the counter stool and hitched up his belt. It had a buckle that looked like real gold, in the shape of a dollar sign.

"You're not gonna finish your doughnut?"

"Are you kidding?"

"Not so loud. Danny's sensitive."

Adler buttoned his pin-striped suit coat, then extended his hand. "You got the job done, Nudger. Thanks."

"It didn't take long," Nudger said. "You've got a refund coming." He reminded himself to deduct the extra forty-seven dollars he'd needed to get his car back from the city after it had been towed from the No Parking zone.

Adler stared at Nudger appraisingly. "Dumb goes with honest almost without fail. I can't prove I gave you that thousand dollars, so keep it. I would, if I were you."

Nudger didn't argue with such ironclad logic. Did that prove he was more honest than dumb? Or vice versa?

He shook hands with Adler and watched him leave the doughnut shop and stride across Manchester to where his gleaming black Cadillac was parked. The man who'd believed in love and the electric instant. What was the blonde woman to him, anyway? A reminder of some childhood imprint even he couldn't recall? Some long-buried Oedipal reflex? A nagging suggestion of something more exciting and satisfying than corporate law?

What was she?

Nudger had his own problems with the female of the species. He asked Danny for a glass of water, then sat at the counter sipping it as slowly as if it weren't free.

Danny walked over and leaned on the counter, took a few listless swipes at it with his gray towel. "You look like you got trouble, Nudge."

Nudger said, "Claudia."

Danny's docile, basset hound eyes rolled their pupils toward the door. "Where?"

"I mean, she's my problem," Nudger said.

"Oh. I thought you meant you seen her coming towards the shop. Crossing the street or something." Danny worked the towel again, moving a few crumbs around, then tucked it back in his belt. "She been going to that shrink again?"

Nudger knew Danny meant Dr. Oliver, Claudia's analyst. The doctor had once told her she should see other men as part of her process of self-actualization. That was when she'd taken up with Biff Archway the first time.

Archway irritated Nudger from the start, and not just because he became something of a romantic rival. The guy was average height but muscular, handsome in a jut-jawed, chesty sort of way. He looked like a former college football star who'd kept in shape and learned how to wear expensive clothes and could afford a spiffy car to impress the ladies. Nudger had checked on him. Archway turned out to be a former college football star who'd kept in shape and spent a large percentage of his schoolteacher pay on clothes and red sports cars. He'd also carried a 3.9 grade point average. He was easy to dislike even when he wasn't hanging around Claudia.

". . . shrink again?" Danny was saying.

"I don't think she's gone back to him," Nudger said.

Danny looked serious. "So is it that Archway bastard?"

"Maybe," Nudger said. "I think he might be going to Claudia's apartment tonight. She wouldn't tell me for sure one way or the other. She says if he is gonna be there, it'll be about the school and it's none of my business."

"If he is? She say those exact words, Nudge?"

"More or less." Nudger wondered what significance Danny saw in that.

"I was you," Danny said, "I'd drive on over there and see what was going on."

"Claudia warned me not to do that."

"Her saying so doesn't mean she really don't want you there, Nudge."

Nudger stared at Danny. Occasionally, with childlike clarity of vision, Danny could be very wise about certain matters. Intuitive if not logical. Nudger sensed this was one of those times.

"I don't follow you," he said, thinking he might glean some further insight from Danny. Some faint clue to the true nature of the universe.

Danny placed his blunt-fingered, flour-whitened hands on the counter and leaned toward Nudger. "I figure she might be testing you, Nudge."

"Testing me?"

"Seeing if you love her enough to go to her tonight and tell Archway to scram."

Nudger said, "That's absurd."

"No, no," Danny said, "women think that way sometimes."

"Not Claudia."

"Even Claudia."

"I wouldn't bet on it."

"But you are betting on it, Nudge, and the stakes are high." He nodded knowingly and pushed away from the counter, leaving two flour handprints on the stainless steel surface.

Nudger sat silently while Danny went back to his baking. What Danny had said was eating on him, along with his conversation with Adler. In some way it was all connected, and Nudger couldn't figure out how.

He walked around the counter and helped himself to a cup of Danny's sludgelike coffee from the huge, complex urn. It wasn't easy getting the stuff down, but he knew it would keep him awake. Alert. His stomach was kicking violently as he walked toward the door.

"Where you goin', Nudge?" Danny called from the door to the back room.

"Following your advice," Nudger said. "I'm going to see Claudia, whether or not she's alone."

"Good," Danny said, beaming and wiping his ghostly white hands on his apron. It obviously pleased him immensely to see Nudger acting on his suggestion. "It's the thing to do. You can't go wrong."

"I've thought that before and gone wrong."

"It'll work out this time," Danny assured him. "I got a kinda sixth sense about these things. Wanna take her some of yesterday's doughnuts? That'll get you in tight. I'll pop 'em in the microwave and freshen 'em up if you want."

Nudger said, "I think not."

There was the sleek red convertible, Archway's, parked on Wilmington right in front of Claudia's apartment. Nudger knew it was Archway's car because there was a Stowe High School parking permit dangling from the rearview mirror.

Okay, Nudger told himself, driving around the block and

trying to ignore what felt like a sharp-clawed hamster fight in his stomach, so Archway was there. With Claudia. She hadn't said that wasn't going to happen, just said that if it did, it would be strictly business. School business. Her business and none of his. She and Archway would be doing whatever teachers did when they got together professionally. Could be anything. Possibly they were discussing difficult students, discipline problems. Nudger remembered being one of those, but unintentionally, as he recalled. His teachers had been upset. Teachers could be sensitive. Maybe the faculty out at Stowe High School was going on strike.

Or maybe the school had too much money and the faculty was trying to figure out what on earth to do with it all.

The truth was that none of those possibilities seemed at all likely to Nudger. He was thinking of the way Claudia moved when she walked, the way she tossed her long dark hair to get it out of her eyes, the way she smelled.

He slammed on the brakes.

An old, stooped fellow wearing a Cardinals cap, watering his lawn even though it was almost dark out, glared at him as he steered the car into a driveway, then backed it out so it was turned around and headed back to Claudia's apartment and the parking space he'd seen across the street from Archway's sporty red convertible. Staring fiercely from beneath the bill of his red baseball cap, the old guy looked about to throw a wicked fastball at Nudger's head. But he merely lost momentary control of his hose, and its stream of water knocked over one of the two plastic flamingos flanking the steps to the porch.

Nudger knew he should keep on driving, turn the corner, and go home. But he didn't. Couldn't. He parked the Granada and climbed out, plucking his shirt away from where it was plastered to his back with perspiration. He stood still then and stared up at Claudia's apartment.

The lights were off up there.

Well, maybe she and Archway had gone somewhere in Claudia's car.

But there was Claudia's little blue Chevette parked down the block. Nudger recognized it by the dent in the front fender.

His stomach did fast loops.

Don't make an ass of yourself, he thought. Don't jump to conclusions.

But suspicion and jealousy had him like a drug. It was dusk, so it had to be almost dark in the apartment, and the lights were out. Under the circumstances, what would anybody think?

He walked down the block a short distance so he could make sure the dining room light was also out.

Darkness there, too.

So what were the options here? Nudger asked himself. He could go up and knock on Claudia's door, but if she and Archway were up to something, she'd hardly answer.

Or he could sneak upstairs and let himself in with his key, surprise them, and catch them doing . . . whatever they might be doing.

But he really didn't want that. He couldn't bear it if he happened to be right. And Claudia would never forgive him.

Still, he'd know where he stood, however painful the knowledge might be. He thought again of Adler, how the poor guy must have felt learning about Doris Vandervort, his brief but true love. What might passion turn into in a situation like that?

Go home, Nudger told himself. Go home and grow up.

He spun on his heel and was about to walk back to the Granada when he noticed the faint glow from the rear of the brick building. Up on the second floor.

He felt his skin actually crawl. Not very far, but it crawled. The rage in his acidic stomach rose in his throat.

The light had to be burning in Claudia's bedroom! And sometimes she liked leaving the lamp on when—

He swallowed bile and crossed the street, striding angrily toward the building. Then, as he stepped up on the curb, he slowed down.

He'd gained enough control of his anger to be devious.

Opening the street door slowly and carefully so it couldn't possibly be heard upstairs, he slipped into the vestibule. Then he took the stairs to the second floor with equal caution, keeping his feet spread wide and placing them near the wall and the banister so the wooden steps wouldn't creak.

He paused outside Claudia's apartment door. Pressed his ear to the cool enameled surface. Heard nothing.

Standing up straight, he hesitated. Should he do this?

His stomach told him he had no choice.

Slowly he slipped his key into the lock, turned it, then took a deep breath.

He threw open the door and leaped inside.

Only an instant was required for him to take in the scene: Claudia and Archway seated side by side on the sofa in the dim living room, their necks craned so they could stare at Nudger over their shoulders. Even in the dimness the surprise in their eyes was plainly visible. Some sort of machine was set up on a card table, a projector. And there was one of those home movie screens that lowered like a shade over a tripod. On the glowing screen was a young girl wearing only shorts and a flimsy gray tee shirt, running across a grassy field, her youthful bosom jiggling with each coltlike stride, her blond hair flying. What was the deal here? Archway and Claudia watching pornography! Suddenly another young girl appeared on the screen, large but muscular, with a malicious expression on her pug-nosed face. She smashed into the first girl, knocking her to the ground, then dashed out of camera range.

Archway, who'd turned back toward the screen, said, "That's definitely not allowed."

Claudia, still staring at Nudger, gave him the same kind of look the old guy in the Cardinals cap had aimed at him, as if the lawn flamingos were being threatened.

In a voice so calm it scared him, she said, "What's this all about, Nudger?"

"He thought he'd drop by and surprise us," Archway said, sounding amused. The creep had figured it out by the expression on Nudger's face. "You bring a bottle of wine, Nudger? Maybe a bouquet?"

Claudia, standing up now, fully dressed in slacks and a sleeveless blouse, said, "I'm going to substitute for Biff and coach the soccer team for a week while he goes on vacation. He was showing me film so I could understand the game."

Archway had switched on the lamp by the couch and was grinning. Handsome bastard, always at ease, his hair slicked back with some kind of grease you could fry an egg with. He wasn't starting to go bald on top like Nudger. "You think we were watching porno movies, Nudger? What a sick mind."

Nudger realized his mouth was hanging open. His rage had turned to humiliation. His stomach hurt.

"You've made a fool of yourself again," Claudia said.

"Maybe he doesn't believe your explanation," Archway said, trying to make trouble. "Maybe he knows something was going on between us."

"Knows?" Nudger said.

Archway, standing next to Claudia now, slid his arm around her waist and said, "Poor choice of words, I guess."

Anger glowed in Claudia's dark eyes. "Do you believe me, Nudger?"

"Of course I do."

"Then get out."

"Wait a minute . . ." Nudger said. He wanted to arrange it so he could leave with a smidgen of dignity. They should allow him that much.

But Archway saw his opening. He took two steps toward Nudger. "The lady said leave, chum."

"Chum?" Nudger said. "We're not chums."

"Don't be a problem, Nudger, please." Claudia, pleading now.

"He's on his way out," Archway said. "Put this jerk in the past, Claudia."

"He's not a jerk." Now she felt she had to defend him.

Anger and embarrassment pushed reason out of Nudger's mind. He planted his feet wide and crossed his arms. "I'm not leaving," he told Archway. "You are."

"Nudger!" Claudia said.

"I'm not leaving you alone with this creep," he told her.

"I was fine until you arrived," she said. She clenched her fists and slapped them against her thighs. "You are a jerk!"

"So long, chum," Archway said, and advanced on Nudger in a crouch. Archway knew karate, or something like it; Nudger had learned that the hard way some time ago.

"You're the one leaving," he said, circling Archway.

Archway spun his body around and tried to kick Nudger in the chest. Did it, too. Nudger said, "Oooomph!" and went sprawling.

He scrambled to his feet immediately. "I said you were leaving," he told Archway, as if he'd been the one who'd landed the blow.

He stepped in and swung hard at Archway's grinning face.

Missed clean and felt something slam into his forehead.

Must have been Archway's fist, he figured, from where he sat on the carpet.

Archway was smiling down at him. "Time to say night-night, Nudger."

Nudger struggled to his feet. Said, "Night-night," and swung at Archway again. Saw a galaxy of stars and discovered he was lying on his back on the carpet. His jaw ached.

"Had enough," Archway asked, "or do you want a nightcap?"

Nudger heard himself groan. He rolled onto his stomach, raised himself to a low crouch, and ran at Archway.

It felt great when his shoulder crashed into Archway's midsection. Both men fell to the floor. Then Archway was on top of Nudger, landing punches to his head and shoulders. Nudger threw him off, tried to stand up and jump on him, but was tripped so that he crashed into the projector. It fell near him and stopped whirring. He thrashed around, tangled in its cord, and stood up just in time to be knocked back down by Archway, who at least wasn't smiling now. Nudger had mussed his hair.

"Both of you knock this stuff off!" Claudia was shouting. She was facing Archway, inches from his face. "Leave him alone, Biff. Go home, please!"

"Me?" Archway looked astounded. "You were telling him to go a minute ago. He's the one who sneaked in here like a terrorist commando. He's the one—"

"The one without sense enough to leave," Claudia interrupted.

"But I don't see why I should go."

"Because I asked you to," Claudia said. "Isn't that reason enough?"

"It's not reason enough for Nudger."

"You're not like Nudger. Thank God."

Archway stood for a minute or so with his chest heaving, trying to sort things out while he flexed his muscles. Putting on a show for Claudia, Nudger thought.

Finally he said, "I'll see you at school, Claudia."

"I'll bring the screen and projector," she told him.

Archway snatched up his plaid sport coat from where it was folded on a chair. "If any of that expensive visual equipment's broken, he's gonna pay for it!" he said, pointing at Nudger.

"My pleasure," Nudger said, rubbing it in.

Archway didn't say goodbye to either of them as he stormed out. Nudger heard him bluster down the stairs, then charge through the street door and let it swing wildly behind him until its pneumatic closer calmed it and eased it shut.

Nudger slumped on the sofa. Claudia had her fists on her hips and was staring down at him with anger, and with some other emotion.

She said, "You would have let him kill you before you'd leave us here alone together, wouldn't you, Nudger."

It wasn't posed as a question, but Nudger said, "Yes." And maybe he would have, he realized. It had been headed in that direction.

"Why?" Claudia asked.

"I don't know," Nudger said. It was something he'd have to think about.

"I know why," Claudia said. She sat down next to him and kissed him on the cheek, surprising him.

She kept surprising him.

A year passed before Nudger learned from Gideon Schiller, an attorney in Clayton he sometimes did work for,

John Lutz

what had happened with Jake Adler after that night at the doughnut shop.

Adler had paid Doris Vandervort's bail, become her lover, then married her and left the law to own and operate a charter fishing boat down in Key West.

Nudger didn't know how to feel about that. It bothered him and he wasn't sure why. Finally he drove to Key West on vacation and accepted Adler's invitation to go deep-sea fishing.

It was a nice boat, about a thirty-footer. Doris was the crew. She didn't know who Nudger was and neither Nudger nor her husband told her. Nudger watched them together. The two of them seemed happy enough, he decided. In fact, very happy. Whatever romantic whimsy they had forged into reality here in the sun must agree with them.

Adler had put on weight and looked fit in his cutoff shorts and unbuttoned blue work shirt. And there was a new contentment in his once wary and calculating eyes as he familiarized Nudger with the heavy tackle for ocean fishing. Doris smiled a lot and bustled around the bobbing deck, now and then ducking below to ice drinks and work up the lunch that went with the cruise.

Nudger had never been deep-sea fishing, yet somehow an hour from shore he felt pressure on his line and reeled in an odd-looking brown fish about a foot long that flopped around listlessly on the deck. As if it didn't much care one way or the other about being caught.

He stared at it with distaste. "What is it?"

The tanned and content Adler smiled. "I have no idea. There are all kinds of unusual things in the sea. That's what makes it so interesting." He turned slightly so Doris couldn't see him and winked.

Doris popped the tab on a cold can of beer and handed it

310

to Nudger. She grinned down at the fish, then at Nudger. "Gonna keep it? Have it mounted to hang over your fireplace?"

Nudger gave her back the grin. "Sure. Why not? I'll ask the taxidermist to make it look like it's leaping."

He didn't have a fireplace, but he didn't see where that made any difference.

So much of life was in the mind.

Additional copyright information:

312